S0-AHK-238

Greetings, Magician!

With those words, Jason June invites us into the world of the Guild and introduces a cast of characters and a universe so delightful I can't stop smiling just thinking about what a treat you have ahead of you in this book.

Filled with magic, romance, humor, friendship, and a Texas-size swagger, this is a magical world we haven't seen before, but one that still feels cozily familiar from the first dazzling spell cast by our heroes: handsome and hilarious Nigel, and gorgeous and sensitive Ori.

I was hooked the moment Nigel received the Guild missive on a soggy napkin (spoiler alert), and I know you'll be equally swept away by this heart-stopping and swoony adventure!

I am beyond thrilled to bring this book out into the world. To me, *The Spells We Cast* is a bright light against the darkness—my favorite kind of story, one that affirms our humanity and shows us the deep and miraculous power of love. To say that reading this book is a joy would be an understatement. It's simply magic.

Good luck with the Culling! Hold on to your horses!

Melissa de la Cruz

THE SPELLS WE CAST

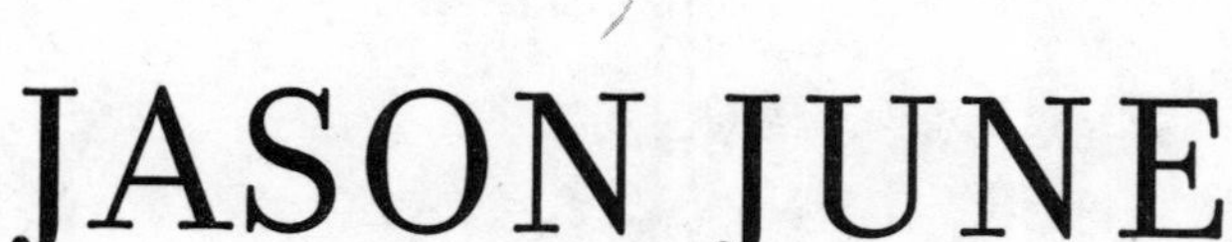

JASON JUNE

HYPERION
Los Angeles New York

First Edition, October 2023
10 9 8 7 6 5 4 3 2 1
FAC-004510-23230
Printed in the United States of America

This book is set in Garamond Mt Pro
Designed by Marci Senders

Library of Congress Cataloging-in-Publication Data

Names: JASON JUNE, author.
Title: THE SPELLS WE CAST / by Jason June.
Description: First edition. • Los Angeles ; New York : Hyperion, 2023.
• Audience: Ages 12–18. • Audience: Grades 10–12. • Summary: Sparks fly when eighteen-year-old Nigel meets Ori during the Culling, a competition that determines whether a magician is stripped of their powers or joins the magical society known as the Guild, but they soon realize the connection growing between them threatens their future, the Guild, and all of humanity.
Identifiers: LCCN 2022032333 • ISBN 9781368089234 (hardcover) • ISBN 9781368089975 (ebook) • Subjects: CYAC: Magic—Fiction. • Contests—Fiction. • Gay men—Fiction.
• Interpersonal relations—Fiction. • Fantasy.
• LCGFT: Fantasy fiction. • Novels.
Classification: LCC PZ7.1.J8754 Sp 2023 • DDC [Fic]—dc23
LC record available at https://lccn.loc.gov/2022032333

Reinforced binding

Visit www.HyperionTeens.com

Logo Applies to Text Stock Only

To Brent,
for working your agent magic to make
all my dreams come true

CHAPTER ONE

I've been expecting something big to happen for weeks. I just didn't think it would be getting dumped.

"I'm breaking up with you," Jeremy says while his mouth is still full of taco, a Torchy's "trashy" taco, so the extra queso it came soaked in dribbles down his chin while he stabs the knife in my back.

My fingers itch to drop the tortilla chip frozen in midair over our shared guac and put a curse on him right then and there. Maybe I'd make that dribble of queso un-wipe-away-able, or, I don't know, turn the jalapeños poking out of his corn tortilla so spicy that no amount of milk drinking, tongue wiping, or praying would ever make it go away.

But no . . . Meema always says to be a Barrett means to never do harm with a spell. So instead I set the chip back in the basket, put my hands out of view below the table, and tug on my leg hair sharp and quick to send a jolt up my shin that distracts from the constricting in my heart.

"Say something." Jeremy's deep brown eyes are round with

worry, but not like he's afraid my feelings are hurt. More like he's concerned that I haven't reacted the way he wants me to. Maybe he wants me to beg him, or thinks I should burst into tears.

"Why-y?" I ask, and curse my freaking throat for catching. Not *literally* curse it, of course, but I'm convinced if I let one tear fall, I'm going to lose it. The last place I want to have a meltdown is a crowded restaurant with an audience of frat boys chugging a pitcher of margaritas one booth over.

"It just makes the most sense." Jeremy starts ticking reasons off on his thick fingers. "We just graduated, you're taking a year off and I'm going to Duke, you said you thought you'd be busy with work this summer. It just seems like we should end it now. Long-distance college relationships never work out, right?"

"So you're just going to throw away the past fourteen months?" My hands are shaking, and it's taking everything in me not to use them to pool magic in my fingers and make devil horns sprout from Jeremy's forehead.

"I thought you'd be relieved," he says. "You've been so busy lately, you've hardly had any time to hang out. Weekly taco dates aren't really enough for a whole relationship, you know?"

"I haven't been busy," I snap, but as soon as the words leave my mouth, I know it's a lie. In between cramming for Calculus and US History tests so I could just barely graduate from Lake Travis High, Meema was teaching me how to create air pockets that would protect her hair from Texas humidity, or to turn the coyotes that like to shred her chickens into harmless armadillos. Ever since high school started she's made me treat magic like a whole other class—like six other periods of class, actually, every day for the past four years. I think she feels like she has to redeem herself after her last student completely failed. Especially since he hovers around the house like a beer-soaked reminder of how she let him down, watching us—his mom and his son—cast spells while he's forced to relive the moment his magic was stripped away from him.

"Okay, maybe I have had to spend a little extra time at home. But you know how Meema gets about me working around the ranch." It's the excuse I gave him all year, conveniently leaving out the fact that I was mucking stalls with magic or gathering eggs from the chicken coop while my nose was shoved in some ancient elven text.

Jeremy gives me those adorable puppy dog eyes, likely perfected while spending hundreds of hours washing dachshunds and Pomeranians at his family's dog-grooming business. Only this time he really does seem concerned, and I instantly feel bad for suspecting the worst of him. "I wouldn't trade the time we had together for anything, Nigel. You and I had so many firsts, and nothing can take that away. But honestly, I kind of thought you'd be relieved. Like, you've been so stressed out this entire year. I thought I'd be one less thing on your plate."

I always knew that being a Barrett would be a lot of work. It's a big reputation to live up to, being a descendant of the first human granted elf magic, a man who created a weapon so strong it defeated one of the most evil monsters this country has ever seen. You've got to be the strongest, cleverest, fastest magician of your generation. But I wanted that *in addition* to a boyfriend. Who wouldn't want a partner who's adorable, dog-grooming, piano-key-tinkling, soccer-playing, all-around perfect? Meema always warned against dating, saying that relationships never work out for apprentices once they start studying for the Culling. But I couldn't just magic away my feelings. I couldn't cast some spell to get rid of the hope when Jeremy asked me out that maybe I could have this slice of a normal life, too.

"Is there anything I can say to change your mind?" The words sound pathetic even to me.

Jeremy reaches across the table, palms up. I give in because this might be my last physical contact with a guy, let alone a guy I really like, for who knows how long. Over the past few months, Jeremy's even graduated to saying the L-word. I've never said it back, and it hits me now how heartless that must have been. How can you not love the person who was your first kiss, your first *everything*? Who asked you to prom by lining up five Goldendoodles painted with pet-friendly purple dye to spell *P-R-O-M-?* in their curly tan fur. But I was too distracted becoming the next great magician to fully give my heart to a relationship that I guess I always knew would end. Even still, I don't want it to.

Jeremy's warm, large hands completely engulf my own, a feeling I've always adored. He held my hands like this that first day we talked, when I passed out from the sight of my own blood after a scalpel accident during frog dissection. I've had this embarrassing inexplicable blood phobia my whole life. So imagine my surprise when it led to my first boyfriend. Jeremy helped me off the floor, and as we walked to the nurse's office he said he'd always had a crush on me. I don't know why, since I pretty much kept to myself, never quite able to connect with anybody or relate to their normal human lives.

"If we stayed together, I think we'd just be delaying the inevitable," Jeremy says. "You're amazing and you always make me laugh. Except it only happens when I get to see you, and that's too few and far between right now. I understand you have to work hard, but if we keep this going, it's only going to get worse. I want my relationship to be more than just texts and the occasional taco."

The defensive part of me wants to tell him that we only do tacos because Torchy's is *his* favorite spot, but I know it's a weak comeback. Without tacos, our relationship *would* just be texts, and I can't expect him to hang on until after the Culling. Because if I succeed and make it into the Guild, how much of my time will be filled with missions stopping demons and the Depraved from wreaking havoc?

The intercom usually used to announce orders ready for pick-up squeals to life, making both Jeremy and me cringe. "Uh, is there a Nigel Barrett here? Nigel Barrett? You've got a message."

Jeremy frowns. "That's weird."

I shoot up so hard my knees knock against the table. Tendrils of pain throb through my legs, but they barely register. It's hard to feel anything over the pounding of my heart. And at least now it's not due to the abrupt breakup.

"I should get that," I breathe.

Jeremy nods, or at least I think he does; I only catch the movement in my peripheral vision. My eyes are focused on the college kid at the intercom looking around for Nigel Barrett to come get his message. For *me* to come get it.

"You do that," Jeremy says, placing his perfect big hand on my shoulder when he stands. "It's been fun, Nigel, and I'm going to miss you. I know whatever's next for you, you're going to be great at it. But some advice? Wait to charm somebody else until you're fully ready for a relationship."

I know I should meet his eyes, I know I should acknowledge the hurt in his voice, I know I should regret all the times he asked me to come over, but I couldn't because I was making it rain over Meema's tomatoes or breaking my pinkie to see if I could mend a broken bone. (I could, by the way, but I fixed it at an angle, so I had to break it *four more times* until I got it straight again.) But instead of saying goodbye to Jeremy, I walk like a spell has been cast over me—somehow both numb and aware of every nerve-ending in my body—toward the cashier holding up an immaculate gold envelope. Only for him it's probably been spelled to look like something else entirely.

"I'm Nigel Barrett," I whisper.

The cashier, whose nametag says RICKY, hurriedly hands

me the envelope. "What took you so long? I've been calling your name forever. Just to hand you a phone number on a salsa-soaked napkin." Yep. I knew it. "You better get some serious action from that."

Ricky moves on to take the order of a mom wrangling a group of middle-school baseball players while I turn the envelope over in my shaking hands. A navy-blue wax seal is on the back, the five-starred symbol of the Guild shining up at me, representative of the five ancestral races of all magicians: elves, fae, goblins, nymphs, and sprites.

I swallow and look up. Jeremy's gone, which dampens my excitement for a second. I didn't even tell him goodbye. But it's not like I could actually share with him that I have magic powers, that if I really wanted to I could turn him into one of the Shar-Peis he washes. Not only is it against the rules to tell Jeremy (or any human you're not married to), but I'm certain he'd run out the door faster than you can say *My boyfriend lost his mind.*

Ex-boyfriend, actually.

I take a deep breath and tap the wax Guild seal. Just like Meema said it would, the stars light up gold, responding to the touch of the envelope's recipient. The seal pops off and the flap opens, a blank piece of parchment sliding out all on its own. I quickly look around; I've never been in the presence of actual working magic in such a crowded place. But nobody's on high alert. The frat boys still chug their margaritas, a toddler cries as a cascade of soda spills on their lap, and only one of the middle-school baseball players looks at me like I've gone completely bonkers. Not because of the magic, but because I'm treating what they see as a dirty napkin like it's the Holy Grail.

This parchment might as well be that legendary relic. Because the words that are now appearing on it in bright, curling cursive will determine the direction of the rest of my life. They'll kick off the journey where I'll end up a magician or a bitter, powerless ghost of a man like my dad.

No pressure, right?

Greetings, Magician—
You've been selected to participate in the Culling.
This tradition keeps our power alive,
our members from death.
Succeed and enter the Guild.
Fail and you will be stripped of all magic.
Participation is not optional.
The first trial will begin shortly.
Sincerely,
The Guild

CHAPTER TWO

The Culling. An annual tradition that's gone on for almost four hundred years (since AD 1648, to be exact) in which thousands of magically gifted eighteen-year-olds are whittled down—*culled* down—to just hundreds. Three trials in just a matter of days that will make or break you, that will let you join the Guild and continue your life with magic running through your veins, or have your power snatched out of you like the last PS5 at a holiday sale.

Why only hundreds? When the Depraved got out of hand and Ancestral races first decided to stop hoarding their power and share it with humans, folks quickly learned there were problems when too much magic coalesced in one place. People died. Humans, magicians, *and* Ancestrals. Animals and plants, too. Meema always says to think of magic like water. It's needed for life. But too much of it and you'll drown. Every last magician in the Guild would drown in their own power if the Culling didn't take place, and every human, plant, and animal would be consumed by magical energy. It's why we dwindle our numbers each year, and why Ancestrals have kept to their own hidden city ever since. With magic dispersed more evenly throughout the world, we were finally able to use these powers for good. Because it's not just magicians who need our magic. Humanity needs us, too. The Ancestrals aren't the only magical beings out there, and many of the others mean to do harm. So while we may have powers greater than humans will ever know, we don't just keep them to ourselves. The Guild protects humans from all those that prefer evil and chaos to light and love. It's a privilege, and a fair price to pay for our gifts.

If you asked my dad, though, he'd call it all a load of shit. I can practically hear him say as much as he glares down from his bedroom window while I park outside our Texas Hill Country estate. It's all pristine, cream-colored limestone that Meema made me spell to prevent any black mold from growing in its crevices and steel-lined windows similarly magicked so that moisture doesn't leave streaks. That last one took me a minute to figure out. The first time I tried it, I broke every window in the family room. Meema wouldn't fix them, either—said we could live without windows until I could clean up my own mess. And it was the middle of August, so everything in the room was soaking wet with humidity. The couch squished when you sat on it. Worst month of my life, and it certainly didn't make Dad warm up to me.

I meet his eyes and wave. Like an idiot, I choose to use the hand that's clutching the invitation—that he must see as a napkin—and mouth, *The Culling*. Wrong move. Dad scowls and turns his back, making me cringe. Sometimes I get this instinct to treat him like he's a made-for-TV-movie dad who will root for me in anything I do. Even though my brain knows he's never, ever been that, my heart still holds out hope.

Instead of bringing us closer together, though, I've just made Dad relive his own trials and his failure in the final task. He was that close. His own dad, my grandpa, disowned him for it; and to her credit, Meema divorced my grandfather for turning away their only son. I don't even call the guy Grandpa because I hardly ever saw him. He died a few years back, in a Depraved battle gone wrong, a reminder that membership in the Guild is literally life or death.

Dad apparently handled his magicless life well at first, living with Meema and trying his hand at becoming a lawyer to represent kids who, for whatever reason, had to be put into the foster care system—sometimes because of a dad like his who decided they never wanted to see their child again, other times because of a parent who wanted so badly to provide for their kids but couldn't. Dad might not have had magic anymore, but he still had a heart. Until it was ripped away by my mom. She gave birth to me and then left the hospital in the middle of the night with Dad asleep by her bedside. Not a word from her since. Meema says she'd never seen two people more in love, or another person more heartbroken than my dad after she left. I mean, she can't have been *that* great if she would just up and ditch her newborn son, right? But apparently I look just like her: tall and stocky, the same deep green eyes, a flash of red in our chestnut hair under the sun. It's yet another reason Dad can't stand to look at me.

Anyway, at least there's Meema. The goofy sound of the Southern title for grandma is ironic, considering she's one of the most powerful Guild members there is and the sole remaining member repping the Barrett family. The name *Barrett* literally means "mighty like a bear," and Great-Grandpa Barrett—the first guy ever given elf magic—had a way with them. He's really more like my great-grandpa eight times over, but it's just easier to call him Great-Grandpa, sometimes Gramps. Anyway, he could use his magic to communicate with bears, to turn himself into a bear, or to create magic ones to fight alongside him. Barretts have had a way with animals ever since.

Meema's no exception, a bull being her animal of choice. As

the sole Barrett left in the Guild, should an evil mega behemoth ever awaken, she's the only magician who'd be able to find G-pa Barrett's enchanted bear claw and end it. Gramps did the same thing centuries ago to the Knife, one of the worst Depraved in history. He used the claw to send the monster into an enchanted sleep. The Knife's snoozing form still lies under Mount Rainier where it can do no harm, and let's just say you'd better hope it stays there. If I make it into the Guild, I'll share the responsibility with Meema, which I'm sure will only piss Dad off more. He's literally the *only* Barrett ever to have had his magic taken away.

I guess I've got to give him credit for trying to make the best of it at first. Wish I could have known that guy instead of the flannel-and-Levi's-wearing ghost whose gaze makes me feel like he's trying to melt me from the inside out. But if I get in the Guild, I'll be out of his sight for good. Not only does Guild membership come with magic powers, it brings in a nice paycheck, too. Hello, rent on my own place; goodbye, depressing dad.

I put my hand against the iron front door with its Texas Longhorn knocker. With a flash of golden light, the door opens. Magic can be a lot less exciting than humans think it is. Descendants of elves, like my family, can perform magic with concentrated thought. No fancy words, no wand waving, just *wanting* it to happen. Most elven texts are about learning to slow your thoughts. Once your mind is calm, you can feel the magic in your blood, and elves pull on it and mold it to do what we want, its expenditure emitting gold light that only magicians can see. Emotions are a part of it, too, confidence and courage making spells stronger, while sadness, fear, and angst make them weaker.

From there, it's practice makes perfect, a lot like working out a muscle by starting small before graduating to the heavy weights. You see if you can gather enough magic to get a spoon to move, then a full water trough, then your grandma's shiny magenta pickup truck, that kind of thing. Just like in weight lifting, you can tire out. You can't use big amounts of magic over and over without taking a rest. When fully charged, though, it's pretty legit what we can do.

But for a human, it would look very anticlimactic. Like if you encountered me on the street trying to make it rain, one second you'd be dry, the next you'd be drenched. You'd have no indication that I was the one to let loose the storm, except maybe that I was staring *really intently* at the sky and moving my hands around a bit. But for me or any other person with magic powers, they'd see a little light show blast from my hands and know I was the guy who'd just soaked them to the bone.

Fae descendants, on the other hand, have more of a tell, since they can only cast spells verbally, usually in rhyme or by singing specific notes. There's more of a musicality to their work. Sprite descendants use effigies to cast spells on certain people or things. They carry a knife in their back pocket and a bit of sprite wood to carve an effigy on the fly. Also, they can disappear with a snap of their fingers. It's where the word *spritely* comes from. Back in the day people used to think some sprite descendant was a super-fast runner, when really they were disappearing and reappearing in the blink of an eye. It's how they carve so fast, their hands blinking in and out to just the right location to make their effigies.

Then there's goblin descendants, the group that humans have *way* wrong. There's so many myths about goblins being these creepy monsters, but they're anything but. They're shape-shifters, and while they can't cast spells on others, just imagine the things they can do by changing into a dragon, or a literal fly on the wall, or your favorite celebrity. You've got strength, secrets, and seduction right there alone.

Last but definitely not least, there's nymph descendants. They're probably the most exciting of all of us. You watch cartoons or listen to Greek myths and you think nymphs are green or blue humanoids who wear togas, are attached to a tree or a river somewhere, and perform plant or water magic. Apparently that's pretty close to how real nymphs look, wherever they are now. Nymph-born magicians, however, look just like anybody else but can perform spells representing one of the elements: fire, air, earth, and water. They can blow flames from their fingers, or create hurricane level winds, or make a cactus grow to the size of a sequoia.

But for my family and me, we're all golden elf power. The front door swings open at my magical push and reveals Meema waiting right behind it. She's in her usual denim-on-denim outfit: tight, perfectly clean blue jeans and a denim shirt tucked in with a red blouse underneath. Cinching her waist is a brown leather belt with a massive, angry gold longhorn belt buckle staring up at me like it wants nothing more than to gore me right through the middle. It looks a lot like her favorite spell, in which she magics a golden bull to defend against the monsters of the world. Meema always says her "Texas pride" is what keeps her alive and kicking.

"Darlin', I've been waiting all day," she says. "I know you've been spending time with that boyfriend of yours, but this is the Culling we're talking about here. Show me your invitation."

It's not a question of whether or not I have it. Just like it's not a question to her that I was with Jeremy despite never having mentioned it—although she doesn't know that he's not my boyfriend anymore. The hurt is too fresh to tell her. Besides, she'd just say it was better that I'm not attached before heading off to the Guild, and just because she'd be completely right doesn't mean the hollow feeling inside of me would ache any less.

Meema—known to the Guild as Senior Magician Adela Barrett—gets to know when things are happening before most everybody else.

Things like the Culling. For all I know, she's the one who spelled that dirty napkin at Torchy's to become my invite. Being in on and getting to decide all of the Guild's moves are perks for any member who makes it a couple decades without being killed by a Depraved magician or clawed to death by an owl demon. Death isn't uncommon in the Guild, but between having magic and dying young or living long enough without magic to become Dad, I'll take the former.

I flash the golden envelope at her and she claps her hands, her expertly manicured, bright red nails catching the light from the purple rhino demon horn chandelier overhead. Her nails perfectly match her cherry lipstick and go with her flaming-red hair (she magics the color over the gray in her roots every morning, but she'd smack me upside the head if I ever said that out loud).

Meema snatches the envelope and holds it reverently, like it's the last known tube of her Fiery Soul lipstick. "This is it, hon," she coos in a voice made raspy by all the cigarettes she smoked until she quit five years ago, the old-fashioned way. (Weird how we can have spells for almost anything, but not to get rid of the addiction to the world's most disgusting habit. I guess that explains why she couldn't magic Dad out of drinking.) "You're going to hog-tie the rest of those apprentice magicians. They won't know what hit 'em until you're sauntering off into the sunset, the latest member of the Guild."

Her eyes gleam with pride just thinking about it. My stomach squirms; I hope I can live up to her expectations.

"When does it start?" I ask.

Meema motions for me to follow her into the massive great room. The living room section runs into the dining room and butts against the kitchen, all of it decorated in a cowboy-magician hybrid aesthetic. A dragon skull hangs beside a pair of longhorns on the wall, a cowprint rug lies atop a much larger demon alligator hide (imagine a gigantic rotting reptile with three times as many teeth) covering the living room floor, and the polished wood kitchen buffet is lined with a rope of braided griffin hair. All flanked by floor-to-ceiling windows that look out onto the expanse of bright blue sky and rolling hills surrounding our estate, two hundred acres with dozens of cattle grazing around it. Any human who walked into our house would just see the Texas-themed stuff, but those with magic in their veins would gawk at the paraphernalia that Meema has accumulated over fifty-five years of Guild membership.

"You know I can't tell you that," Meema says as she reaches into the refrigerator to grab a pitcher of her world famous sweet tea. (Her secret? She spells it so it only tastes sweet without any extra calories. As she says, she's got to maintain her feminine figure. Even among magicians you'll find outdated gender and body tropes.) "Nepotism is frowned upon in the Guild."

"Uh, the whole Guild is Nepo Baby Central. We're literally *all* descendants of humans that magical beings gave their powers to. How bad would it really be if you told me what the first challenge is?"

Footsteps stomp down the stairs, and it's like a dark cloud sweeps over the kitchen.

Dad.

Even though he had his magic stripped away, he's still got a power all his own to bring the mood down. My heart drops; I feel nauseous. Even more so when he catches my eye and his scowl furrows deeper. I taste something bitter, metallic, like Dad's resentment is trying to claw its way into my throat to choke me.

"Finally deciding to grace us with your presence," Meema says, looking at her watch. "Jesus, Reggie, it's almost six o'clock." She gives him an up-down, taking in his wrinkled flannel shirt and dirty Levi's with a blotchy stain on the knee. "You haven't even taken a shower."

"Get off my case, Ma. You should be focused on wonder boy

over here, anyway, 'stead of worrying about me, right?" Dad claps his hand on my shoulder, but by how hard he squeezes anyone could tell it's not a supportive father doting on his son kind of movement. It's an I-would-pulverize-you-to-dust-if-I-could kind of grip. It's for sure going to leave a bruise, and even though I could spell him so his fingers feel like they've been shocked, I don't have the heart to do it. I'm sure that Dad hates me—he's never said "I love you" or given me a birthday or Christmas card that would hint at the fact—but I don't hate him back. I feel sorry for him. No magic, no partner, no friends. Just memories of when he thought his life might turn out different.

Sometimes I wish Meema would erase his memory so that maybe he'd be a normal person. A normal father. But Meema says a person can never grow if they just forget the bad things that happened to them. And he was born into this world of magic, its rules forced upon him, just like I was. So I'll let him be. Hopefully, I can get out of his crushing sadness once and for all through the Culling.

Dad finally lets go of my shoulder and pours himself a bowl of cereal. He adds milk but spills it over the sides, most of it splattering onto Meema's krakenhide boots. She jumps back and he stomps upstairs like he didn't leave a mess—literal and emotional—in his wake.

"That boy, I swear," Meema mutters.

I gather magic in my hands and pull it into a square. A magic hankie. I wipe it over Meema's boots and relax into the familiar tingle of a spell well-performed, this elation in your blood that makes your heart soar and your chest puff with pride. It's a nice feeling after Dad sucked out all the good energy in the room.

"Don't pay your father any mind, you hear? The best revenge is doing well, and when you're a member of the Guild, all he'll have is decades' worth of regret and a beer cozy. You're gonna be something, darlin'. Now, as for telling you when your first trial is going to start, I can't. But just think about everything *I've told you* and you'll be right as rain." She slows her voice down—slow as molasses, she'd say—when she says *I've told you.* She follows it up with a wink. Way to be subtle, Meema.

"You've told me?" I repeat, and she nods.

"Yes. Think of everything I've told you about concentrating the mind, about casting spells, since you were knee high to a grasshopper. You know I've never stopped preparing you for this. Think of what I've said *today even.*"

There she goes again, laying it on thick.

"Today?"

Her eyes practically bug out of her head. "Jesus, boy, have you got wax in your ears? Just think of all my lessons, all my statements about *magicians.*"

My brain must still be slowed down by thoughts of Jeremy because I can't get my head straight. His goodbye echoes more in my mind than anything Meema mentioned since I got home.

But who am I kidding? Mom and Dad didn't work out, Meema and my grandpa neither. Coming from a mother and a grandfather who both ended up abandoning their family has to be some cosmic sign that I'm cursed when it comes to romance, so I just need to *focus.* What has Meema said today? That nepotism is frowned upon? She's doing a poor job of sticking with that if she's willing to give me hints. Not that I'm complaining.

"Nigel, I'm just gonna have to tell you again, aren't I?" She takes a deep breath, probably questioning whether she should really be giving me this clue. But she takes one look up at the ceiling, through which we can hear Dad stomping around his room. Just as badly as I want to be out of this house, out of range of his sulking drunk hauntings, I know Meema wishes she could get her son back. But, just like magic can't cure addiction or heartache or being a miserable asshole, magic can't turn back time. I'm her last shot at making up for her perceived mistakes, so she says again, nice and molasses slow, "You are going to hog-tie the rest of those apprentice magicians."

I mean, to a human, hearing the phrase *apprentice magician* might seem weird, but that's a title Meema has brought up literally every day since my magic first manifested. I was angry when Dad took the remote from me to switch my cartoons to some college football game, and I stewed and stewed about it. I thought of what it would be like for that remote to come flying back into my hand, and in a burst of light it did. I'd never heard Dad yell like that before, and he locked me in the pig pen. Even in my little six-year-old heart I knew his anger had more to it than just being mad about a remote.

When Meema got home and found me crying in the pen, she magicked Dad to the barn—the first time I'd seen her use her powers in front of me—and dunked him into the trough, holding him down with her power until he nearly drowned. She placed a spell so he could never touch me out of anger again, then made Dad check into rehab.

It should have been a really depressing time, but while he was gone for three months, Meema showed me the basics of magic and how I could help out with the animals around the farm without breaking a sweat. Cows, chickens, horses, pigs, and whenever they'd get rowdy, she'd tell me to "hog-tie 'em" with my magic. Find ways to bind their legs so I could safely put them back in their pen or stall or coop. She only ever used that word when I had to wrangle up an animal on the farm. And said I could "hog-tie" Dad if he ever got out of hand again, too. Which he did. That rehab didn't work.

"Hog-tie?" I try.

Meema's Fiery Soul lips break into a grin. "That's a smart boy."

"What? Am I going to have to like, hog-tie a pig for my first trial?"

"Don't be ridiculous, Nigel, of course not. The Guild wouldn't waste its time on pigs. On farm animals of any kind, for that matter."

"But . . . there will be some kind of animal, right? Maybe a demon?"

It's one of the two main functions of the Guild. First, kill demons before they can kill you. They're not scary beings from the underworld, or hell, or anything like pop culture would make you believe. Demons are made from human souls, literally. All those years ago, when humans thought they didn't have magic? They were wrong. Their hate and cruelty can make spirits, bad ones that need to possess a vessel and use it to create fear in human hearts, because that's what feeds them. We call those spirits the Depraved. Void of any love or compassion. And they like to possess creatures that could do damage, like alligators, elk, and mountain lions, warping them into grotesque Depraved Monsters, or demons for short.

But all the damage demons can do is nothing compared to when a Depraved spirit gets so strong that it becomes its own physical form. They're humanoid, with elongated, freakish features, rotten green skin and eyes, and they smell like death. We just call them Depraved, and when they're fully formed, they love to fight with their evil magic, causing fear and panic to feed on. Their favorite targets are other magical beings.

In fact, the rise of these evil creatures is the entire reason the Ancestrals shared their magic with humans: to fight the Depraved. When settlers first came to America, cruelty was on high, as you can imagine. Genocide of the Native populations, enslavement everywhere you looked. The awful beginnings of our country created Depraved in numbers the Ancestrals had never before reckoned with. And that's to say nothing of the Knife, a Depraved so huge, it towered over mountains. Those ancient magical species decided to give magic to humans—of all races and from all walks of life—who were willing to unite and fight to keep the country from total Depraved destruction. So that's the second duty of all Guild members: finding and killing the Depraved before their numbers get so big that humanity doesn't stand a chance.

It's a mission I'm proud to be a part of, and have been ever since I first saw Meema fight a Depraved on the ranch. It was that same day Dad went off on me when my powers developed. Before Meema had a chance to throw him in the water trough, a thick, greenish sludge coated Dad's arms, leaking from his pores before coalescing into a mottled mass that floated in the air. A Depraved spirit.

Dad's hatred was so strong that the spirit took its humanoid form pretty quickly. But Meema ended it fast, magicking a life-size golden bull into existence to kick its head so hard its neck snapped. As the years went on, just how important Meema's work is became increasingly clear. I watched her as she decimated the Depraved, or the skunk, bull, and coyote demons Dad's hovering hate would create. I learned how she used her magic to end those monsters quickly so they couldn't hurt more humans. I vowed to help her in that work as soon I could get into the Guild. And the time has finally come.

Meema mimes zipping her lips. "I told you I'm not saying a word. But a little studying wouldn't hurt. Perhaps, I don't know, at the library."

For as long as I can remember, Meema has taken me to the Perry-Castañeda Library at UT Austin to get extra studying in beyond her elven texts of meditation, concentration, and emotional manipulation. You'd be surprised how many humans have studied up about magicians and monsters and folklore, thinking it's all myth, but really a lot of their academic analyses can be helpful. And I guess by the way Meema is looking at me, the library is the place I've got to go to make sure I pass this first test. That, or she's really got to get that eye twitch looked at.

CHAPTER THREE

From the outside, the Perry-Castañeda Library doesn't look that inspiring. It's made of thick gray cinder block reminiscent of a prison. And honestly, the inside isn't much better. Old beige bookcases form row after row across unremarkable industrial carpeting. All that's to say, studying up for the Culling isn't, like, poring over ancient tomes in drafty castles where generations of magicians have studied before you. It's kind of the least magical experience you could imagine.

As I walk into the building that night, the rush of cool air from the AC is a relief. It's practically eight thirty, but outside it's still wet and in the nineties. Even though the shirt clinging to the sweat on my back is finally starting to dry off, my insides are melting. Flipping through old-smelling books in the near-empty library just really hits home Jeremy's point that I'm never available to do normal things. I should be outside right now, enjoying my one summer break after graduating high school, going to Barton Springs with Jeremy and splashing around at sunset until I fall in his arms and his wet hair tickles my face while we kiss.

He was so right to dump me. He should get to enjoy his last summer before college, too. Maybe he's already found some new guy to swim with, someone else to kiss in the cool waters. My heart squeezes just thinking about it, and even though I know sweet, puppy-dog-grooming Jeremy deserves to have that, I can't help thinking that if I cursed the water into mud nobody else would get to enjoy those lips and that slightly gap-toothed smile.

"Oh my god, did you see that?" A guy decked out in Longhorn orange runs down the aisle to the windows. He gets so close his breath fogs the glass. "What the hell is that?"

A stampede follows. Well, more an excited rush of the only other students—three, total—from this floor. It could just be some stupid college antics, but there's enough commotion that I can't help but see for myself.

"No way," I breathe.

All this time I should have been studying on the ranch. Not reading about snake monsters, but corralling *horses*, of which we have plenty on the estate. Because down in the square—galloping and whinnying so piercingly it stings my ears four floors up—is a crystallos, a magical horse-like ice creature from the far reaches of Antarctica. Its hide is made of shockingly blue ice, and it stands twelve feet tall on massive hooves that come to a point. If that thing stomped on you it'd spear you clean through, right before it ripped you apart with the fangs slashing out of its muzzle. The humans stare at it, open-mouthed. They might not be able to see our power, but they sure as hell can see living, breathing, magical creatures.

Something slips out of the book on fairy lore dangling from my hand. It's an old-school checkout card from the 1950s that turns into a shining gold envelope with the five-starred symbol of the Guild when it hits the ground. I quickly glance at the college kids, but their faces are all pressed to the glass in wide-eyed wonder.

As I snatch the envelope off the ground, the blue seal snaps off, and that bright cursive font of the Guild writes itself into a set of instructions.

Greetings, Magician—
Welcome to your first trial of the Culling.
This beast has been released by the Depraved
to cause havoc and fear.
Subdue it.
Succeed, and it will lead you to the Guild
for your remaining tests.
Fail, and you will be relieved of your powers.
Best of luck for the former.
Sincerely,
The Guild

Subdue it. Seems simple, but I'm sure it will be anything but. I've done this a thousand times on the farm, with animals ranging from squirrelly pigmy goats that refused to get back in their pen to irate emu who'd rather peck out your eyes than see you take one of their massive eggs for Sunday morning breakfast. But I've never wrangled a magical creature alone. Either way, step one on the ranch has always been to assess our animals' energy and figure out the best way to get them to do what I want, so I take a good look at how the crystallos is behaving surrounded by so many humans.

Just moments after its arrival, the scene's relatively calm. Students and tourists walk around the square staring at the crystallos in awe, unsure what to make of it. The way the setting sun flashes off its icy skin is really pretty, actually, and several people seem to think the creature is some kind of ice installation. But then the crystallos gallops right toward a small group of cheerleaders practicing a routine, so engrossed in their choreography that they haven't noticed the stunned silence. When the ice horse gets within feet, they finally look up, just in time to see a cold blast of air burst from the whinnying critter's mouth. And when that air touches the three cheerleaders, it covers them in frost and ice, freezing them in place in a perfect split-lift, looks of terror carved into their expressions.

The awed silence lasts for just a heartbeat longer while the crowd takes in the cheerleader ice sculpture. Then the screams start. Just like the Depraved wanted. The cowards are probably off somewhere soaking up the fear and chaos to feed their evil magic.

"Did that just happen?" the guy in Longhorn orange asks, glancing at the other students around him. I think he even pinches himself. "Dude, that really just happened. Frozen solid."

I don't stick around for any more of his astute observations. I barrel down the stairway. Students from the lower levels are running up, trying to get as far away from the crystallos as they can.

As soon as I make it outside, I'm nearly shoved backward by a wave of heat. It's hard to believe that a frozen creature could survive in these temperatures, but that's magic for you.

Students, joggers, tourists, and food truck employees try to dodge or find places to hide, but in the ninety seconds it took me to get from the mythology section to the square, the crystallos's magic has frozen at least five other people and coated the entire ground in a layer of ice. People run in place, slip and fall on their butts, or land hard on an elbow or wrist. I think I hear a couple bones crack.

The crystallos gallops in a panicked frenzy, huffing its cold breath on anyone in its path. The poor animal is scared, as much a victim of the Depraved as the humans. It's my job to make it right.

Time to hog-tie this snow blower.

Growing up on a huge Texas farm means Meema didn't just teach me magic. She taught me how to lasso, too.

I start to mime the act of coiling a rope around my elbow and call magic to my fingers. I have my left arm crooked, my hand held open so that the dip between my thumb and my pointer finger creates the perfect resting spot for the rope I'm going to create. Then, I circle my left arm with my right hand, going from thumb dip to elbow, over and over, while I concentrate on an image of a rope. Pride and determination at beginning my Culling journey fuels my power. Soon, gold light coalesces in my right fingers, then spools from my hand as I trace it in the shape of the coiled rope. It gets firmer with each wrap until I have a bright gold rope looped around my arm. The whole process takes seconds—fifteen, tops—but it's enough time for the crystallos to freeze a security guard just after the electric strings of her Taser bounce harmlessly off its side. Nice try, lady, but even bullets would ricochet off this thing's icy hide.

I quickly tie my magicked rope into a lasso, creating two overhand knots and looping them through each other to create a space big enough to fit over the crystallos's head. I swing the loop above my own head, 'round and 'round, readying to let it fly. All I need now is the crystallos's attention.

"Hey, Twilight Sparkle!" I shout, but there's enough commotion from screaming students and approaching police sirens that the horse doesn't hear me.

Fortunately, there's a spell for that. Using my left hand, I wrap my fingers around my throat and think, *Magnify.* A burst of golden light is followed by a blast of warmth that oozes down my neck as my magic takes hold.

"OVER HERE, FUTURE GLUESTICK!" My voice booms across the courtyard. Everyone's heads turn in my direction. But the gaze locked on me the hardest is the crystallos's, and angry bursts of ice billow from its nostrils. For the record, I don't support turning horses into glue, but magical creatures are proud, and one of the easiest ways to get their attention is with an insult or two.

The crystallos's mouth opens wide, blue drool dripping from its fangs. It looks like it wants to eat me whole. Which is exactly the reaction I want.

Rearing up on its hind legs, the crystallos lets loose another ear-piercing whinny. Everyone not frozen in the square covers their ears, and I'd join them if I didn't have to keep this lasso in the air.

The crystallos drops to the ground, ice cracking under the force of its hooves. It gallops at me, ready to trample me flat. But having calmed quite a few bucking broncos, I know this critter doesn't have anything on me. Sure, it might have four fangs about a foot long each, but I've got a rope, and I'm good with ropes.

But then another movement catches my eye. Someone appears behind the crystallos, like he blinked into existence, running straight for the horse. *Gaining* on it, even. His pale white skin glistens with sweat, his thick mop of dark brown hair flying behind him, and his cheekbones stand out on his angular face as he sets his mouth in a determined line. His dark eyes, focused solely on the crystallos, are framed by eyelashes so long I can make them out from here. For a brief second I feel like I'm betraying Jeremy for noticing another guy's eyelashes, and my adrenaline moves aside for the pang in my heart at the thought of my very recent breakup. The least the Guild could have done was wait to start the Culling until I had a couple days to mourn the loss of the one person I had connected with. I mean, I haven't even been able to have magical friends. Meema stopped inviting people over after Dad's negativity created that Depraved. Sure, she can vanquish the demons his anger summons, and magician guests could help, but she'd never risk the embarrassment of her peers seeing the monsters her magical failure of a son creates.

The sadness comes on quickly and unexpectedly, and I'm so lost in thoughts of loneliness that by the time I snap to, the crystallos is practically on top of me. Too close for the amount of energy I've got going in this lasso over my head. If I flung it now, it'd fly right over the horse's body, only to loop around this long-lashed guy running toward danger.

"Hey, you gotta move!" Long Lashes screams. "You got a death wish or something?"

He's right, I'm about to get pulverized and fail the Culling as soon as it started. But Long Lashes is quick enough for both of us. He flings his backpack from over his shoulder and pulls out a toy horse. It's one of those cheap plastic things you'd find at a Buc-ee's gas station, clogging the shelves with all the other sad toys desperate parents buy to keep their kids occupied during the endless drive from one end of Texas to the other.

This really doesn't seem like the time to be busting kiddie bribes out of a bag. I don't think the crystallos is going to be swayed.

Long Lashes waves his hand over the toy horse and it's bathed in bright pink light. He grabs the toy's left front leg and snaps it off. Inches in front of my face, just before a breath of icy wind freezes me solid, the crystallos's left front leg glows pink and breaks away from its body, sending it tumbling onto its side. Its crystal leg flies and crashes into the front doors of the library, shattering the glass into pieces that blend in with the ice covering the square.

"Holy shit," I say, staring in awe at the crystallos thrashing in front of me, trying to gain purchase with its remaining three hooves. "He's a sprite."

This kid used that toy horse as an effigy, casting his magic over the figurine so that whatever he did to it would also happen to the crystallos in real life. I've never heard of that before. Sprite descendants usually have to create effigies themselves, their magic binding to an object handmade out of sprite wood. But honestly, I'm glad this guy didn't have to take the time to carve a little horse. If he did, I'd be a Nigel-cicle right about now.

"I know it's shocking to see one of these things in the flesh, but you've got to move or it'll kill you!" Long Lashes is in my face now, giving me a look of concern. Or is it pity? Being a sprite, he has to see the magicked lasso in my hand. He probably thinks I'm not cut out for Guild work if I stand there like an idiot when finally faced with a magical beast.

He pushes me back, gently but firmly. "Keep your distance. I've got this covered." My chest buzzes where he touched me, probably in desperation to cling to any boy's touch after getting dumped. It's so distracting that I don't pay attention as I step backward, and I slip on the ice. My legs fly out from under me, the magic rope flies from my hands. It slides across the courtyard, its gold light reflecting off the frozen surface, and gets tangled in Sprite Boy's legs. We both go crashing to the ground, me landing flat on my back, him hard on his butt. The wind is knocked out of my lungs, the air so cold from the crystallos's magic that I can see my breath fan out in front of my face.

"Oh, that hurt." I moan, craning my head up to see how far away my rope is. I've got to move fast and hog-tie this crystallos now that it's writhing on the ground.

Only, it's not writhing anymore. That breath of air fanning out in front of me wasn't mine after all. It's a cloud of icy magic that pours from the crystallos's mouth to hover over the area where its leg used to be. In the blink of an eye, the magic freezes into a new leg. Now, with four legs completely intact, the crystallos spears its pointy hooves into the ground and hoists itself up in one fluid movement. Its hulking body replaces my view of the twilight sky with the murderous glare of a predator that's ready to devour me.

It opens its mouth to breathe deadly Frosted Flakes over my body, just as Sprite Boy yells, "Hey! Over here!"

He holds out a red BIC lighter triumphantly and flicks it open, its itty-bitty flame flickering to life. The crystallos huffs again, this time like it's laughing at this guy for thinking that tiny fire could do anything to stop it. I'd laugh, too, if I wasn't on the verge of being frozen to death.

"No offense, but I don't think that's going to work," I say while the crystallos is distracted. I've got to get to my lasso so I can tie this creature up and cast some sort of calming spell over it. If it keeps thinking we're foes, there's no way I'll be able to get it to take me to the Guild.

"While I *appreciate* the feedback, so far I'm the only one getting anything done." The bite in his tone makes it clear that appreciation is the last thing he feels. "Just watch."

Sprite Boy snags the horse toy from the ground—still throbbing in the pink light of his magic—then holds the flame under it. The plastic starts to warp and melt, just a millisecond before the crystallos lets loose the most ear-piercing whinny yet.

It bucks and writhes and stamps its hooves as a small red glow blooms in the center of its stomach. As I watch, the glow steadily grows, each pulse of red light sending the ice horse into an even greater frenzy.

The flame is burning the creature from the inside out. Water starts to form on its sides, small drops at first that eventually coalesce together and pour down the horse in rivulets. This guy has turned the crystallos into a living, breathing, panicking fountain.

If the spell goes on much longer, he's going to subdue the ice horse before I can, and I'll be left standing here like a moron, watching him ride off to the Guild while senior magicians strip me of my power. I've got to get in on this action or I'll be stuck at home with

Dad, creating twice the number of demons with our combined anger and disappointment.

Sprite Boy gives me a satisfied smirk. "See, I've got this in the ba—*oof!*" This smug sprite careens backward as the thrashing crystallos's head collides with his. Even if this guy's fire spell has melted the ice creature to the size of a quarter horse, that means he was still bowled over by a regular-size equine. As I know from the dozens of times I've been bucked off, kicked, and bit, that does not feel good, and this guy isn't nearly as burly as I am. I can already see the beginnings of a bruise spreading across his left cheek as he picks himself up off the ground.

"Hang on," I say. "I got this." It was one of the first spells I mastered on the estate, thanks to the scars, bruises, and broken bones that came out of the aforementioned horse incidents.

My hands glow with magic, and I hold them out in front of me, palms parallel to each other. My chest heaves with exhaustion and the strength of my magic starts to dwindle. But there's got to be enough left for me to muster this last trick. I imagine the crystallos's head in between my hands, then point my middle fingers inward, resting them on the temples of my mentally conjured horse.

Calm.

Meanwhile, Sprite Boy is anything but chill. He's slid over to me to put his hand on my shoulder, ready to pull me back. A jolt goes through my body, and I wonder if Sprite Boy's trying to curse me, but I'm too deep into this calming spell to hold him off. "Your magic *literally* tripped me up before," he says, "I do not need your hel—"

I don't know what stops him. Maybe it's the fact that I'm casting magic of my own and he wants to see how it will go down. A warm golden orb appears in the air between my hands, surrounding the imaginary horse head in my mind. The crystallos immediately stops thrashing. Its whinnying quiets and its breathing slows.

I glance over at Spritey and see that he's swaying on his feet. His eyelids have drooped, fluttering, and a gentle smile pokes up the corners of his lips. Somehow, his bruise has gone, too. He's entirely at peace, the human mirror of the look on the crystallos's face.

Oh crap. I don't think I just spelled the ice horse. I spelled this magician, too.

Sprite Boy, the crystallos, and the entire square is pleasantly quiet. A few grackles lazily squawk in the background. Now that I look around, *everyone* has that glazed over look on their face. The college students who were previously cowering behind the statue of the university founder, the people who were watching the icy mayhem through the library windows, even the cops who just pulled up on the side of the street. Each person stands there, looking at me with that dumb grin on their face like they're simply curious—not at all concerned—about what will happen next.

My magic hit each and every person as far as I can see.

This has never happened before. I mean, sure, I have messed up magic in the past, blowing out the windows in our house or accidentally turning all the eggs in our chicken coop to pudding cups. But I've never had a spell's effects magnified to hit every creature in reach. Magic has its limits, and such widespread power usually belongs only to the most powerful and practiced members of the Guild. But I just spelled dozens of people, a few birds, and one ice monster like it was nothing. Even after using up a good amount of power.

Maybe I'm stronger than I thought.

The good news is the crystallos is completely calm. It stands there, looking at me like it hopes I've got an apple in my pocket that it can eat from my palm. I am supposed to follow—or I guess, ride—this thing to the Guild, so I figure now's as good a time as any to approach. I extend my hand, fingers up, palm flat, and move in slow so the fanged beast knows I'm coming.

"Good horsey," I breathe, inching closer and closer until my hand lies flat on the ice horse's forehead. It leans into my hand, letting out a snowflake-filled huff that cools my arm but doesn't freeze it solid. So we're headed in the right direction.

The bad news is I've now got an audience of mind-numbed humans and one dazed apprentice magician to handle. To be honest, the get-them-before-they-get-you attitude of the Culling makes me almost want to leave Sprite Boy here. He *was* about to tell me he didn't need my help, after all. But if I ride off into the night and let him stand here until my spell fades, senior magicians will find him and take his power away for not completing the first trial. If someone loses magic because of their own mistakes, that's on them. But I'd feel awful being the reason someone had their magic taken. Besides, I'm not sure how easy it would have been to ride the crystallos if Sprite Boy hadn't shrunk it with his effigy-lighter trick first. This was a team effort.

Plus, he looks way too innocent batting those long lashes for me to leave him standing here defenseless.

I give the crystallos a reassuring pat. "Stay," I say, then saunter over to Sprite Boy and wave like he hasn't been staring at me this entire time. But instead of smugly smirking like I'm sure he would if he wasn't spelled, he just smiles and waves back.

"Hi," he says. He sounds like he belongs on an after-school special, all sarcastic vibes erased.

"What's your name?" I ask.

"Orion Olson, but most people call me Ori. What's yours?"

Ori. My brain clicks with recognition as I realize I met this long-lashed smirker years ago. It was before my magic manifested and Dad's hatred got out of control. Ori came to the ranch once, with his older sister and his mom, Meema's fellow Guild member. I can't remember their names, but I do remember Ori and me playing with some baby goats. He was much less sarcastic and not nearly this cute. Wait, I did not just think that. Anyway, that was the last time I ever had a potential pal over.

"Nigel Barrett," I finally answer, "but most people call me . . . Nigel." I wince. Real smooth. If he was his normal self, I'm sure Ori would laugh, or make some comment about how my name sounds like it should belong to some ancient white guy running Downton Abbey. Which is totally accurate, but you hear it enough times and it really starts to get old. With the exception of Dad—who his father insisted be named after him since Dad took Meema's last name in order for the Almighty Barrett Family to live on—all the men on Meema's side of the family were named Nigel. A tradition started by . . . well, ancient white guys.

Anyway, Ori doesn't seem fazed. "I thought so. Nice to see you again, Nigel."

I was right. It's baby goat buddy Ori.

I hook my thumb over my shoulder. "So, we should probably catch a ride on the crystallos to get to the Guild. You up for coming with me?"

Ori nods. "Sure!"

"Have you ridden a horse before?"

"Nope! But it looks like fun."

I've ridden horses all my life, and if this were just me, I'd be able to ride bareback, my body moving with the ice horse so my legs won't feel like they're going to fall off after the ride. But Ori is going to have a time of it depending on how far we have to go, so I bring magic to my palms and mold it into the shape of a saddle. Before long, a golden seat is in my hands and I throw it over the crystallos's back.

"Let me give you a hand up." I link my hands together to form a hold that Ori steps into amiably, and I boost him up into the seat. I'll sit in front of the saddle and try to keep the ice horse calm.

The first step to that is giving this beastie a name. Animals are most calm when you speak to them like equals. That's something I'm used to. Without any friends, animals have always kept me company, so talking with them like people just comes naturally.

"What should we call you, buddy?" I ask, putting a comforting hand on the crystallos's neck. They lean into me (now that I know they're not going to eat me, calling them *it* feels a little heartless), and I shiver. Like they can sense my discomfort, the crystallos warms their icy skin so that I won't get frostbite. They huff out a breath again, this time warm even though there's still snowflakes in it.

"You think you can thaw out our friends . . . Frosty?" Frosty and Snowflake are the only ice-related names I can think of. Both extremely unoriginal, but coming up with a good name is not part of the Culling.

Frosty huffs warm air again, but this time their breath billows and builds until it forms a cloud that covers the square. Thankfully, it doesn't *smell* like horse breath—more like sunshine breaking through a crisp winter day. The cloud glows with a silver light, and then everything starts to melt. The ground goes from a slippery ice rink back to cement, every frozen human thaws and color returns to their skin, and their horrified expressions soften into that same simple calm that's on Ori's face.

Leaving them in a magicked stupor might actually be a good thing. Not that there's a point system in the Culling or anything, but it couldn't hurt to lend a hand to the senior magicians who'll come in and wipe these folks' memories, and surely calming them down ahead of time will be a help. Meema says there's an entire branch of the Guild dedicated to memory altering and technology tampering, making it so that no trace of magical power lives on in the minds or phones of anybody who sees us on a mission.

Though, there'll be a lot more work for them if I just ride off into the streets of Austin on a mythical horse. I've got to turn us invisible, but my magic's waning again; no wonder after I blasted this entire square into sweet serenity. At least using a spell I'm familiar with takes less of a toll than trying to make my magic do something new. I let my power pool in my hands, then stretch it out into my trusty hankie, a cowboy's favorite sidekick. Only, there's no way this is big enough to cover me, Ori, and the horse, so I pull on it, thinking *Invisible* the entire time, until it's about the size of a horse blanket. That should do. I throw it around Ori's back, draping it over us like a cape, the sides long enough to hit Frosty's hide. On contact, I see the edges of our bodies blur. The spell's working.

The invisibility horse blanket starts to slide though, so I clutch it in my fist, my hand balancing on top of Ori's knee. A warm, tingling sensation cascades up my arm. It's peaceful, and I feel my power gaining strength as I run my freehand through the air, drawing an arrow. Then, with the snap of a finger, a little rooster pops up on top. It's a glowing magical replica of the weather vane on top of our barn. I tap it and say, "To the Guild," and it spins in circles a few times before pointing east. With my magic somehow seeming stronger than ever despite all the spellcasting, I snap my fingers again, willing both Ori and my new horse to come to their senses. Ori's eyes flutter and that small smile drops into a frown.

He's back, all right.

I click my tongue and squeeze my knees against Frosty's sides. "Move along, buddy."

Frosty breaks into a trot just as I hear a biting, "What is your hand doing on my knee?"

I snatch my hand back, being sure to keep the spelled blanket clutched in my fist so we're not revealed to the downtown crowds around us. Warmth washes over my face, and I'm thankful I'm facing forward so Ori can't see the blush lighting up my cheeks. We may be invisible to humans right now, but we can very much still see each other. I can only imagine what's going through Ori's head when he came out of a calm stupor to find some kid he hasn't seen in over ten years with a hand pressed to his leg. "Chill out," I say. "I was just making sure you weren't spelled anymore or spotted by humans. *And* I helped you through the first trial, by the way. I'm not as helpless as you thought."

"Neither am I, and I told you I didn't need help." I peek over my shoulder to see him cross his arms like an obstinate toddler. "And you *spelled me*?!"

"It was an accident. I can just put you right back down on the ground and ride off to the Guild without you if that's what you'd prefer."

Ori opens his mouth, probably to make some snarky comeback, but then stops. He furrows his brow and mutters, "No, thanks." He knows as good as I do if he gets off Frosty he only has minutes before a senior magician comes and strips him of his powers. But that smirk returns and, before I know it, he pokes me in the back, hard. "Just don't magic me again. It's rude."

"Ruder than jabbing someone in the kidney? If you keep that up, I'm going to have Frosty buck you off."

"Frosty?" He scoffs. "That's original."

"This is going to be a long ride, isn't it?"

Ori smirks. "You bet."

CHAPTER FOUR

"So, where are you from?"

I wince as soon as I ask it. Of course my way of easing out of kidney-jabbing tension is to act like some awkward middle schooler at summer camp orientation.

But Ori doesn't seem to have heard. So I try again, this time tilting my head toward him.

"You're not from Austin, right? I think I remember you visiting the ranch from some other city."

At first I think maybe the commotion of traveling through town on a bustling summer night has covered my words. Traffic whizzes by, bluegrass bands play on bar patios, the ever-present screeching of grackles in towering oak trees pierces our ears.

But when I glance behind me and ask again, I know he's heard because his scowl deepens and his lips press into a tight line.

"Oh, so you're one of those, huh?" I say.

"One of what?" Ori snaps, then grimaces when he realizes he's broken his silence.

"One of those apprentice magicians who's only out for number one." Meema warned me that about half of all Guild-hopefuls take this approach: sneering and scowling and closing off to any other apprentice who might be competition. Many see connection as weakness. You connect to someone, you start to trust them, and just when you think you've found your new BFF, they turn around and stab you in the back. She also said these closed-off apprentices were the ones most likely to sabotage you in the Culling, to try to get in your head at best, or to "unintentionally" aim a spell at you at worst.

Meanwhile, connection is *all* I want. It doesn't make sense to me to shut everybody out when some of them could end up in the Guild with me. So many other apprentices have grown up knowing one another all their lives, even vowing to help each other out during the Culling. But thanks to Dad's constant demons, I never got the opportunity to make those friendships or allies. And with Jeremy whipping our relationship rug out from under me, Dad never warming up to me, and a lifetime of feeling different in the human *and* magical world, I'm done being closed off from people. I'm going to use the Culling to prove that I'm worthy of friendship, that I'm nothing like Dad. That I do belong.

So I persist.

"How's your sister?"

Silence again.

I take another peek back to see Ori's pursed his lips. I can't help but notice how deep his Cupid's bow is and the fullness of his bottom lip. Even when pressed together so firmly, they form a delicate pink heart. If only his attitude was as heart-filled as his face.

"What about your mom? She's still in the Guild, right?" God, what a dumb question. Of course she is, unless she— "Oh crap. She didn't die, did she? Meema says the Depraved are getting stronger. Demons, too. I didn't mean to bring up a sore subject, if, you know . . . That would be awful. God, now I'm rambling and I'll just—"

I mime zipping my lips shut, even if Ori can't see with my back turned to him.

Ori finally mutters, "Meema? So you still act like a five year-old."

I huff, wishing my breaths were as powerful as Frosty's and could freeze the smug expression I *know* is on Ori's face right off it. But while I may not have ice sighs, I do have one skill I know Ori doesn't, based on the way he fidgets every few seconds, despite the saddle I conjured.

He's hurting from riding a horse. Meanwhile, my body's moving with the crystallos's gait, gently bobbing up and down as Frosty takes step after step through Austin. We're heading up Lamar Street, past the gas-station-slash-barbecue-joint Rudy's, following my magic weather vane toward who knows where. If I sent Frosty into a nice gallop, I'm sure Ori would go from condescending to hanging-on-for-dear-life in no time flat.

I get ready to press my thighs on either side of Frosty's muscley blue hide, but the second before I do—as if they read my mind—Frosty takes in one deep breath and speeds forward. Austin's streets blur by as we gallop down the sidewalk.

"Ha!" I call, loud and sharp, the thrill of a full equine sprint sending a jolt to my heart. This is the best feeling on earth. This and being in Jeremy's muscular arms.

"Help!" Ori calls, and as if *he* could see the heart-panging vision of Jeremy cradling me against his chest and wants to serve as stand-in, Ori wraps his arms around me.

I gasp, his touch sending tingles up my spine. It's the same warmth when I touched his knee, only *more*. The sensation is so strong it must travel back down my spine and through my legs, because it's like Frosty can feel it, too; their already-galloping legs go into overdrive. My invisibility spell flies out of my hands, but we're moving so fast I'm sure all people will see is a split second of an icy blue blur.

"Slow down, slow down, slow down!" Ori shrieks, and his tingle-inducing fingers become claws gripping my side. I can feel Ori bounce so high with Frosty's increased speed that he lands behind the saddle. He starts to slip, his torso inching away from me and down Frosty's body. I try to reach around to grab him, but I've got to keep both hands gripping either side of Frosty's beefy neck. It would feel more natural to wind my fingers into their mane, but that's just wisps of snow, so this is all I've got or I'm certain I'd fly off, too.

But Frosty knows what's up. The crystallos's blue hide glows even brighter and lumps of ice form around my hands. In seconds, they're covered, as are my thighs. The cold starts out sharp as knives, and after I suck in a breath, warmth spreads where the ice covers my body, but the horse's skin never melts.

Frosty's frozen me in place. Ori too. He's now awkwardly frozen right over Frosty's butt, his own rear against Frosty's and covered in ice. I don't know if it's punishment for being so snarky, but Frosty hasn't covered Ori's arms or legs, so his limbs are flailing about like some car dealership air sock with arms billowing wildly. His backpack slaps against his back with every stride.

"Ha!" I call again. This time it's a laugh, but Frosty takes it as encouragement and snorts before putting one last burst of speed in their legs. I don't know how fast we go, but I can no longer discern any shape around us. The world's a blur until the only thing I know is we're out of the city and there's just inky blackness and smears of starlight and the moon. I've ridden a lot of horses before, even a wild mustang or two, but none has ever been this fast.

This is magic.

Until suddenly, it stops.

The world comes into focus, and the ice holding us in place gently melts back into Frosty's body. My muscles instinctively adapt to Frosty's new pace, a steady trot, but Ori can't keep up. He slides back, his jeans slicking against the crystallos's skin until he falls off and lands hard in the desert dirt with a heavy *thud*. He tries hopping up but tumbles right back down, dust billowing around him, illuminated by the moonlight.

I chuckle. "Don't worry. It's normal. The first few days I rode, I couldn't feel my legs. But you'll get used to it."

Ori just scowls and leans to the left, massaging his right butt cheek. He moans and I bet he's feeling those pinpricks as blood seeps into his muscles and feeling slowly comes back.

"Just a heads-up, you're going to be sore for about a week," I say. "But the more you ride, the more you get used to it, so—" I stretch my leg out from atop Frosty's back so he can grab it and hoist himself up, but he just swats me away and dusts off his white sneakers before slowly—so, so slowly—getting to his feet. He looks like a baby trying to stand for the first time, and it's actually kind of adorable. I can't help but laugh, even if he still has that perma-scowl on his face.

My chuckle only makes Ori frown deeper. "Yeah, no, I'm never getting on that thing again."

Frosty grunts in indignation. They're *definitely* proud. It occurs to me that it might be an issue if I've got a standoffish ice horse following me around when I'm trying to make friends. But in this case, I'd have to agree with the crystallos. "I never really trusted people who don't like animals," I say.

"Good. You shouldn't trust me. Because I don't trust you. I won't trust any of you people until I make it past the third test and I'm solidly in the Guild."

I shrug. "Suit yourself. I guess I'll just gallop off to the Guild without you." I scan the horizon, but all I see is silvery desert bathed in moonlight and that inky-black sky. "Which is where, exactly?"

As if on cue, a solitary light blinks on in the distance. Whoever or whatever the light belongs to is too far off to see from here.

I take a deep breath and center my mind. Then I bring my hands out in front of me, creating circles by pressing my pointer fingers to my thumbs. As I bring the circles over my eyes, I let my magic pool in my hands. A round trail of light traces the shape of my fingers, and when I pull my hands away from my face, the light stays over my eyes. A band of golden magic connects the two circles so it's like I'm wearing a pair of glasses spelled to work like binoculars. I look to the orange light on the horizon. A small, square adobe building sits there. Its glass door is flanked by two large windows, a few purses and high heels illuminated by the light that pours through them. Designer wear in the middle of the desert.

"It's the Marfa Prada store," I say. Instantly, a pang hits my heart. This is one of the places Jeremy and I said we'd check out over the summer, exploring Texas like a totally normal couple before he went off to college. Maybe when all this is over I'll tell him I saw it. Maybe he'll tell me he wished we could have gone together. Maybe he'll say breaking up was a mistake. Maybe he'll—

"Are you crying over the sight of high-end handbags?"

I swipe the magic glasses into my pocket and rub the tears welling in my eyes. Ori is looking at me like I've lost my mind. Or like he has no idea how to comfort someone who gets upset over purses and stilettos.

"No. No. Sorry. Dust in my eye. From when you flopped on the ground. When you fell off Frosty." Any trace of concern leaves his face while I clear my throat. "Anyway, if you're sure you can make it on your own, I guess I'll see you in the Guild."

I click my tongue and tap my heels against Frosty's side. "'Yup," I say. That's a shortened version of *giddy up* that's stuck after years of saying it so fast the first part always seems to get lost.

Frosty doesn't move. They just huff once, then curve their neck around to give me some serious side-eye.

"So the friendship's over, is that i—"

I'm smacked off Frosty and land on my back, hard. Frosty's piercing whinny fills the night as they're knocked off their feet, too, a hoof missing my nose by centimeters. I turn my head just in time to see the moon blocked out by a huge, blue, scaley belly, attached to four legs that end in crystal claws.

We were knocked down by a dragon.

A tiny green dot leaps off the giant reptile just before the dragon curves hard and flies off into the night sky. The green jumper lands on my chest softly before hopping off.

A frog. But in a flash of silver light it changes into a teenage girl, my age, East Asian, her black hair in a layered bob, wearing a Ziggy Stardust shirt and studded black pants.

She's a shape-shifter. A goblin-descended apprentice.

"Sorry," she calls with an apologetic wave. "That dragon was kind of all over the place when I hitched a ride. Little known fact, frogs scare the crap out of dragons. Anyway, see you inside, I guess." She shifts in another silver flash, this time to a cheetah, and books it toward the Prada store with a growl.

Ori saunters by while I get to my feet. "Oh no, she doesn't," he says under his breath. In the blink of an eye, he's gone. He reappears a second later, fifty feet away. In another blink, he's so far away I have to pull the magic glasses out of my pocket to find him. As I do, I can see he's passed the goblin-cheetah and made it to the front of the Prada store. He tugs on the door, but it doesn't budge. Locked.

Giving me time to catch up.

I walk over to Frosty, who's also hobbled to their feet, looking left and right nervously.

"No more dragons, buddy. Promise."

I place my hands on Frosty's ice-cold side and ready myself to push onto their back. But just as I launch into the air, my foot gets yanked behind me, and I'm on the dusty desert floor for the second time in as many minutes.

A thick, brown-green vine has an unbreakable grip on my ankle. Which is entirely surprising, because with the exception of a dried-up shrub here and there, this desert has little to no plant life.

I move to unwrap the plant from my ankle, but when my fingers brush the rough stalk, its grip tightens. My foot starts to throb as my circulation is cut off. At another sharp cry from Frosty, I look up to see that all four of their legs are covered in the same thick vines. Every time Frosty bends down to freeze one of the plants with their breath, another vine shoots from the ground with a burst of green light to snap Frosty in the face.

Gripping the vines around my ankles at their base, I try to pry them from the dirt. Their stalks only grow thicker, this time blooming with thorns that stab my palms, dark blood glistening in the moonlight as it falls to the ground. I instantly feel lightheaded at the sight of it.

"Not sorry!" a grating voice calls, followed by a chorus of cackling. Over my shoulder, two kids around my age point and laugh, while a horned troll sulks next to them, attached to a vine leash. One of the girls is white with long auburn hair braided into sections that dangle around her waist like the vines she controls with her fists. She's a nymph, obviously. One that has the power of earth.

The harder she squeezes the fingers of her left hand, the tighter the vines become around Frosty's and my legs. From her other hand, she releases the vine looped around the troll's neck. "Thanks for showing us the way, pal." She says it with acid in her voice, and the troll looks like it could rip her limb from limb. But one look at her partner, who seems ready to strike, and the troll hobbles off into the night.

The girl next to the nymph is South Asian, with warm brown skin and black hair that pours past her shoulders. As soon as the troll takes off, she cups a hand to her mouth and sings.

"Lie back, dumb boy.
The earth is your bed.
Dirt is your pillow.
Rest your head."

Purple light glows from her throat, and I have just enough time to register her music as fae magic before a warmth spreads over me and my body acts on its own. My legs stop struggling, my back goes rigid, and I lie down, crossing my arms like Dracula settling into his coffin.

"Gorgeous song, babe, as always," the nymph girl says to the fae.

"This team work makes the dream work," she replies, and I roll my eyes at the typical fae apprentice need to rhyme. But the vines continue to coil around me—up my legs, past my knees, over my thighs—a new sting with every inch as their thorns pierce my skin. The fae's persistent humming keeps me rigid, unable to flinch or protect myself from becoming a human punch card. It won't be long before I'm completely covered in vines and bloody thorn wounds.

As the vines circle my waist and continue up my stomach, I can't help but wonder what's going to happen when they reach my neck. Will I be choked to death? Will the vines get stuffed down my throat until I suffocate? Will thorns pierce my jugular until I bleed out?

But they wouldn't kill me, right? It's against the rules for apprentices to intentionally kill one another. Still, Meema's warning echoes through my mind.

"They don't want the injuries to be fatal, but the Guild encourages Cullingmates to cast spells against each other. It makes you think quick on your feet, and the quicker you are, the more Depraved you can whup. So when it's you against the other magicians, just be sure you're fastest."

Right now, these two are definitely winning. The nymph's vines crawl past my chest, wrapping around my neck. In seconds, they're over my mouth, then my nose. While she's not shoving them down my throat and the thorn wounds aren't fatal, the vines are so thick that they completely cover my airways. I try to gulp in oxygen, but I can't. I try to struggle, but I can't. The fae's song is still working, so even though my brain is desperately trying to get me to move, my body won't listen.

But then the vines cover my ears, curling to a stop at the top of my head. I'm a vine-covered mummy, and while air and moonlight can't get in anymore, neither can the fae's song. It's silent.

Time for magic.

The only problem is, my magic requires movement. Concentrated thought and a wave of the hands and *bam!* Magic. Some elf descendants, like Meema, can channel their magic with thought alone, but come on. I'm not even a member of the Guild yet; how on earth am I supposed to be as skilled as a denim-loving magical cowgirl in her seventies? With my hands and feet so tightly bound together, I can't direct my power.

Making matters worse, my chest tightens as my lungs gasp for air. Deep breaths are what centers me, and there is no chance in this nymph-induced hell of that happening.

Suddenly, the ground falls out from under me. Or rather, I'm yanked off it. The tension squeezing my limbs together vanishes as the vines snap at their base, and I fall a few feet to land on Frosty's back. They take off instantly while I suck in a huge breath. My lungs fill, relief and magic flowing through me once more. I glance up in time to see a pony-size version of the dragon I saw before booking it back to the Prada store. It must be the goblin girl turned dragon, and while she may be tiny, her crystal claws were just sharp enough to get me out of my thorny prison.

"Thanks—for the—assist," I shout through heavy breaths, and the shape-shifter growls a low rumble of acknowledgment that's immediately met by a frightened whinny.

"Hey, buddy," I coo. "I know I promised no more dragons, but I swear that one is a friend."

Meema always said I was like a therapist to the animals on our farm, feeling their wants and needs before ever casting a spell, but to not expect the same of magical animals. They've got thoughts and feelings as complicated as humans', and don't take to people lightly. But as I coo, Frosty's frantic dash turns into a confident gait, and before I know it we're in front of the Prada store.

Ori doesn't bother to look up from inspecting the building, and the shape-shifter changes back to her human form in a burst of silver.

"Thanks again for the rescue," I say.

She scuffs her tattered black Converse in the dirt. "It was nothing."

"Not everyone would do that," I reply. "Why did you?"

Goblin Girl shrugs. "Jaleesa, that fae, and her girlfriend, Laurel, shouldn't have done that to you. They're always trying to get in other apprentices' heads. It's playing dirty. Even if the Guild encourages them."

"Well, I owe you one." I put my hand out to shake. "Thanks . . ."

"Bex," she says, rings on every finger catching the light streaming through the store windows. "Bex Sasaki."

"Nigel Barrett."

Bex's eyes go wide. "You're the Barrett kid! Shouldn't you have been able to, like, disintegrate those vines with your magic? You're supposed to be from a super powerful family."

My face instantly heats up. Even Frosty turns to me with round, judgmental eyes, like they've got some animal instinct telling them I'm not as great as Gramps.

"I mean, it doesn't work like that. He wasn't instantly powerful or anything. So I've got to, you know, work up to it." I don't think listing accomplishments like growing our rooster to the size of a rottweiler or mucking the stalls in one swish of a conjured rake would impress her. Not compared to my great-grandpa, who went down in history for putting the Knife into an enchanted sleep. That legendary Depraved nearly wiped out every human in the burgeoning United States until G-pa Barrett stepped in. And I clearly can't even thwart one wood nymph and a fae.

Bex's face goes as red as I assume mine is. "Sorry. Didn't mean to put you on the spot like that, honest."

She seems like she genuinely means it. Not at all like those apprentices who tried to kill me or the snark I get from Ori.

As if on cue, Ori's voice drips with sarcasm as he says, "I hate to interrupt this tender moment, but we've got company." He points over my shoulder. I turn to see Jaleesa and Laurel, so close that no magic glasses are required.

"Let's get inside before they try to kill me again." I jump to the door and jiggle the handle. The glass rattles as the lock catches on the jam.

"That's your big move?" Ori asks. "Shaking the door?"

I glare at him. "Doesn't seem like you've come up with any bright ideas in all the time I was *fighting for my life*. You weren't too keen to help me out with those apprentices, either, despite the fact that I got you here in the first place."

Ori shrugs. "What was I supposed to do, attack them?"

"Yes! They attacked me first. It would have been self-defense. Or defense of an innocent apprentice, at least."

He bites one corner of his bottom lip, making it pillow out even farther on either side of his canine. That flush rises in my face again, and god I wish I knew a spell to make it stop.

"But maybe you would have taken each other out," Ori says. "It was a win-win for me."

"Bless your heart," I say—letting my voice drip with that Southern sweetness that can turn to condescension on a dime—then get back to inspecting the door.

There's no key hole, so I can't conjure a key and open it that way. If Ori has been trying to get in this whole time and wasn't able to hop inside with his sprite magic, I assume that means a teleportation spell is out. And if Bex can transform into a dragon, albeit a small one, but is still standing outside with us, that must mean crystal claws and fire won't do anything.

Fwip! Whap! Fwip!

Three thorns shoot past, just barely missing my head. They're so elongated and pointy that they look like spears. One inch closer and they would have skewered my eyeballs in the world's most gruesome kabob.

Instead, the thorn spears slam against the Prada store window and shatter without leaving a single mark. But I'm so surprised that I jump, falling face-first into Ori's arms. He catches me on instinct and pulls me to his chest. It's awkward and fumbly since I'm a good six inches taller than him, and about twice as thick, but I'd be 100 percent lying if I said there weren't butterflies in my stomach from feeling just how firm his pecs are. Even if he did sort of wish me dead earlier.

Ori clears his throat, an eyebrow cocked. "Something got your attention?" I'm saved from having to come up with an excuse by Laurel's nasally voice.

"Shoot, just missed."

"You'll get him, don't you worry." Jaleesa looks at me with a demonic grin. "Think of him like target practice. Get him while he scurries."

I groan. "That's near rhyme, Jaleesa. You can do better than that."

Ori laughs, and my heart flutters knowing that I made it happen. But Laurel completely ruins the moment when she flicks her wrist like Spider-Man and more thorn spears fly toward us. Bex, Ori, and I dive, and the desert ground scrapes my elbows raw.

Jaleesa and Laurel cackle as I roll onto my back, just in time to see a thorn hit the store window again. While the thorn shatters in a shower of wood, a wave ripples over the glass. A wave of magic. Purple light—*fae* light—shimmers across the surface.

"It's a portal," I say, propping myself up on my elbows just as I see understanding dawn on Ori's face.

Fae portals. Their magical ability to transform a seemingly ordinary object—a tree, a rock, an undersea cave, a designer store in the middle of the desert—into an entryway to another space. You just have to know how to activate it.

And fae always love to sing. With clear lyrical intention. And rhyme.

"Listen, I may love David Bowie," Bex says, catching on. "But I'm no singer."

"What about you?" I turn to Ori, who has started dancing on his toes like he's playing Ground Is Lava while Laurel's vines sprout left and right in an attempt to ensnare his ankles. Won't she just tire out already? I mean, come on!

Ori scowls, but it doesn't seem to be directed toward our

attackers. Not even when he opens his backpack and pulls out a Barbie, only for Jaleesa to sing it out of his hand with some stupid "Gimme the doll so we don't brawl" line. Instead, Ori's looking right at me, like I'm the one who just thwarted his attempt at making a Mattel effigy.

"Okay, fine, I may have an idea," he says, then drops his voice. "I'm swift."

"Yes, we know you're swift, all sprites are fast!" A thorn pierces through the edge of my jeans, just barely missing my shin, and pins my leg to the ground. "Get on with it!"

"He didn't say he's swift, he said he's a Swiftie," Bex clarifies, dodging plant projectiles of her own. "As in, a major Taylor Swift fan."

"I don't see how that's pertinent to this situation," I say, trying to tug my leg free. But Laurel's attention is on that spear, her fist closed and pulsing green, keeping the thorn rigid and in place. I'm not going anywhere.

I turn to Frosty who, based on what I saw them do in the UT square, could really do some damage. "A little help?" But they just bend down and nibble on a tumbleweed, turning their back to me so all I have is a view of their icy ass. "Thanks for nothing."

Then Ori's voice wobbles, hideously offkey, to the tune of Taylor's "Love Story."

"Portal, please take me somewhere we can be alone.
A nymph is attacking, all there's left to do is run.
You'll be the savior, I'm the apprentice.
To the Guild safely, Portal, just say yes."

The store front glows a weak purple, portal magic triggered.

"It's working!" I cry. That was some seriously quick thinking on Ori's part. Still held in place by the thorn, I'm just able to stretch and press my palm against the window. It gives just a little, but a fully activated portal would let my hand go all the way through. Maybe this has something to do with the strength of Ori's singing. It doesn't help that he has to warble through huffs and puffs as he hops back and forth avoiding Laurel's vines.

So I guess that means I have to join in.

"Portal, please take me," I begin, but not before sucking in a breath as a new vine crawls its way up my ankle and a thorn pierces my skin. Thank god it's under my jeans, or else seeing blood would make me pass out and I'd be done. But the pain snaps me back to the present, enough to see that in two big steps Laurel and Jaleesa will be on me—and I do not want to find out what other tricks they have in store.

Fortunately, Laurel miscalculates a vine's location and it whisks right through Frosty's tumbleweed snack. They glare at Laurel, and one thing is perfectly clear:

They. Are. Pissed.

"Have at 'em," I say, and dramatically point at our attackers. Frosty huffs in assent, then charges. The two dive out of the way, Laurel's thorn spear falling to the earth, though her vine still clings tight. Jaleesa opens her mouth to sing a spell, but Frosty rears up on their hind legs and bats their icy hooves in her face. She ducks and dodges, the effort preventing her from belting out a tune. This is our opportunity to fill her silence.

I take a deep breath and sing, Bex joining in. Ori hops over to my side, his shoulder brushing against mine. An entirely pleasant shiver runs up my spine that I'm attributing to magic well-cast. The fae wall glows brighter and brighter, the purple so intense I have to squint. When we finally get to the last line—*"Portal just say yeeeeeees"*—the magic pulsates with so much force that the glass in the store front windows bursts.

Glass shards fly everywhere, severing the vine at my ankle and nicking my skin in the process.

But the portal's finally open, and with a call of "Frosty! Come," Ori, Bex, and I, all battered and bruised, limp through the wall of fae magic and into the Guild.

Task one of the Culling complete.

CHAPTER FIVE

The second my feet are through the portal, I feel a pull, like suction cups cover every inch of my skin. The glass and thorn scratches sting from the pull one second, but they're nonexistent the next. I have just enough time to see my wounds seal shut—portals have healing powers, I remember reading—before everything is gone in a blur. The world is just a swathe of purple, my body soaring through who knows what, then my feet slam onto solid ground. A shock runs up my shins to my knees, making me fall to the floor, my palms smacking against cool white marble streaked with veins of gold. Scattered among the gold are blotches of dull gray. I squint, trying to get a closer look. They look an awful lot like bones, but . . . that can't be right.

We've landed in the center of a pentagon. Five gold-streaked marble walls loom around us, a large pointed archway at the base of each, intricate bronze artwork framing them. An elf stands tall in one, her ears pointed, casting a spell with long fingers stretched in front of her. There's a nymph with vines for hair over the next arch, making plants grow in a desolate field; another of a fae with delicate wings behind him singing to a crowd of bewitched onlookers; in the arch to my right there's a goblin taking the form of a hydra in the midst of a battle at sea; and lastly, a sprite, looking tenderly at a pile of wood that they carve in their lap. An archway for every Ancestral species. I follow the walls up, tilting my head back as far as it will go. The ceiling must be at least twenty stories up, balconies circling the pentagon along the way at every new floor, with dozens of people crowding each to witness our arrival. Over their heads, looking down on all of us from the ceiling, is the five-starred symbol of the Guild.

Somehow, each of those stars feels like they're boring holes into my soul, judging my magical performance. I feel this fire in my belly to prove myself, to show the Guild that I am worthy of my powers. I think of my future, decimating the Depraved with Meema by my side, living up to my family name, keeping the world safe from evil. This is where I belong. This is what I've trained my whole life for, to jump headfirst into the Guild's heroic mission like thousands of magicians before me. No more sulking around under Dad's heavy gaze. I finally get to put my power to good use.

If only I can make it through the Culling.

"The first three," a male voice grunts. A perfectly manicured hand with thick white fingers grabs me by the chin. I look into his pale green eyes, then notice his auburn hair, impeccably styled, and his stubble, expertly conditioned. I recognize this face: It's Alister Baumbach, a US senator from Wyoming who seems to want his mug on cable news as often as possible. I once asked Meema why there were so many magicians who were famous or successful in the human world, suspecting they'd used their powers to get ahead. But she said while we can use magic to enhance what we're already good at, it's against the rules to manipulate humans except to hide evidence of magic. It's why magicians never stepped in when horrible people held the worst views: racism, sexism, homophobia. We can't take away someone's free will, even if they are terrible and create the Depraved we work so hard to fight against. So if Alister was elected, it was fair and square. Per usual, nothing about his appearance is out of place, except for his lip, which curls in disgust before he snatches Bex's and Ori's chins to inspect them as well. "Not mine," he drawls. "What a disappointment."

"Get your hands off me." Bex's arms transform into gorilla limbs, and she shoves Alister away. "Who do you think you are?"

Alister grins, all cool condescension. "I'd be careful if I were you."

"Oh, I'm so scared." Bex shifts back, putting her now-human hand to her mouth as her eyes widen with fake horror. "Get a life, jerk."

My stomach churns. I don't know about sassing a top magician who could do a lot to make our Culling experience a living hell. But before he can snap back, two new Guild members join Alister. All three appraise us like we're pigs in a 4-H competition, but at least they keep their hands off. Alister's face is full of disdain. A Black man, who I know is elf-descended, best-selling author Jameson Adebisi looks at me with curiosity. The third is a woman with russet-brown skin, her hair shaved. She's Pallavit Devi, world-renowned opera singer who, surprise, surprise, also happens to be fae. She looks at me with a gleam in her eye, excited and hungry.

"What an entrance," she says, a musicality to her voice. "What an *entrance*! Unlike any we've seen in years. So much power. Of course, I'd have loved if my daughter had beaten you here. She was so close. But I've got to hand it to you. That was impressive."

So she must be Jaleesa's mom.

"I wonder, though, if the glass exploding in the storefront was intentional," Jameson says softly, pensive. "You seemed surprised."

"*Or* you were trying to cheat," Alister says. "Trying to *destroy* the portal before others could get through. My daughter was right behind you, but where is she now? Dealing with your blatant sabotage, no doubt!"

I see the resemblance between Alister and Laurel, and while I really can't stand their open contempt, my stomach clenches at the idea of *anyone* thinking I'd stoop so low as to try to ruin the Culling for everyone else. Does Alister really think we meant to prevent any other apprentice from succeeding in the first task? Sure, this is a competition, but more than just *three* apprentices need to make it into the Guild. I believe in the cause of this organization, fighting Depraved everywhere, and I'm not so delusional as to think that three apprentices are enough for that. I can't have this seed planted in the minds of the hundreds of magicians watching from above, either. I need them to know I'm a team player, that I take the responsibility of using magic for good seriously. "It was a total accident!"

Pallavit laughs, bright and cheery. "I think that was pretty obvious! You should have seen the look on your face when that glass exploded." Her eyes go comically huge, her mouth dropping open in a mock-stupor. "Don't worry, Alister. The magic is linked to the glass. If Laurel and Jaleesa can repair the window, they'll be fine. And just think, if we can harness their powers, these three could be seriously beneficial to the Guild's mission."

A bit of the weight on my shoulders lets up. I could be *beneficial.* Some members of the Guild could actually want me.

"Besides," I say, getting to my feet with a little bit of bravado now. "We didn't try to destroy anything. *Your* kid"—I direct my own accusing look at Alister—"tried to kill me!" Sure, Jaleesa was in on it, too, but with Pallavit backing me up I can let that slide.

"Us," Ori corrects. "Or did you think I was just having a tickle fight with Laurel's vines?"

Alister smirks, I guess proud of his daughter's attempts to get rid of us.

"All's fair in the Culling," he drawls. "And they had to fight back. Commanding your beast to attack Jaleesa like that, what else were they supposed to do?"

So they *were* watching all this go down—but clearly Alister's put his own revisionist history on it. Frosty lets out an indignant snort.

"They're not a beast," Bex says on Frosty's behalf. The crystallos grunts and nods in approval, stamping a hoof for emphasis.

"Come on, Alister, give it a rest," Pallavit says. "I've still got the scars from one of *your* vines during our year." She points to a small, inch-long slash on the back of her scalp. "These things happen."

Bex crosses her arms in front of her chest. "It sounds to me like you're just jealous we did better than your kid." She shrugs. "And that's on her."

I want to reach out and hug Bex. It's like her personality can shape-shift, too. One minute she's this welcoming, warm apprentice giving me a hand, the next she's standing up to one of the most intimidating magicians in the world. Meanwhile, Alister's icy glare reminds me entirely too much of Dad looming over me whenever I performed magic, making me feel bad about my gifts. My heart whips back and forth between loving Bex for standing up to Alister and shame that I can't stand up for myself.

"Keep yourselves in check," Alister says. He puts a hand on Ori's and my shoulders, pressing hard. Yeah, speaking of reminding me of Dad. Tears spring to my eyes, and I swear he smiles when he sees them.

"ALISTER!" a familiar voice bellows through the hall. I've heard it that loud so many times, spelled to blast across our two hundred acres so I could hear her no matter where I was on the property. Meema fumes as she stomps into the hall.

"You better wipe that cow-pie-eating grin right off your face," Meema demands. "This is tampering with the Culling, plain and simple. You're telling me you're a corrupt politician *and* magician? I have half a mind to call a tribunal right this second and have your magic removed."

"Oh, please, Adela, don't be so dramatic," Alister says, not budging an inch however close Meema gets. "It just seems odd, doesn't it, that so much power should be concentrated in these apprentices? They destroyed the portal. This one"—he gestures to Ori—"can make effigies without sprite wood, and *he*"— Alister's finger whips toward me—"spelled dozens of humans during the challenge."

"Is that . . . *bad*?" I ask. Isn't this whole challenge about seeing who's the strongest to begin with? Why am I being treated like I did something wrong, when all that magic felt so right?

Meema turns, her fiery lips pursed in that way she does when she's trying to figure something out. "Not bad at all darlin'," she finally says. "Just unusual, to be so strong so young." She turns back to Alister, smug. "But maybe not for a Barrett. We've got history, after all."

"The history *I* remember is your son not cutting it," Alister snarls. "And even in the very unlikely scenario these are God-given gifts, he can't just go strolling through human streets with an ice monster at his heels." He snaps a judgmental finger at Frosty. "It would attract entirely too much attention to us if we had dragons and unicorns and *crystallos* by our sides all the time."

Meema waves him off. "More Barrett lineage showing itself, hon. We have a way with animals. If you're really worried about people seeing the creature, there's a spell for that, Alister, Jesus."

"We should consider the animal's wishes here," Jameson adds.

"It could be considered disrespectful to the creature's intelligence and independence to have it stay here, in the Guild." He doesn't say it with an air of accusation, but rather curious pondering. Still, it puts me on the defensive.

"I'd say the only disrespectful thing is y'all talking about Frosty like they're not right here." Frosty whips their icy mane to the side, wisps of frost and snow elegantly cascading over their neck. A total show-off moment in the best way. "And it's not like I brought them here. They just kind of do what they want. They followed me, isn't that right, buddy?"

Frosty huffs, and Pallavit says, "Well, it is pretty adorable, isn't it?" She turns to Alister. "Technically there's nothing in the rules against this. I say we allow it. A simple invisibility spell will shield it from humans. And honestly, it'll spice things up a bit. Aren't you getting tired of seeing apprentices try the same tricks each and every year?"

Alister just quirks an eyebrow.

Meema's face is set with conviction. "The only thing strange I see is the first apprentices to arrive successfully being interrogated like they're criminals."

Her chest puffs, and for the first time in my life I feel the thrill in my heart of making her proud in front of other magicians.

I can do this. I can prove that the Barrett family is one to be respected, not laughed at or hidden away thanks to Dad's failures.

"Depraved attacks are occurring more frequently than they ever have before," Jameson says. "Perhaps it's time we tried fighting them in new ways. Maybe Nigel and his companion are the way of the future. Ori as well, with his unusual gifts."

"Or maybe these boys' powers will be the end of us," Alister growls. "Power so uncontained, uncontrolled, it exposes us to the world. Causes chaos and fear among humans that only feeds the Depra—"

Alister's lips suddenly seal shut. He stumbles in wide-eyed surprise, the first time I've seen him out of sorts, running his hands over his face and grunting his distress.

"Would you please shut up?" Ori sits on the ground just beyond the bickering magicians, a G.I. Joe at his feet. A smear of pink light coats the toy's lips. He's magicked it.

Ori pushes himself up off the ground. "I thought *we* were supposed to be the angsty, hormonal teenagers. But wow, you sure love the sound of your own voice."

Alister looks like he's ready to attack, but Jameson gives a bemused smirk, and Pallavit's shoulders shake with barely suppressed laughter. Meema's grinning so wide all her teeth show.

"Sometimes you just got to get people to calm down and listen," Ori says. "We didn't *do* anything, except kick ass in the first challenge of the Culling. I've been able to do this"—he motions to his action figures—"for years now, and I don't know why. I just can, and I'm ready to use this ability to stop the Depraved. If there's anything in the rule book that says I can't do that, or that we can't make your kids look like second-place fools, show me. But if not, can we please just move on?"

The hall is silent at first. Bex looks ready to shift again in case Alister attacks, my stomach gallops with nerves, and Ori just inspects his nails. Then someone floors above us bursts out laughing. It's loud and obnoxious, but it's the release on the pressure valve that was needed. The other magicians lining the balconies follow suit, until the entire hall is echoing with laughter. Ori only gives a small, self-satisfied smirk, then snaps his fingers. The magic coating his action figure effigy washes away and Alister's mouth unseals.

"How dare you!" Alister yells, but it's barely audible over the laughs of the crowd.

"Oh, give it a rest, Baumbach," someone calls from above.

Alister seethes and gets right in Ori's face. To Ori's credit, his smirk never drops. "I'll be watching you." He whips his head to me, then Bex. "All of you."

"You're a drama queen, huh?" Ori says, digging under a nail. "By the way, I could come up with a spell to freshen that breath, if you want. Trust me, you need it."

Alister cracks his knuckles, a small pulse of green light bursting with each pop, and a red flower that I swear has teeth starts to grow at his feet. But then—

Wham!

Laurel and Jaleesa appear in the center of the hall, Laurel crashing into her father, sending him sprawling to the ground as she makes it through the portal. I bet no person in America has ever seen Alister this disheveled before.

"Excuse *you*," Laurel says, peering down to where Alister picks himself up off the floor. "Oh! Dad! L-let me help you."

Alister's fall makes the already cackling senior magicians lose it even harder.

"There's a reason we watch from up here, genius," somebody shouts.

Jaleesa looks up, scoping out the magicians in hysterics, her forehead bunched in confusion.

"What did we miss?"

CHAPTER SIX

It quickly becomes apparent that we're going to have to move or else get flattened by arriving apprentices. They pop onto the platform in the center of the hall one by one, moving out of the way until there are dozens of us crowded within the five walls. Then hundreds. As each competitor arrives, the applause gets louder. While I want to be happy for these magicians, who have waited eighteen years just like me for this first magical accomplishment, I'd be lying if I said it didn't sting. We were interrogated upon arrival. Everyone else gets cheered on like they just won the national rodeo. I already feel like an outsider, and I haven't even been within the Guild's walls for an hour.

"Where was our grand welcome, right?" I say to Ori, trying to laugh it off. But I can't deny the sad sort of desperation that tinges my words.

Ori only shrugs. "What does it matter?"

"It's just that everybody else gets brought in with open arms, while we were practically thrown in the dungeons. I mean, if this place has dungeons. It seems like the kind of spot that would, right?"

Ori scowls, his favorite facial expression. "Look, I know we came here together, but I'm not looking to make friends."

So much for Southern hospitality. "I just thought since you helped me out back there. You know, with sealing Alister's mouth shut? That was amazing. Thanks for having my back."

"It's not like we're going to become besties and braid each other's hair and use our magic to pop popcorn and gossip, all right?" Ori's face softens, though, for just the briefest moment. "But Alister shouldn't have come after you like that. Or me. I just couldn't stand listening to him drone on. Still, we're in a competition. And it's best if you don't forget that." His face goes colder than Frosty's.

Speaking of my icy friend, they're sauntering through the crowd, shoving their face into people's pockets, looking for snacks. I've tried getting them to stay, but it's clear they have no interest in listening to me. Bex is somewhere else, having been beckoned a while back by her dads to give them a play by play of her first challenge, so I'm over here with no pals, human or horse.

"Got it," I say. "We're not friends. But still. Thanks. Insert Taylor song here about you being my hero."

Oh god, did I really just say that?

Ori crosses his arms firmly over his chest. "Don't bring her into this." He leans coolly against the marble wall, looking anywhere but at me, and for once I'm thankful to be ignored. I don't know what it is about this guy that makes me so fumbly and awkward, so the less I say the better.

I distract myself by inspecting those dull gray splotches in the otherwise glittering walls. This close I can see they definitely *are* bones embedded in the marble. One just over Ori's shoulder looks like an elongated skull, and it's creepy as hell. I want to talk about it, but Ori's body language makes it clear that conversation's over. Forever, apparently.

I turn to the person next to me, a girl with light brown skin and long black hair. "What's with the walls?"

She gives me some serious side-eye, then nudges the white boy beside her. "This was the one Laurel mentioned, right? The elf who tried to destroy the portal so the rest of us couldn't get in?"

A multitude of feelings flash through me. Frustration that Laurel is spreading this rumor already. Annoyance that the portal clearly *isn't* destroyed, yet other apprentices still want to treat me like it is and it's my fault to boot. Embarrassment that my magic got so out of hand it allowed Laurel to start the rumor to begin with. And the most prevalent feeling of all, sadness that this place that I thought was going to be where I finally belonged is turning out to be anything but. I set out to prove that I'm worthy of being a part of the magical community, but one challenge in and I've already convinced people I'm a screwup.

"Look," I start, "it was a total accident. I didn't mean to—"

I'm cut off once again, this time by the guy, who leans around his friend and takes me in with judgmental blue eyes. "That's him, all right." Then he takes a small wooden figurine carved into the shape of a human from his pocket. He glares at me while he rubs his thumb over the arm of the wooden man, a pink trail of sprite magic left in his wake. On my same arm, an uncontrollable itch blooms, and I scratch so hard I'm shocked I don't leave tracks of blood.

The sprite and his friend cackle while I go to town on my forearm.

Bex shoulders through the crowd until she's next to me and notices my scratching. "What happened there? Laurel's plants poison ivy or something?"

"Sprite curse," I say, tipping my head in my still-laughing attacker's direction.

Bex glares at them, her face erupting in rich brown fur when she does. Her nose lengthens, her teeth grow, her eyes turn a sickly yellow. She's become a werewolf. Well, her head has, while the rest of her body is still David Bowie–loving Bex.

She growls, then snaps her fangs in the sprite magician's direction, tendrils of saliva stretching between teeth that could clearly chomp off that guy's effigy-holding hand in one bite. "Watch yourself," Bex grunts, and the sprite and his friend instantly stop laughing. He swipes his thumb over the figure, the pink light and my itching gone.

"Thanks," I say.

Bex is back to normal in a silver flash. "Don't mention it. I owed you one, what with you having my scales back there. I can't tell you how thankful I am I didn't have to face Jaleesa and Laurel alone." She peers across the room to find Laurel, who's deep in conversation with her dad. Their heads are leaned in close, and the more her dad talks, the deeper Laurel's frown gets. "I've never liked her. All the Baumbachs think they're some gift to magickind since they've never had a family member fail the Culling." She points through the crowd to where Jaleesa stands, a half-dozen apprentices in between her and Laurel. "Jaleesa used to be cool, until she and Laurel started dating last year. The stuck-up rubbed off and now Jaleesa's just as bad."

While I appreciate Bex giving me the backstory, it also sends a stab to my heart. If Meema hadn't shut me off from the whole magician community, I'd know this stuff already. But then Bex's eyes go wide, totally at odds with how I'm feeling because I know if she still had a werewolf head she'd look more like an excited puppy than a man-eating beast. "Wait, we could do that, too. I mean, not be total asses to everyone, but we could have each other's back until we both make it into the Guild."

A sense of relief washes over me so completely that I almost think it's another spell. I need an ally. I need a friend. Especially since the one guy I tried to warm up to made it very clear he is colder than Frosty.

"I'd like that," I say. "A lot."

Bex grins, friendly, warm, so different from everyone else here. "It's a deal." She puts her hand out to shake but snatches it back as soon as Meema's loud voice booms through the hall, "ATTENTION, CULLINGMATES."

The room snaps to attention, backs straightening, eyes zeroing in on Meema as she paces the center of the hall. It must be three hundred feet wide, but her commanding presence makes it feel like she's right next to each of us. It's something I'm used to, and I know what a softie she is at heart, so it's funny to see how intimidated these apprentices are. They all look so serious while I'm grinning like an idiot. At least there's one magician here I know something about that the others don't.

"We've reached sunrise," Meema says, her voice echoing as she turns periodically to send her perfectly mascaraed stare at every cluster of apprentices. "Which means that's it. Four hundred sixty-one of you have passed the first test."

The spell of her speech is temporarily broken while the crowd breaks out in cheers and whistles. Bex pops back into her werewolf head and lets out a triumphant howl.

"That's right, y'all, this is an achievement," Meema says, her magically magnified voice loud enough to drown out our celebration. "But don't go counting your chickens before they've hatched. The apprentices who didn't make it to a portal are currently being stripped of their magic. The thing that defined them—the thing they lived for—taken from them in an instant. That could be *you*. That will be *most* of you."

Talk about killing the vibe. Any hint of pride or excitement has completely left the hall. The senior magicians crowding the balconies look down on us, their faces just as serious as Meema's while she continues.

"It's all in the name of balance. Of protection. Of the mission of the Guild. To protect our world and mankind from magical threats. Of which *we* are one. Magic can bring light, health, expediency to everyday tasks. But it likes to coalesce, to feed and grow off itself. Too much magic in the world and we'll all drown in our power. We have to cull ourselves, get our membership to a manageable number, so our magic won't transform the world for the worst."

Pallavit steps forward, the clacking of her heels the only sound as everyone holds their breath. "The Culling lasts five days. One for each Ancestral race. The most auspicious number known to magic-kind, representing the five points in a star, the source of our ancestors' magic millennia ago. Over the course of three challenges, your numbers will be dwindled down to just five percent of what we began with, the amount to sustain magical balance. It's a noble sacrifice. One for the greater good. Because that's what this organization of magicians is all about: upholding good. At times, we must sacrifice ourselves, but the payoff is great."

Pallavit motions above us, directing our attention to the adults watching. "Look around you. The thousands of magicians you see succeeded in your same trials. They made it through all three tasks and have committed their lives to magic and protecting the earth. To balance, to weeding out evil before its magic can coalesce and destroy. It's a dangerous life, but well worth it. As you grow with the Guild, so too does your strength and power. But only roughly one hundred of you will succeed. You must prove yourselves worthy of the responsibility and the rewards to come."

Meema saunters over to a wall, where she points to a skull just like the one over Ori's shoulder. It's longer than a human's would be, the teeth sharper. "You'll be reminded of your great responsibility everywhere you look," she says. "These bones are those of the Horde, the Depraved army the Knife led centuries ago. We were able to destroy those soldiers, and we embedded their bones in these walls as a constant reminder of what we're up against."

Each apprentice has a stable's worth of emotion written on their face: awe and wonder at Pallavit's and Meema's words, fear that we'll have to face the Depraved head-on someday, apprehension at the realization that we're going to have the weight of making sure evil doesn't destroy human and magickind on our shoulders soon.

Pallavit's expression, however, is full of pure glee. If you thought all opera singers were serious and stuffy, you thought wrong. "Get ready to kick some Depraved ass!" She's clearly in love with magic and the mission of the Guild. Totally the energy you'd want from a mentor while competing in a challenge that will determine the course of your life.

"Now, get some rest," Meema says. "A representative of each of your magics will take you to your designated wing. Sleep fast and hard. Training begins soon." Meema walks to the nearest pointed archway. Even though it looms a dozen feet over her head, she seems to fill it with her presence. "Elf apprentices. With me."

She moseys through the arch without a glance back to see if we follow. But every single apprentice hustles, elves following Meema, fae after Pallavit, sprites and nymphs after their own senior magicians.

"Gotta follow my dad," Bex says, nodding toward a man who has the same everyday rocker vibe as Bex, goblin apprentices gathering around him. It's Yamato Sasaki, senior goblin-descended magician and fashion designer known for creating clothes for all body types since day one. "See you when I see you, I guess," Bex says before she dashes off, too, a veiny pair of bat wings blossoming behind her so she can fly above the crowd. Apprentices swirl and push like the contents of a roiling cauldron, the occasional flash of magic bursting over our heads as annoyed apprentices cast spells to avoid being bumped into, nymphs blasting fire, wind, and water in the face of anyone who gets in their way. I finally find Frosty, stubbornly unmoving and making the crowd part to walk around them.

"Hey, bu—" I start, but instantly stop when I realize who's on the other side of Frosty's hulking body.

Laurel and Alister. I can just make out their conversation.

"You would have been first, Laurel, if you didn't distract yourself with that girl."

"Her name's Jaleesa, and if you'd just give her a chance, you'd see we're stronger together. We almost had that Barrett kid."

"Almost isn't good enough," Alister snaps. "Keep distracting yourself with this abhorrent behavior and you'll lose everything. The Guild, your power, me."

With that he turns on his heel, leaving Laurel looking the complete opposite of how I met her: defenseless, weak, cut to the quick. And why wouldn't she, after being called abhorrent? What's even worse is that Alister *knows* the Depraved shit that can go down because of that kind of hate. So Laurel's got a future of having to fight not only the Depraved, not only bigots at large, but her dad as well.

Frosty chooses that exact moment to trot over and eat a clump of stinging nettles some nymph sprouted to get folks out of his way. So now I'm exposed, staring like a moron right at Laurel.

"H-howdy." Ugh. What is wrong with me?

Laurel's face instantly snaps from defenseless to pissed. "Screw you, Barrett." Her glowing green pointer finger slashes through the air, and a twig smacks against my ear. "And quit eavesdropping."

So much for feeling sorry for her. Laurel stomps off, and I'm left to hustle after the rest of the elf apprentices. I'm the last in the crowd slowly filing through the archway to our designated arm of the Guild star. Ori stands under the bronze sprite, last in his line, like me. He's practically through the archway, but I can still see his facial expression clearly. The scowl is gone, and there's no trace of triumph on his face after making it through round one of the Culling. Instead he looks almost . . . sad. He stares off into the distance, not paying attention to the hall around him. He's clearly somewhere else.

For whatever reason, I want to ask him what's up. I know he said we're not friends, but we've gone through so much together in just a few hours.

Then again, I was never that person people turned to for a shoulder to cry on in school. I never let anyone get that close. I couldn't really relate to their normal problems; I mean, how do you care about someone's crush not asking them to Homecoming when you regularly watch your grandma battle deranged fox demons created by your father's negativity?

But if I really want to make connections in the Culling, maybe I should check on him. Maybe he's acting so closed off just to defend himself from the folks who might trick him into trusting them and then stab him in the back. I'm not that kind of person, though, and I can prove it.

I hesitantly step toward Ori as he stares off into the distance. Of course my brain picks this moment to think about Dad. Maybe it's because I just heard Laurel's father ream her out, or maybe because I'm nervous, and if Dad were here, I know he'd have something to say that would make me think less of myself. Just thinking of him makes my palms sweaty by the time I reach Ori.

"H-hey," I say, but my voice catches. I take a breath, clear my throat. "Hey." I even tentatively tap his shoulder.

The moment my finger connects with Ori's shirt, the room goes out of focus. My vision is fuzzy, like a thick fog has descended through the hall. A figure materializes in the mist with the same pale skin and sharp cheekbones as Ori. It's his sister. I recognize her from the one time we met on the ranch, only in this vision she's older, around the age I am now. Her name comes to me like a bolt of lightning.

"Cassie."

A pressure builds in my chest, an emptiness in my heart that I know can never be filled. Tears well in my eyes, a sadness like I've never felt before rising in my throat. I'm going to get lost in it, I'm going to be sucked into this despair until—

"Reggie."

Hearing Ori say my dad's name makes me jerk away. The room comes back into focus. Cassie and the fog are gone.

Ori seems stunned, his arms limp by his side, his eyes almost sympathetic as he looks up at me.

"Your dad," he says. "He's . . . awful."

He shouldn't know that. He never met Dad, the one time his family came to visit. Meema made sure he was away so he couldn't ruin my first and only chance to make a magical friend.

"He is," I say. "And your sister. What happened to her?"

That's all it takes for Ori to clam up again. His scowl's back and he turns toward the sprite arch. "I don't want to talk about it."

He walks away without looking back, but so many questions linger. Where did that vision come from? What did he see with my dad in it? And why is Ori so sad when he thinks of his sister?

He might seem confident—he even bewitched one of the most

intimidating magicians in the Guild—but from what I just saw, something about her causes him pain. And like a complete idiot, instead of considering he might have as much family baggage entering this Culling as I do, I asked if we could be *friends*. No wonder he looks like he's staring at the world's biggest cow pie whenever he lays eyes on me.

I'm nearly alone in the entrance hall now, the last of the elf apprentices having vanished through the archway, and I hustle to follow after them. Ori didn't stick around to see what just happened between us, so I guess my questions will have to wait. Besides, I don't want to miss some pivotal instruction. But when I step through the arch, I'm completely unprepared for how jaw-dropping the elf hall is.

Meema always said the Guild headquarters was impressive, but I never imagined *this*. The elf branch stretches as high as the main hall, but our arm of the building looks like the inside of a mountain of gold. Gone are the Horde skeletons, replaced by deep, thick veins of the precious metal that run through rocky walls, ranging in shade from a dark bronze to a brilliant white. The entire space seems about as wide as the main entry hall, with various caves in different sizes and shades of gold dotting the walls. In one near the top, a large group of senior magicians eats around a golden table; in another, a few practice spells. Individual magicians float between the caves; there seem to be no staircases here whatsoever. Lining the walls all the way to the top are smaller caves with plush cushions and blankets.

"She's a looker, ain't she?" Meema says, taking in our amazed expressions. "Welcome to the elf arm of the Guild. It's fashioned after the golden mountains our Ancestral predecessors called home. The first elves claim their magic came from enchanted metal like this, that they lived among the star-charged rocks for so long that the magic seeped through their skin, creating the first of their kind.

"Note the communal caves for eating and practicing your magic. A small study room on the top floor is where you can read up on elven concentration and spells. The only areas you will have to yourselves are your individual alcoves. They're first-come-first-serve, and they are reserved for Culling apprentices, as full members return to their own homes and only report here for missions and training. But be warned, the alcoves will not offer you any privacy. It's Guild policy that no space within these walls is to be hidden from view of another magician. It prevents conspiring or corruption within this building, and makes it so that, Guild-forbid, any magician who turns against the organization can't sneak up on us from the inside. You'll find the same transparency in the main hall. Nothing is hidden from view: prisons, tribunals, training rooms. Someone is always watching. And it's best not to forget that."

A hand raises in the crowd. "But what about when we have to go to the bathroom?"

"Being put in a tight spot is when we learn our most useful magic tricks," Meema says. "You'll figure it out."

Wow. I did not expect to be thinking about magical ways to pee on my first day in the Guild, but here we are. And I definitely do not want my talents at mucking out horse stalls to have to come into play here.

"In the meantime, find yourself a bed and get some shut-eye. Training could start at any moment, and you'll need your wits about you."

She saunters out of the archway, sweeping her hand above us as if to say, *Have at it.*

Everyone gets to work casting their own spells, small blasts of golden light reflecting off the walls with each burst of their magic.

Some conjure steps in midair, taking them one by one and making their way slowly up the walls. Others try molding the gold protrusions that sporadically jut out of the stone into staircases. A few attempt floating like the senior magicians above our heads, but nobody can quite seem to figure that out. They hover a few feet off the ground before crashing to the floor.

Frosty finally clops into the hall and adds to the commotion by ambling around the room, sniffing everything and licking veins of gold. Does this horse ever not think about eating?

I decide to conjure my lasso. If I can hook different parts of the wall and swing myself upward, maybe even create a bit of wind to boost me along, I might be able to make it to one of those alcoves. I start looping my hand around my crooked elbow, getting ready for my golden rope to appear, when I'm bumped from behind. I whirl around to tell whatever ticked Cullingmate is trying to mess with me to back off. But instead, I'm met by a cold huff of air as Frosty nudges my arm.

"Not now, buddy."

Frosty bumps my wrist again, this time with enough force that my hand soars over their head and lands on their back. The ice horse seems satisfied with that, wiggling a bit, inviting me to hop on.

This could be a total trick. I've met more than a few stubborn horses who play nice only to buck you off when you climb on their backs. And I do not need to be made a fool of in front of all the other apprentices. But god, am I tired. I may not be scratched and bruised anymore, but I expended so much magic tonight. It'd be nice not to have to tap into it just to finally get some sleep.

"All right, Frosty. Don't make me regret this."

I reluctantly hop on the crystallos's back. Frosty jumps and lets out a breath of ice, the gust of air solidifying into a solid brick before them. We bounce higher again and Frosty repeats the magic, making ice steps that they climb in no time at all. Within seconds, we're up to the highest alcove. Talk about a Frosty flex. And I didn't have to use a single drop of magic.

This high up the rest of my Cullingmates look like ants, staring at me with what must be jealous glares or frustrated grimaces. One even magically magnifies their voice to echo around the hall as they say, "There he goes again, cheating. Where's *our* animal sidekick?"

Frosty seems to decide that's the perfect time to dump on the competition—literally. A snowball drops out of their butt and splats on top of the head of our naysayer.

It won't get any easier to make friends if my horse keeps literally shitting on people.

I slide off Frosty's back and into the cave, which is just beneath the senior magicians who are eating together. They wave with looks of approval, apparently as happy as pigs in mud to watch apprentices piss each other off. Meema wasn't kidding when she said spells against Cullingmates were encouraged. I wave back while Frosty settles in atop the plush cushions that cover the rocky, golden floor. Their body takes up more than half the space, and they peer smugly over the edge of our pod at the apprentices still trying to make their way up.

"You're causing way more trouble than you're worth," I say.

Frosty doesn't care. They just close their eyes like they're ready for a nice long rest.

I curl up against Frosty's side, half expecting them to push me away. But they lean into me, sending a comforting wave of warmth through their hide. Maybe it's that being this close to an animal reminds me of the many times I fell asleep with livestock in the barn, or the fact that I spent my day taming this ice horse and fighting off a nymph and fae that want me dead, but my eyelids suddenly feel entirely too heavy. I wouldn't be able to keep them open if I tried.

The last thing I think about as I close my eyes is Ori's scowling face, and I vow again to figure out what happened between us before I finally fall asleep.

CHAPTER SEVEN

"Y'ALL ARE ABOUT AS USEFUL AS A STEERING WHEEL ON A MULE, sleeping all day like this!"

I shoot up and look over the side of my alcove in time to see Meema turn on her boots and walk into the main hall. In seconds, apprentices begin dropping from their alcoves like flies. Nobody wants to miss anything that might have to do with the second Culling test. Frosty is nowhere to be found—probably off somewhere looking for breakfast—so I guess it's up to me to find a way down.

After a few hours' sleep, my magic feels charged and ready to go. Apparently other apprentices feel the same way, because they're jumping out of their caves with abandon, spelling parachutes or magic versions of those little hats with propellers on them, or springs that allow them to bounce harmlessly off the floor and out of the arch.

Maybe I'm just homesick for the farm after spending a few hours nestled against a horse, but my mind goes to chickens. Sure, they can't *fly* fly, but they can float, which is as much as I need for a soft landing a couple hundred feet below. I take a deep breath and let magic flow to my fingertips. With my right hand, I trace feathers on my left arm. Then I switch hands and repeat. I haven't made wings, exactly—I've never been able to transfigure my own body completely—but picturing all those chickens getting just enough lift to escape a sticky situation back home imbues my magic feathers with purpose.

I jump from my cave and my stomach instantly leaps into my throat. A free fall from this high up is *terrifying.* I flap with all my might, but I'm too freaked out. I've never plummeted like this before, and I can't stop imagining myself breaking apart completely on the unforgiving floor.

But then Ori's face pops into my head, reminding me that we're all in competition, that I can't ever forget that. It would be unbearably embarrassing, even if I were dead, to know that I got knocked out of the Culling because I splatted myself against our dorm floor. Meema and the Barrett name would never live that down. Steely determination flows through me, and with it, a smirk pulls at my lips. One that's probably an awful lot like Ori's.

I flap harder, sweat beading on my forehead. And finally, I gain a bit of lift. Not much, but enough to send me arcing toward a golden protrusion on the nearest wall. My feet hit it at a totally reasonable speed, and I jump off, flapping to control my fall as I bounce from outcropping to outcropping until I land on the ground. Not flattened, no splat.

"Ba-kaw!" I mean for it to be a triumphant *Ha!*, but it comes out more like a squawk. "I did it!" I'm going to build the chickens the most luxe new coop as soon as I get home.

My magic feathers fall to the ground as I look around to see if anybody saw that bit of perfectly performed spellcraft. Apprentices around me just stare, until one of them finally says, "You. Became.

A *chicken*!" He bends over double, cracking up. The entire room follows, their derisive laughter filling the hall. My mind plays the worst trick on me by picturing phantom Dad heads on all their bodies. He'd do this exact same thing. Instead of encouraging me, he'd constantly laugh at the ridiculous way I moved my body to control my spells. Even though he couldn't cast a spell himself, even though he was once unskilled enough that his power was taken, he could always make me feel small. Just like I do in this moment. I should be feeling the thrill of magic well-performed, not wanting to shrink away.

I rush into the entry hall before I can combust from humiliation. The place is packed, and I wonder if I can get lost enough in the crowd to escape my Cullingmates' ridicule. Apprentices pour from their varying archways, and senior magicians pop in using the same central platform we arrived on last night. The older Guild members climb to balconies above using various magics: ropes made of vine, singing to levitate, shifting to great horned owls, you name it.

"Now that you're rested, it's time you learned your way around here," Meema says, waving her hands to get the elves' attention. "It's simple, really." She gestures to the five archways. "Resting and eating areas for each type of Ancestral descendant."

As soon as I follow Meema's finger toward the nymph arch, a familiar glare locks with mine. Laurel looks poised to attack, and magic instinctually pours to my fingertips as I remember just how brutal her spells can get. But as Laurel stomps over, I see Frosty trotting right behind her, munching on a bundle of hay that the nymph consistently makes grow.

"I believe *this* belongs to *you*."

"Right," I say, blushing as all eyes turn toward me once again. I snap my fingers and click my teeth, the same thing I do to call horses back home. "Get over here," I whisper. "I really could have used your help back in the dorm. Good to know you'll ditch me for food."

Frosty gives a whicker that I swear is yet another laugh at my expense.

Laurel continues to glare as Frosty sniffs my pockets for more snacks. "Isn't it sabotage letting your monster off leash?" she asks. "It broke into the nymph branch and started eating our entire forest."

Frosty stamps their hoof, and a bit of ice builds around their muzzle. It grows to the size of a baseball, and Frosty takes a breath like they're going to blow this rock-hard projectile at Laurel's face. The last thing I need is for my ice horse to start a full-on war between me and a nymph who has already tried to take me out once.

"Oh, no you don't." I pluck the ice from Frosty's mouth, then quickly trace a rectangle of my power to create a magic hankie and make it disappear. If only my embarrassment could be wiped away so easily.

An elf apprentice raises his hand. "If that crystallos can wander around willy-nilly in here, what about the Depraved?" he asks. "Or humans, for that matter? How do tourists at that Prada store not just fall in?"

Pallavit joins Meema, her fae apprentices mingling with our group. "As magicians, entering the Guild will become routine, but there are a number of protections that prevent our organization from being breached. Thanks to sprite magic, the portal is constantly changing location, and can even be in multiple locations at the same time. With goblin gifts, it's always changing shape. One day we're a tree in Yellowstone National Park, the next a retail store in the desert. Any portal location is protected by nymph power that keeps unwelcome visitors away via earth, wind, water, and fire. And lastly, the fae-created portal can only be activated through a song, sung by a magic wielder, with lyrics specifying the intention to enter—as you all learned in your first challenge. You see the power we have when all types of magic are combined?"

"What about elves?" I ask. "Everything you listed came from other Ancestral gifts, but no elves."

For the first time, the other elf apprentices actually look like they agree with me. It's a nice change.

"Hopefully, you'll never have to see that bit of magic in action," Meema says. "I pity the unlikely bastard who gets through the first four defenses and falls victim to our last." She points to the platform at her feet, the gold-flecked marble refracting the light so it almost looks like it's moving. "This isn't just some pretty pattern to waste on our shoes. All these gold lines? Those are elf magic. An elf *curse*. If anybody not invited or accompanied by a magician gets through the portal, they'll be incinerated the moment they set foot on this floor. Literally burned, from the inside out, until they're nothing but bones. It's not pretty, I'll tell you what."

That gives the elves around the room a little extra confidence. Several of them puff out their chests and look at the other apprentices like, *That's right. Incinerated.*

"But, we're getting ahead of ourselves," Pallavit says, her usual eager expression lighting up as she turns to take in the gathered apprentices. "Some of you are about to join the greatest magical organization the world has ever known. Over the next few days and two challenges, those of you who succeed will demonstrate power that proves your worthiness to join this organization." I swear at that moment she gives me a wink, and I can't help the smile that tugs at my lips.

I can do this; someone here already thinks so.

"Today, it's all about boot camp. You'll be given a crash course in how the Guild works, what enemies you can expect to meet, and how they will attack. You'll be asked to demonstrate the skills you've honed all these years while awaiting your invitation to the Culling. It's all in preparation for tomorrow's second task.

"But first up, it's time to see how we operate, and what you're up against."

Pallavit lets out a long, clear note and soars into the air. She hops off on the tenth floor balcony, about a hundred feet up.

"A word of warning," she calls down. "Don't expect getting around the Guild to be easy. You're going to have to use your magic for it to get stronger. The building is spelled to challenge you, to test the limits of your power. Meet me in Dispatch to see what I mean."

She takes a few steps onto the tenth floor until a solid wall of the Guild's gold-streaked marble springs up behind her. If we want to find out what Dispatch is, we're going to have to get up there and bust through that rock.

Nobody moves at first. Some glance around like they expect an elevator to pop out of thin air.

"You coming, or what?" Pallavit's voice reverberates through the hall. Immediately after, a huge gust of wind nearly knocks Frosty into me. It's the goblins, all of whom have shape-shifted into flying animals: owls, hummingbirds, bats. I catch sight of Bex just before she transforms into a small pterodactyl and takes off.

The rest of us get to work trying to mimic the senior magicians above, who hop from floor to floor as though taunting us with how easy it is for them. Elves cast spells, fae sing, sprites blink, nymphs use bursts of wind, jets of water, or crawling vines to get up as high as they can.

You can tell how much competitors have practiced their magic at home based on how quickly they get up to the tenth floor. For some, the trek is a breeze; others are panting, sweat dampening their shirts in moments.

I lick my lips, about ready to cluck to summon Frosty, when a biting voice comes from behind me.

"God, cowboy, you really are an idiot, huh?" Ori sidles up next to me with that smug smirk on his face as he watches the pandemonium. All the goblins are up, as are most of the fae and a smattering of the rest of the magician types, but about half our Cullingmates are still making their way.

"Good morning to you, too." Why is it that when Laurel makes fun of me, I want to spell her lips shut, but when Ori does it, this tingle in my gut reaches catastrophic levels?

"You can't just gallop through here, ready and raring to go at all times," Ori says, taking in the struggling apprentices. "We were everyone's target yesterday. Magicians so strong we almost broke the portal. They think we're enemy number one. Best to look a bit helpless now, even things out. Get back in the middle of the pack. Then just slip by in the second challenge and dominate in the third. Guild membership, here we come."

My heart flutters at the way he says *we*.

Ori's nose scrunches, almost like he smells something bad, but I can't help noticing the way it makes his smattering of freckles stand out. Then he gives me this pointed look and says, "You going to say anything, or are you always this awkward?"

What is wrong with me?

"Oh, uh, th-thanks, I guess. That's actually a pretty good idea."

Ori nods once. "All my ideas are. Now we're even."

"Even for what?"

Ori's eye roll is epic. "Keep up, Nigel, come on. You didn't have to take me with you yesterday, but you did, and I've still got my magic because of it. Now I've told you how to escape apprentices *accidentally* maiming you in the Culling. We're even. And I can go back to literally never thinking about you again."

I know that should make my heart drop, but instead, my stomach bubbles. It must have something to do with the way Ori's lips pillow with his small smile, even if it is from him thinking he has an upper hand on me.

Holy shit. Is this what a crush feels like?

I mean, sure, I liked Jeremy. A lot. But I never got those tingles when I first saw him, or when we first touched. When Jeremy told me he'd liked me for a while, I figured, why not. And then my feelings grew slowly, over time. But this? Whenever I'm around Ori, there's this not-entirely-unpleasant buzzing inside of me. Like how I feel after a nice long ride around the ranch. My legs might be jelly, but it's still nice.

Frosty chooses that moment to stop sniffing my pockets and nuzzle Ori instead. Clearly the crystallos is not at all the fearsome monster that appeared yesterday in the courtyard. But right now they're not the standoffish, proud creature I've started to get used to, either. They're curious, almost open, looking between me and Ori expectantly. Ori must feel their openness, too, because he pats Frosty's back, making my knees weak. It's like when I first saw Jeremy pampering his French bulldog, only *more*. Something about a guy being kind to animals gets me all worked up.

"Yeah," I finally say when my chest settles. "We're even." I try my luck with a smile, and Ori's drops as he rolls his eyes. But he doesn't walk away, so I guess it's a start.

"Well," I say, after yet another moment of awkward silence. "I'm going to head up."

Frosty gets it and kneels down so I can hop onto their back. I look over at Ori. Maybe I can push this friendship even further and not have him revert to I'd-curse-you-if-I-could vibes.

"Want a lift?"

Ori scoffs. "What, you think you're just going to carry me through this whole thing? Guess again." He cracks his neck, bending it from side to side. "As if you and that bag of bones could beat me." Ori takes a step back. "I'll even give you a head start." He unzips his backpack and takes out a small cup of blue Play-Doh.

A challenge. This I can do. I'm used to the cowboys in rodeo competitions who won't respect you until you beat them. Maybe that's what it will take for Ori to finally let his guard down with me. "You're on."

I squeeze my thighs against Frosty's sides and click my tongue. "'Yup!"

Frosty jumps, leaping up their icy staircase until we're in the thick of the apprentices making their way to the tenth balcony. We'll be there in no time.

I look down to see Ori still standing on the first level, just one of many sprites and nymphs trying to make headway. But even though I'm about two-thirds of the way up, it'd be shortsighted to think Ori's going to make this easy.

I see him fiddle with the Play-Doh in his hands, and in a heartbeat he has two enormous wings, cobalt and glistening, longer even than he is tall. In no time at all he's become this beautiful angel, and it makes every apprentice stop what they're doing to look. Even Frosty slows to watch.

In one graceful movement, Ori spreads his wings wide. One flap, two, and he's airborne.

I don't stand a chance. Stunned by his grace, by his hair dancing in the wind, I watch as he flies level with me, then higher, in just three wing beats.

On the third, the tip of his wing grazes my shoulder, and if I thought my heart fluttered before, it has nothing on the way it beats against my chest now. As his feathers slide against me, I see the deep blues, purples, grays, and blacks that all swirl together there. Literally. My vision goes fuzzy, until I see her again.

Cassie.

Ori's sister.

Only this time, she's being held underwater by a rotting Depraved.

"Cassie," I whisper, just as Ori flaps his wings again, his touch gone as quickly as it began, his feet up and over the tenth-floor balcony.

"'Yup!" I urge Frosty into a gallop to follow. As soon as their hooves hit the floor I swing off, landing on my feet. In normal situations, I'd hope I looked as much like a smooth, hot cowboy as I felt—but right now, there are more important things to think about.

"Ori! Your sister. She's being attacked!"

I expect Ori to go wide-eyed with worry, to race to some Guild member to find out how we can help her. But instead, his face falls, his mouth forms a tight line, and his wings disappear with an angry snap as he balls the Play-Doh effigy in his fist.

"No, she's not," Ori says flatly. "She's gone."

CHAPTER EIGHT

"Gone," I whisper. The way he says it, I know it's bad. Not gone as in "We haven't spoken in a while." Final *gone*. Permanent.

She's dead.

No wonder he's been closed off this whole time. The second I met him I rambled on and on about him losing a family member. It must have been a bucket of salt in the wound.

"Ori, I'm so sorry."

I try to catch up to him, but the floor's packed with arriving apprentices. All of them work on their own spells to make it through the solid marble wall. Goblins have taken to transforming into gargoyles if they're strong enough, their crystal claws able to cut through stone. Fae attempt to craft portals from one side of the stone to the other and sprites try blinking. You can tell who's successful, because those who fail pop right back to where they started. Ori doesn't pop back, and I watch any hope of really apologizing disappear to the other side of the wall.

Elves are trying all sorts of spells, from crafting stone-cutting knives to making themselves incorporeal in an attempt to float through the wall. Most are unsuccessful. Jumping up ten stories has already spent a lot of magic. Since I rode up here on Frosty, my magic is ready to rock.

Sometimes, the best spell to solve a problem is the simplest, and the best way to get into any room is through a door. The first that comes to mind is a barn door like the ones I've slid through my whole life. And maybe this can be my chance to earn some good will.

With power in my hands I hop back up on Frosty's back, tracing a line parallel to the ceiling. The crystallos seems hesitant to move at first, but magicking an apple to levitate in front of their face gets them going. I guide Frosty to the left, creating a new line down to the floor, then do the same on the right. Before long there's a twelve by twelve golden rectangle glowing on the wall. I center myself, taking a deep breath, and imagine my magic clinging to the marble and moving it all to the side. Then, with a big exhale, I push. The marble slides, but just an inch or two. This isn't like the greased wheels of the barn doors back home. I push from on top of Frosty's back, and once I magic their apple through the small opening, the crystallos leans their icy head down and puts their back into it with me. So, *so* slowly, the door slides. When we've managed a three-foot opening, we stop. I'm exhausted, sweat dampening my flannel and sliding down my crack. It's disgusting, and I won't be able to craft another spell for a minute. I wish I knew how to trigger that supercharge I felt yesterday in the courtyard, but for now, this will have to do.

"Hey, y'all." Every head turns to me, and I shrink under their glares. I try to give a friendly smile. "Um. You can use this door here if you'd like."

Frosty and I clop through, and I don't have the heart to see if anyone follows. Instead, I spot Ori in the crowd and direct Frosty his way.

Unfortunately, my crystallos stops responding to me thanks to the salad bar laid out before us. Plant life coats the floor, stretching farther than the confines of the building should allow. Nymphs have clearly been at work here. So it's travel on foot for me.

On this side of Pallavit's conjured wall, plush grass covers the ground. Dotted here and there are majestic marble fountains. Water gurgles from statues of Ancestrals and magicians in various stances, battling demons or the Depraved. There are dozens of fountains, each at least ten feet across, and the water pouring out of them creates a sort of water screen in which images flash. Pictures of poison-toothed bob-cat demons, of Depraved stalking humans, of Guild members arriving to destroy evil creatures in bursts of colorful magic. Toadstools ring each fountain, grown to a size comfortable for sitting to view the action playing out on each watery screen. Suddenly, the judgmental glares of my Cullingmates—who are begrudgingly pouring through my barn door—seem insignificant, overshadowed by the heroic deeds of the organization I've worked my whole life to join.

"Welcome to Dispatch," Pallavit says. "This is where we monitor demons and Depraved. The fountains let us know where they are formed and when they attack."

All of us apprentices seem spellbound by the images. The only sound in the room is Frosty ripping up a clump of grass, roots and blades snapping, followed by steady chewing. Until . . .

A scoff.

From Ori.

"Something you'd like to add, son?" Meema asks. She's sauntered up next to Pallavit, Jameson following, Alister and Yamato not far behind. I really hope this doesn't mean Bex's dad is all buddy-buddy with the senior member who most clearly hates my guts.

Every head turns in Ori's direction, but he doesn't shrink under the attention. Not like I would.

"It just seems that Dispatch could use a little work," Ori says. "Since so many folks die at the hands of demons and the Depraved while you're up here watching it all go down. You're obviously not doing your job right if you can't stop the worst from happening."

I know right away he's talking about his sister. It doesn't take a genius to put together that the Depraved holding her underwater is the reason she's gone. It must be awful for him to talk about the monsters like they're theoretical when he watched one take away a person he loved.

Gasps ripple through the crowd. Even Frosty picks their head up in response to the room's energy shift. Nobody breathes, all eyes darting between Ori and the senior magicians. The only movement is in the fountain image before us, the scene showing a dark alley where a Depraved coats a woman with mottled-green power. She claws at her throat, clearly choking. The Depraved's eyes glow a sickly green the more she struggles, feeding off her panic. I think I even see its muscles bulge as it soaks up her distress.

Then, a magician appears out of nowhere, silver magic glowing when she transforms into an elephant. In one swift movement, the goblin tackles the Depraved and slams it against a wall. Her thick, leathery trunk grabs the Depraved's head and twists, snapping its neck. The monster crumples to the ground before disintegrating into a pile of bones.

We've all gone from nervous breath-holding to straight up awe. That Guild magician worked so quickly, so efficiently, saving that woman and ridding the world of one more evil spirit. This is what we're here for. For the chance to become that sort of hero. It could happen in just a matter of days.

Pallavit turns from the fountain, a gleam in her eye as she takes in Ori. "You were saying?"

But Ori doesn't back down. "Sure, you save people. But you also fail, too. Or are you not going to show us that part?"

A hand raises in the crowd. Bex. I'm taller than most folks here, giving me the perfect view of her determined face.

"I agree. We need to see what we're getting ourselves into, right? It's only fair that we know both sides of how this works."

I glance at Yamato, thinking he might be upset that his daughter is talking back. But he seems almost playful. His lips quirk up as he glances between his colleagues and his kid with interest.

"It's not like we're trying to hide it from y'all," Meema says. "You've all heard stories of humans who've been victims of the Depraved, or you know someone who has died in service of the Guild. It's a part of this life."

It's true. My grandfather, Meema's ex-husband, died just four years ago on a Guild mission. Of course I wish he hadn't died, but his death felt more like a fact of magical life than a tragedy to me. He rarely came back to Meema's ranch after they divorced, too ashamed of Dad's failures to want to see him, or me apparently.

Jameson glides forward. "What good would it do to show you those deaths? To cause fear? Panic? Hatred? What do all those emotions have in common?"

Laurel's voice rings out. "They're what the Depraved feed on. So I guess we know who Ori's most concerned about."

"Bex too," Jaleesa adds. "And I, for one, don't want to fight alongside someone who's more concerned about the Depraved than me. Do you?"

Jaleesa looks around the room, and a chorus of *No way*s, *Of course not*s, and *Hell no*s ripples through the crowd.

"That's not what they were saying, and you know it." The words are out of my mouth before I can stop them. My whole body flushes with heat, and I wish Frosty were here to cool me down. But there is nothing that can stem the fire of over four hundred angry apprentices.

Or that of Meema. She's not giving me that fiery-soul smile, or a wink that says she's got my back. Instead, she's looking at me like she wishes she could lock my mouth shut as firmly as she locks the gates on the ranch.

"All right, enough squawking!" Meema yells. "Or do you honestly think a bunch of whippersnappers have the Guild more figured out in one day than the magicians who've been putting in their blood, sweat, and tears for decades?"

Everyone looks at Ori, but he doesn't object. His mouth is set in a tight line. Still, as soon as Pallavit begins speaking again, his gaze wanders over to mine.

My eyes dart away. This is just great; I've been caught staring. Why is it that my default state is creepy? But then, completely against my will, my eyes move toward him again. I'd say it's some spell, but I know better.

Ori's still looking. Glaring, actually.

Oh shit. Did I screw up? I was just trying to help. My eyes flick to Bex, and at least she's grinning at me.

"So, now that it's been established that death is a very real consequence of Guild membership," Yamato says, "do you want to know why? Depraved and demon attacks are at an all-time high, and the monsters are becoming stronger than ever before. They have constant fuel thanks to humanity's ever-increasing population and the hate and cruelty that can come with the human experience. Add technology to that mess, and you create a breeding ground for these monsters. With social media broadcasting hateful actions and opinions, you can find cruelty anywhere you look."

Pallavit takes a deep breath and her chest puffs with pride. "But that's where you come in. Don't let this information feed your fear. Let it stoke your commitment to doing what the Guild does. To fighting for the greater good. There's no better counterbalance to negativity than that."

"Which leads us to your next lesson," Jameson says. "Let's see up close just what monsters mankind's savagery can create." He motions to Yamato, who transforms into an eagle.

"Follow me," he clips through his beak.

Yamato's off toward the balcony in a flap of wings, and the room bursts in a kaleidoscope of apprentice spells as everyone scrambles after him. Three figures, however, move against the crowd, dodging toadstools, fountains, topiaries, and Cullingmates to march straight for me. Ori, Bex, and Meema. Unfortunately, it's my grandmother who reaches me first.

She. Is. Pissed. I can feel the energy crackling off her. It makes me so nervous that my eyes dart to the ground.

"You look me in the eye, young man," she snaps in the tone she usually reserves for Dad. It'll only be worse if I don't listen, and I can't risk any apprentices seeing me get owned by my grandma. The second I bring my eyes to hers, she launches into a hurried and hushed reprimand.

"Darlin', don't go making enemies from the jump. Alister's already fixing a squall behind the scenes, making senior members suspicious of you and that Olson boy. He's clearly got his daughter doing the same thing among the apprentices. And now here you are, sassing back like that, questioning the Guild in front of God and everybody. What were you thinking?"

She's never in my life made me second-guess myself. She's always said to trust my instincts, to lean into a challenge. And what was that back there but a challenge?

"Ori had a valid point," I say. "I couldn't stand by while he was ganged up on like that. Aren't we supposed to be a fellowship of magicians that work *together*?"

"Yes, *after* you make it in. Until then, every magician here will do anything and everything to trip you up so they can have your spot. Don't be stupid."

"I don't see how it's stupid to question tradition." Bex has finally arrived, and her expression matches the one of Joan Jett holding a cherry bomb on her T-shirt. She looks ready to blow it all up. "If the Depraved feed on inhumanity, wouldn't it make more sense for us to work together? To encourage friendship rather than distrust among one another?"

Meema's eyebrows furrow deep. I know it's testing her magic to its limits to keep her forehead from crinkling. But no amount of magical Botox could take the venom from her voice.

"Healthy competition isn't inhumane," she barks. "If it creates hate in your soul, maybe you're not made for this work, *sweetheart*." The word drips with sarcasm. "Guild membership is about accepting the realities of the world. Realities like the fact that not everyone who's born with magic gets to keep it. Or do you want people to think that not only are you a Depraved sympathizer, but that you want magic to get out of whack and destroy the planet?" To me, she says, "Use good judgment, darlin'. And that should start with your friends. I'm not sure you've picked the best ones."

She doesn't wait for a reply. She just marches over to the balcony, summons her magic bull, and bounds off to a floor above. But what does she expect me to do? Choose between making her happy or finally having real friends in my life? Abandonment by my grandma or abandonment by my Cullingmates?

Thanks, Meema.

Ori, who hung back while Meema reamed me out, makes his way over. I guess he decided to skip face-to-face time with another senior magician, and I can't say I blame him. At first I think he might be coming over to thank me for speaking up for him, but the second he opens his mouth, I know I'm sorely mistaken.

"Listen, cowboy, I do not need help." His cheeks are flushed and his eyebrows are raised so high they're practically lost in his hair. "Don't go sticking your neck out for me expecting it's going to make me *warm up* to you."

"I just thought—" I can't get my brain to stop swirling. In any other circumstance, I'd take the hint and leave before I can open my mouth again and dig this hole deeper, but boy howdy, crushes are wild. It must be some bizarre magic all its own that makes me stammer into an explanation. "It seemed like you were getting hung out to dry, so I wanted to step in."

"Give it a rest, already," Ori says.

"Whoa, whoa, whoa. Boys." Bex steps in between us. "This is not the way to start the Resistance."

The way she says it, you can *hear* the capital *R*.

"The what?" Ori looks at Bex like she's said the dumbest thing in the world, and for some reason that makes me feel good? Not that I want Bex to be treated badly, but it's nice to know that Ori gives everybody the same level of disdain.

"The Resistance," Bex says simply, not backing down from Ori's standoffishness.

Ori rolls his eyes. "The Guild will never change its ways."

"It's got to start somewhere, right?" Bex throws her arm around my shoulder, then does the same to Ori, pulling us into an impromptu hug. Ori starts to push away, but Bex's arms shift to unmovable gorilla arms in a heartbeat. "Don't try to fight it. Why see everyone as competition when we could see each other as friends? The Guild focuses so much on avoiding the emotions the Depraved use for strength when they could be creating emotions that could *weaken* them. If hate creates stuff for the Depraved to feed on, friendship, trust, love must taste really bad to them, right? That's my mission. To make it into the Guild and change it from the inside out, with love." Her arms flash back to normal, and Bex looks at us expectantly.

"Nobody said anything about love." Ori shakes off Bex and takes a step away. His eyes dart to mine, and despite his overall demeanor, I swear his scowl softens just a bit. "That is not what's going on here."

Bex isn't fazed. "But it could be. If we started to work together and stopped seeing one another as the enemy. We're *all* magicians."

Ori scoffs. "We're *apprentice* magicians, and if you go getting all googly-eyed for each other, you can bet the both of you will have your power stripped in no time."

"Oh come on." Bex changes again in a flash of silver light. "How can you resist help from a lovable koala?"

Except Ori doesn't look like what he sees is lovable at all. He gives a yelp, takes a step back, trips on a toadstool, and lands hard on his back. The wind gets totally knocked out of him. He's flat on his back in the grass, taking deep breaths, his eyes screwed up tight.

Bex pops back to her human form. "What just happened?"

I lean over Ori, getting a good look at just how long his eyelashes are, just how perfectly disheveled his hair looks, how his freckles are spattered across his face like constellations.

Then his eyes snap open, making me jump back.

"See something you like?" Ori says—back to his smug self, just like that.

"N-no, I just . . ." I've got nothing.

Bex looks back and forth between us, then bursts out laughing. "Wait a minute? Are you afraid of koala bears?"

"Shut up," he says through gritted teeth as he gets to his feet.

"Oh my god, you are," I say. It's just too good to see a guy so cocky have such a surprising fear.

"Nothing that small should have claws that big!" he says, defensive. "It's not natural."

Bex is trying hard to contain her laughter, but she's completely failing. Her shoulders shake as she throws a hand over her mouth.

"So I guess we know the key to fostering friendship and starting the Resistance is *not* through koalas," I say.

Bex grows bat wings, her whole body still shaking with laughter as she floats into the air. "This is just too good. See you guys upstairs." Bex's laughs echo through the hall as she follows the rest of the apprentices to her dad's demonstration.

Ori, meanwhile, is all tight-lipped and scowling as he unzips his backpack.

"Put that away," I say, motioning to his bag with my own sorry attempt at an eye roll. I click my tongue and Frosty actually walks over instead of ignoring me for more feasting. They even bend down so I can hop on. "If you're all about strategy, it's stupid to waste your magic when you're being an offered a ride. Why not save your power for the next task?"

Ori sighs, then swings his backpack over his shoulder. "Okay, fine. But don't go thinking this means I owe you one."

"I wouldn't dare."

Ori's lips twitch, the beginning of a smile. Maybe we're getting somewhere. I stretch out my hand to give him a boost, but he just scowls at it before blinking behind me, taking extra effort not to touch.

"And we're off," I say, squeezing Frosty's hide beneath me,

paying extra attention to the coolness of their skin to get the heat away that's crawling through my belly. Frosty breathes their icy steps, per usual, and Ori instantly starts slipping backward.

"Oh shit!" Ori flings his hands around my waist.

So much for trying to push away that heat.

I feel my magic recharge, my heart gallop at full speed.

I feel like I'm flying.

And it has nothing to do with the ice horse giving me a lift.

CHAPTER NINE

"Demons."

Jameson says the word quietly, almost a whisper, but the room is so focused on him it's as if he yells it. Partially we're quiet because we're exhausted from having to spell the balconies floating around the room to stop moving so we could get on them. The other part is, well, Jameson. He's cerebral, he's captivating. I can totally see how his fantasy worlds become best-selling novels even without touching on the actual magic he sees every day. His enchanting personality is enough. We're hooked.

This level became an auditorium the minute we set foot inside. The floor extended out until the open space of the Guild tower was completely covered. A platform rose at the center of the new floor, like a stage, on which Jameson and Yamato stand. The ceiling lifted another fifty feet, and small balconies holding three or four magicians popped up to do a bucking balcony dance until most of us made our way onto them. Bruised and panting, Bex, Ori, and I lean against the railing of our balcony, taking in Jameson's speech.

"There are certain common demon species you'll encounter as Depraved spirits possess wildlife across North America," Yamato says. He's back in his human form, with tight black jeans, disheveled hair, and a strategically ripped t-shirt from his YS line. "Animals are the perfect vessels for weaker Depraved spirits because many creatures have appendages that can do severe damage when warped by Depraved magic, and most lack the intelligence to fight off the possession." I know if Frosty were here, they'd stamp an indignant hoof at that. So would Doodle, the outrageously stubborn rooster on our ranch. If Doodle ever become a demon, we'd be cock-a-doodle-doomed.

"I'm here to show you what you're likely to come across in the field," Yamato says. "Some of these forms may be freaky, but don't worry. I'm not here to hurt you. Only inform."

In a flash of silver, Yamato transforms. Upon first glance, I think people would call this creature a wolf. But it's mangy, grotesquely skinny, its ribs visible through patchy gray fur. It's also about the size of a cow, with claws nearly a foot long, oozing rotten liquid that leaves streaks on the floor as Yamato prowls back and forth. Drool drips from his crooked fangs.

"Coyote demon." Jameson's totally calm, despite the appearance of a blood-thirsty monster just inches away from him. "Claws laced with poison that will kill you within sixty seconds of a scratch. Fangs that will turn *you* into a coyote demon if bitten. Best destroyed by fire, or silver entering the bloodstream."

"It's a *demon*-stration," Bex says, loud enough for the room to hear, while nudging my shoulder. "Get it?"

If it's Bex's mission to make the Guild a friendlier place with puns, it at least works on me. I bark out a laugh, while everyone else remains stone-faced, including Ori.

"Tough crowd," I mumble.

"Yes, Bex, indeed," Jameson says, a slight smile quirking his lips. "Humor in the face of the monsters that would kill us is a wise strategy. What better way to push back fear—which the Depraved love—than with a laugh?"

"Good work, babe," Yamato says with a wink at his daughter.

With flash after flash after flash of silver, Yamato shifts while Jameson describes what we're seeing. Porcupine demons whose quills burrow into skin and flay humans from the inside out. Grizzly bear monsters with such brute strength one smack of a paw would shatter a skull. Possessed skunks with acid spray that can dissolve skin. Demonic alligators whose bite fills humans' lungs with water, drowning them on the spot.

Each demon is more horrific than the last, but fear isn't the emotion rippling through the room. With every transformation, apprentices take notes, call out spell ideas for thwarting the latest demon. Determination steels their shoulders as they imagine vanquishing each monster. Maybe it will be different when we see these beasts in person, but right now, our shared mission to uphold the Guild's duty and protect the planet from Depraved threats is exhilarating.

Yamato transforms back into his human form. "I may be stating the obvious, but remember that demons will not go easy on you. They will feel your magic and aim to kill. They know we are their greatest threat. So act first. Always. And when you're fighting them, remember to steel your heart with the strongest of emotions: love." Now I know where Bex gets it. "Especially when you come across the worst of them all. A Depraved."

We all gasp as Yamato morphs one last time. Instead of becoming animalistic, he becomes humanoid but ragged, wrong. Gone is his perfectly white smile, replaced by jagged yellow teeth, canines long enough they could do damage. His eyes go from rich brown to a grotesque green. His light brown skin turns a rotten chartreuse. His fingernails are cracked and bloody as he holds his hand in the air and gathers the green energy of Depraved magic in his hands. The power crackles and pops as it grows, and Yamato lets loose a maniacal laugh, high-pitched and grating, that sets my teeth on edge.

The determination that was so obvious just moments before is now replaced by doubt. Some apprentices look sick, others like they might faint. A few are unfazed, Bex among them. But surprisingly, not Ori.

He sways on his feet, and I know from the way his eyelids flutter that he's going to pass out. He looks like I feel whenever I see blood.

"Ori?" I take a step toward him. "Are you all right?"

Ori goes down, but I'm close enough now that I can catch him. He falls into my chest, and we both collapse to the balcony floor. The ground is hard and unforgiving, but the pain is gone almost before it started. It's replaced by the most soul-crushing sadness. My heart clenches in my chest, a lump rises in my throat, and tears well in my eyes. It's the all-encompassing pain of loss. It's *Ori's* pain. I can feel it.

Then an image. Ori and his mom, standing over a tombstone. The image comes on so suddenly it's disorienting. Nothing else matters. Not the Culling, not the Guild, just Ori and making this pain go away.

"Nigel! Nigel!"

A wet slap completely clears my vision, the red flare of pain snapping me out of wherever it is I just went.

"Ow!" My hand flies to my face as my eyes snap open to find Bex above me. She's completely normal except for the slimy tentacle where her arm should be, ready to go in for another slap.

"A tentacle? Really?"

"What? Gorilla arms would be too strong, so this was the next best thing. You and Ori went down like that." She tries to snap her tentacle but you know . . . no fingers.

"Ori!" I glance down and find his head on my chest.

He didn't hit his head. Good.

The relief that moves through me is quickly pushed aside by the butterflies swarming in my gut.

Ori's lying on top of me.

In front of everybody.

I gently nudge his shoulder, and his head turns in my direction.

His eyes are bloodshot, rimmed red.

He's crying.

"Ori?"

He just shakes his head, swallows, and sits up.

"Awwww, would you look at that." Laurel's nasally voice brings the rest of the room back into focus. Mainly, the fact that four hundred-plus apprentices are staring at us, some with great vantage points from their balconies above. "Little Ori and Nigel are scared of the Depraved. Some magicians you'll be."

"Guess the Barrett name doesn't mean much, after all," Jaleesa says, and apprentices around the room snicker.

Ori slowly gets to his feet, takes a step back, then another, until he's on the opposite side of our small box. With each step, the sadness inside me grows.

But it's no longer Ori's.

It's mine.

Bootcamp takes a break for lunch, which offers yet another chance for the Guild's physical setup to test our magic. We're pointed to the ninth-floor dining hall, a sparkling geode cavern of pinks and purples and blues, complete with tables and chairs made out of the same stones. Only it seems everything here is imbued with goblin power. Trays of sandwiches shape-shift into snapping crabs at the last minute; one clamps a claw right over my nose. As soon as Bex and I settle into our chairs, they transform into cacti, leaving both of us pulling spines out of our butts.

"Prickly little buggers, aren't they?" Meema says as she passes a table of fae who all met the same fate. "The trick of this room is to anticipate when the chairs are gonna shift and counteract it with a spell of your own."

She glances over to my table, her face melting into a frown as she takes in Bex and Ori beside me. But I don't have long to think about it, because my sandwich chooses that moment to sprout pincers again. I use that trusty transformation spell I learned on the farm and turn mine, Bex's, and Ori's snapping crabs into pudding cups. It might not be a lot to eat, but at least they won't fight back.

Ori doesn't eat a bite and only responds with a grunt when I ask again if he's okay.

Meanwhile, Bex speculates about the second challenge.

"Maybe, given Dad's demonstration, we'll be fighting off demons. I don't think they'd have us go after a Depraved yet. My dads say that's usually the last task. And it's when the most apprentices fail. Some of them are killed."

At that, Ori pushes his pudding over, a brown, blobby mess splattering the table as he sulks away.

"Shit. Ori! I'm sorry." Bex's eyes follow Ori's retreating back. "I forgot about his sister." She shakes her head like she's trying to clear it. "I don't want to become like the rest of them. I don't want to be so nonchalant about death."

She's right. Maybe that's part of leaning into love. Challenging the Guild's impulse to just move on from death and really feeling the loss instead. But before I can say so, noise echoes through the hall.

"Apprenticeeeeees!" a singsong voice calls out, and completely out of my control, my head snaps to the side to see Pallavit, her throat glowing purple with fae power. "Who's ready to see some more magic? Meet us at the fifth-floor medical bays."

The room erupts with movement, Bex jumping up instantly. "Medical bays. That's got to mean curses. Or gruesome injuries. Let's go."

She bursts into a canary with a puff of feathers and flits away. I let Frosty roam Dispatch for lunch of their own, so I don't have their help to get around. Instead, I bewitch some of Ori's spilled pudding to make it extra sticky and coat my shoes so I can march down the walls, praying to the Guild that my magic doesn't give out while I trek the few floors down. I can feel my power depleting with each step, and it gives out entirely when I'm one step away, making me fall unceremoniously on my ass. But if there was anywhere in this place to bruise my tailbone, this would be it.

Circling the balcony are small rooms separated by shimmering, diamond glass. They almost look like doctors' offices, minus the horrific overhead lighting and sterile walls. Each cubicle has a cushy bed, a handful of softly glowing orbs floating near the ceiling, and a curio cabinet stocked with bottles in a variety of shapes, all filled with liquids or objects glowing in every color of the rainbow.

Apprentices gather around Alister, who stands ramrod straight, with his back up against the glass of one of the medical bays. He looks at his wrist, bored, while the rest of us crowd around to see what's about to happen.

"Humans cursed by the Depraved are brought here for treatment, before their memory is erased and they're returned home," Alister explains. "Dispatch signals us to expect their arrival through our Guild Marks." He holds up his wrist, where the Guild star is tattooed. "You'll receive one, too, should you succeed in the Culling. Now . . . victim arriving in three, two, one."

"AAAAAAAAAAAAAH!" The shriek makes most of us jump, and the hairs on my arm stand on end. It's coming from below, where a senior magician and a writhing, screaming man have appeared on the entry platform. As they levitate to the fifth floor, I can see blood completely covering the man's face. They float over our heads and into the medical bay.

By some stroke of cruel luck, I'm close enough to the bay to see all the action. I'd much rather be one of the apprentices in the back, or on the opposite side of the floor. Instead, I get a front row seat to the blood dripping steadily from the man's nose, pooling and glistening with the reflected light of the glowing orbs. It's so much blood. Too much. I get woozy and duck down to put my head between my knees.

"If he can't handle the sight of a little blood, he'll never make it in the Guild," Laurel says, of course directing everyone's attention to my mini-freak out. I can't pass out in front of them. I'd never hear the end of it. I take a few deep breaths and shakily get to my feet.

A circle has crowded around the bloodied man, who seems to have had some calming spell placed on him. Red liquid continues to pour from his nose and ears. It slides down his face, soaking through his sheets and smattering the pristine marble floor. I stare at the man's feet, zeroing in on the pattern on the bottom of his shoes to distract myself.

"Stay back," Alister commands. "This man has been cursed by the Depraved." He gestures toward the rivulets of red snaking out of the man's body. "Some curses are easy to identify, like this one. It's called the Blood River's Run. He'll bleed out until there's not a drop left in him."

Oh god, oh god, oh god. I look to the ceiling, breathing in

through my mouth and out through my nose. *Keep it together, Nigel.*

"You'll have to think on your feet when you find a Depraved victim. Some curses work fast. Others like to fight back. But with time, you'll have an array of knowledge at your disposal. For example . . ." Alister curls his fists and a half dozen small pink flowers with bright yellow centers burst from a vase on the bedside table. Alister pulverizes the petals between his thumb and forefinger. "Pixie primrose. A magical plant known for sopping up liquid-based curses." I glance down as Alister stuffs the petal dust into the man's nose and ears. It bloats deep red as it soaks up the blood, but the petals harden like a scab before falling away. The bleeding has stopped, and now I need someone to take these red-stained sheets away immediately.

The man gasps, his eyes snap open, and he bolts upright. The crowd of apprentices jumps back as he wipes at the blood on his face, smearing it around more than getting rid of it. My stomach clenches, but I refuse to let this get to me. The only shaky hands here should belong to the formerly cursed human with the pale white face, and yet his breaths get steadier with each passing moment.

"Hello, sir," Alister says, kneeling down beside the man and placing a calming hand on his shoulder. "Seems you got yourself into a bit of a tight spot. But don't worry, we'll get you cleaned up and home, good as new."

The man looks up at Alister, his face twisted in confusion. "D-don't I know you?"

"I don't believe so."

Alister twirls a finger in midair, and a stalk of lavender appears before him. He blows on it, and its petals dance around the man, putting him to sleep. Alister's grip is firm on the man's shoulder as he lowers him gently to the bed. Any trace of the kindness in the senior magician's eyes has vanished, replaced by his typical judgment and stone-cold seriousness.

"It looks simple, but it takes practice," Alister says. "If you let it, the wicked magic of demons and the Depraved can take you under along with their human victims. Curses are like a virus, latching on to whoever they can to spread fear and panic. You've got to stay strong, let your magic overwhelm the curse. Your ability to do just that will be tested in the second challenge. You will each be randomly assigned a cursed human to cure. You'll have one hour. Because the Depraved strike at random, this challenge will be spur of the moment. But there will be plenty of victims for each of you tomorrow. On average, these last several years, the Guild has dealt with hundreds of cursed humans a day. That's how active demons and the Depraved are. Should you be unable to identify your victims' curses, or if you require assistance to cure them, a senior magician will step in to get the job done, and you'll be drained of your magic."

Alister points over his head, as if we can see through the ceiling. "You'll find ample texts regarding curses in the library on the twenty-fourth floor. Hopefully, your guardians have already taught you well, but you'll have the next couple hours to study and practice countercurses as you see fit. Learn as much as you can, because you never know what the Depraved will throw at you."

Nobody moves, every apprentice waiting to see if any clues will be given.

Finally, Alister sighs. *"Go."*

Apprentices sprint in every direction, dodging and pushing to get to the library first.

I know I should be following after them, but I don't move. Something about everyone's blatant disregard for the blood on the floor doesn't sit right with me, even if the pool of red does make my stomach squirm. It's like they think their magic is more important than the presence of human suffering. If they weren't magicians, would the horror we just witnessed impact them more? Would they rush to clean up the blood, or stop to think about how close that man was to bleeding out and dying? Or does it stop mattering when you can cure someone with a bundle of magic flowers shoved in their ear?

I kneel down next to where the cursed human sleeps, his blood still streaking the floor. I can't look at it directly, so I squint until my vision blurs and try to convince my brain I'm simply looking at red carpet. I still have my magic hankie tucked into my back pocket. With a few swipes over the marble, the blood is gone, and I can finally exhale.

"That's right, Barrett," Laurel's nasally voice booms. She's magnified it somehow, her throat glowing purple—I guess with the help of Jaleesa, who floats beside Laurel in the center of the hall. "Act like the janitor we know you are."

"It's smart to practice," Jaleesa says. "You'll be able to start your custodial career the second you fail. Or when you're scared by your first demon and decide to bail."

The clack of Meema's boots overtakes their cackling as she stomps over to me, clenching her fingers around my arm and yanking me up. "What are you doing?" Her eyes dart to where Alister watches with a scornful look to rival his daughter's, while Jameson and Pallavit peer our way with obvious curiosity.

"We wouldn't leave a mess in the coop if a fox got in and killed a chicken. We can't give a human as much respect?"

Meema's eyes soften. "It would have been cleaned. You just get used to the sight of blood in the Guild. Missions comes first, like your next task. You should be studying." She stamps her foot and points upward. "Now git."

After she lets go I wander to the balcony, trying to settle my squirming stomach. If I cast magic now, I know my nerves will get in the way, so I've got to give it a minute.

I rest my forehead against the cold stone banister. I take deep breaths in and out, my stomach calming, my heart rate slowing, the dizziness leaving my head. I don't look up until I feel someone move next to me. On instinct, I prepare for Laurel to try to launch me over the railing. But I turn to see a much more welcome guest.

"Ori."

"Hey," he says, giving me a nod in that effortlessly cool way I'll never be able to muster.

"Howdy," I say, then cringe. Yep. Never cool.

"You're for real, aren't you?"

He looks at me with no trace of a scowl. No smirk. No biting remark on the tip of his tongue.

"What do you mean?" I ask.

"Back there. With all that blood. You didn't have to clean it up, but you did. It seems so . . . un-magicianlike."

I shrug. "It just didn't sit right. Magicians aren't the only ones worthy of being treated as human." The irony of it all.

"Show me somebody who agrees with that here," Ori says. He looks around, his eyes wide with mock searching. It makes me laugh, and he gives me a soft smile before saying, "But seriously, that was—" He stops, takes a beat. Like he's fortifying himself. "That was cool of you." His face screws up immediately after saying it.

"Wow, it's really hard for you to give a compliment, huh?"

Ori just crosses his arms. I can't help the urge to fill the silence, so of course, this gem pops out of my mouth. "No one's ever said I was cool before."

"Yeah, you're definitely not cool." I completely set myself up for that. But then, Ori says the unexpected, "But you do have a heart, I guess."

This seems like the perfect moment to get to know Ori better, to show him that the heart he's talking about is concerned about him, too. A chance like I never had back at Lake Travis High, where I was always too busy with my magic training to worry about human concerns. With Ori, it's different. We've worked for this moment all our lives. And we've both had our share of pain in the past because of it.

"Hey."

Ori quirks an eyebrow.

"I just, I wanted to say . . . if you ever want to talk about your sister, I'm here for you. Okay?"

Ori's silent, that scowl creeping back onto his face. When he doesn't say anything for a solid thirty seconds, I figure I've totally blown it.

I turn on my boot heel, and just as I take my first step away, Ori finally speaks. "I don't. Talk about her. And I never wanted whatever *this* is, between us, to show her to *you*." The way he says *you* makes me feel like the scum of the earth. "If you bring her up again, I'll curse you so hard even your precious Meema won't recognize you."

CHAPTER TEN

Curses to take away your senses. Curses to keep you from ever finding your way home. Curses to cover you in spiders for the rest of your life. And the totally unrelated curse of seeing Ori's rage-filled face behind my eyelids every time I blink. I try to stop thinking about him as I slowly make my way through the library, reading about each evil spell and how to get rid of it, trying to memorize as much as I can. Most cures are about intent, the books giving examples of how other elves have channeled that into their spellwork. I definitely learned curses back on the ranch, Meema occasionally surprising me with different ones that I'd have to counteract. But here, there are literally *thousands* of curses to read about, ones I've never heard of. If Alister thinks a night of cramming is enough to prepare us for what we'll face tomorrow, he's got to be kidding himself. I'll be lucky if one of the curses I read up on just happens to be what's afflicting the victim I'm assigned.

Not to mention how lucky I'll be to even remember a single

countercurse with this constant distraction of Ori. I know he didn't mean it when he said he'd curse me to a pulp (well, at least I *think* he was exaggerating to make a point), but still, I want to give him space. Yet for some reason every time I wander into a new aisle, there's Ori, like an invisible force is trying to pull us together.

On the fourth time this happens, Ori snaps, "Are you just going to follow me around all night, or what?"

"No! I swear I'm not trying to. I just want to study."

"Oh so that's what that face is?"

"What face?"

"Any time your nose is in a book your face gets all screwed up in what I think is supposed to be determination? But it's coming across more like constipation. Do you need to excuse yourself?"

"Ha-ha," I deadpan. But wait. If he knows what my face was doing, that means he was looking at *me*.

Let the butterfly stampede commence.

In all honesty, every time I've run into him, I couldn't help stealing glances at him, either. "Go back to playing with your toys."

Ori's been rummaging through his backpack while I've been reading. Sorting his action figures and various household objects, picking up different items to add to his collection as we make our way through the library: a pencil here, a stapler there, random office supplies that I'm surprised to find in a library full of ancient magical texts. But as Meema always said, sometimes it just makes sense to go the human route. Why expend the energy to magically staple papers together when you could just . . . *staple* them, in less than a second? And besides, the more you get used to doing human things that actually make sense, the less likely a human will come across you casting a spell and looking like some weird mime.

"They're not toys," Ori growls.

I squint at the old-school G.I. Joe he's got in his hands. "Oh really?"

"Fine, *technically*, they're toys. But you've seen what I can do with them."

"And just fiddling with them in your backpack is enough to be prepared to fight off curses? I don't know the ins and outs of sprite magic, but that seems a little . . . easy."

"It's not *easy*," Ori chides. "It's about organization, making sure you're ready for anything. I've got all sort of figurines lined up for spellwork, cursing, et cetera. Besides, curses are my specialty. I've been studying up ever since—" He stops himself midsentence, and the way the glint in his eye dims gives me a solid enough hint as to where his mind went. But Ori told me loud and clear he doesn't want to talk about his sister, so I let the moment pass. "Anyway," he continues, "I've got different first-aid equipment for curing sickness and most curses. Gauze, bandages, Band-Aids."

"Wait, wait, wait. You think you can counter a curse by *putting a Band-Aid on it*?" Ori comes off as cool and confident, but now I think he might be living in a different reality entirely. "No offense, but if anyone should be worried about how they're going to get through this next stage of the Culling, it should be you."

"Not just a *Band-Aid*. I wrap it around an effigy and infuse it with magic. I healed my mom's broken foot with only a doll and an Ace bandage once. Do you know how powerful that is? It saves so much time, not having to carve an effigy from sprite wood. I can do things no other sprite has before. *None* of them."

Ori's chest puffs with pride. Sure, it's cocky, but he can back it up. I *have* seen him in action before, turning that horse toy into an effigy of Frosty.

"How do you do it? When nobody else can?"

His self-assured glare falters. He looks seriously troubled, and I think I may have overstepped. *Again.* This whole trying-to-make-a-meaningful-friend thing—or, who am I kidding, having-a-crush-on-a-guy thing—is not going well.

"Hey, you don't have to tell me. It's none of my business."

I mime locking my mouth shut and throwing away the key. Ori's eyes actually follow the imaginary trajectory. When he looks back at me, his face sets into its typical furrowed position before his mouth stretches wide, like he's about to roar.

But it's a yawn. I immediately follow suit.

"It's getting late," Ori says, his voice deep and garbled.

"Yeah, we should get some rest." I just hope getting in and out of my alcove will be less eventful tonight than it was yesterday. "Knowing Alister, our next challenge will probably come when you and I are dead asleep, so we'll be extra groggy. Everything's *so fair* in the Culling, right?"

Ori's lips quirk up. "Right."

"Good night, Ori." Part of me wants to reach out, feel those sparks like every other time we've brushed against each other. Well, not just *part* of me; my whole body feels like it's being pulled toward Ori, yearning to close the distance between us. Even if this is just a simple crush, it's *intense.* Does everybody feel like this when they meet a person they instantly like? Even if that person always looks at them like they're a massive cow pie? My body almost takes an involuntary step forward, but after all the time he's been closed off, I figure I should let him come to me. If he ever wants to, that is. Hell, maybe this won't just be my first real crush, but my first unrequited one to boot.

So I take a step back and turn on my heel. As I round the corner, leaving Ori in the aisle, I hear him say, "Night, Nigel."

"WAKE UP!"

I jolt up so hard I hit my head on the unforgiving rock ceiling of my little cave. A white burst of pain flashes behind my eyes, and Frosty whinnies in a way that's definitely a laugh. I figured after yesterday's chow-down in Dispatch, the crystallos might have fully recovered from their ordeal in the first Culling task and decided to finally head home. But they curled up next to me in the middle of the night. Apparently, just so they could make fun of me in their special horsey way.

"Screw you," I mutter, my hand flying up to gingerly test the place where I smacked my head. I wince—that's for sure going to leave a goose egg—but at least there's no blood. When my hand pulls away, Frosty leans forward and huffs a cool breath onto my forehead. "Okay, I take it back. Thanks."

"COMBAT TRAINING!" Meema's magically magnified voice slams through the room like her bull, who's currently stomping and thrashing. "ENTRY HALL IN FIVE MINUTES OR YOU'RE DISQUALIFIED FROM THE CULLING."

That gets everyone into action. Elf apprentices dive and climb and spell themselves from their alcoves. One just leaps from her bed, freefalling until she spells a flock of birds to catch her in midair. She's out the archway first.

Frosty lets me hop on their back and we're not far behind. Somehow, though it hasn't even been a minute, the hall is already packed. I'm not sure what time it is, exactly, but it feels like it's only been a couple hours since I collapsed, exhausted. And everyone else seems to have been woken up in the middle of a deep sleep, too. Several people have wicked bedhead, some are still in their pajamas, a handful of cute guys are shirtless, and someone has such intense morning breath I'm not sure it isn't a spell to gross us out and throw us off our game before whatever is about to happen.

Alister swings down into the entry hall on a vine, landing gracefully, like he's done it a million times before. He probably *has* done that a million times before, but either way he moves with the confidence of a person who's never made a mistake in his life. He snaps his fingers and a giant bright yellow sunflower bursts from the floor. It extends twenty feet up, level with the first balcony. Then its petals begin to drop, one by one, steady and ominous.

"Time's almost up," he calls. "Whoever is not here by the time the last petal falls will be stripped of their magic. Demons wait for no one. The Depraved certainly don't either. And if you waver in the face of evil, there are consequences. It's a lesson you need to learn now."

Everyone starts counting off their friend groups, making sure those closest to them have made it. For a moment, it makes my heart sink that no one is looking for me. Apprentices call one another's names and clap each other on the back when they find who they're looking for, but no one calls out *Nigel* or gives me a relieved squeeze.

Just then, someone bumps my shoulder. I assume it's a Cullingmate trying to curse me, or Frosty searching my pockets for something to eat. But I turn and find Bex, wiping gunk from the corner of her eyes.

"God, they couldn't have let us sleep a few more hours?" she says. "I'm not gonna be much of a fighter if I don't get my sleep. I snooze like a sloth, literally. A solid fourteen hours and I'm good to go."

"Have you seen Ori?" I ask.

I can't find him. I don't know if it's because the crowd is too thick or because he's actually not in the hall.

Bex scowls. "Jeez, I'm right here."

"Sorry, it's just—" I motion to the ticking sunflower of doom.

Quick as a flash, I hop on Frosty's back and survey the room. I don't see his perfect dark eyes under his furrowed forehead. I don't see his judgmental scowl as he takes in our Cullingmates.

He's not here, and the petals are down by half.

My heart gallops in my chest. I know he wants to come across as this tough guy, but a magician's power is so much a part of our identity that I'm positive he'll be devastated if it's gone. If not, why compete in the Culling in the first place?

Ten petals left.

Nine.

I'm so anxious that I hop off Frosty and sprint for the sprite arch.

Seven.

Six.

Just as I pass the fae arch, Jaleesa and Laurel run out, hand in hand, and I'm perfectly positioned to get clothes-lined between them. Heads snap in our direction as I fall with a shout. Apprentices laugh, but the most noticeable reaction comes from Alister.

"Laurel!" he barks. With a snap of his fingers and a green burst of light, a bloomless rosebush grows between his daughter and Jaleesa, thorns piercing their linked hands. Their fingers snap apart, Laurel's face going beet red as she hurriedly joins the other nymphs, leaving Jaleesa to blankly stare after her. I can feel the rejection radiate off of her. Guess I'm not the only one around here who has feelings for someone who's hot and cold.

But there's no time to comfort her. I race over to the sprite archway, hoping beyond hope Ori will get here in time.

Three petals left.

Ori's not going to make it.

Two.

Bam!

A body flies through the sprite arch and slams into me. I fall to the floor for the second time, a body pinning me to the ground, and my elbow lands hard on the marble. But, like so many times before when we've touched, all pain fades away. And the room's replaced by a silhouette.

As it comes into focus, I realize it's not Cassie this time.

It's me.

Ori lifts his chest off mine, and my image goes with him. As he picks himself up, his normal scowling is replaced with embarrassment. He temporarily shields his face, which I swear is redder than usual behind his fingers.

Am I making him blush?

He doesn't say a word while I stare up at him from the ground. "Are you okay?"

Ori nods once.

"I saw something. When we touched. Again. It was m—"

"Me." He gets that smirk. "I had a vision of my own handsome mug."

My stomach does somersaults that have nothing to do with the tumble I just took. Is it possible these visions show each other what we're thinking? Because I *was* definitely just thinking about Ori. So I guess I won't be keeping this crush a secret.

But then, if I was thinking of him, and he saw his face, that means that when I saw mine, he was thinking about *me.* As in, the irresistible, grumpy guy I can't stop thinking about also happens to sometimes think about dorky, cowboy me. I have no idea what is going on between us, or why we see these things, but I definitely know Ori makes me feel as hot as a barrel full of chili peppers when he's around.

We're saved from an awkwardly too-long silence when a guy skids into the hall from the fae wing. He looks completely disheveled, bedhead all askew, and he rubs his eyes so hard it makes the white skin around them a bright red.

"Sorry I'm late," he pants. "I overslept."

"How he could sleep through a hundred fae singing wake-up spells is beyond me," Jaleesa says. So much for feeling bad for her. Laurel laughs from somewhere across the room, but the rest of us have gone silent. We're all looking at a procession of senior magicians traveling down from one of the topmost floors. They may be using different magics, but their pace is even, steady, the five of them traveling as a pack.

When they hit the first floor, it's clear their path is set on the late fae. The way all five magicians have their eyes locked on him only adds to their pack-like vibe, wolves honing in on their prey.

Any nearby apprentices clear the way, giving the senior magicians a wide-open path.

"Wh-what's happening?" the boy stutters.

Meema sighs. It's full of sadness and regret, not the glee that I see on some of the apprentices' faces.

"We told you anyone who is late is out, sweetheart," she says. There's no sarcasm in that *sweetheart*. It's soaked in empathy, tinged with disappointment.

"No!" he cries. The apprentices closest to him jump away, like expulsion from the Guild is contagious. "It was an honest mistake." Tears pour down his face.

"Rules are rules," Pallavit says, but she, too, looks genuinely sad. "Being late in the field can have consequences. Irreparable, terrible consequences. And you all need to learn that now."

As one, the five senior magicians spell the fae. He's held in place by vines from a nymph, stunned into submission by an elf's spell.

A sprite uses her knife to carve an effigy of him and glances over at a fae magician, who sings a short, high staccato note over and over while the sprite presses into the carving's hands, head, heart. With each touch, the boy writhes and shouts.

"Stop! Stop! Please!"

With one final press to the carving, the boy falls to the ground, unconscious. A goblin magician changes into a moose, and the boy is loaded onto his back. The moose gallops away, disappearing through the portal at the center of the hall.

As they leave, I feel a part of me leave with them. Not that I was connected to that fae boy in any way. I didn't even know his name. But somehow it feels real now, having seen firsthand what happens if we fail. I don't even like to imagine what that would feel like. Magic's part of me, sends a thrill through me, makes my heart beat stronger every time I use it. To have it stripped away would be like having a piece of my soul removed. Which is why—even as much as he directs his misery my way—I can't bring myself to ever say I hate my dad, even though I have no doubt that he hates *me*.

I can't meet that fate. I can't.

Nobody in the hall makes a sound, not even the senior magicians now returning to the balconies, their work done. I take in all the apprentices' faces and know their thoughts are on overdrive. Some faces—like Ori's—are set in a determined glare. Some have heartless smirks of satisfaction. Others, like Bex, have horror written across their features. Regardless of the reaction, we all have one thing in common: None of us wants to be in that boy's shoes.

The only problem is, most of us will be. And as we all take in the sheer number of apprentices in this room, I know everyone's having the same realization. In order to not be the next to have our powers stripped, we've got to win. From the quirked eyebrows, suspicious stares, and crossed arms of so many, it looks like most of us will avoid that fate by whatever means necessary.

I've never felt so unsafe in my life.

"Weaknesses!" Meema's booming voice snaps us back to reality. "Just like butt cracks, we've all got 'em." A few people snicker, but when Meema's face doesn't budge, they quickly stop.

"I'm serious," Meema continues. "Your weaknesses out in the field will mean life or death. Demons and Depraved will exploit them so they can kill you. And there is only one thing that will save you from your weaknesses."

She pauses, all of us leaning in to figure out just what can save us from certain death.

Pallavit steps next to Meema. "Your fellow magicians," she says, and Meema gives her an appreciative smile. I'm surprised by the pang it sends through me to see her obvious friendship with Pallavit. While I struggled to relate to nonmagical peers and never had a chance to make friends with my own kind, *Meema* clearly got to have a full magical life. Meanwhile, I was basically hidden away on the ranch. My friendship with Bex could have already had a years-long head start instead of only beginning now.

"Which leads us to why you're all gathered here," Meema continues. "You're about to find out y'all's weaknesses so you can avoid any pitfalls in the field." She has her classic mischievous glint in her eye. "By fighting. Each other."

CHAPTER ELEVEN

The room erupts in shouting, but Laurel's voice rises above the clamor. "I know who I'd like to fight." She looks right at me. "When can we start?"

She takes a step toward me, but with a flash of gold light, she stops in her tracks. Jameson saunters behind her, and with a snap of his glowing-gold fingers, Laurel slides back a good ten feet.

"Your partners will be chosen for you," he says with a bored look. "But do keep in mind that whomever you're paired with will also be your partner in the second task."

"It's a safeguard," Meema adds, throwing daggers at Laurel with her eyes, and for a second I forget my frustration and appreciate that she's trying to have my back. Jameson too. "You'll be fighting your partner for the second challenge for two reasons." She holds up a perfectly manicured finger. "First, fighting lets you learn your partner's weaknesses and find where you can fill in the gaps in their magic." Another finger joins the first. "Second, it prevents sabotage.

You can fight, but we're not here to deal fatal blows. And just in case anyone gets carried away, if either member of your duo becomes so injured they can no longer compete, you're both out. Stripped of your magic and taken out of the running for Guild membership. Got it?" She peers around the room. Like she cast a spell, the entire room says, "Yes, ma'am."

"All right then," Yamato says. "Senior magicians will be walking through the crowd to pair you together. Like will not be paired with like. You already know your own magic's pros and cons, so it's time to switch it up."

Meema and her colleagues make their way through the room, shuffling Cullingmates around with bright bursts of magic. Frosty tosses their head and eyes the action nervously, like they think they might be the next creature to be moved against their will. My stomach churns, too, at the looks the unpaired apprentices give me. Most seem like they're raring to whup my ass, Laurel most of all. Her dad struts up next to her, and it's clear they're arguing again. She motions over her shoulder at me, and Alister gives me a cool, appraising look before shaking his head.

"Fine, then Jaleesa." Laurel moves closer to her girlfriend, and Alister's look turns red hot.

"No." He uses that parental, don't-push-it tone. And even though we're all newly adults who can make their own choices, nobody could blame Laurel for taking a step away from Jaleesa, who visibly deflates.

"That's so messed up," Bex says, loud enough for Alister to hear, and when he catches her eye, Alister's look turns from anger to slick confidence once more.

"Oh good, a volunteer." At the flick of his wrist, a tendril of ivy pulls Bex to his side. To his daughter, he says, "Try not to leave any marks."

But Laurel's lost in some unspoken conversation with Jaleesa, who never takes her eyes from Laurel's as her mom pushes her through the crowd toward a water nymph partner.

Alister, meanwhile, turns his attention to me.

"Oh shit. This can't be good," I mutter, turning to Ori. "What do we do?"

He shrugs sarcastically. "I'm not your knight in shining armor. You figure it out."

There's no time to think. I don't know if the crowd parts or if it's just that everyone's been paired up, but Alister has a clear, unobstructed path to us.

"Would you look at that? The Wonder Boys." He grins wickedly, making my stomach sink. "I think you'll make a fine pair."

Wait. What? That's just about the best scenario possible. And it's thanks to *Alister*?

Ori, on the other hand, seems anything but pleased. "Great." He sighs. "I'm going to end up dead."

Alister looks like the cat that ate the canary.

"We can only hope," he drawls.

Alister turns away without another word, while nearby apprentices eye us hungrily, likely hoping that Alister's wish comes true.

"We haven't killed each other yet," I say to Ori. "There's no way it's going to happen now, right?"

"Oh, I don't know." Ori rolls his eyes deeper than Dad ever has. "You spelled me into a stupor when we first met, then nearly destroyed a portal in the first challenge. I'll be lucky if I walk out of this alive."

A righteous anger swells in my belly. "*We* destroyed that portal."

"I've thought about it some more, and it wouldn't have happened if you weren't there with me. *I've* got my shit together."

Frosty decides that's the perfect moment to nudge me in the butt, making me fall into Ori. My face smooshes against his shoulder, rubbing against his backpack strap, and Frosty snickers. That heat in my stomach turns from anger to twitterpated so fast that I'm too disoriented to reprimand them.

I keep slipping, but Ori's arms circle around my waist, tightening so I can't fall farther. "Jesus, Barrett, you can't even stay on your two feet? Guess I'll be able to kick your ass pretty quickly then."

Ori looks genuinely annoyed, but he doesn't let go. And maybe it's this weird connection we have, but visions of the two of us working together flash through my mind. Bursts of our individual power shining together, gold and pink blazing bright like a choreographed routine.

Ori breathes in deep. If I didn't know any better I'd swear he just took a whiff of my hair. But then he lifts me onto my feet, keeping me at arm's length. I shake my head. He was obviously only taking a breath to steady himself before hoisting me up. I'm so much bigger than he is. How many times had I done the same thing when I'd run out of magical energy on the ranch and had to carry bales of hay the good ol' fashioned way?

"Get it together, Nigel," Ori huffs.

Right. He's definitely not feeling the same things I am.

"All right, then." Pallavit clears her throat and belts out in song.

"Hurry up now.
No time to waste.
Stairs to the top.
So we can make haste."

As her song rings out, glowing purple stairs appear, leading to the fourth balcony.

"I've decided to make getting there easy on you," Pallavit says. "Fourth floor training room. Everyone up."

The crowd stampedes the stairs, but I waver. There are no railings or banisters.

"Aren't you guys coming?" Bex asks, dashing behind Laurel, who works overtime to avoid eye contact with us.

"It's just . . . I don't think it's that much of a stretch to imagine someone pushing me off those stairs if they got the chance."

Ori nods. "Now you're thinking right. We're all in competition. When we're gasping our last breath through a broken neck, they can say, 'Whoops! It was an accident.'"

"You go on ahead," I tell Bex. "We'll be there in no time."

I click to Frosty, but they eye me warily.

Ori smirks. "See? Even Frosty thinks you might blow them up into ice cubes."

"Frosty," I say through gritted teeth. *"Come on."* Ori savors every last second of this awkward staredown. But finally, *finally* Frosty clops over and lets me hop on their back.

I give Ori my own smug look. "You were saying?" I pat Frosty's side. "Great-Grandpa Barrett had bears, Meema has bulls, and I've got ice horses. It runs in our blood."

Ori shrugs, unimpressed. But if we're going to work together in the second challenge, we can't waste time with him being all broody. It's a really, *really* attractive broody, but still.

I put my hand out. "Let's go."

Ori crosses his arms, quirks a judgmental eyebrow, and gives me that inordinately cute smirk. "I don't knoooow." He lets my hand hang in the air with his elongated vowel, and it's torture. My hand is *this close* to his body and every inch of mine is dying for him to take it.

Damn. Crushes are wild.

I almost take my hand back. Why wouldn't he simply blink behind me like he did yesterday? But surprisingly—*thankfully*—Ori's long, skinny fingers wrap around my chapped and scarred ones. The boost of energy that goes through my body is enough to yank Ori up in one movement. I picture him wrapping his arms around me again, but he just balls up my shirt in one fist and holds on to it like makeshift reins.

God, I wish Frosty would douse me in ice right now. I try not to think too hard about Ori behind me—how I could just lean back into him—because I need to focus on this next exercise. But *wow* is it hard. Multiple things are hard, if you know what I mean. But Frosty takes off to the fourth floor, and the sight of the combat space wipes away all (okay, *most*) of my thirsty thoughts.

We've arrived at what looks like a coliseum. Peering over the balcony, I can see the Guild in all its gold-streaked, skeleton-filled glory, but on my other side there's a training field where I wouldn't at all be surprised to learn lions once ate gladiators. Just behind the railing are massive marble steps that lead down to a sports court of some kind, with multiple large gold circles marked inside with glowing elf power. They look like magic wrestling rings. A number glows from the center of each, with 1 directly in front of us. To the left and right, the circles wrap around the floor in a massive ring, and more steps rise on the far side of the space—I guess for spectators. In total there are twenty-five rings, and at the foot of each is a senior magician with the same mischievous glint in their eyes. These Guild members must get some serious enjoyment from telling apprentices they have to kick each other's asses.

Ori and I hop off Frosty's back as Pallavit gives instructions. "Partners, find your assigned ring. The first number you receive indicates the ring you should report to. The second is the order in which you will fight." She calls a long clear note, and glowing numbers appear on each of our chests. I can't help but notice the shadow Ori's pec casts, highlighting the lean muscle there. It's nice. *Really* nice.

"I guess that means we're first," Ori says.

"Huh?" I shake my head to clear it. Now is not the time to

imagine what Ori's torso would look like if he removed his loose gray cardigan and white tee.

"Front and center," Ori continues, tapping his finger next to the purple light over his heart, which now reads 1–1. He looks down the steps to the ring with a glowing 1 in the middle. "So much for trying to stay under the radar."

A crowd has already gathered in the seats on the opposite side. They clearly can't wait to see what damage we'll deal each other. *Nobody* else has an audience.

"Looks like you're the popular guys," Bex says, eyeing the crowd. She has her own glowing purple 2–1 over her chest. So while we're going to have an audience, the one person who might cheer for me has her own battle to fight.

As if on cue, Laurel shouts, "Bex, are you trying to get us disqualified, or what?" A thorny vine grows at her feet. "Don't make me pull you down here."

Bex sighs. "Oh, joy. I guess making the Guild a friendlier place starts with finding the good in our nemeses, right?" Bex turns to go, but not before adding, "But that still doesn't mean I can't kick ass."

"Nigel! Get your rear in gear!" Meema stands beside the shining number 5 ring, just at the edge of my vision. She's giving me the wide-eyed What-in-tarnation-is-taking-you-so-long look. It's day three, and she's barely spoken to me except to say that senior magicians are suspicious of my power, that she doesn't like my choice of friends, and now she wants to treat me like an idiot while everyone's watching. I know she doesn't want to have too many private chats and risk folks saying she helped me in the tests. But does she have to go out of her way to get in my head?

Alister stands in the middle of the first circle, cheesing at the apprentices in the stands, knowing he has an audience. "Need directions, boys?" His sneer grows wide as the crowd laughs.

"Coming." Damn it, I sound like a little kid, yet again. I turn to Ori. "I guess we should get started."

Ori smirks. "That eager to see your defeat, Barrett?"

There's no malice in his words. Bite, sure, but nothing like what Laurel and Jaleesa or any of our other Cullingmates have thrown at us. This bite is tingle-inducing, like the playful nip Jeremy always liked to give my bottom lip when we kissed. A promise of something to come, something to look forward to.

And I want to know what that something is.

"Is that a challenge?" I ask.

Ori opens his mouth to speak, but bamboo shoots burst from the ground and push us forward. It takes all my concentration to keep from face-planting on the marble. From the corner of my eye, I spot Frosty happily crunching on the bamboo.

"How lovely of you to join us," Alister says when Ori and I stumble into the ring. Without waiting for a reply, Alister turns back to the crowd. "The rules are simple. Two of you will enter each ring, but only one of you will win. The first to get their partner to step foot outside the gold border is the victor. Though you are not to incapacitate your partner, injuries are to be expected. I expect to hear no complaints. The Depraved certainly won't ***ask nicely*** for you to bend to their whims. Get used to pain now; it's a part of Guild life. You will be healed."

Alister finally turns back to us. He looks so hungry to see us fight that I swear he licks his lips. "Take your places." He motions toward two small versions of the Guild symbol glowing about ten feet apart on the floor. When Ori and I each take one, Alister crows, "Begin."

I swallow nervously, running through all the spells I know in my mind. Meema taught me lots of curses, but my instinct is to avoid hurting Ori and use defensive magic instead. I could box him in, but how would that get him *outside* the circle? Ridiculously, the next thing I think is that I could try turning him into a pudding cup like I did our chicken eggs all those years ago, but what happens if I accidentally knock him over? I don't know that I could put him back whole if I get pudding all over the floor.

Ori, however, doesn't hesitate. He shrugs his backpack over his shoulder and unzips it in one swift movement. He snags an action figure, an old-school Ken doll, and drops his bag at his feet. I'm flattered that he'd ever think I'm as unnaturally ripped or coifed as that plastic dude, but Ken has got to go. I know what Ori can do with his effigies. My only hope of winning this match is getting every action figure he's got out of his reach.

Lasso it is.

I take a deep breath and let magic pool in my fingertips. Warmth cascades up and down my arms, making the hairs on them stand on end. Ori's centering himself, too, his long fingers poised over the Ken doll while pink light flows to his hands. As his power gathers, I see him register the gold light flowing through my own body, and he watches as I coil a magic rope around my crooked elbow. His eyes settle with recognition.

Crap. I forgot he's already seen this trick.

It's a race to see who can cast a spell first.

Ori bathes the toy in pink light while I finish creating my rope. I grab one end and flick the length of it toward Ori's hand just as he pinches the Ken doll's left leg between a finger and thumb and twists.

My leg falls out from under me. I topple over, and Ori grins wickedly, proudly, sexily. But the expression is short-lived. The free end of my rope finds its target, whapping Ken right in the face. The doll flies from Ori's hand.

"Yes!" Then, "Ow!" A slap to my cheek catches me off guard.

"Ha!" Ori's laugh is quick and sharp. "Smacked by your own trick."

He's right. Ori has magicked the doll to be *my* effigy, so any damage I inflict on the plastic figure is going to be felt in my very real body.

"Clever," I say, a grin spreading across my stinging skin, and Ori smirks back. He's in it to kick my ass, but something in my belly still lights up, a new warmth adding to the pleasant tingles left behind from using my power. For a moment we're both frozen, grinning at each other like idiots. Then, a second before me, Ori lunges, diving to the floor after the Ken doll.

But I'm quicker. Years trying to wrangle sheep on a farm teaches you how to get somewhere first.

I kick my leg out just as Ori's fingers are about to wrap around the figure's arm. The doll flies out of Ori's reach, but not before I feel a kick in the ribs. I hear a slight crunch, but it's covered by a wave of laughter from the crowd. I must be giving them some serious physical comedy, launching my body forward to cast a spell, then pulling away just as quickly when I hurt myself with it.

My kick sends me airborne, matching the trajectory of the Ken doll. My lasso falls out of my grip as the toy and I skid to a stop just inside the boundary of the ring. I shove the doll into the pocket of my Levi's, but Ori doesn't miss a beat. He just dives for his bag to find something else to spell me with.

Okay, no more Mr. Nice Elf.

In order for Ori to spell me back, he needs to get his fingers on his toys, so I've got to keep those hands occupied. And there's nothing like fire ants to get you scratching with both hands.

I take a deep breath, my determination to win fueling me, pulling up every last drop of magic I've got. Just like all spells, curses are powered by emotion, and there's nothing like the fire of competitiveness to add extra bite. With power glowing in my palms, I smack my hand to the floor. A spear of golden light snakes through the marble from my skin, racing toward Ori, until it bursts at his feet. Thousands of tiny gold ants erupt from the stone to crawl up Ori's legs. He drops his backpack in an instant, swiping at the magic coating his jeans. But that's the thing about curses. You can't erase their effects without magic of your own, or until your curser tires out and their spell dwindles.

But Ori keeps at it, swiping and swiping, until he loses his balance and falls hard on his butt. He takes in a sharp breath, winces and rubs his tailbone.

He looks truly pained, and I instantly regret it. Suddenly, that extra bite to my magic is gone, the energy disappearing as quickly as it came. I'm overcome with the urge to race over to Ori and see if he needs any help with . . . his butt, I guess.

"Are you o—" I begin, then notice that Ori has landed inches from his backpack. It doesn't matter that Ken is snug in my pocket when he's got access to his whole arsenal of toys.

My lasso is too far away, so I try to call on my magic to make another one, but I'm tapped out. I've still got legs, though. I jump to Ori's side and kick his bag, knocking it away. A handful of items spill out as the bag skids past the boundary of the ring, where Ori can't retrieve it without being disqualified. But he still has a paperclip, a cup of Play-Doh, and a roll of duct tape to work with.

Our eyes lock. I can see a twinkle in Ori's. I just have to anticipate what he's going to do next.

That smirk is back. "Bet you can't tell what I'm thinking," he mocks.

My eyes snap to his trio of goods, then back to him. "Betcha I can."

We both move at the same time, fast as lightning. Of what he has left, Ori has got to be able to do the most damage with the Play-Doh.

I've seen how quickly he molds that stuff into an effigy. So I lunge for it and throw it out of the ring.

"Told ya," I say, but the smile falls right from my face.

Ori went for the paperclip. While my attention was on the trajectory of the Play-Doh, his fingers were fast at work twisting the clip into a makeshift stick figure. With one burst of magic from his fingertips, the clip effigy is coated in pink.

"This is it, Barrett," he says, a wicked grin popping up that's equal parts infuriating and captivating.

Ori sets the figure on the marble and slides it across the floor, the paperclip-cowboy flying past the boundary of the ring.

With a tug in the center of my gut, I feel my body jerk backward, straight for the boundary. I'll be there in no time if I don't act fast.

My path is going right past my fallen rope. I snatch it, swing it over my head once, and send the lasso flying, hoping my years of rodeo practice honed my intuition enough to account for the growing distance between me and my target.

Time seems to slow. I see the crowd's eyes follow my golden rope, see Ori's smirk turn to a scowl of confusion and then an unmistakable *Oh shit* when he realizes the loop is right over his head. Gravity brings the rope downward, below his face, neck, and chest. I tug and it cinches around his waist.

I'm jerked to a stop, even though I can feel Ori's sprite magic still trying to pull me backward. It feels like having anxious butterflies in my belly, but *hellbent* on getting me to *move*.

I'm not budging, though, and my butt is just in front of the golden boundary. I'm still in this.

"Ha!" Instinct takes over once again and I spring to my feet, suddenly in ranch mode. And when I successfully lasso a pig or goat, I get right to work before they can wriggle away.

I yank Ori toward me. He stumbles a few steps forward, and with his arms pinched to his sides he has no way to get to the single roll of duct tape that's still in the ring.

This match is mine.

Ori is just a yard away, and I know I can end this with one final tug. I can pull him toward me and gently push him outside the boundary, taking the first win. But when I give that last pull on my rope, Ori stumbles over a shoelace that's come undone. He falls forward, right toward me. My arms fly out to catch him and he lands hard against my chest.

The second we collide, the wind is knocked out of me. The impact wasn't that hard, but there's nothing I can do to fill my lungs. Still, when Ori's deep brown eyes meet mine, I don't feel panicked. I don't feel worried. I don't think about the Guild, or the crowd, or the remaining two challenges that will determine my fate. I don't even think about myself. I can only think of Ori, as his face swims in my vision before everything vanishes.

CHAPTER TWELVE

This isn't like being unconscious. Or being asleep. It's not like one minute I was awake, the next minute out.

I'm aware of everything. I'm aware of the fact that there's not a single person around me, that I'm somehow standing but there's no floor beneath my feet. But most of all, I'm aware of the faint pink light that seems to tinge everything. Or, seems to tinge nothing. Because that's all there is.

Just me and the pink light.

But then, as suddenly as I appeared here, wherever here is, someone else does, too, and I'm not in that pink void anymore. I'm standing next to a younger Ori, probably six or seven. He's playing with action figures in his living room, pretending to do magic on them while Cassie, around ten, uses a rough wooden figure to cast actual spells on their mom, Lyra. Cassie has the same wide eyes and self-satisfied smirk as Ori as pink magic pools in her fingers.

Lyra looks on tenderly, nodding every now and then while Cassie smears her magic over the figurine. It's rough, wood shavings are scattered around her lap, and a small pocketknife rests gently against her side. She clearly just carved the figure herself.

Cassie worries at the fingers on the effigy's right hand, and a bright glow of pink on Lyra's same hand tells me the magic is working. Cassie whoops when a chipped nail on Lyra's pointer finger becomes whole again.

"Great work, Cassie," Lyra says, bending down and sweeping Cassie up in a hug. She laughs and Ori sets down his toys to join them.

"You did it, sis, you did it!" Ori's missing a front tooth, making him lisp. The family is wrapped up in a jumble of hugs and laughter, and warmth cascades through me. It's not magic. It's love.

The vision jumps, pink light surrounding me until figures materialize once more. Ori's older this time, maybe ten years old, and he sits on top of a Spider-Man comforter, action figures of all kinds lining his shelves. But Ori is working on a block of silvery-pink wood, carving an effigy.

Cassie, fourteen, leans against the doorframe. "You can do it, Ori," she says. When Ori catches her eye, the look of confidence on his sister's face gives him the boost he needs.

He makes one last cut on the wood and the human shape is complete. Gathering sprite magic in his thumbs, he rubs them over the figure's feet. Cassie's shoes start to glow, and then she rises into the air. It's too fast, and she knocks her head against the ceiling.

"Ouch!"

Ori springs off the bed. "Sorry!" He loses his concentration and Cassie drops, but she lands on her feet, beaming at her brother. "Those demons won't stand a chance with you knocking their heads in." She reaches forward and pulls Ori into her. "We'll be in the Guild together before you know it."

Ori looks up at her, complete admiration written all over his face.

The scene fades, everything bathed in pink light once more until it's washed out by gray, by jagged streaks of lightning. A thunderstorm rages overhead, and I recognize the water those flashes of light reflect in. It's McGovern Lake in Hermann Park, right in the middle of Houston. Ear-splitting thunder crashes overhead, but still, I can hear the screams. *Ori's* screams as he watches a Depraved hold his sister under the lake. I've seen just a speck of this memory before, but now every detail is crisp. The monster's sickly green skin is lit up by each flash of lightning, and the magic pouring from its fingers to keep Cassie underwater is a matching, ghastly color. Ori fumbles over a block of sprite wood, but his hands shake. He can't make a cut with his pocketknife.

A boom behind us mixes with the thunder, and I turn to see Lyra standing over the corpse of another Depraved, her pink sprite magic fading. She catches sight of her daughter and screams her name.

"Cassiopeia!"

Fear and dread threaten to swallow Ori whole. I can feel it, and I know without ever being told that Lyra never says Cassie's full name. Never. Not even when she's mad. Only when she's truly, deeply afraid.

With the next burst of lightning, I see Ori realize that his sister has stopped thrashing. Her face is turned toward him, one eye above the water, boring into his own, letting him know everything is going to be okay. Even if she's not going to be around to tell him that after this night. They can do that sometimes. Communicate without saying a word.

I love you.

Ori swears that he hears those words in his sister's voice, even though her mouth is underwater, even though she's not moving, even though the thunder rages above.

Lyra blinks and reappears behind the Depraved attacking her daughter. Lyra grabs an effigy from the pocket of her billowing red coat and breaks off the figure's head. In a second, the Depraved's neck snaps, a crack and the unnatural angle of it signaling its death.

Lyra throws the effigy to the side, blinking again and reappearing with her arms around Cassie, next to Ori on the lakeshore.

"Cassiopeia! Cassie! Open your eyes!" Lyra shakes her daughter violently, but it's no use. Her body remains limp, her mouth hanging open.

The most gut-wrenching wail pours out of Lyra's throat. "My baby. My baby. My baby."

Ori watches on, his fourteen-year-old fingers resting upon his sister's lifeless hand. A sadness like I've never known seeps into my gut, eating me from the inside out.

Ori's convinced this is his fault. That if only he could have carved an effigy, he could have stopped that Depraved before it killed his sister.

Ori wants to let loose a wail of his own, but he can't make a sound. Emotion clogs his throat, chokes him, makes him feel like he can't breathe. I can feel his heart stop, and I know he wonders if heartache could kill him.

Then, an intense fire builds through his chest. It's different from the heartache. It's a pressure. No, a *presence*. Something inside him—next to, over, and in his heart. It doesn't do anything to alleviate the emptiness Ori feels now that Cassie is gone, but it reminds him of her. He's not sure whether that's better or worse, to have this entity within him that won't let him ever forget his sister. He knows with certainty he'll relive this moment, again and again, for the rest of his life.

And he'll hunt down and destroy every last Depraved until the day he dies.

A need for revenge so strong and so bright overwhelms the sadness. Not diminishing it, but keeping it in check, guiding him, setting the course of his life, shaping his power. That hot, angry determination is so strong it makes me gasp.

I take a heaving, gulping breath, and the Guild coliseum comes back into focus. There are pale, thick fingers on my shoulder, and I look up to meet Alister's glare. He's pulled me and Ori apart.

"What happened?" I mean it for Ori, who looks at me like he's trying to see into my soul. Or maybe like he was just in *my* soul, and is reliving what he saw. Just like I'm doing.

But, typical Alister, he thinks the world and every question in it is meant only for him. "I pulled you off each other before you could kill your partners!" He points to my coiled rope, now sliced into golden pieces. "You nearly broke Ori in half with your lasso. Meanwhile, you"—he turns his glare to Ori, who finally pulls his eyes from mine to meet Alister's—"practically bashed this one's skull in!"

As if his words brought the pain to life, the back of my head throbs. I gingerly place my fingers there, and they come away damp with blood.

"Whoa." My vision blurs, but this time I'm definitely just woozy. No visions, but good ol' fashioned blood phobia.

"Nigel." Ori snaps forward and wraps his hand around my wrist. "I'm so sorry."

On contact, my vision clears. Something pops softly in my rib cage, in the exact spot where Ori's effigy made me knock my own rib out of whack, like a puzzle piece fitting into place. And the throbbing in my skull dulls until it's gone. I use my free hand to feel the back of my head again. My fingers come back dry.

"Healed." As I say it, I see bloody raw gashes on Ori's arm—imprints that match the woven pattern of my magic rope—seal over and heal.

"How are you doing that?" Alister's eyes snap accusatorially between us, as if healing is anything but a miracle after we beat the crap out of each other.

"I don't know," I say, my voice dripping in uncharacteristic sarcasm. "Magic?"

Ori laughs, loud and bright, the sound completely at odds with the anxious faces of everyone in the stands, not to mention the other fighters, who seem to have left their rings to hover around ours. Bex is there, and her nervous stare softens when she meets my eyes.

"Bex? Did you see what happened?"

"I only caught the last second, right after I beat Laurel." She says it without any hint of pride or smugness, but the nymph huffs anyway. "You pulled Ori into you with your lasso. But the second you touched, your rope started squeezing Ori, and you blasted backward. You only stopped when you and that paperclip effigy slammed against the wall. But you had such a hold on Ori that you took him with you. It seemed like you were both blacked out until Alister tore you apart." She doesn't seem concerned . . . more like she's in awe. "It was all from your touch." She glances at her dad as he joins the ring, who nods once, I guess encouraging her to go on. "Your magic magnified. Exploded." There's a wave of movement as apprentices in the stands scoot apart. I guess nobody wants to risk their own magic being set off by contact with a Cullingmate.

Meema pushes through the crowd.

"Horse manure!" she says. "That's not how it works. Magic doesn't explode."

"But it *does* magnify," Laurel says. "Too much magic in one place and it takes everyone out with it. These two clearly can't control their power. They should be culled immediately."

"Come *on*!" Ori and I say together. It's almost one of those lol-we-just-said-the-same-thing moments, except for the whole someone-might-want-to-rip-my-power-from-me thing.

"That could be a possibility," Alister says with an approving look at his daughter. "At the very least, they tried to kill each other despite clearly stated rules forbidding it. We should expel them both."

"Isn't that what you wanted?" Ori sneers. "For us to kill each other?"

Alister waves his hand dismissively. "It's called hyperbole. This level of violence cannot be tolerated among our own."

"Oh, come on, Ali," Pallavit says. Hers seems to be the only face filled with excitement rather than dread. "Sometimes magic just gets out of hand. That's why they're here. *To practice.*"

Ori takes in our accusers, a furrow of confusion creasing his forehead.

"But who won?" he finally asks.

"Technically, you," Bex says. "Nigel's butt fell outside the ring first. So . . . congratulations!"

If this were any other competition—the rodeo, 4-H, Future Farmers of America—the other apprentices would be good sports and congratulate the victor, too. But looking around, none of our Cullingmates seem likely to join in. Instead, they look suspicious, wary, even *scared* of us.

So much for making friends.

Meema claps her hands. "Everybody, back to your rings. You've got some butt-whupping to do." Nobody moves, and from the doubt-filled glances they give one another, I'd guess they're wondering if theirs will be the next power to get out of hand.

"NOW!" Meema barks.

The crowd finally disperses, giving Ori and me space to climb into the stands, Bex close behind.

"Ori," I mumble as we make our way up the steps. "I saw it. What happened to your sister."

He doesn't look me in the eye when he says, "I saw your dad. Screaming at you."

A dark cloud hovers over me that has nothing to do with the thunderstorm a water nymph just cast over her competitor.

"He's, uh . . ." I fiddle with the seam of my flannel. How do I describe Dad? "Not the best."

Ori nods, then abruptly turns to Bex as we're about to sit.

"Switch places with me, will you?" he asks her, and moves so she's in between us. Ori and I are only a yard apart. But somehow, it feels like miles.

CHAPTER THIRTEEN

OUR CULLINGMATES AVOID US FOR THE REST OF THE DAY. THEY STAY at least four rows away while the remainder of our Culling class fights. It's like they're afraid that, at any moment, we might spontaneously combust.

Ori seems perfectly fine with it. The smirk on his face grows wider every time someone climbs the stairs but changes direction when they see us. For me, all I can think is how wrong I was about what the Guild would bring me: friends, connection, belonging. I'm just as lonely here as I was back home.

Bex notices my mood and tries to reverse it. Whenever someone gives me an evil eye, she nudges my shoulder and says, "Screw 'em. Don't let it get to you."

Which makes Ori say, "I told you that none of us are here to make friends. The point of this place is to take out demons and Depraved. Every last one of them."

I catch his eye, and he looks away. He knows that I know why he wants to destroy them all. Which means he must also know why I long for connection here, after seeing my dad. If his time in my memories was anything like my time in his, he must have felt my despair in the moment Dad first saw me use magic, must have felt my betrayal and loneliness. He must know that above all else, I fear I'm going to be abandoned. Again. First by my mom, then Dad, then my grandpa; even Jeremy left me, too. And now everyone but Bex is treating me like I don't exist. And the one guy who does all sorts of unexpected things to my body and heart doesn't want to look for answers. Doesn't want to get closer. He saw the worst things I went through and is acting like it never happened. I'm sure Ori would just say that our purpose here is greater than wrestling with daddy issues.

Adding insult to injury is the distrustful looks I'm getting from not only my Cullingmates, but from Meema as well. She keeps glancing over from the ring she's supervising, appraising me like she's never seen me before. It makes Laurel's words run through my mind on repeat.

They can't control their power. They should be culled immediately.

"You don't think it's true, do you?" I ask. "That our power is building on each other's? Magnifying to dangerous levels?" I look at Ori, who still won't look my way. "What if we *are* a threat to the Guild? To the world?"

I ask it so quietly I'm not sure he heard. Ori scowls off into the distance, while Bex gently takes my hand, lacing our fingers together.

"Don't internalize their shit," Bex says, "or they win." She squeezes my fingers and holds our clasped hands up. "See? You didn't destroy me. I didn't blow up. Anything anyone else thinks of you is on them. If the goal is to make the Guild a more positive place, you need to believe you're not the monster they say you are. You've got to believe in *yourself*."

I give her a weak smile, but I can't ignore the tiny spark of hope her words create. I've never had this before, this platonic closeness. I lean into Bex's shoulder, which she pops into a gorilla arm to really pull me close.

"Careful with my ribs," I wheeze. "They've been through enough today."

Ori glances over at that, an apologetic smile on his face, the first bit of warmth he's shown since our fight. Butterflies go wild in my stomach as my body casts its own spell on me. One that I like quite a lot.

"It was some good magic, by the way," I add, hoping to keep this warm Ori instead of the one who can be colder than Frosty. "You whupped my ass with those effigies."

Ori's lips quirk higher. "It was pretty good, huh?"

"This is what I'm talking about!" Bex bursts. "The Guild should be all about flirting, not hurting."

My face burns like a forest fire while Ori rolls his eyes.

"N-nobody was flirting," I stammer, and Ori grunts, "What are you, fae?"

Bex shrugs. "All I'm saying is, this is *your* magic!"

I guess I never thought of it that way. Flirting, having a crush, as a type of magic. It's kind of sweet.

But Ori squints warily. "Why'd you say it like that? *Your* magic?"

Bex doesn't reply, just transforms her other arm into a gorilla limb and pulls Ori in, too. When there's no possible way for us to get any closer, her ears pop into elephant ears and she drapes them over us, creating the world's most bizarre cocoon.

"If this is your version of flirting, it's really creepy," Ori says.

"Shut up," Bex snaps. "I'm going to tell you something, and you can't tell a soul, all right?" Her voice drops. "Word can't get out about this."

"I don't think you're going to have to worry about anyone talking to us ever again," I say, and my heart squeezes with a pathetic pang.

"Just get on with it," Ori snips.

Bex's eyes dart left and right, as if she could see anyone approaching through our gray-skinned bubble. "There is a type of power that isn't talked about a lot," she whispers. "It's a power that I think *you two* have. You know how you can meet someone sometimes and there's this instant connection? You just feel butterflies in your stomach and know you like somebody even though you've never met them before. And you feel sort of boosted and invincible and on top of the world?"

Ori and I briefly lock eyes before we both look away. She's describing literally everything I've felt since we met. My entire body heats up and I squeak out, "Sure, yeah, I've heard of that."

Bex grins. "I'm sure you have. There's a magic version of that, too. Your whole body lights up when you meet that *someone*, and in magicians, it boosts their power. It's what I was telling you before. There's a power in love. A love *magic*."

"Not this again," Ori says. While my heart skips a beat, Ori's face furrows. "That's ridiculous."

"Y-yeah, so stupid." The last thing I need is for Ori to think I'm even more of a desperate idiot than he already does.

Bex gets this knowing look in her eye. "But there *is* something going on between you, isn't there? Let me guess: You see things sometimes when you touch, your power gets stronger when you have physical contact, you can heal each other's wounds when you're holding on to each other. I mean, I literally saw that with my own eyes just an hour ago."

All the visions of Cassie, the way I was able to calm that entire UT plaza when Ori's hand was on my shoulder during the first challenge, Ori and I watching our cuts and bruises disappear after our showdown. None of it has made sense. Unless what Bex says is true.

Ori has his bottom lip between his teeth. When I realize I'm staring at it, I glance up and meet Ori's eyes. "Based on how often I catch you gazing longingly at my face, I'd say you have a thing for me," he says.

Jesus, Nigel, get a hold of yourself.

I rush to change the subject. "How do you know all this, Bex?"

"You have to swear on your lives not to tell anybody." In two silver flashes, her eyes shift to eagle eyes that she uses to stare us down with. "It happened to my dads. They were a few Culling years apart, but when they got assigned their first mission together, they felt a spark like yours. Power overload. It blew Depraved to smithereens. But nobody in this place trusts a magician who's noticeably stronger than the rest. So my dads have made a conscious effort to lessen their power in front of others. When they're not on missions, they dedicate a lot of their time to researching what's going on between them. And from everything they've told me, you two are showing the exact same signs they had when they first met."

I think back to that moment when Bex described what happened between Ori and me in our matchup. Bex gave Yamato this long look, and it must have confirmed that Bex's dad thinks we have that same type of connection he has with his husband.

This is . . . kind of a lot of pressure. I mean, to be told you have love magic with your crush is a lot, especially when you've only known him for three days.

Bex takes in my worried energy and Ori's doubtful eyebrow. "It's not like you have to go ahead and get married or anything. It's just permission to, I don't know, give in to the feelings you've got. At the right time, I mean. Not when it's going to attract fear and suspicion from other Guild members. But, when all this is over and you make it into the Guild, my dads will be on your side. I promise."

"But how does nobody else know about this?" I ask. "Wouldn't the Guild want to harness some extra strong type of magic against the Depraved?"

"I mean, think about it. We're taught to distrust one another from the very start, to see other magicians as competition." She gives a very pointed look at Ori, who just shrugs. "My guess is it's kinda hard to fall in love in that environment, you know? So not a lot of people have stumbled into this magic on their own.

"That's why I'm here: to get in the Guild, keep my magic, and change the way this place operates. We need to encourage *love*, not competition. It'll be a long game, but the more people I can get on my side, the quicker we can harness love to battle Depraved hate. To battle hate everywhere, in and *outside* of the Guild."

Bex pops back to her normal self, and lets out a long sigh. One of those sighs that you can tell has so many meanings to it.

"You can talk to us," I say. "We're here. If you want."

Bex fidgets with the rings on her fingers, staring at her hands while she speaks. "Sometimes it seems impossible to tackle all the hate in the world. I have gay dads, one of whom is trans, and we're a happy queer Japanese American family. But no matter where we go, there's someone out there trying to tell us we don't belong. People creating laws that affect Pop's access to healthcare, and Dad can't even post a photo of a new design without getting called some slur. It's so disorienting to live in a world where hate creates *literal* monsters, when to me, the worst monster of all is how people try to actively make us feel less than. So my whole mission doesn't just start and stop with the Guild. We've got to stop hate everywhere, in the human world *and* magical one; we've got to encourage love and connection everywhere we look. I know it's such an intangible goal, but I've got to go after it. Because hate has real fucking consequences. So many more than just what this organization claims to fight. That's what I'm doing. That's my life's work. Even if it is an impossible task."

Bex finally looks up from her hands, a sad smile on her lips.

"Bex, I—" I don't know what to say. How do you follow an epic speech like that with something that has any real significance? It's not fair that she has to deal with that kind of hate from the world at large. That she not only has to fight the monsters it creates, but also the sadness and fear and insecurity. And the way so much of that weight gets thrown on the shoulders of queer people of color. Even though this group is made of magicians, we're still humans too, and the consequences of homophobia, racism, transphobia are all still felt by our members whether or not we can shapeshift or create effigies or turn chickens into pudding cups.

Magic can't solve everything.

But we've got to try, in any way we can.

"I'm here for you," I say. "I know it's not a lot, I know it can't change the whole world in this one moment, but I'm here for you." I lean into her shoulder, and she puts her head on mine.

"That's a start," she says.

We both look at Ori. No smirk is there. No cocky assuredness. Just concern.

"Me too," he finally says. "And I guess that means we can look into whatever this magic between Nigel and me actually is."

Bex cackles, then does the last thing I expected her to after pouring her heart out.

"Bow chicka bow wow," she sings. "That's what I'm talking about! Explore that looooove, baby."

I crack up, while Ori hides his face in his hands.

"Bex, you truly are the most magical person. And it has nothing to do with being a goblin descendant."

"Never a truer word," Bex says. "But let's see if the magic between you two can come anywhere close to as magical as I am. Bow chicka bo—"

"Jesus, make it stop." Ori snaps up to his feet, lunges across Bex, and grabs my hand, lacing his fingers through mine. This isn't at all like when Bex did the same thing. Ori's fingers brushing my own cause my heart to beat against my chest and make my hand break out in sweat. This is the kind of contact my body's been hoping for this whole Culling. And it's the kind of contact I thought Ori would never want.

But I'm so glad to be wrong.

"I expect a full report," Bex calls after us while Ori marches me over to the balcony, away from the remaining competitors duking it out in their rings. He looks over the railing, his face screwed up in concentration. Each floor is packed with magicians. People go in and out of Dispatch, tend to injuries of their own or of human victims in the medical bays, hop onto floors that I haven't even set foot on yet. Ori lets out a dramatic "Aaaargh," drops my hands to throw his in the air, and even stamps his foot. I know he's frustrated, but it's actually kind of adorable.

"Damn it, there's nowhere to go in here where we can be alone."

I shrug. "Someone's always watching."

"Fine, then." Ori gets close until our noses are barely inches apart, his lips just a heartbeat away. I look up into his eyes. It's the first time I've seen Ori frazzled. I can smell his minty breath as he whispers, "Okay. You win."

"Win what?"

"You're going to make me spell it out, huh? I felt it all, too."

He says it hushed and fast, glancing down at the floor as soon as the words are out.

Seeing him like this is a trip. The best kind of trip, and I want to milk it for all it's worth. I cross my arms smugly. "Felt what, exactly?"

Ori huffs, his eyes squinting into a glare. "You know what. The pull, the warmth, the visions. Your dad. I've seen it. I've felt it all. I've been trying to ignore it, refusing to get closer to you, but I guess I can't. We're"—he rolls his eyes—"written in the stars, or whatever. So I guess we should see what this means. Do what Bex says and use our powers for good. We can start in our next challenge."

"You mean it?"

I know I sound like such a little kid, desperate for affection. But after a lifetime of disappointment and distance, it's incredible to hear someone say they want to get closer to me. For once. And to be able to return it.

Ori nods, tucking a stray bit of hair behind his ear. "But don't go getting all *boyfriend* on me. This isn't a relationship, and don't forget it. Once we get through the second task, I'm looking out for myself in the third. Maybe you can make it into the Guild, too, but if it comes down to you or me, I choose me."

I understand completely, thanks to the visions. His need to get into the Guild is crystal clear.

"For Cassie," I say.

He nods again, the only noise the sound of his swallow.

"What the Depraved did to her?" I gently hold his fingers in mine, allowing him the opportunity to let go if he wants. "It wasn't your fault. You were just a kid."

Ori's not scowling now. The browns and ambers and golds of his irises are open, tender, hurt. "I've never told anyone about that day. The only person I've ever talked about it with is my mom."

"How is she doing? After Cassie?"

"Hellbent on destroying every last Depraved, while simultaneously hating the Guild for putting Cassie in a situation where she could be killed in the first place. She doesn't want me to be here.

Doesn't want to lose both her kids. But magic is the only thing I think I'm any good at, and if I don't join the Guild, they'll take it from me. Mom thinks a life without magic is better than no life at all. But I'm not so sure."

"Trust me. It isn't." The words are out of me before I can stop them. I don't want to come across as insensitive when we're talking about his sister.

But Ori gets it.

"Your dad . . ." he says. "Didn't handle the adjustment well?"

I laugh lightly, a pressure gripping my heart. "That's an understatement."

"Parents sure know how to fuck us up." Ori squeezes my fingers. His cardigan brushes against the exposed skin of my forearm, where my flannel's rolled up past the elbows. It sends goose bumps all along my body. Ori watches and that confident smirk returns. "I did that, huh?"

"Okay, let's not get cocky."

Ori shrugs. "It's not cocky if it's facts."

He tugs me closer, just an inch. Our lips are centimeters apart.

"Hey," he breathes.

"H-hey." I want to curse myself for my voice breaking, but Ori just smiles. Not a smirk. Not judgmental.

"You're cute, cowboy."

From the way my heart soars, I could swear my body flung itself over the balcony. But then I feel the toe of my boot anxiously tapping against the marble floor. I'm here. This is real.

"APPRENTICES!" Meema's voice barrels through the coliseum floor. Ori and I jump back, cold air whooshing between us, my fingers itching to get within reach of his again. "Eat, rest, study for the remainder of the day. No spellcasting. You'll need all your energy for when you're called upon to retrieve and cure your cursed victims. Stay ready."

My anger at Meema flares back to life, unjustified as it may be this time. She's kept me from magician friends for so long, and now she's done something I never saw coming:

She's become my first magician crush cockblock.

CHAPTER FOURTEEN

I'm flustered the rest of the day, antsy as I anticipate seeing Ori again, though we're all forced to wait in our individual dorms until being called upon for the second task. My leg jiggles with energy while my head swirls with thoughts of Ori's mouth just centimeters from mine. If our magic magnifies when we touch, what will happen if we *kiss?*

Hours go by and apprentices are summoned one by one. I'd hoped to be called first since that's the order we fought in, so at least I'd get to see Ori sooner rather than later, but of course it doesn't work out like that.

Frosty apparently spent the whole day snacking and is now ready for a good sleep, like I should be. They keep trying to stop my legs jiggling by nipping at my Levi's, and eventually they freeze the fabric to our alcove to force me to keep still. The way the gold light of the dorm reflects off the ice is just the distraction I need. I follow the glittering patterns until I finally calm my whirling thoughts enough to close my eyes and try to sleep.

Only, once I close my eyes, all I see is Ori. Ori at ten, doing magic for his sister. Ori at fourteen, seeing her die. Ori, the way he looked at me when Alister pulled us apart, empathy in his eyes after seeing my dad. Ori, any time we touch, the sparks and tingles and magic that follow. Ori calling me a cute cowboy, complete with that playful smirk and judgmental eyebrow that's cocky and hotheaded and freaking sexy.

He fills my dreams when I finally doze off. In one, we're fighting the Depraved together, saving his sister. In another, we're back on the Barrett farm, and I'm showing him how to ride a horse. When he falls off and skins his knee, my touch is all it takes to heal him. He moves my hand from his leg, his skinny fingers wrapped up in my thick ones, pulling me closer to him until our noses almost touch. He leans forward, his full lips parted, until—

"Get up!" Something grips my shoulder so tight I'm sure it has claws. My eyes snap open to find a bramble bush growing around me, its thorns making a pin cushion of my arm.

"Cut that out!" The bush recoils, snaking across my alcove floor. Frosty leans over and picks at the blackberries, plump and dark, that are laced in between the thorns. "Nice to know you have my back," I say, while Frosty chews happily.

"Get down here!"

I peer over the edge and find Alister leering at me from the first floor. All the other caves seem to be empty, even though it's the middle of the night.

"You don't have to be so rough about it," I growl.

"I don't have time to wake you gently," he snaps. "Your second task of the Culling starts now. Or would you prefer to dillydally and let your Depraved-cursed victims die?"

That snaps me awake. Frosty climbs to their hooves, sensing my alarm. I grab my flannel shirt from the corner and throw it on before Frosty and I follow Alister to the empty entry hall. It's weird and unsettling to be the only two people in the vast space, and for the first time I realize how smart it was for the Guild to set this building up so no one room was secluded. The way Alister keeps glaring makes me think he'd love nothing more than to spell me to death right here, and I hate that there's no one around to see us, just in case.

"Come here," he barks.

"Where's Ori?" We're supposed to do this together.

"Already at the site. Let's go."

With green nymph magic pooling in his fingers, Alister hums. It's deep, and surprisingly warm for someone whose voice is usually tinged with cynicism. The platform in the center of the hall glows purple, and Alister sings clear and strong, *"Hatred, fear, Depraved at their worst; take us to where the victims have been cursed."*

A beam of purple light shoots up from the marble floor. Alister motions to it. "After you."

I hop off Frosty's back and try to shoo them away. The last thing I need is for Frosty to get in the way when they start searching our cursed victim's pockets for food. "Go on, bud. I'll find you a midnight snack when we get home."

But, Frosty being Frosty, they don't budge. Instead, snow billows around their muzzle and they push me with their now freezing-cold snout. It's so cold it burns, making me jump through the portal, my stubborn crystallos following right behind. There's a flash and the entire Guild is gone. My stomach flip-flops as we travel through the rays of light. When my boots land on solid ground, the sound assaulting my ears only makes my nausea worse.

Screams. Human. At least two, by the sound of it—one higher pitched, the other low and scratchy. They're screams of pure, unadulterated fear. Or pain. Like whatever is happening to these people is ripping them apart from the inside out. Alister said Ori was here, and I hope that neither of those screams belong to him.

It's too dark to find their source. My eyes take long seconds to adjust, each filled with those soul-ripping bellows. It's my first time out of the Guild in three days, and the chaos is jarring.

My eyes finally adjust enough to see we've landed in a forest. Trees all around us block out the moonlight and make it hard for Frosty to move freely.

"What do we do?"

"Quiet!" Alister snaps. "Or you might attract the—"

SCREEEEEEEEE!

"Demon."

The monstrous shriek comes again, ear-splittingly high-pitched. Mixing with its cries are crashes, branches snapping, trees ripped up by their roots as if it's barreling through the forest.

Frosty tosses their head, the whites of their eyes showing. They're freaked out, and I can't blame them. I try to call on my magic and center myself for a calming spell, but my pulse is racing too high.

"What's a demon doing here? I thought we were just coming to get the cursed victim."

Alister looks at me like I'm a complete idiot. "Demons are drawn to human suffering. They feed off it. Now, are you going to ask questions all night, or are you going to get ready?"

Alister raises his green-glowing hands and clears a path through the trees. Sky-high trunks fly out of the way like they weigh nothing. Next, he folds his hand into a downward U and pulls up, a massive Venus fly trap blooming in front of him. Thick, viscous poison glistens in its center over the deep red of its mouth. Spikes around its borders are at least as tall as I am. Frosty rears back, and I'm too thrown off by the screams and demon shrieks to stop their panicked movement from pushing me to the ground. I land on my back, hard, the air knocked out of me.

Frosty's truly freaking out now, rearing back and stomping. I have to duck and roll to avoid my own horse trampling me. But I've been here before, thrown from the back of broncos countless times at the ranch or the rodeo.

This is my element.

Magic pools in my fingers, and I spring to my feet. Middle fingers extended again, an image of Frosty's head in my mind, I calm them.

"There's a good buddy," I coo. Frosty huffs and paws at the ground. I create a circle with my forefinger and thumb and blow out three glowing bubbles so we'll at least see the demon before it catches us by surprise.

SCREEEEEEEEE!

The demon's closer, its cry so loud that I'm amazed my eardrums don't burst. Alister's mouth is moving, but I can't hear what he says.

"What was tha—" The question is knocked right out of me. Literally. I'm flying through the air. Tree branches whip and nick me until I'm so high up I break through the tree line. Moonlight finally illuminates my surroundings, enough to see our enemy as it bears down on Alister.

It's an elk demon, its horns three times as wide as a normal elk's, its body hulking, patches of fur falling off to show rotten, dead skin. Its eyes glow such a bright green that I can see them from up here. I can also see how sharp its horns are. The horns that I'm quickly free-falling toward, ready to skewer me through.

My fingers glowing gold with power, I put them into my mouth and blow. A whistle loud enough to match the demon's cries sings out through the forest. A summoning spell. I've used it countless times to call animals back home, and now, it gets the elk demon to move right where I need this fleabag to be.

"Oof!" I land on its back, but I have to dig into the decaying green flesh of its neck to keep from being thrown off.

SCREEEEEEEEE!

This thing can buck all it wants, but I'm not budging. In its frustration, the demon charges Alister's Venus fly trap, its horns piercing through the plant's meaty flesh. Alister tumbles out of the way as the demon careens toward him. In a flash of green light, the trees closest to Alister lean together and their bark thickens, creating a wall between him and the elk monster. The demon bashes it over and over, but Alister holds steady.

The monster rears back in anger, slamming to the ground and charging the first thing it lays eyes on.

Frosty.

My crystallos might be stubbornly confident back in the Guild, but when faced with a demon hellbent on destruction, Frosty freezes. Ironic, coming from an ice horse. Rotten green magic builds in the elk demon's muzzle, and I've only got seconds before it melts Frosty into a puddle.

I take a deep breath and summon more magic. It's slow to respond—I've used a lot in the last minute—and for a brief instant, I think all is lost. But then Ori's face fills my mind, that perfect smile spreading across his lips as he called me cowboy.

That's just the inspiration I need.

Using the ounce of magic I have left, I create a magic horse bridle—or demon bridle, I guess.

SCREEEEEEEEE!

The monster barrels down on Frosty, shrieking in glee, and with its mouth open, I let the bit swing into the elk demon's jaw. Just as it releases its stream of evil magic, I yank with all my might, turning the demon's neck just enough so that its power blows a tree into matchsticks instead of my crystallos into ice cubes. Frosty takes advantage of the momentary distraction to gallop off into the woods, and I think this might be it for my ice horse companion and me. Who would stick around after realizing demon death traps might become a daily occurrence?

This monster bucks and thrashes, and I grip my reins to hold on for dear life. If I slip off this beastie's back, there's no way I'll be able to avoid getting trampled by its hooves.

The demon pounds the earth, deep grooves gashed into the dirt. From atop its back, I can see down Alister's cleared path to where blasts of purple and pink magic dot the darkness.

Sprite and fae magic. Ori and someone else.

Then green, jagged streaks of light.

Depraved.

I can't tell if my vision is just scrambled from this bucking psuedo-bronco, but it looks like there's more green magic than purple or pink. Evil is winning.

How could they be here? We were just supposed to retrieve our victim, not fight off their attackers. But as more bursts of green power light up the night, I know I don't have time to question it. I've got to kick some serious Depraved ass.

"Ori! I'm coming." I squeeze my thighs on either side of the demon's belly and yank my reins hard in the direction of Ori and his attacker. "'Yup!" I pull on the reins, and we sprint down the path.

"Good demon." I pat the beast's back and a mass of decaying green fur pulls off in my fingers. "Gross demon."

SCREEEEEEEEEE!

As we get closer, it's clear we got here just in time. Pallavit lies among the trees, a gash in her side. There's only one Depraved, and its hands are pulsing green with magic, pointed right at Ori.

I have no magic left, but I have pure will, damn it. This fucked-up monster is not about to take away the first guy I've ever had a real crush on.

"NOT TODAY, VARMINT!" I spur the elk demon forward and we gallop straight for the Depraved, getting its attention just in time. The monster whips around as a stream of green power pours from its fingers. I've got to move, now! I hoist myself up and jump off the demon's back at the exact moment the Depraved's power hits the twisted elk's heaving chest.

The Depraved's magic is so strong I feel the elk's body heat as I hit the ground and roll. In seconds the demon combusts from within, leaving nothing but ash and decaying fur.

"Nigel!" Ori yells as I tumble head over boots into the forest. I catch a brief glimpse of him, worrying at an effigy in his hands, but I can't tell what he's doing.

That is, until my tumbling stops and I'm pulled upward by the wings that sprout from my back. They're fluffy and white and huge, practically glowing from the way the moonlight reflects off them. A pair complementing the ones he gave himself just yesterday.

As I clumsily flutter to the ground, I finally spot our victim. Well, *two* victims, actually. A boy and a girl, probably a couple years younger than us, writhing on the forest floor and screaming hysterically. Their eyes are clamped shut tight, but still they shriek like whatever they see behind their closed lids is terrible. The sounds of their cursed panic set every nerve in my body on edge, the hairs on my arms standing on end, a bitter taste of metal filling my mouth.

But the Depraved closes its eyes and smiles. It takes a deep breath and waggles the fingers of one hand, as if conducting a beautiful symphony. Taking joy in the pain of others, feeding off it.

A light flicks on in the distance. A cabin. With others behind it.

Some resort, or maybe a summer camp. How others aren't hearing our battle is beyond me, but we've got to take out this Depraved before it goes in search of more victims.

I turn to Ori. "What do we do?"

"I've got this," Ori says, and with the sound of a sealed lid popping off, my wings fall from my back. Ori has his Play-Doh in hand, his long fingers smooshing the clay into a new figure.

But in a heartbeat, the clay is gone. Zapped into nothing by a snap of the Depraved's fingers. It laughs, a metallic sort of clacking sound.

The Depraved's just taunting us now. Its head keeps twitching every which way, taking in me, Ori, Pallavit getting to her feet, and Alister sliding into the scene from his cleared path.

"Any ideas?" I turn to Alister, but he only laughs.

"This is your challenge, kid. I've just been given the unfortunate task of making sure you don't die."

I look at Pallavit, who has a burn mark along her throat, weeping pus.

"I can't sing," she croaks.

"Nigel! Watch out!"

I'm thrown through the air and land hard on my back. The oxygen whooshes from my lungs. At any moment I expect to feel my body combust. But a pink glow catches my eye. Ori brought his Ken doll back, and he's thrown it across the forest floor, taking me with it. There's scorched earth where I just stood.

Ori saved my life.

I am *sick* and *tired* of these near-death experiences.

"Ori, catch." I toss the Ken doll back, hoping he can use it against the Depraved—and giving myself some help closing the distance between us. I soar through the air and land next to my crush in a heartbeat.

The Depraved shrieks and lets loose a string of magic bursts, hellish lightning stretching across the sky. Ori and I jump apart, just barely avoiding getting hit.

"I'm out of magic!" I yell.

Ori's face falls. "I don't have much left." He swipes his hand over the Ken doll twice, once to wipe it clean, the next to make it glow with his power, resetting the effigy. "Got it!" He raises Ken triumphantly.

"It's time for you to *stay. Put*," Ori says, bending the Ken's left arm down to its side. The Depraved's arm whips to its side like a magnet pulled it there.

But the Depraved seems unfazed. Its power just shifts to its right hand, and with the set of its sickly eyes I know we're seconds away from it dealing a death blow.

That cannot happen.

Bex's words echo through my mind. Her insistence that our magic magnifies with our touch. Her telling us to *lean into* this connection, to see what the sparks between us can do. The whole point of Ori's and my showdown was to learn how to compensate for each other's weaknesses, and the biggest takeaway was that when we're stretched thin, contact will bring our power back tenfold.

Just as Ori grasps the effigy's right arm, I put my own arm over his shoulder and pull him into me. My body lights up, enough electricity running through my veins that I'm sure I could power the whole city of Austin. Ori glances my way, that smirk creeping up his lips, and I know he feels this, too. He slams that plastic appendage to the doll's side.

I've never heard a more enraged and agonized sound than what comes out of the Depraved's mouth. Never heard a scream and known for certain that whoever was yelling was about to die.

I watch, open-mouthed, as the Depraved's arm slams into its

side. At first, I feel pride that Ori and I subdued it together. This is what we were meant to do, stop monsters in their tracks. As we watch, the Depraved's body begins to fold, bending at an unnatural angle. A sickening crack lets us know its spine has broken, its shoulders meeting the back of its legs.

This is more than just a fused arm. This whole creature's entire body is folding in on itself.

But then, movement to the right. A new cry of agony joining the Depraved's.

Pallavit. Her screams hoarse from her injury.

Her own arm is pinned against her side. And some unseen force is bending her back. Exactly like what's happening to the Depraved.

Our magic, gone wide, catching her in its net. Our magic—about to kill her.

"Make it stop!" I shout, but Ori's as confused as I am, wide-eyed with worry.

"That's not how effigies work," he says. "They're for one person only." He yanks the arm up again, but nothing happens.

"Boys! Enough!" Alister commands.

More screams as the Depraved bends forward this time. Pallavit too.

Then, with a flash of blue, Frosty gallops into the clearing. They butt Pallavit off her feet, then freeze her to their back when she lands unceremoniously on top of them. Frosty carries her away, and I see her back straightening the farther she gets from us. Her screams subside, and relief rushes so strongly through my body I can practically hear it. I'm going to find a spell for an infinitely refilling trough when Frosty and I make it through the Culling.

Meanwhile, the Depraved's not as lucky. Our magic has taken hold, folding its body again and again and again.

Crack.

Crack.

Crack.

Red bursts of blood.

Ori bends over and throws up.

I want to look away. I want to tell him we've done good, that we're doing what we've always been taught.

But I can't tear my eyes away from the Depraved's horrifying last moments, brought on by us.

So I watch until all that's left is a small cube of bone, rust-colored, stained with blood, the last remnants of the first monster I killed.

CHAPTER FIFTEEN

I DON'T KNOW HOW LONG WE STAND THERE. I DON'T KNOW WHEN Ori's vomit turns to white, foamy bile. Why don't I feel more like celebrating? I mean, I feel good in a way; we just stopped a Depraved. Meema's going to love that. This is what we're supposed to do as members of the Guild. There's something magical—no pun intended—about Ori and me working together and ridding the world of evil. Our magics magnified, just like Bex said they would. I was nearly tapped out, but one touch with Ori and that Depraved was gone in seconds. Though staring at the leftover cube of bone makes my stomach turn. Especially considering how Pallavit almost shared the same fate.

My blood turns cold as ice.

What we have . . . it could be dangerous.

With a high-pitched whinny of triumph, Frosty canters over. My shoulders sag with relief to see Pallavit beaming from her position on their back like she wasn't almost killed.

"What a wild ride, baby!" Even hoarse, her voice swells with excitement. She climbs off Frosty, laughing to herself the entire time. When her feet touch the ground, she practically runs over to give both me and Ori a squeeze.

"I've never seen such quick handiwork!" she says. "You've got to be the strongest apprentices in years!"

"They certainly are." Alister's expression is strange. Confused. Maybe even disappointed.

I glance at Ori, but his face is blank, as if he didn't hear them.

"But . . . what about you?" I almost don't want to break the spell of victory. It's the first time I've really been praised since starting the Culling. But I need to know what happened back there. "We almost turned you into—" I gesture to the Depraved cube.

Pallavit waves me off. "So you don't know your own strength. We'll figure out a way to harness it." She gives both of our shoulders a shake. "The Depraved won't know what hit 'em."

"No time to celebrate just yet, Pallavit," Alister says. "They still need to cure their victims."

"I thought there'd only be one," I say.

Alister looks at me like I'm an idiot. "Oh yes, *restraint* is what the Depraved are known for." He motions to Ori. "You get the girl." Then he gestures for me to carry the boy.

Now that we're not fighting for our lives, my ears finally register the victims' screaming again. They've been yelling this whole time, but I don't know if that battle took five minutes or five hours. The victims' eyes are still closed, their minds still seeing whatever horrors the Depraved cursed them to. Their yells do nothing to chase the memory of the Depraved's tortured scream, much less Pallavit's, from my mind.

Alister shakes me. "Move!"

Ori walks forward as though spelled. There's no confidence in his gait, no perfectly cocky grin tilting up the side of his mouth. He makes an effigy of the girl from a doll in his bag and uses it to have her float next to him. When he looks my way, his face twists in disgust.

"What did you do?" he hisses. "I had it covered. You saw. Its arm was glued to its side, just like I wanted, but then you grabbed onto me and—" He waves back to the bone cube we're both avoiding looking at and then toward Pallavit.

"Seriously, don't worry about me. You completely dominated." Pallavit's so pumped she actually laughs. "When you two are in, I call dibs on having you on my missions."

A war wages inside me. Part of me wants to believe Pallavit and celebrate that I really am meant for Guild work. But the other side wants to promise Ori we won't get so carried away a second time. He has to know I'm as in the dark as he is. He has to know that we can figure this out together.

"Ori, neither of us meant for that to happen. We can practice, coordinate better next ti—"

"You do realize this is a timed exercise, right?" Alister snaps. "We need to get back to the Guild. Quickly."

I try to clear my head, to get myself back into the second Culling task. But I can't ignore Ori's suspicious glare, like he thinks I *meant* to do this. Then Ori's face morphs into Dad's, and he's grinning. I know he'd say this is what I get for thinking I was the most powerful magician on the ranch, for thinking I had it all figured out.

"Good, Barrett," Alister says. I look down and see that, without thinking, I've magicked the boy to be light as a feather. My power is as strong as ever after Ori's touch. I cradle the guy in my arms, a faint gold glow surrounding him. He seems like he could be a high school junior who expected to enjoy his last summer at camp before senior year and graduation. Who could have guessed what awaited him?

Alister looks to Pallavit. "Let's go."

The fae clears her throat and winces a bit, her hand going to the red burn mark on her skin. Even still, she's able to summon enough power now to imbue her neck with a purple glow.

"The battle's won.
Enemies bone.
Signal the portal
To take us home."

A knot in a nearby tree glows purple and molds into the shape of a door knob. She twists it and a pane of purple light shines behind the spelled door. She steps through without looking back. Ori and his floating ward go next, then me and mine, his screams now just white noise in the background of my stampeding thoughts.

The second our feet land on the Guild's marble floor, my thoughts are whipped away by dozens of angry voices.

"What in blue blazes is going on here?" That one's for sure Meema's. Her hands grow gold with gathering magic as she barrels toward Alister. "A demon *and* Depraved at the site of their victims? All threats are supposed to be confirmed contained before apprentices are sent to retrieve them. Combat is reserved for the final task. You know this!"

I see in her eyes what I've been hoping to glimpse for days: concern, worry, love. Not embarrassment, not anxiety that I'll continue to blemish the Barrett name.

"Wait, wait, wait." Pallavit's so worked up now she's shaking. The burn on her neck is gone, healed by the portal, and her enthusiasm rings clear through the hall. "You've got to hear this."

"You know as well as I do, Adela, that Depraved are growing more powerful by the day," Alister says. "Dispatch confirmed all threats were contained. But new foes must have been drawn to the humans' suffering while we were in transit. Still, you should have seen how well the boys performed. They are very promising apprentices."

Whoa. Did Alister really just say that? About *me*? Maybe I judged him too quickly. Maybe he just needed to see how strong I can be before believing in me.

"I saw it all in Dispatch," Meema says, her eyes shimmering as she appraises me. I hold my breath, knowing however she takes this news matters more than anything. If she's proud, I'll finally feel like I'm living up to the Barrett reputation. If she's horrified at what we nearly did to Pallavit, I'll know that my power is just as much of a disappointment to her as Dad's total lack of it.

Finally, she laughs. "Whooee!" she cries. "Getting rid of varmints in a flash!" She pulls me in for a hug, and for a moment I feel like I'm actually meant to be here. "That's my boy! The greatest magician in generations!"

"Let's not get carried away," Alister drawls, snapping back to his usual self. "Or was it my imagination that my daughter's power nearly overtook your grandson's during the first task? This challenge was not about battling the enemy, as impressive as their performance may have been." He looks lazily at his immaculate gold watch. "There are humans to save. Clock is ticking."

"He's right. Hop to it, you two." Meema taps her foot. "Take these victims up to the medical bays. You've got fifty minutes to keep your naysayers from getting exactly what they want."

She turns without another word, giving me a cold shoulder that feels more like the Meema I've gotten used to the past few days. Alister leaves just as suddenly, but Pallavit gives us an encouraging wink before she follows. It's just Ori, Frosty, and me in the entry hall now, staring at each other, unable to move after all the intensity of the last—I look at my phone—eleven minutes. It feels like I've been awake for a week.

"Hey," I say, putting a reassuring hand on Ori's shoulder, but he shrugs it away. Even the way his hair bounces with the movement seems angry. If it wasn't for Frosty's cool snout nuzzling my neck, I'd feel seriously burned.

"Uh, was it something I said?"

"Don't touch me," he says flatly. "Just don't. We can't let that happen again."

"Okay. But this doesn't have to be a bad thing, Ori. You heard what everyone said. The two of us? Together? We could be the greatest team the Guild has ever seen."

Ori's judgy eyebrow is anything but playful now, full of disgust, like he'd rather be anywhere than here. It feels like a pitchfork to my gut.

Ori finally turns his attention to the screaming campers at our feet. "We'd better get them cured. I can't let anyone else suffer because of us." The pitchfork digs deeper, but Ori doesn't care. "Let's go."

Using his effigy to make her weightless, Ori bends down and picks up his victim. He's got her by the hand, and I'd be lying if I said it doesn't sting that he's able to have such close contact with a stranger, but he's completely shut me out.

The two of them blink out of existence and reappear on the first-floor balcony twenty feet above.

"Show-off," I mutter. I click my tongue gently to get Frosty's attention. "How you feeling, bud? Been through a lot, huh?"

Frosty huffs as if to say *You're telling me.*

"You up for a ride? I can find another way if you're not."

But Frosty bends down, letting me climb on their back. Something's changed for us, and I don't think I'll be dealing with the same stubborn ice horse in the future.

"You and your *horsey* are no match for me," Ori calls from the second floor. It's wild how much difference tone makes. Yesterday, Ori could have said the same snarky words and they would have been playful. Now, they're demeaning, like he wants to get under my skin. It works. And it hurts.

I snap my fingers and the screaming boy, still under my spell from the forest, is in my arms, wedding-style. I imagine Ori there instead, and my stomach gurgles guiltily as I remember the look he gave me when I tried to touch his shoulder.

I shake my head to clear it. "Stop feeling sorry for yourself," I whisper, and Frosty sends a burst of warmth through their back, like they know I need a friend right now. "Thanks, buddy. Ready?"

In response, they bound into the air and gently freeze my legs to their side all at once. We've found our rhythm now, and I don't know how I ever imagined going through the Culling without a crystallos. When we make it to the fifth floor, I send them off to the nymph hall to gorge themselves on all the plants they can get their muzzle on, Laurel be damned.

"Took you long enough," Ori barks before ripping open the Guild envelope that sits on a silver pedestal beside him. Its curling cursive details the next challenge:

Welcome to your second Culling task.
The cursed have been inflicted by a Depraved's evil spell.
Reverse it.
Or the humans won't be the last to meet an unfortunate fate.

"That's it?" I ask, while Ori scoffs, "That's dramatic."

I take the card from Ori (who snatches his fingers away from mine way too quickly) and flip it over. "Nothing tells us what the curse even *is*?"

"Right, because the senior magicians have held our hands so much up to this point." He rolls his eyes, then directs his attention to the rest of the medical bays. About half of them are filled with apprentices inspecting their own victims. Bex and Laurel work a few bays down, hovering over a woman with pea-green pus oozing out of her pores and soaking the sheets beneath her. Bex looks like she might puke, and Laurel shoves her out of the way as she makes different types of plants appear, chewing their leaves or tearing them apart and applying them to different spots on the woman's body.

"Let's go." Ori leads the way to the nearest empty bay. All it takes is a gentle touch on the shimmering glass for us to enter. Once inside, all other sounds cease. The walls are opaque, blocking out the rest of the floor. It smells clean, like freshly laundered sheets, and the calming babble of a stream fills the room. Until our victims' screams drown it out.

"We've only got forty-five minutes to get them cured," Ori says, and he lays the girl on the bed. I position the boy next to her while Ori and I stand on opposite sides of the room. Plenty of distance between us, just like he wanted.

I rack my brain for anything I read about curses that make people scream themselves to death. I draw a blank, so I march over to the cabinet stuffed with books. "Let's start by identifying the curse. Maybe there's something about it in one of these."

Ori stops my hand before I can grab the nearest spine. Warmth cascades through my fingers and up my wrist. A faint smile pulls at his mouth, just for the quickest second, until he realizes he's broken his own rule and snaps his hand away.

Ori clears his throat. "Curses are my specialty. This is a

Nightmare Coma. The inflicted are put in an enchanted sleep. They'll dream of their worst fears until they die. Literally scared to death."

A shiver gallops up my spine. "How long does it take? Until it kills them, I mean?"

Ori shrugs. "Depends on the fear. For most, about a day. Eventually, a mist of blood starts to come out with each new scream. Their heart will pump faster and faster as their fear gets worse until—" He slams a hand against the cabinet. "Their heart stops. But the Guild won't let that happen. It's us we should be worrying about."

"Right." Instinctually, magic moves into my fingers. "Let's get started."

Ori looks down at the girl, her face twisted in agony. "I'll work on this one. You see how far you can get with him."

If our magic really is stronger when we're touching, maybe . . . "Don't you think, if we worked togeth—"

Ori snaps his hand up to stop me. "What happened last time we worked together?"

"We stopped a Depraved."

"And we nearly killed another magician in the process. What if we do it again? Do you want to kill these kids, too?"

"Of course not. I just thought—"

"No," Ori says flatly, then riffles through his backpack, ignoring me. Rejected, I turn to my side of the bed.

For a second, with magic in my hands, I feel good. *This* is why I'm here. To use my powers and make people better, to battle the evil of the Depraved. For the first time in my life, I have a real chance to be a part of that. All those years of practicing around the ranch, of enduring Dad's negativity and the demons he brought to our property, finally being put to good use.

I just have to get started.

"All right, uh . . ." I realize I don't know this guy's name, and calling him "the guy" when I'm trying to connect and bring him out of a curse feels too cold. "Vic. Vic, let's get this curse out of you."

"Did you just call him Vic?" Ori's giving me that judgy eyebrow again.

"What? It's short for *victim*. I just thought he needed a name."

Ori scoffs, then turns back to the girl. I'll call her Cursula. But Ori doesn't need to know that.

I get to work, trying everything I can think of. If Vic's eyes have been sealed shut to allow for nightmares, maybe I need to cast a counter-spell to open them. Smearing my right thumb in two straight lines like an equal sign against my left palm, I craft two pieces of magical tape and try to stick Vic's eyes open with them. He looks freaky with his eyelids pulled back for about point two seconds before a green tinge worms its way up my golden tape and dissolves into a rotted mess. Vic's eyes slap closed.

I try Sweet Dreams, the spell Meema would use on me when I was little and had nightmares about demons. I place a hand around my throat and my neck glows gold. I lean down and whisper into Vic's ear.

"There's nothing to fear. You're safe. You're in a lush green meadow, winds gently blowing through the grass, the blades softly tickling your legs. Unicorns graze in the distance, and a bird's angelic melody fills your ears. The sun is bright and warm on your face. Sleep softly."

If anything, Vic's screams just get louder. So much for that.

Maybe an extraction spell could help. I use the basic spell all the time on the ranch, whenever a dog bumbles into a patch of pricklers or I get a splinter in the barn. I hover a hand over Vic's face, my fingers and thumb forming a downward U, like a pincer poised to pull the curse out.

In order for the extraction to work, I have to clearly visualize what it is I'm trying to remove. I have to tune out Vic's screams and imagine what his fears could be. I close my eyes and center myself, letting the golden warmth of my magic fill me up from the inside out. I try to place myself in Vic's thoughts. There's no way I can know what scares him most, but I try to let my body feel the symptoms of fear that haunt Vic's mind. I think of my heart racing, my palms sweating, my breath coming in short bursts. The extraction spell poised in my hand latches on to something. I can feel an energy gather between my fingers, something that makes my hand go clammy. It has to be Vic's fear.

I don't open my eyes, not wanting to break the spell before it's complete. Since magic is influenced by emotion, I let myself get deeper into the fear. I imagine a life without magic. I imagine fighting the demons and Depraved that would haunt our property twofold thanks to both Dad's and my Culling failures. I remember Dad screaming at me that first day my magic appeared, my realization that not only had my mom left me physically, but that any hope of my dad being there emotionally was gone, too.

The fear is so thick now it feels like a baseball in my hand. I pull up, hoping all of Vic's fears are coming with it. The gold light behind my eyes wavers. I feel a slight pinch of warning, but before I can react, the gold in my vision shatters. Those mottled green tendrils of Depraved magic overtake it until all I can see is a murky gray-green haze, like swamp water filling my soul.

I snap my eyes open. Well, I *try* to snap my eyes open. But they won't budge. Fear pierces my heart. I want to open my mouth and call to Ori, but the words won't come. All that leaves my throat is a scared moan.

Alone, unable to control my body, unable to communicate, fear runs hot through my veins. The dull green light behind my eyes mutates to form new images. More visions of an angry dad. More despair at being magicless. And then: bones crushing, blood spurting, as Ori and I kill not the Depraved, but Pallavit.

It doesn't stop there. I see death after death, each more gruesome than the last. Magician, human. Everyone I hoped to save. And at the end of each vision I see myself, gold magic pouring from my fingers. Every last murder happens at my hand, with Ori by my side.

Are these visions of what's to come? Do I have any real choice? Either a life without magic, or a life with magic that is used only to kill?

Something in my heart tells me that yes, these are my only options. That I won't ever be a hero who destroys evil. That I *am* evil. Ori's been right all along. I can't be trusted.

My moan builds to a gut-wrenching scream. I scream until my throat gets raw, my eyes still sealed shut as I drown in that rotten green light. Maybe the time for the second task has already run out. Maybe my magic will be taken from me at any second. And maybe that's for the best.

I scream and scream and scream until I feel a pressure in my head. Maybe there is so much fear and despair in me that I'll actually burst.

The pressure builds until finally, *finally*, there's just black.

CHAPTER SIXTEEN

"NIGEL. NIGEL! NIGEL!"

Sensation floods in.

Hands. On my shoulder. Shaking me.

Screams. Not my own. My throat is scratchy and raw, but the screams are coming from somewhere else.

Light, behind my eyes. Not green, or my golden magic, but light from the room sifting through my eyelids.

I blink until my surroundings come into focus, until what's right in front of my face comes into focus.

Ori.

His expression worried. His forehead scrunched. Holding me so close that I can see the different swirls of brown and amber and russet in his eyes. Holding me so close that a stray lock of his hair brushes my cheek.

"What happened?" I croak.

"You were a complete and total idiot!" Ori yells, but there's so much concern in his voice. "You tried to *extract* the curse. You can't just pluck it out. Nightmare Comas are like the most infectious disease. If you try to take another's curse out of them it just brings nightmares to you. What were you thinking? Why would you do that?"

"I—I was trying to make it through the Culling." I sit up so hard I almost bash my forehead against his chin. "How much time do we have left?"

Ori glances at a clock on the wall. "Seven minutes." While we stare at it, the minute hand moves again. "Six."

I launch myself off the floor so fast I get lightheaded. "Whoa." I move to catch myself on the bed, but Ori's up just as quick to steady me with a hand. The dizziness fades almost instantly, a buzzing in my stomach replacing it.

"H-how? How did you get the curse out of me?"

Ori sighs. "Yet again, this mysterious connection doing its thing. You started screaming and collapsed. I caught you just before you could smash your head on the floor, so you're welcome." He looks at me like I caused a scene on purpose, but as he continues, his face creases with worry. "I sat here with your head in my lap, and the longer we sat like that the quieter you became. Until the screams stopped. You were shaking and then you weren't. Your breaths became even. I guess this healing thing also works with curses, but slower."

"Do you think if we touch the campers, they'll heal, too?" I reach out and grab Vic's wrist, but his screams don't stop.

"You know that's not how curses work." He says it like he's explaining the ABCs.

"Well, it worked for us!" I snap.

"That's because of . . . whatever's going on between us. I don't know how to unlock it any more than you do. All I know is, when we touch, our powers react. Magnify."

The vision I saw in my nightmare flashes through my mind. Ori's hand on my shoulder while we cast spells that murdered magician and human alike.

"We can't do that," I say flatly.

"Oh, so now you agree with me." Ori looks at the clock again. "Five minutes. Maybe it's for the best. Cassie wouldn't have wanted it this way. She wouldn't want me risking innocent lives, even if it was to take out the monsters that killed her."

He looks at me, and for the first time, doesn't try to hide his sadness. He's been dead set on keeping his magic for years, seeking revenge on the Depraved, and that dream is going right in the manure pile in a matter of minutes.

"You didn't have any luck with your effigies?"

Ori shakes his head, pointing to a pile of discarded toys, clay models, and paper clip figures. All of them are tinged with that same rotten green hue that invaded my golden magic.

I take a shaky breath. "So we just . . . give up?"

Ori's eyes wander, but he nods slightly. "I just never thought it'd be like this," he says. "Ever since Cassie—" His voice breaks, and I avoid his eyes, allowing him this moment alone to compose himself. "Ever since she died, I promised myself I would take up her mission. She wanted to be in the Guild so bad. And you know, I always thought she blessed me from beyond or something, because everything I can do with those"—he motions to the pile of used up toys—"started after she died. It was always sprite wood, until the day of her funeral, and then it wasn't. I made an effigy of my mom out of this Captain Marvel figurine in my room. I didn't even think it would work, I just wanted her to get her hands away from my collar and stop trying to adjust my suit. I expected Mom to be so angry, but we both laughed until we cried. Cassie would have loved to know I could do more than other sprites. And Mom and I agreed it was a gift left behind by Cassie."

Ori laughs now, derisive, mad. "But the way that gift almost killed Pallavit? It's messed up. A cruel fucking joke. Cassie would *hate* that. *I* hate that. It's like, time after time, I get slapped with these shit choices. First, it's join the organization that led to Cassie's death or have the thing that linked us together—our magic—taken away. Now it's keep that magic, but only at the risk of innocent people getting hurt. I know Pallavit and the senior members lit up when they saw what we could do, but damn."

He looks at me again, and there's so much hurt, sadness, anger in his eyes. It's the most vulnerable I've seen him. It makes me want to open up, too.

"When those nightmares came, I saw things," I say. "*Worse* things than what we did at that camp."

"Well, at least that means you have a heart."

"What do you mean?"

"That's the point of the curse. To show your worst fears. And if you're afraid of getting out of control . . . again . . . it means in your heart you know what I'm saying."

I nod. "I do."

Ori seems to soften, a look of resignation spreading across his face. He glances at the clock again. "Three minutes." But he looks content to just sit here with me, at least now that he's sure I have a heart.

Wait a minute. I *do* have a heart.

"The Heart of Health," I say. "Meema would use it when one of the animals on the farm got hurt bad. It's a magical heart, spelled to heal someone on the verge of death, or at the very least restore enough strength for their body to naturally do the rest. I saw her use it on some cattle who tripped down a ravine after heavy rain. They practically leaped from the ground afterward. I'd never seen a cow move like that in my life."

Ori is incredulous. "You think a cow spell can wake these two up?"

"Yup."

Ori bites his lip. I can tell he's fighting an internal battle, too. Part of him wants to avenge his sister, and part of him is desperately afraid of losing control again.

"I have a theory," I say.

Ori motions for me to go on.

"Our magic is about intent. It has been from day one. What we tried to do back there, at the camp, was destroy—and our spell got out of hand. But what we're trying to do here is heal. To awaken. Those are *good* things. So when we touch, our intention will be magnified again, but for the right purpose this time. Nobody will be harmed."

"What if you're wrong?"

I throw my hands up. "I don't know. I can't lie to you and say I have this all figured out, but we at least have to try, right? It's not about the Guild anymore. It's about proving it to *us*. If we can do this one thing right, we'll know that we can use whatever's going on between us for good."

"But how is this Heart of Health going to work when the curse has wiped out everything else?"

I grab Ori's hand and that warmth of our connection bubbles up in my stomach. "Because we'll be working together. If your touch took away my curse, maybe mine can prevent the curse from taking over your effigies. And then I'll craft these hearts and put them in one of your toys, and it'll work. We'll do good."

Ori worries at his lip, glancing between me and the clock. It ticks down one more minute. Like a bull unleashed from his pen, Ori jumps into action, pink light building in his fingers. "We have two minutes left. Hurry." He reaches into his bag and pulls out a couple tiny figures, barely an inch tall each. "These are all I have left."

Ori lays the fingers of his free hand flat, maneuvering the little plastic people so they lay side by side. He wipes his thumb over them, making the figures glow with magic. Instantly, a matching light pink haze hovers over the campers, but it does nothing to silence their screams.

"This is the moment when the Depraved's magic has kept wiping out my own," Ori says, giving my fingers a squeeze. For a brief instant, the pink fades from around the toys' feet, a greenish tinge working up their toes to their mini plastic knees. But as Ori squeezes my hand tighter, the green subsides. "It's working. With you here."

My mouth goes dry. Butterflies flit through my stomach.

And then Ori's all Ori. "Come on, Nigel, we're under a time crunch. No time to get sappy now."

With one minute left, I get to work. I feel clumsy using only one hand, but extra strong from the buzz pouring into me through Ori's touch. I pull on that warmth while I trace a heart in midair. It glows gold, and with a squeeze of my hand it begins to pump.

"One down."

"Make the other." Ori's palm is damp with sweat. "Thirty seconds."

"Don't get your boots in a twist. I got this." I quickly trace another heart and give it a squeeze. The two hearts pump in rhythm.

Buh-bum.

Buh-bum.

Buh-bum.

Buh-bum.

Feeling Ori's pulse beat against my wrist, I realize that ours have synced. The steady rhythm of the magic hearts, my real one, and

Ori's makes me feel the most right since being here. This is going to work.

"Ten seconds."

Ori's words aren't panicked. They're not hurried. They're confident. He knows this is going to work, too, that every heart in this room is coming together exactly as they should.

"They're too big," I say, then quickly pinch the sides of the hearts together, almost like I'm resizing an image on a computer, until they're the right size to fit perfectly on the tiny figures' chests.

"Five," Ori says.

I pluck the hearts from the air and look to Ori. When our eyes meet, my own heart skips a beat, like Ori reached inside my chest and gingerly touched my soul.

I think two thoughts over and over as I set my miniature magic hearts on top of Ori's effigies.

Awake. Heal. Awake. Heal. Awake. Heal.

With one second to go, our magics meet. The pink and gold combine and turn a brilliant abalone, like the inside of a shell. It's not our power weaving individually, side by side like I imagined. It's them melding together to become one. And our combined power shines so brightly I have to shield my eyes. But it doesn't feel dangerous. It doesn't feel out of control.

It feels good.

My heart is so full I think it might burst.

The light finally dims and I'm able to open my eyes. Ori's are still closed, but his free hand, gently clutching his plastic figures, is right over his heart. I think he felt it, too.

It's quiet.

"Did it wo—"

I'm interrupted by two contented sighs. Vic and Cursula, breathing easy. Slight, peaceful smiles spread across their faces.

"It worked." Ori's eyes are open now, and he stares in wonder at the campers. At what we did. "They're dreaming. Not screaming." He lets out a laugh, loud and so sudden it makes me jump, which only makes him laugh harder. "Those fae are rubbing off on me." He takes me in, from boots to ruffled hair. "We did it!"

"We did," I say, and a nervous giggle escapes my lips, too. "We passed the test. We're not being culled."

"One challenge left." Ori looks the most ecstatic I've ever seen him, joy lighting up his face. God, he's so cute. Then his beaming smile turns to a sarcastic smirk again as he says, "You really said *Not today, varmint!* back in that forest. You are such a cliché."

My face blazes with embarrassment, but I know Ori's cackle isn't to make fun. It's a playful tease, and without thinking, I use our clasped hands to tug Ori in for a hug. Our hearts beat against each other's chests, and I swear with our torsos pressed together, mine beats stronger.

"Seriously though," I say, resting my chin on Ori's head. "How does this bond work? I could touch any other magician and what we just did would never happen."

"I don't know," Ori says. "But it does."

"It does," I whisper.

Our noses practically touch. Ori licks his lips and I want so badly to know what they feel like. What his tongue feels like.

My body leans in all on its own, and I know with a deep certainty that Ori wants this, too. We're millimeters away, our hearts picking up the pace. Ori's lips part and—

Wham!

Frosty slams into me, bursting through the medical bay wall with a happy whinny. I thought this critter finally had my back, but now they're teaming up with Meema as a cock-ice-block. Frosty nuzzles my neck, and the rush of cold is disorienting after Ori's heat. I guess they didn't trot off to the nymph hall, after all.

Pallavit, Alister, and Meema enter just behind.

"Good work, boys!" Meema sounds ready to take on the world. She pulls me in for a hug, the horns in her belt buckle digging into my hip, but the sharp pain does nothing to dampen my mood. I'm meant to be here, and Meema knows it, too. Finally. The rest of the group's doubt may have affected her, made her wonder if I'd end up just like Dad. But now she knows what I can do. She knows I'll live up to our family name. Like she read my mind, she says, "That's a Barrett for ya."

"And if memory serves, it's also *Barrett for you* to fail at the last second, in the final task." Alister's voice is silky smooth. "I almost thought you boys were going to bite the bullet and fail now. Really, it would save us all a lot of trouble."

"Are you sure you're not fae, Alister? Because you sure love to make a lot of noise," Meema says.

"Rude," Pallavit quips. Alister cocks an eyebrow and opens his mouth to retort, but Meema magics two stretchers out of thin air and places the campers on them. The spelled apparatuses are so large that Alister and Pallavit are forced to step back to the side of the room.

"Last second or not," Meema says, "this was a win. And we need to get these humans back before anyone notices they're missing. I'll enhance their dreams on the way, make them forget their nightmares."

She pushes the stretchers out of the bay, but not before giving me one last wink. "I'm proud of you, darlin'."

As we make our way out into the hall, I'm blinded by the light reflecting off the white-and-gold walls. A Depraved skeleton stares at me from within their depths, and I stare back, defiant. I'm meant to be here. Ori and I *can* control our power and fight for good.

Echoes of excited chatter bounce along the balcony as apprentices celebrate their wins. I'd totally forgotten about the others curing curses of their own. But a pit sinks in my stomach, because we could see couples who failed, too. We were so close to becoming one of them.

"This is bullshit!" Bex's voice reaches me from across the floor. I whip my head around, and my heart practically falls out of my butt.

Bex, who only hours earlier looked ready to take on the world, now looks like she wants to blow it all up. Angry tears well in her eyes, a glare like I've never seen directed at Laurel. The nymph just stares back, smug as ever.

"We could have saved them!" Bex says to Jameson with conviction. "Two others got cursed!"

A crowd gathers around Bex and Laurel, and I take advantage of Frosty's bulk to push apprentices and magicians out of my way. Ori follows right behind, occasionally grasping the hem of my flannel when the crowd threatens to separate us.

"Bex?" She locks eyes with me as soon as I say her name. "What happened?"

That's when the flood comes, her angry tears pouring out. She chokes on them, snot dripping down her face, when she finally says, "I was seconds away from bringing them back here to safety when *she*"—Bex flings her hand out toward Laurel, magicking her accusing fingers into claws—"pulled me through the portal back here. She left them to die!"

"Bex," Jameson says, his tone as flat as ever. "The loss of lives is terrible, but death walks hand in hand with our work. We try to avoid it at all costs, but sometimes that's not possible."

"But this *was* avoidable," Bex screams.

"I did what we were told to do," Laurel snaps. "We were assigned *one* victim, so I brought that one victim back."

"We had time to get the others." Bex gets right in her face. "But you snaked that vine around my waist and brought me back here."

A green burst and Bex is pulled back, just like she described, only this time by Alister, pushing Bex away from his daughter. "It's a timed exercise. Laurel has broken no rules."

"Don't you dare touch my kid!" Yamato shoves his way through the crowd, arms transformed to stone to push people out of the way. But his husband gets there first, using his air-nymph abilities to whoosh to Bex's side in a rush of wind. He uses a quick burst of air to slash away Alister's vine.

"Ah, Kenneth," Alister says coldly. "Nice of you to join us."

"Wish I could say it's nice to see you, Ali," Kenneth says, taking Bex's head in his hands and hugging her against his chest. "Why were so many cursed there?"

"Neither I nor the other magician keeping the Depraved at bay with me anticipated other humans being at that bridge so late in the night," Jameson explains, and for once I'm grateful that his tone is so mellow, easing some of the tension. "The assigned victim was inflicted with Flyer's Folly."

Ori sucks in a breath. At my confused scowl, he says, "It makes the cursed get this insatiable need to fly. They're sure they can, so they jump off the highest thing they can find, only to fall to their death."

Jameson nods, somber. "The girls were just about to retrieve their victim when a car passed by and the passengers saw the man about to jump. The humans got out of their vehicle and tried to grab him, but the curse infected them as well. Laurel retrieved both Bex and their victim before triggering a portal back to the Guild, just as the newly cursed jumped."

"And why didn't you intervene?" Kenneth asks.

"Senior magicians are assigned these Culling tasks for a reason!" Yamato adds.

"A commuter bus was approaching from the opposite direction," Jameson says. "Full of dozens of humans who could also have been infected. We had to make a judgment call on who to stop. We decided we should save the multiple lives as opposed to two."

"No one would have had to die!" Bex shouts. "I could have shifted! I could have saved them if she hadn't stopped me! We had plenty of time!"

"Laurel did nothing wrong here," Alister insists. "She was just completing her Culling task." He motions toward the man that Laurel and Bex saved, snoozing peacefully in his medical bay. "And you're lucky, girl, that she didn't melt into hysterics like you did. Otherwise, you'd both be out of the Guild for good."

"Maybe that's what I want," Bex says, quietly, pushing away from Kenneth.

Murmurs ripple through the crowd.

"Bex." Kenneth's voice is low, warning. "Not here."

"You don't mean that," Yamato says, and he tries to put a hand on his daughter's shoulder. But she shakes it off, even transforming her head into a werewolf's so she can snarl.

"Get off of me," she growls, feral. With a flash of silver, she's back to her normal self. Or, well, her completely emotionally destroyed human self. "I can't be in an organization that values *winning* above all else. Who cares about the stupid fucking Culling when there's lives to be saved? I can't believe I even have to explain this!"

"But a life *was* saved, darlin'." Meema pushes through the crowd. "Because of you." She spells her voice so that all the surrounding apprentices can hear. "This is a lesson you would have had to learn eventually. I'm sorry you had to learn it now. But there are times when humans interfere, acting in ways we couldn't anticipate, becoming casualties in our fight against evil. It doesn't happen often, but it does happen." She gives a loving half-smile to Bex. "Don't beat yourself up over it. You couldn't help it."

"Yes, I could. I *can*," Bex says. "I'm out."

"Bex!" her parents shout together.

"You can't," I say.

"This is too much." She doesn't hang her head. She doesn't look sad anymore. She looks determined, defiant, as she turns her gaze up toward the ceiling, where a rustling grabs my attention.

It's that same set of senior magicians, the wolf pack, descending to the fifth floor to once again dole out *balance*. The full reality of the Culling comes back into focus. People are about to have their magic taken away. From the looks of it, about half of our class, as the ones who succeeded shuffle away from those who failed, looking at the pack with dread. A couple hundred apprentices whose magic dreams stop here. Some stumble meekly out of their medical bays, having failed to cure their cursed victims. Down on the first floor, others who failed earlier cry or wail or stand in shock.

And Bex is *choosing* the same fate. A life without magic.

"Bex!" When our eyes meet, she gives me a weak smile.

"Guess this is it," she says. She's so calm. Resigned. Sure of her decision. She looks at her dads. "I told you there was another way."

I watch Yamato and Kenneth have an entire conversation in glances, without saying a word. They aren't moving. Why aren't they stopping her?

"Ori." I turn to him, and he just stares at Bex with his forehead furrowed, like he can't imagine ever making this decision. "We have to do something."

"What can we do? We're not here to tell her what's best for

her life." He says it so certainly, but I can't just let Bex go that easily.

Laurel scoffs. "Who cares? Just leave. That's one less person we have to worry about in the final task."

"Meema." I look over my shoulder at my grandmother, who's returned to talking to Jameson like it's any day at the office. "There's got to be some way to help Bex."

She doesn't even spare an apologetic smile for me. She simply shrugs. "It's her choice."

"Don't worry about me," Bex says. "I know what I'm doing."

The pack has landed on the balcony now and stopped right in front of her. The remaining failed apprentices, shepherded into a flock by senior magicians, lose their shit completely. As the pack gets to work, their screams are worse than those of our cursed humans. I can't imagine how empty they'll feel, how miserable, how utterly incomplete. Even if they are my competition, I would never wish this fate on anybody.

But then, by the end of this, most of us will walk away without our magic. And so the pack continues on their way. Cries grow louder throughout the hall as more and more are rid of their power. The pack's goblin member has transformed into a six-armed giant and stands in the center of the hall tower, holding his palm out for each newly magicless apprentice to step into. They all cry or stare into the void like a zombie.

It's awful.

And somehow, finally, even though she was closest to the pack when they arrived, Bex is the last apprentice left standing.

Maybe it's because she never moved from her spot. Maybe, because she chose her fate, the senior magicians knew she wouldn't put up a fight. But as they surround her, she smiles, her eyes bright as ever. She's not going to cower and wail. She's sure of her choice.

Her fathers step back, letting the pack in. Kenneth watches, blank-faced, while Yamato sports a defiant grin, nodding at Bex, I guess supporting her decision even as silent tears slip down his cheeks.

"We'll see each other soon," Bex says, locking her gaze on mine. "I promise."

Then she turns to face the pack head on. The fae member's throat glows purple, but before a spell can be cast, Bex grabs something from her pocket and throws it to the ground. She's instantly shrouded in purple smoke. It glows brighter than any fae magic I've seen yet, then vanishes completely, taking Bex with it.

Poof.

She's gone. Just like that.

The hall erupts into chaos. The pack cries for everyone to find Bex; senior magicians leap into action. Yamato laughs, loud and hard, and Kenneth seems to sag in relief. I'm right there with them. I can't help but feel proud of my friend for running with her magic. The world can probably withstand *one* more magician keeping her power without falling out of balance, right? But then my stomach rumbles with nerves. I hate to think of the weight of the Guild crashing down on her when she's found.

Then her words come back to me.

We'll see each other soon.

She said it so confidently, but how? When?

Another rumble. It vibrates through my bones, up from my feet. It's not just my nerves, then.

The floor is shaking.

I have just a handful of seconds for the feeling to register before the floor bursts apart completely. Stone cracks not just beneath my feet, but on the ceiling, out of the wall next to me, hunks of broken marble flying in all directions.

And then I can't breathe. A bony hand—belonging to one of the thousands of skeletons that were once embedded in the walls—clutches my throat.

Choking me.

CHAPTER SEVENTEEN

Creaking bone fingers squeeze tighter around my windpipe, my Adam's apple pressing painfully into my throat. It makes me gag, triggering a spike of panic. Frosty's by my side in a heartbeat, spinning around and kicking. The skeleton shatters in a shower of bones.

Air floods my lungs and I cough, nausea and relief rising simultaneously. "Thanks"—cough—"buddy."

Frosty neighs briefly, but the sound is drowned out by a keening like nails on a chalkboard, emanating from the destroyed skeleton's skull. Its jaw and neck bones glow that mottled-green color of Depraved magic, and the pile of bones rattles as individual pieces slide across the floor *toward* one another. Toes reform and attach to a foot that clicks into place with an ankle bone. This freak is reforming.

"We've got to get out of here." I take a step forward but instantly trip. The floor is shattered, slabs of marble obliterated and jutting at angles where skeletons have emerged. The entire hall looks like it's been ripped open from the inside out. Everywhere I can see, skeletons battle with magicians and apprentices alike. Their shoulders and elbows seem to protrude farther than should be possible, forming glistening, sharp points that the skeletons use to slash left and right, trying to slice magicians in half.

It's chaos.

Pallavit races past me, hopping between jutting marble slabs, and approaches a quartet of skeletons that close in on Alister. Even over the din of spellcasting and bones breaking, I hear her song.

"Life gone.
Go back to bed.
You're only bones.
Remember, you're dead."

But the skeletons rage on.

Alister whips vines up from the ground. Two zoom into the eye sockets of separate skeletons, wrap through the gap in their noses, then slam together. Their skulls break apart into a thousand tiny pieces, and when their bodies collapse, they don't rise again.

"Destroy their skulls," he yells, his voice hardly carrying through the noise of the battle. "Defeat the Horde!"

My heart jumps to my throat. The Horde. The minions of the Knife my great-granddad destroyed all those years ago. How are they rising?

Alister's words are drowned out by that horrific Horde call as shattered skeletons reform with piercing shrieks. I see Ori make an effigy out of a femur and force a skeleton to kick its buddies. Meema's bull rampages a floor down, scooping up skeletons in its wide horns. A dragon flies above—a shape-shifted goblin, the sight of which sends an ache through my heart for Bex—and breathes a burst of flames at a dozen enemies. The fire does nothing to burn their bones.

Again and again, even if every last bone is detached from their bodies, as long as their skulls remain intact the skeletons glide back together to attack again.

"Frosty, let's go." My crystallos leaps into the air the second I swing a leg over their back. Frosty bounds into the center of the tower, breathing an ice platform that gets us out of reach of the battle. With magic in my fingers, I grasp my throat to amplify my voice and shout, "Destroy their skulls. Destroy their skulls. Destroy their—"

I'm cut off by something that sounds like hundreds of lions roaring, a thousand off-key trumpets blaring, and a factory full of rusty gears grinding together, all at once. It blasts up from the entry hall, drowning out all other sound. Hundreds of skeletons keen from the ground floor, tilting their heads to the ceiling, their jaws open and bellowing. Every skeleton in the building stops what they're doing to join in, and that green light of Depraved magic begins to build over the remnants of the entry platform. A rectangle of that light appears, the size of a theater screen.

A portal.

The skeletons on the ground floor are already running through it, disappearing to who knows where. The Horde members on other floors jump over balconies, breaking apart on landing and slinking back together before rushing for the portal. They push past magicians, slicing anybody in their way.

"Stop them!" Meema yells, her own voice magically magnified. "We don't know where they're going! We can't let them through!"

The tide shifts instantly. Now instead of fighting the Horde, we're forced to *chase after* them. It's so much like chasing after cattle at a rodeo that I instantly feel in my element.

A magic rope is looped around my arm in no time.

"'Yup!" Frosty bounds down the center of the tower until

we're on the ground floor, skeletons falling around us like demonic rain.

The second Frosty's hooves hit the marble I let my rope fly. "Ha!" It loops around my first target, yanking the skeleton back just as it pokes a bony foot through the portal. I've cinched the rope at its neck, and it hits me that I can do more than just stop this monster from getting away.

I can defeat it.

I yank with all my might, and the Horde soldier's neck snaps, its skull clattering to the ground. Frosty lunges forward, knowing exactly what to do. With a triumphant whinny, Frosty slams their icy hoof down and the skull shatters into a million pieces.

"That's right!" I yell, while Frosty rears back in victory.

Time to get to work.

I whip my lasso left and right, yanking skulls off necks while Frosty stomps. We've stopped ten soldiers in a matter of minutes. When my rope gets snagged on a stray Horde bone and yanked from my hands, I spell a magic cattle prod that sends jolts of power into skulls and shatters them on impact.

But the triumph I feel with each decimated skeleton is short-lived. There are just *too many.* For every soldier that I kill, half a dozen run through the portal, letting loose their monstrous victory cry. And with each varmint I take out, my energy drains, until finally the magic prod in my hands blinks twice before disappearing entirely.

It's the same everywhere I look. The wood nymphs are doing their best, using all types of plant life to rip skulls from Horde bodies. Water and air nymphs are using well-aimed bursts of their elements to knock skulls from spines. But eventually, vines become stems and jets of water become trickles as we all use up our energy. Meanwhile, others try to block the portal entirely, but nothing they do works. With every barrier they craft, the Horde's portal jumps to another location. There's no way we can put up an effective block without injuring magicians in the process.

Meema is busy floors up, riding her bull and stomping skeleton heads. Sprites are using effigies to behead soldiers, but the sheer number of them is just too large. And the majority of the magicians in this building are apprentices; most of the senior members are home now, in the middle of the night. No one comes to aid us.

I feel a pull in my heart, a sensation that something is ***wrong***, forcing me to turn as Frosty lands another death blow.

"Ori!"

He's surrounded in front of the portal, a group of a dozen skeletons descending on him. One of the Horde soldiers has his backpack of would-be effigies over its arm, pierced by one of its sharp shoulder protrusions.

Ori's defenseless and the Horde is closing in. Maybe their magic has limits, too, because they don't appear to use it for anything other than creating that portal and reforming. But their skeletal blades work just as well. They fling their bony limbs in every direction, slashing, slicing. Ori tries to dodge, but a leap too far in any direction would send him into the knife-like arms of another skeleton. He has no way out.

I squeeze my thighs hard on either side of Frosty. "'Yup!"

We gallop forward, bones flying everywhere as Frosty charges through our enemies. They're so sure-footed on the uneven floor, bursts of ice magic cascading from their hooves when they can't gain purchase on the marble. We barrel through the group surrounding Ori, toppling them like bowling pins.

"Strike!"

Ori grabs my outstretched arm so I can hoist him up behind me. The second we touch, the magic within me blooms outward from my chest, from my heart, and I know we're back in this fight.

"You are so cheesy!" Ori says, but he moves quickly as Horde members turn their focus to us.

With our arms touching, I see the cuts on Ori's body heal. "This will never not be convenient," Ori says, then flings himself to the side.

"Ori!" I'm sure he's about to fall back into the skeletal melee, but Ori cries, "Frosty, catch me!" and Frosty freezes him in place, hanging off the crystallos's right side, perfectly positioned to pluck his backpack off the shoulder spikes of his bag thief.

"Up!" he commands, and Frosty's ice shifts into a seat that brings Ori upright. Why is it so hot when a guy strikes up their own relationship with your favorite pet?

"We need to work together again," I say, lassoing as many Horde skeletons as I can while Ori gets to work coating a LEGO man in his power. "Combine our magics. We could stop them all."

"Not gonna happen," Ori says quickly, never taking his eyes off his work.

"Come on! We don't have time for this!"

Ori pops the head off the toy in his glowing hands, and the skeleton lunging at us loses its skull. Frosty uses the opportunity to bash it to bits.

"Use your head, Barrett!" Ori says. "We want to destroy these things. We don't know how to control this yet. Who knows how much collateral damage there'd be. Who we'd hurt."

I see flashes of my nightmare, of Ori and me killing so many people. But that wasn't real. "You said yourself that my visions of the harm we could do were just nightmares. We need to work together!"

I know we can do this. I was so focused back in that medical bay. Our magic cured our victims, exactly the way we intended.

"All we have to do is focus," I say, zapping another skull with a newly conjured prod. "Say exactly what we want. Like in the test. I kept thinking *heal. Aw—*"

"Awake. Heal. Awake. Heal. Awake."

"What the hell?" We screech to a halt in the middle of the floor as the words I focused on in the medical bay echo back at us.

"Heal. Awake. Heal. Awake. Heal. Awake."

They're not coming from me. They're not coming from Ori. They're not coming from any magician at all.

They're coming from the Horde. Now using their monstrous voices to add my words to their portal-making call.

A horrible sinking sensation fills my stomach. "You don't think . . ." I can't finish the sentence.

But Ori can.

"We did this," he whispers. "Our magic woke them up."

Bile rises in my throat, and it takes everything in me to swallow it down. "We can't control it." A gut-wrenching scream comes from my right as a magician is stabbed by a Horde soldier. A potentially fatal wound that never would have happened, if not for me. "We caused all this."

My nightmare wasn't just a bad dream. It *was* a vision. Even when we intend to use our magic for good, it does evil in the process. No good without the bad.

I've always been told magic is about balance, but this is too much.

Terrified screams come from behind us. "Somebody help! Help!"

It's the apprentices. The *former* apprentices. The ones the pack rid of their powers just before this attack. They're surrounded. One clutches a wound in his stomach while another stands over him protectively, her fists balled and her eyes shut tight like she's trying to summon any last drop of power to fight back. But the pack was swift and efficient. The failed apprentices are defenseless.

"'Yup!"

Frosty springs into action, but a flurry of auburn hair and green light reaches the group before we do. I can just make out Alister among the vines whipping left and right.

He may be a giant prick, but he's not a coward.

Alister loops his vines through the eye sockets of four skeletons at once and flings them against the wall. As they shatter, more and more plants grow and reach for the Horde, tripping them up, squeezing their skulls.

Ori snaps a few skeletons in half using the toys in his bag, while Frosty charges what's left of them. But so many skulls slink away before Frosty can shatter them to bits. And the soldiers still standing take the opportunity to book it through the portal.

Every single one of them.

The noise of battle stops as suddenly as it began. The final hundred or so Horde members run, chanting my words, through the sickly green portal. When the last of them staggers through, I swear their words—*my* words—still echo through the Guild.

"Medic! We need medical attention here!" Alister hovers over the stabbed apprentice, whose hand is soaked in blood as he clutches his stomach.

New chants replace the Horde's as magicians call for help from every direction.

"And here!"

"More injured!"

"She's going to die!"

Apprentice and senior magicians alike get to work. Bursts of magic in every color flit throughout the hall with their healing spells.

Alister leans down and places his hand on my injured Cullingmate's shoulder, true concern etching his features. "You're going to be okay. Help is coming." His palpable worry takes me aback—I'd have expected him to look down on this apprentice for failing the Culling. But here he is, hovering over the magicless former magician like a worried parent, making flowers bloom in his fingers, using them to stem the bleeding. Despite how terrible he can be, Alister must truly believe in the Guild's mission of helping defenseless people everywhere.

Pallavit locks eyes with Alister, hobbling through the rubble to join him, her throat glowing purple.

"That's all now.
Dry up blood.
Suture. Heal.
Stop the flood."

The stabbed apprentice's whimpers turn to a groan of relief as his skin knits itself back together. He's not going to die.

Thank god. I can't have a life on my hands. Not when the destruction of the entire Guild is on my head already.

"Don't just stand there!" Meema's voice pulls everyone's attention. "We have to go after them!"

She gallops down from the fourth-floor balcony on her bull, shining gold with power like some seventy-year-old, denim-wearing superhero. She barely looks back before slipping through the Horde's portal herself.

For one second, there's stunned silence.

Then we spring into action.

Pallavit's first to step up. "I need a dozen fae to stay with me and heal the wounded."

Alister's next, his commanding politician's tone drawing the whole room's attention, even without magical amplification. "Anyone who can walk or fly, follow me. We must stop the Horde—before they awaken the Knife."

CHAPTER EIGHTEEN

A SHIVER RUNS DOWN MY SPINE. THE KNIFE. THE MONSTER MY Great-Grandpa Barrett stopped all those centuries ago. I may have just counteracted every last bit of good he did for human- and magiciankind. Have Ori and I alone just caused the greatest catastrophe of our time?

A finger jabs me in the rib. "Move!" Ori says, and Frosty takes off through the warped Horde portal ahead of my command. Magicians run in front of, behind, and beside us. I brace myself for the pull of the portal, but this is unlike any fae magic. I still feel that pull in my gut, but deep despair fills me along with it. My head squeezes, so hard I think my own skull might crack. Vomit rises in my throat, and just when I'm convinced I'm about to pass out, Frosty's hooves slam on rock. For the first time, I lose my balance on Frosty, falling to the ground to throw up.

"Nigel, on your feet!" Meema's scream is desperate, in a way I've never heard from her.

I move on instinct before a streak of green light explodes right where I was, leaving a burn mark in its wake.

The sounds of battle resume. Fae song, Horde cries, and this time, laughter. Hysterical, bone-chilling laughter.

Members of the Horde use their monstrous magic to open new portals at the peak of the craggy mountaintop we've been transported to. Living, breathing Depraved step through each. As if their undead skeleton siblings weren't bad enough.

"What do we do?" a fire nymph apprentice shrieks, nervous flames flashing from his fingers. A Depraved whips its head in the boy's direction, its maniacal grin showing pointed teeth. It breathes in deeply, and I swear its eyes glow brighter with delight as it bears down on the frightened apprentice. The nymph gathers a ball of flame in his hands and sends it shooting for the Depraved, but it just glances off the creature's skin.

"I'm going to kiiiill youuuu," the Depraved croons in a twisted singsong. I've never heard them speak before. Its tone is twisted, soaked in cruelty. My blood runs cold.

The nymph takes a step back. "N-n-no you're not." Nobody believes the guy—not even me, and I'm on his side. He sounds terrified, and the Depraved keeps inhaling as though smelling something it likes, its eyes glaring brighter, its back getting straighter.

"Retreat!" Meema yells. "All apprentices retreat! They're feeding on your fear. Senior magicians, whup their asses!"

A fae opens a portal, and apprentices run to it like it's the last lifeboat on the *Titanic*. Well, every apprentice but two. Laurel and Jaleesa fight on, side by side. Jaleesa's singing spells, Laurel's bringing plants to life; they could almost be using their powers in sync. I watch them take out two Depraved on their own. It stings to see them work so seamlessly together without adding to the chaos. Not like Ori and me. Those girls may be colossal jerks, but they clearly have their shit together. They're not letting fear get to them. They're just doing what's right. I never thought they'd be my inspiration for anything, but I've got to show the same strength and resilience that Laurel and Jaleesa do.

I glance up at Ori, still frozen to Frosty's back.

"You thinking what I'm thinking?" I ask.

Ori nods. "We started this."

"We've got to finish it."

There are roughly three dozen senior magicians still with us in the fight. I have to shield my eyes when they move as one, launching a multitude of attacks stronger than any I've seen before. Jameson coats boulders in golden power as he levitates them over our attackers and squashes the monsters to bloody bits. Alister spots a patch of weeds and makes them grow lightning fast, their prickles now enormous barbs that pierce the Depraved through. Meema is working on a curse of her own, gathering gold magic in her fingertips and shooting it at the monsters' eyes, blinding three Depraved with one curse. Two of her victims stumble off the side of the mountain, falling who knows how many feet to jagged rocks below.

There's no hint of fear from any of the adults. They're practiced warriors. They've done this their entire adult lives. They know what to do.

I'm filled with pride for all of them, for the Guild. This is the work we were meant to do. Destroying evil, one Depraved at a time, and not giving them a bit of negative emotion to feed on.

"Let's do this," I say, wanting to reach out and grab Ori's knee, wanting our magics to combine, for that abalone burst of our power to reassure me that we'll walk out of this alive. But my arm won't move. My body knows now, after awakening the Horde, that no matter what Ori and I intend, our linked powers are dangerous.

Ori blinks off Frosty's back and appears next to the patch of weeds Alister brought to life. A half dozen Depraved are tangled in them but still launching magic attacks. As they're distracted by a goblin turned griffin dive-bombing from above, Ori makes a Play-Doh man. Bathing it in his sprite magic, he plucks the arms off his effigy. The Depraved nearest him yelps as both its shoulders dislocate, preventing it from aiming any more spells. It turns its fiery eyes to Ori and mumbles under its breath. A curse.

Unknown to him, a small storm cloud begins to form over Ori's head. It crackles with energy that makes Ori's already disheveled hair stand on end.

"Ori! Now!"

Ori looks up, sees the bolts of electricity building above him, and plucks the head off his effigy.

Crack.

The Depraved's head twists at an unnatural angle and it falls to the ground. Unmoving. Lifeless.

"Nigel, move your ass!" Meema hollers just as a duo of Depraved sprint toward me. I leap on Frosty's back and gallop out of their reach.

Two blasts of white-hot magic shoot by, so hot they melt a bit of Frosty's side. I need to act fast before I find myself sitting in a puddle formerly known as my ice horse.

Varmints sneak on the ranch all the time. Rabid coyotes who creep in to kill as many chicken or sheep as they can. And when those critters get out of hand, I always change them into something sweeter. I can do that here too.

I gather a bit of power, letting it sit on my palm like a ball of clay. Ori and I may not be able to combine our powers, but that doesn't mean he can't inspire my next trick. Channeling Ori and his effigies, I mold my power into something resembling a bunny.

"'Yup!" I cry, and Frosty makes a hard turn. "CHARGE!" We

barrel toward the two Depraved, but they don't seem fazed at all. Not by me, not by this ice horse ready to ram them head on. They just grin those sharp-toothed grins and let loose their high-pitched laughter.

Frosty has no problem keeping their footing, despite the craggy mountaintop. They're in their element, dashing through the snow reflecting the moonlight. Frosty is pure power, and I can sense how confident they feel—which makes *me* feel confident, unstoppable.

I buoy myself with this assuredness and get ready to send my spelled rabbit toward the Depraved when—

Wham!

Frosty spills forward, their front legs melted by a blast of Depraved magic.

Our momentum sends us flying, Frosty tumbling hooves over wispy mane, me right behind, until *whack*! My skull slams against a rock. Stars dance in my vision, and my ears fill with that maniacal laughter. My head wobbles. I feel like I could hurl. And when I try to sit up, the entire world spins.

The rotten green eyes of the Depraved swim before me as they get closer, deadly magic building in their fingertips. They're savoring this moment, taking their time. They know as well as I do that I'm no match for them now.

As the Depraveds' cracked toenails come into view, I know for certain that I'm going to die. I close my eyes and see Ori's face in my mind, his playful smirk calming my swirling thoughts. Let this be the last thing I see before whatever comes next.

Then, a tickle, a small brush of softness against my palm. I crack one eye open, my right lid lifting slowly. The Depraveds' feet are still swirling in my line of sight. Their hideous laughter continues, and I resent them for spoiling my last moment of peace before letting go. At another brush against my hand, I look down and see the little magic rabbit I made, still tucked against my chest, hidden from the Depraveds' view. It looks up at me with innocent gold eyes, and the fog in my brain clears enough that I know what to do.

My hand flops down, and the rabbit softly hops off of it, my intention directing the spell.

"Somebunny wants to see you," I mumble, just as the rabbit jumps onto the Depraved. In a flash, my magic soaks the evil magician's foot, climbing up its entire body. With another burst of gold, the Depraved is gone, and an innocent brown rabbit stands in its place.

"Hey, buddy," I say, my words floaty and croaky. "I mean ***bunny.*** Ha-ha."

I am out of it, but I can't help the pleasant warmth trickling down my head from a spell well performed. Or is that blood? I try to lift my hand, but I only get it about halfway before it falls back to the ground.

"So tired." My vision tunnels until I can't see beyond the Depraved-turned-rabbit hopping through a mound of snow and out of sight.

"Nigel!" A hand wraps around my ankle, and my head clears almost instantly. Just in time to see the other Depraved I was up against hovering ominously, prepared to deliver a death blow. Another squeeze on my ankle and I see Ori, free hand busy working with something. But he'll never make an effigy in time. Not with the Depraved ready to fire, a victorious glare in its green eyes.

"I have to thank you." The Depraved's voice is gravelly and grating, like jammed tractor blades gnashing together. It's completely unsettling. Somehow it's worse than their ear-splitting laughter.

"Th-thank me?" I can't have heard that right. My head must not be healed yet.

"Look what you've done," it hisses, using a gnarled finger to point past the mountain peaks. "You fell for our distraction!" I follow its finger to see a swirling mass miles below us, lit by the stars in this cloudless night. Trees crash to the ground as the Horde tramples through the forest. Thousands of Depraved skeletons making their way to who knows where.

"Off to awaken their master. *The Knife.* All because of you." Its green eyes flash toward Ori. "You and your little friend." It laughs that hysterical laugh. "Oh, but you're so much more than friends. You can do so much together. Already have done so much. For us." It sucks in a deep breath, and mine comes in shorter and shorter gasps. *We did this.* "All this havoc. I can still smell the fear of your comrades. I can taste it. *Devour it.* The Guild continues to help us." I want to punch the grin right off its face. "Every day."

The sound of galloping hooves cuts the Depraved off, and Frosty crashes so hard into it that I can hear bones crack. It flies backward, lifted over the edge of the cliff, its last high-pitched shriek echoing through the mountains.

Frosty huffs—a clear *And stay out!*—before trotting to me and nuzzling my neck.

I rub between their eyes. The repetitive movement helps slow my breathing, but my mind wanders, the Depraved's words echoing over and over.

I've helped them grow stronger. Have helped *feed them* from the chaos Ori's and my combined magic caused.

"How *could* you? Feeding the Depraved!"

Alister stands just feet away, his eyes wide with anger. I want to tell him that it wasn't intentional, but it all just sounds like a flimsy excuse.

"Well?" Alister demands. "Say something."

"I—"

I'm cut off by the most frightened animal screech I've ever heard.

Too fast for my exhausted mind to comprehend, a jagged tendril of Depraved magic shoots over the edge of the cliff. It's knotted to fit perfectly over Frosty's neck.

A lasso.

Mocking me.

Frosty bucks wildly. I can feel the heat of the Depraved magic, can hear the water pour off Frosty's hide as their icy skin melts.

Frosty bucks in a frenzy, thrashing and throwing their head. Ice billows from their mouth in a desperate attempt to compensate for their melting hide. Their formerly sure-footed hooves scrabble against the cliff.

But nothing helps. Too fast for me to stop it, the evil power pulls Frosty to the edge, and they plummet out of sight, a streak of blue that's gone in a flash as gravity takes hold.

"Frosty! No!"

The Depraved may not have been able to save itself, but it claimed one last victim.

My heart feels like it's been ripped in two. Surely the despair and hate I feel could feed hundreds of Depraved. I'm only making things worse. Worse for the Guild, worse for the world, worse for this innocent animal that against all odds warmed up to me.

Frosty's final, panicked neighing echoes through the mountain until it cuts off suddenly, like someone flipped a switch. My stomach roils thinking about them scattered in chunks of ice, gone.

Out of the corner of my eye, I see Alister dashing off, maybe on his way to help the other injured magicians—doing exactly what I *should* be doing instead of sitting here, tears welling in my eyes.

The silence of the mountaintop roars in my ears. We're alone. No more Depraved. No more Horde. No more Frosty.

Looking around, I see a fae cradle Meema to her side, my grandma's denim blouse stained with blood. I can't lose the person I love most seconds after my horse. I try to leap to my feet, but Ori's hand is still around my ankle.

"Let go!" I bark—panicked, sad, angry. "Meema's hurt."

Ori's hand snaps back. "She'll be fine," he says. "Look."

Propping Meema up with one arm, the fae hums a long, steady note. Her throat glows purple, as does Meema's side, right under her ribs. My grandma sighs, then wobbles to her feet. The bloodstains remain, but her injuries are gone.

"I can't believe we fell for it," Ori says, looking down the mountain, following the path of destruction left by the Horde. "I can't believe *I* fell for it. I've seen firsthand the shit the Depraved pull. But when I saw you lying there . . . I couldn't focus on anything else. I thought you were dead."

He meets my eyes, and my mind whirls with emotion. Horror that the Depraved was right. Guilt at what we've done. So much sadness that Frosty is gone.

"We are never, ever, ever casting spells together." I think the Taylor reference is accidental. Ori definitely doesn't say it to be funny. The sky starts to lighten—it's nearly sunrise—and the brightening rays are totally at odds with the dark truth sinking over us. "I knew this would happen," Ori continues. "I could feel it."

"Ori, I—"

"No. You tried to convince me I was wrong before, and look what happened. That Depraved asshole knows something about us that we don't, and I'm not about to be used by the very monsters I've vowed to fight. It's not you and me anymore, Nigel. It's me and it's you, cleaning up the shit we started, but not together. You got it?"

I can't say a word. Losing Frosty, almost losing Meema . . . and who knows how many magicians are injured or worse, all because of my bright idea to use our magic together back when Ori was already against it. This *is* my fault.

But I'm spared from having to agree by the approach of senior magicians. They surround us in a flurry of blinking sprites and bursting magic. Alister steps forward, commanding vines from the ground to twist around my wrists.

"Separate them!" he shouts. "Separate them immediately!"

CHAPTER NINETEEN

Alister's vines dig into my skin and yank me away from Ori. He's ensured there's no way I'll reach out, grab Ori, and spell them all right here. He doesn't know that that's the last thing we'd do. Not when whatever it is pulling us together led to this. We tried to be a force for good, and in half a day we've made it clear that we never will be. What can we be but tools for the Depraved?

Jameson approaches, his dark hands bathed in gold. The sight of elf power would usually comfort me, but now it feels ominous. He crafts a rope. At a flick of his wrist, the rope binds me like a mummy, only my face left uncovered. I feel something else constrict inside me as my power is locked away by his spell. I know it's within me, but whenever I try to call it, it stops before reaching my hands. This feels wrong, a violation for something that's so *me* to be controlled by a twitch of someone else's fingers.

But then, part of me knows that this is for the best. Even if I did have access to my magic, I can't control it.

Meema jogs over. "Jameson, what in tarnation are you doing? My grandson just *fought* the Depraved. He stayed behind and showed true bravery! Now he's being bound, for what?"

"He unleashed the Horde!" Alister says. "With the sprite boy. I heard the Depraved say it myself! I knew there was something wrong with them, from the night of the first challenge. Now look what's happened!"

Meema's look of shock is enough to make my heart sink farther than I'd thought possible. "Nigel. Is this true?"

I swallow, the Horde's chants of *Awake. Heal. Awake. Heal* echoing through my mind along with the words of the Depraved who killed Frosty. I can't bring myself to answer her.

"This can be resolved easily enough, back at the Guild," Jameson says. "We can determine what to do with the boys there. Ingrid?"

He motions to a fae. She sings open a portal in the craggy rock wall of the mountain and magicians quickly file through.

Jameson snaps his fingers and I float behind him. Ori's been bound the same way, his eyes shooting daggers at the elf dragging him more like a bale of hay.

Even the portal's healing powers do nothing to make me feel better. Cuts and bruises can heal, sure, but the distrust of the Guild, my guilt at unleashing the Horde, the sadness at Frosty's death? Not so much.

I land hard on my back in the entry hall. I have a perfect view of all twenty-five stories, straight up to the ceiling, every level perfectly in order. No more uneven, broken floors. No more walls with massive cracks where skeletons burst from them to wreak havoc. It's pristine, like nothing ever happened—but without a single bone left embedded in the stone. Alister's crocodile boots click hurriedly along the white-and-gold-streaked marble.

Wait. The gold streaks. The remnants of magic that Meema said would destroy any enemies that made it inside the Guild. Maybe it's because I don't want to accept the full blame for what happened today, but a flare of anger rises in me. Where were the Guild's supposed defenses? How could two apprentices produce magic so strong that spells cast by experienced magicians don't stand a chance?

"What about the elf curse?" I ask. "Why didn't it destroy the Horde before they could get out? What's the point of having that magic in the walls if it's not even going to work?!"

"I guess elves aren't as brilliant as you thought," Alister says, stepping over me, a leg on either side of my body so his towering figure is all I see. "The magic was designed to keep away any enemies trying to come *in*. It did nothing to stop monsters that were already hidden within our walls."

Ori shouts from the opposite side of the platform. "And what idiot thought it was a good idea to put the skeletons of Depraved warriors inside the Guild in the first place?"

"It was a reminder," Jameson says, his tone somehow *still* even despite the tension. "Of our mission, of the strength of our enemies. We thought they were truly dead and gone. But you showed us they weren't."

"Exactly. Little did we know that two of our own apprentices would work against us." Alister raises his hands over his head, calling the attention of the apprentices and senior magicians gathered in the entry hall. "The asinine trajectory of this Culling ends here. Many of you have seen your children stripped of their powers while *these boys*—who are in league with *the Depraved*—are allowed to remain in the competition as they tear down the Guild around us. No more!" The room is silent, all eyes on Alister as he puffs his chest with conviction and shouts, "I invoke a tribunal! To determine if Nigel

Barrett and Orion Olson are guilty of treason, their powers removed as punishment."

My heart stops. I escaped having my magic stripped away in the second task. I escaped being decapitated by a resurrected skeleton. I escaped being burnt to a crisp by the Depraved. But now, after everything, my magic could be taken away by the very people I spent my whole life thinking would want me.

"I second the motion."

Another barb-wire grip of betrayal pierces my heart.

"Meema?" It ekes out of me, the squeak of a scared child. Am I truly that bad? Is my power so warped and awful that even the woman who loves me the most would *advocate* for it to be taken away?

"Don't give me that, Nigel!" Meema's yelling, so angry that her magic bull springs to life, huffing and stamping. The sight sends a pang to my heart; I was starting to form that type of bond with Frosty, but they're gone now. I truly have no one on my side anymore.

"I didn't mean—"

She snaps her fingers, silencing me in a second, not with magic but with sheer intimidation.

"I told you from the start your priorities weren't straight. I told you to stick to yourself, keep your head down, and focus on the mission of the Guild! But what did you do? Made nice with that girl who constantly ran her mouth off at the Guild." She points an accusing finger at Ori. "You got cozy with this boy who doesn't know how to control himself any more than you do. Instead of listening to me, you go and do *this*?" She motions to the Guild walls, indicating the absence of the Horde bones. "You're an even bigger embarrassment than your father. At least he *tried*. You've treated the Culling like some meaningless game from the start."

I'm cut to the quick, but Meema takes a deep breath, like she's going to continue yelling. Only her final sentence comes out as a whisper instead. "I'm just so disappointed in you, darlin'."

No one makes a sound. Not one tiny noise that might distract me from the pain of Meema's words. *I'm an even bigger embarrassment than Dad.* My whole life I've been trying to prove I'm better than him, and in one sentence Meema's declared to the world that I've failed.

And the worst part?

I know she's right. I got caught up in sparks, in crushes, in friendship. All completely meaningless if Ori and I can wreak so much havoc with the spells we cast.

"It's nice to see us in agreement for once, Adela," Alister says coolly. "Does anyone here object to our tribunal summons? Does anyone think we should *not* look into how these two boys unleashed the Horde after they've been resting within Guild walls for hundreds of years?"

Nobody moves. Nobody comes to our defense.

I wouldn't either.

Alister grins. The fox who's broken into the chicken coop.

The gathered magicians work quickly, and it's overwhelmingly clear that Ori and I are seen as criminals. Jameson snaps his fingers again and we both float higher and higher. As floors whiz past, I realize this is probably the last time I'll ever see the Guild tower. I try to take in every last mesmerizing detail before I'm shut out for good. The forest-filled Dispatch center, the calming medical bays where I once thought Ori's and my power could be used for good. The floors fly by too fast until we stop at one I haven't paid attention to before. Lining the floor all the way back to the marble walls is row after row of benches. When Jameson sets me down, the floor stretches until the tower is completely covered, a platform rising from the marble, two empty chairs popping on top out of thin air. All the benches face the platform where Ori is being shoved into one of the seats. The same magic-constricting ropes that bind me tie him to the chair.

Jameson nudges me toward the platform. "I'm sure this must be intimidating." There's something like sympathy in his voice, I think. It's hard to tell. "Just speak your truth. That's all you can do."

"Thanks?" I mean what else am I supposed to say?

"Fancy seeing you here," I say to Ori as I shuffle to the chair beside him. A little levity before our doom couldn't hurt, but Ori's grim mouth doesn't budge. He just looks up at me blankly, then down to my empty seat.

"Let's just get this over with."

Shut down and bitter, I thunk into the seat. "Fine." More glowing gold ropes burst from the chair, wrapping along my forearms, my wrists, across my chest, over my thighs and shins and feet. I'm not going anywhere. And I'm definitely not going to be able to use any magic to fight back if the senior magicians decide I deserve to be culled.

And maybe I do.

I finally look straight ahead and take in our audience.

"Holy hell."

There are way more magicians on the floor than I even knew were in the building. Way more than I've ever seen gathered in one place. They're all around, filling the polished wood risers, tier after tier after tier of them. Thousands. Tucked away to my right are the rows of remaining apprentices. While the crowd of senior magicians looms large, this group feels small. Not the almost five hundred we started with. I spot Laurel and Jaleesa, separated again and sitting rows apart, their bond clear nonetheless thanks to their matching expressions. They'd love nothing more than to see me go down.

They might get their wish, but I'm more concerned about the

apprentices who've already lost their magic, who were cowering before the Depraved skeletons with no power to defend themselves. Where are they? Where is Bex? Maybe with the Guild distracted by cleaning up my mess, she'll have a better chance of escaping their wrath. I scan the crowd and see her dads a few rows from the front. Why are they here instead of helping their daughter? I'm glad Bex got away before the Horde attacked, but who knows if they'll still be able to get her as they rampage through America. Which, come to think of it—even if I *am* worse than Dad and deserve to have my magic stripped away—that seems like the biggest concern at the moment.

"The Horde," I call. "What's going on? Who's stopping them? You're here questioning us, when undead skeletons are on their way to free the Knife? And where were all of you when we needed help battling the Horde in the first place? Don't you need to get your priorities straight?"

"Nigel Barrett," Meema's voice snaps. "Don't sass. Do you honestly think we don't know what we're doing?"

I clamp my lips shut, flames rushing to my cheeks while Ori tilts his head up and says, "It kind of looks that way, yeah."

I feel the briefest flare of pride that Ori can keep up his spirit in all of this. But here I am, crumbling under the weight of my grandma's disappointment.

Pallavit sends a piercing glare his way from her seat next to Meema in the stands. "*Orion.* Your sister died for this organization, and this is how you respect her memory?"

That takes my breath away. How dare she bring Cassie into this? All I can see in Ori's eyes is rage. He's the bull in the rodeo that's ready to gorge a cowboy straight through the middle. And I don't blame him at all.

There's another rustle of movement in the crowd. All heads turn toward one person. A woman with the same pale skin and angular face as the boy who sets my body on fire. The boy who set the world on fire with me.

Ori's mom. Lyra.

Her glare perfectly matches her son's, her arms crossed firmly over her red jumpsuit, her body language daring Pallavit to say that again. Ori makes eye contact with his mom, but the moment she stares back, Ori's eyes dart away. Lyra stares at her son a moment longer before Meema's twang grabs everyone's attention.

"Most of the members you see before you *are* responding to the calamity the Horde is causing, as they were before, working on contingency plans should we have failed to prevent the skeletons *you* unleashed from leaving our headquarters," Meema explains. "You're seeing a phantom of their consciousnesses. A spell that allows the souls of Guild members to be in two places at once and still know full well what is going on in each. And *make decisions* in them. Like whether or not to expel you both from our ranks."

Alister looms in a seat that towers above the stands, a gleaming gavel in front of him. Each pound of that gavel is a nail hammered into my coffin.

"Enough talking!" Alister bellows. "As the member who called this tribunal, I will preside over the proceedings. Nigel Barrett. Orion Olson. This tribunal has been assembled to determine your eligibility for the Guild. You are charged with being in league with the Depraved, with the Horde, and with their master, the Knife. How do you plead?"

I'm too nervous to speak. I know that we made a terrible mistake, but we aren't in league with anybody. I'll never cast magic with Ori again, if that's what it takes. I won't keep digging into whatever those sparks are between us, however desperately I want connection.

But I can't have my power taken from me. I can't become a resentful, magicless, bitter man like Dad. My magic *is* me.

Ori takes a deep breath, and I know he's going to channel his anger to get us out of this.

"Guilty," Ori says, loudly, clearly, confidently.

Well, shit.

CHAPTER TWENTY

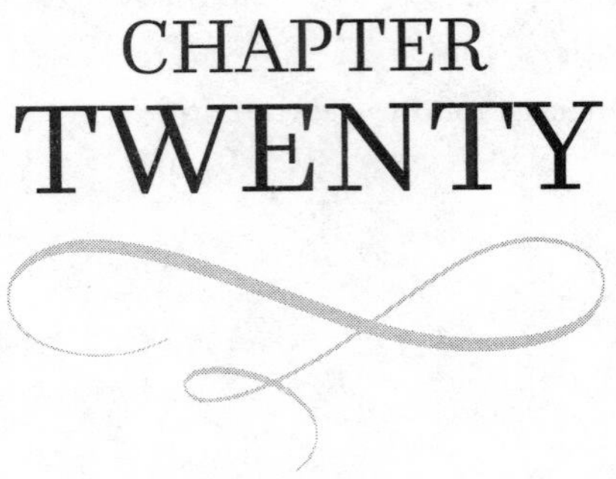

The room erupts into chaos. Shouts of "I knew it!" and "Take their power now!" fly from every direction. A few goblins transform into their beasts of choice and let out angry roars. Alister bangs his gavel, pure glee written across his face.

When the squall finally dies down, Ori adds, "But not how you think."

Meema shoots up from her seat. "Enough with the theatrics!" She gives Alister some serious side-eye. Then, to Ori, "Enough with the games! There's an easy way to learn the truth." Meema makes her way to the platform, thousands of pairs of eyes—both phantom and real, though other than the apprentices and the few senior magicians I do know, it's hard to tell which is which—following her every move. "The Weight of Truth."

I know this spell. Meema threatened to use it when I was a little kid and I'd lie about having snuck into the barn at night. When I'd come back into the house, a bit of dirt caked in my boots and hay in my hair, smelling like animal and dew, she'd ask what I was doing all night. I knew she didn't want me to sleep in the barn, so I'd tell some story about getting up early to do my chores, and she'd give me her piercing stare and ask me if I'd like to revise my story before she made me feel the Weight of Truth.

She's giving me that same stare now, like she's trying to read my mind. I'm sure she's imagining all the ways I could further humiliate her in front of the entire Guild, once she makes me spill. All I can do is beg her with my eyes to trust me. It hurts that she doubts me at all, but I guess after your grandson's magic has a hand in waking a centuries-dead skeleton army, it's a natural response.

Meema sighs, and golden magic pools in her hands. She stretches and pulls it until it's a flowing rectangle the size of a blanket. She drapes it over my torso, gently, tucking me in like she did so many nights when she found me asleep on the couch after reading elven texts.

As Meema's spell settles on top of me, I'm instantly at ease. It's soft, warm, buttery, like a fresh baked biscuit. The angry eyes of the Guild don't seem so intimidating, the memory of releasing the Horde doesn't seem so monstrous. Things are going to work out. If we just talk it through, everything will be fine.

Meema steps back so I'm in full view of the assembled magicians. I feel a contented smile lift my lips, and as I take them all in I break into a wide-toothed grin.

I say the first thing that comes to mind. "It's great that we can all be here together, isn't it? As magicians, I mean. I haven't met many of you before now, because Meema's been such an anxious mother hen. But now I'm surrounded. It's good to know I'm not alone. Though, a lot of you aren't very nice."

Scattered chuckles come from the group of apprentices, but the senior magicians remain stone-faced.

"What's got you all so serious?" I ask.

"I don't know," Ori says, "maybe it has something to do with the fact that we nearly destroyed the Guild? Or that a skeleton horde we woke is running through America right now?"

"Oh yeah," I say. "That."

"Nigel." Meema waves like she's trying to get the attention of a distracted toddler, and I giggle.

Oh *shoot.* Am *I* the distracted toddler?

I pick at the spelled blanket over my shoulders. "What's in this thing, anyway?"

"The Weight of Truth puts you at your most comfortable, your most childlike. You're disarmed, and you'll answer any question I ask you. Are you ready?"

I nod a lot. "Sure thing, Meema."

More laughs from the apprentices, and I can't help but join them.

"Did you knowingly and willingly unleash the Horde?" Meema asks.

My agreeable nodding turns to vigorous head shaking. "No way. Absolutely not. That was entirely an accident."

Meema's tension visibly eases, her shoulders dropping away from her ears. "Thank God," she mutters to herself, too quietly to be heard by the crowd. I smile at her, but she doesn't smile back, which I don't get at all, seeing as how we both know now that I'm not some Depraved sidekick.

"Isn't that good?" I ask.

"Don't rush it, now, boy, all right?" Meema glances over her shoulder at Alister, and the two share a look that's hard to read. Alister still seems suspicious, but he motions for her to proceed. "Have you now, or at any time in the past, been knowingly in league with the Depraved?"

A wave of indignation flows through me. "God, no. You know I wouldn't do that, Meema."

"I'm sorry I doubted you, darlin'," she coos, and I can tell she really means it. "But we've got to be sure we're good and thorough in this tribunal so you're not accused of this bull again. Alister says he overheard you speaking to a Depraved. What did the creature say to you?"

"It thanked me for helping it," I say, giving her another smile of contentment at delivering the truth.

The room gasps. Alister barks, "Just as I told you!"

Meema's face falls, her bright red lips dropping into a frown. "Th-thanked you?" She never stutters.

"Yep!" I look at Ori pleasantly. "Ori was there, too. Weren't you, Ori?"

Ori sighs, his hair swaying as he nods.

"What did you help it with, Nigel?" Meema presses.

"It was really freaky, Meema, I'll tell you what. I thought the thing was going to kill me, but instead it said my magic helped cause chaos that the Depraved could feed on, that there's something happening between Ori and me that helped release the Horde, and that all those skeletons are for sure going to free the Knife. Which, I guess, would cause even more fear and destruction to boost them, huh?"

"Yes, Nigel. Yes it would." Meema paces, her boots clacking heavily against the marble floor. "But you're saying, even if you spoke with a Depraved today, you have never interacted with one before, never intentionally helped them, and never would again?"

"Never before and never would intentionally, ma'am, that's right."

Meema gives me a triumphant look.

"Did I do good?"

"Very," Meema says simply, then whips the Weight of Truth

off my shoulders with a flourish. As soon as its buttery softness is gone, I'm cold. Well, every part of me except my cheeks, which are now burning with embarrassment. *Did I do good?* What a desperate-for-attention-little-kid suckup I was. My eyes bounce from Jaleesa to Laurel, then to the rest of the apprentices, and I know they're thinking the same thing. This should be a win, but I can't help feeling totally revealed, like one of those nightmares where you're doing perfect in your 4-H pig presentation only to look down and realize you're naked.

Back in front of the stands, Meema takes in every magician. "I understand why y'all doubted these two. Hell, I thought for a moment my own grandson had turned against us. But we've heard now that Nigel and Orion are not in league with the enemy. Their status in the Culling and the Guild should stand."

Many of the senior magicians nod along. There are too many in the stands for the majority opinion to be clear, but it seems like a sizeable chunk of them agree.

"I know I've been their champion the past few days," Pallavit begins, her face somber, "but you didn't see how many apprentices I had to heal while you were fighting the Depraved. I nearly lost half a dozen. It was one thing when the boys' magic threatened a capable senior magician. But to endanger these beginners? I was shortsighted. They're more dangerous than I realized." She takes in Alister looming over all of us, and her face settles in determination. "Alister was right. We can't let that sort of power go unchecked." She meets my eyes, giving me an apologetic smile. "I truly am sorry to have to change my tune, boys."

There's a chorus of agreement with Pallavit.

"That's true," Meema says, gently nodding. Those jabs of betrayal start to pierce my heart once more. She's going to cave that easily after my embarrassing yet vindicating performance with the

Weight of Truth? But then, "There is one key we're missing here, however." She turns to me and Ori, still bound in our chairs. "This only happens when the boys use their power together. Separately, they are just like any other Guild hopeful. Technically, they have broken no rules, just gotten a little out of hand."

Alister scoffs. "*A little?* Seriously, Adela?"

"All right, they've really fixed a magical squall," Meema says. "But by simply keeping them apart, we can guarantee it won't happen again."

My body convulses at the suggestion. I know she's right; I know what happens when we work together. I agree that we never, ever, ever should cast spells together. But even still, every iota of my being is pulled toward Ori, and the thought of being separated is excruciating.

"What does it say about us if we can't even give our own the benefit of the doubt?" Meema continues. "They're basically kids. They didn't know what their powers would do, neither." Some of the folks who'd been so quick to side with Pallavit now look around guiltily. "Let them complete the Culling separately. If they both succeed, we can decide how or even if to explore this unknown power later."

"The Culling?" Ori says suddenly. "You're still worried about that when an army of dead Depraved are ransacking America?"

"The Culling *must* continue," Alister says. He looks around the room, and now, every single head is nodding with him. No contingent of magicians seems to think otherwise.

"But why?" I ask. "Ori's right. We have bigger priorities."

"Balance." Jameson says it quietly, ominously, like a thick thundercloud hovering before it unleashes a Texas-size storm. "Or else we'll have more to deal with than just the Knife."

Magical imbalance. What good would it do to fight off the Knife if we just let magic run wild and kill us all?

Alister slams his gavel. "We've heard what everyone has to say. It's time. The Guild knows there's nothing I love more than democracy." He chuckles to himself, like a total prick, before gesturing to Pallavit, who clears her throat to sing.

"Accusations made.
Suspicions of note.
A tribunal called.
It's time to vote."

Purple light pours from her mouth, coalescing in the air and forming a massive scale. On one side, *Guilty* is spelled in delicate cursive. On the other, *Not Guilty*.

"The choice is simple," Alister says. "Vote guilty and these two will be disqualified from Guild membership and stripped of their powers immediately. Or, not guilty and allow them to continue to compete in the Culling."

Thousands of members eye us up and down, analyzing Ori and me as they make their decision. I've been judged before, stood by while a group of farmers looked over sheep I showed, but this is a whole other level. And while we sit, bound like animals, I can't help but imagine what my life will become if they take everything away. Meema will be devastated. I'll have to sit by and watch while others clean up the mess I made. While other magicians *die* trying to clean it up, and human lives are destroyed. I saw what happened to Dad when he simply failed his test. What will happen to me if I fail on such an epic level that the Horde can't be stopped? That the Knife is unleashed? I can't sit by. I have to help.

"Wait!"

"The time for discussion is over," Alister yells.

"Please, just hear me out! If anyone should have to clean this mess up, it's me. This is my fault. Please don't take my magic before—"

"Ours."

I turn to Ori, and he's truly looking at me for the first time since we got on this stage. His nostrils flare, and he seems ready to fight. Ready to fight *me*, and I don't understand why. But even with his eyes shooting daggers, the steadiness of his glare sends sparks through my belly.

"It's *our* mess," Ori says. "You didn't do this alone. Don't get all chivalrous on your own, either. If this is getting cleaned up, we're doing it together."

Together.

"I like the sound of that."

Ori scowls. Jesus, I said that out loud. I'm even *smiling.*

I clear my throat and quickly look away, calling back to the group. "Right. *Our* mess. Let us fix this. If our combined powers brought this on, they might be needed to make it stop. We can be supervised the whole time, though. You can guide us, but don't take our powers away yet. Please."

Meema stares at me, her face unreadable. She has to know I mean it. I won't let her down.

"What an *uplifting* speech," Alister says, his voice dripping with sarcasm. "May we continue, or would you like to go on hijacking this tribunal?"

"No, I—" My cheeks blaze. "Sorry."

Alister gives one sharp pound of the gavel. "Vote."

Light erupts around the room in every color of magic. Gold, purple, silver, pink, red, green, whooshing throughout the hall, reflecting off the marble floor as they pile up on the scales. It would almost be beautiful if it didn't make me nauseous.

Ori stares straight ahead, eyeing his mom, trying to communicate something to her as she mulls. How can she even be debating this? But with one snap of her fingers, a ball of pink light shoots from her hand and lands in the guilty pile.

My heart stops cold. I know Ori said she didn't want him in the Guild, for his own safety. But if Ori's own mom voted against us, how on earth are we going to make it out of here with our power?

I can't bring myself to look anymore. Instead, I watch Ori's eyes fill with hurt while colorful votes pile up, reflected in his irises. The longer we wait, the tighter Ori's jaw clenches. That can't be good.

When I can't take it anymore, I finally face the scale.

Small dots of light are piled high on each side, the weights gently bobbing up and down, over and over, no side dropping and overtaking the other. Eventually, they even out and still, side by side.

It's a tie.

"Has everyone voted?" Alister calls. He looks over his shoulder, eyes scanning the room. "Everyone?"

"Hold your horses, Ali." Meema's voice rings through the hall, triumphant. She holds out a compact and reapplies her Fiery Soul lipstick. "I was just getting primped for this moment. Here's that last vote you're looking for."

With a smile bigger than I've ever seen, Meema snaps her fingers and a golf ball–size speck of gold flies across the room in a smooth arc. It lands on the side marked NOT GUILTY, the vote that tips the scales, making the tray descend. When the other side careens upward, the magic votes against us scatter across the room, leaving only the votes in our favor to glow brightly and proudly over our heads.

We did it.

We're still in.

The binds melt from our wrists, receding back into the chair. I pump my fist, whooping like I just hog-tied the most finicky goat, and look around the room expecting others to join in. But the thousands of senior magicians who watched the proceedings just moments ago have vanished. All that's left of our audience are the few dozen senior magicians who were physically present to begin with—and none of them look too happy. Maybe they didn't vote for us, having seen the destruction our magic caused firsthand.

The apprentices look pissed, too. They didn't lose us as competition, after all.

I expect Ori to be as pumped as I am, but he's just staring at the pile of magic—the votes in our favor—his mind clearly somewhere else.

Meema claps her hands, and all the resentful stares turn to her. "All right, sourpusses, don't get your knickers in a twist. We've got some monsters to kill."

CHAPTER TWENTY-ONE

"To Dispatch," Meema calls. Now that I'm in the clear—at least for now—she seems energized, barking out orders. "We've wasted enough time today already."

A fresh pang of guilt stabs me in the gut. All that time wasted, because of *us*.

Meema stomps over and takes me forcefully by the hand, pulling me out of earshot of anyone else.

"You've got to be on your best behavior now, you hear me?" Any grandmotherly concern she showed during the tribunal is gone. She's stone-faced, her Fiery Soul lips a straight, stern line. "I meant what I said in there. Something strange is going on between you and Orion, and if you can't control that, darlin'—that's it for the Barrett family. I don't care how goddamn twitterpated you are. Got it?"

I've never seen Meema stumped by anything magical. She's always had new spells to show me, new methods of concentrating to make my magic second nature. She assumed I'd be a force for good.

But now that we're both faced with the chaos I've caused, it's like she doesn't know who I am anymore.

"Bex said it was some kind of—" God, am I really going to bring this up now? The world is on fire because of me, but I'm thinking about a boy? "Some kind of love thing? Have you heard of it?"

She shakes her head hard and fast. "*Do you hear yourself, Nigel?* This isn't some happily-ever-after fairy tale, so don't you go getting your head caught up in the clouds at a time like this. That's ridiculous. That girl never took the Guild seriously, from the start. I told you not to, but here you go letting her fill your head with nonsense. And your nonsense is deadly." She grips my forearm hard, making me wince, reminding me of all the times Dad grabbed me like this. Stern. Without love. "You listen to me, Nigel, and you listen good. You've messed up everything I've worked the past eighteen years to put in place. Training you, pushing you, making sure you were ready for this. And in one challenge, you've thrown all that away. You're the only one who can fix what you've done now. The fate of the Barretts depends on you, and if you don't keep your head in this"—she stamps her foot for emphasis—"it's not just you and me who are going down, but the whole country. Maybe even the whole world. Ya hear?"

I want to tell her so many things. I want to tell her that if she hadn't hidden me away my whole life, maybe I wouldn't have been so desperate to find friends like Bex and Ori. I want to tell her that her impression of them is wrong, that they both want to fight evil in their own way. But . . . she's not *entirely* wrong, is she? We woke the Horde. The responsibility to fix that lies on my shoulders.

Meema stamps her foot again. "*Nigel.*"

"Yes, ma'am," I whisper.

"About time." She snaps her fingers and her longhorn comes to life. The hulking bull heaves in front of us, and Meema jumps on like she's a rodeo champion, not a woman in her seventies. She reaches down and pulls me up. "Let's get to it."

Her bull jumps over the balcony, and I feel a hollowness at the sudden memory of flying on Frosty's back. We're down to Dispatch in no time, Meema's bull vanishing when our feet hit the grass. The gurgling fountains and lush green plant life do nothing to calm my nerves knowing we're about to see the extent of our mess.

The looks I'm getting from everyone else certainly don't help. As Meema and I make our way to the nearest fountain—where Ori, Pallavit and Jaleesa, Alister and Laurel, and Jameson are all gathered—I get doubt-filled stares from every single person in Dispatch. Not just from the people who clearly voted against me, but from those that must have voted for me, too. Nobody knows how this is going to work out. I physically feel the pressure, a weight on my shoulders. I feel it radiating from every last soul in the Guild.

Then there's Ori. I take the toadstool next to him, and Meema dashes off to join Jameson and Pallavit for a hurried conversation. Ori doesn't say a word. I feel a gentle buzz being near him, but he's still closed off. He's true to his word, refusing to talk to me ever again. Even though he took half the blame during the tribunal, I get the sense that he still feels this is all my fault, somehow.

"Attention, magicians!" Alister's voice echoes around the room, magically magnified thanks to Pallavit's power. An image takes shape in every gushing fountain: the Horde, thousands of skeletons ransacking a quaint town that lies next to a river, a snowcapped mountain looming in the distance. Panicked humans flee while the skeletons destroy shops, decimate homes, and knock over powerlines. Small fires dot the town. More humans have barricaded themselves in schools, churches, and the town hall, all of which are being swarmed by Horde soldiers and more Depraved, clearly lapping up the humans' fear. It's pure mayhem. And it never would have existed if it weren't for me.

"Hood River, Oregon," Alister says. "Feeling the wrath of the Horde on their way to free their master. We were lucky—"

Ori scoffs. "*Lucky*. Right."

Alister raises his voice a notch as he continues. "We were lucky that the Knife's soldiers are more brute force than brains. They misjudged the location of their master's prison and directed their portals to Mount Hood instead of Mount Rainier. Their mistake has bought us time."

The fountain images change to show hundreds of magicians in the forest surrounding Hood River. Nymph descendants set traps, elves and fae cast spells, goblins prowl the woods in various beast forms, and sprites blink in and out of existence, placing effigies to use in battle.

"The Guild has the city surrounded, and members will do everything in their power to prevent the Horde from leaving. We're building a barricade as we speak. But if the Horde makes it to their master, we will have much bigger problems on our hands."

Alister takes in my Cullingmates, who are crowded around their own fountains throughout the floor. "As stated in the tribunal, in an effort to not contribute to *more* problems, the Culling must continue."

The fountains change, showing a new town, magic of all colors coating buildings, clothes, the ground. And skin. Humans and magicians alike burn as it touches them, pure energy making them writhe in agony until holes are literally bored through their bodies. It saturates the air, too, and as people breath it in, they're destroyed by magic from the inside out.

It's horrifying.

"The Culling is carried out each year for the greater good, allowing us to harness our power before it destroys us. So we can use it to fight evil, like the Knife. No matter what catastrophes present themselves, we must always be ready to maintain magical balance.

"There's no more room for the fear many of you showed on that mountaintop," Alister continues. "If you are not up to the task of tackling the Horde, you can leave now. I'll summon the magicians to sap you of your power. It will be much easier to defeat our enemies if we don't have to worry about inexperienced apprentices getting in the way. Any takers? Anyone want out?"

Nobody moves. I'm pretty sure the apprentices don't even breathe. A knowing smile creeps up Alister's face before he says, "That's what I thought. Now, it's time for a makeover of the third Culling task. The third test has always been to face down a Depraved, and speed determined the winners. Now, it's about numbers. The half of you who destroy the most enemies will be in. That applies to Horde soldiers, demons, *and* the Depraved. You'll have to face them all."

"This is so messed up," Ori says.

Alister swoops down on him, getting so close his nose practically touches Ori's. "Something you'd like to share?"

Ori leans back, a judgmental eyebrow cocked. "You're making this a game. Doesn't that seem a bit *twisted* to you? This isn't about racking up points, it's about saving lives."

"Well, lucky for you, your mission is different," Alister sneers. He turns to my grandma. "Why don't you tell them, Adela? About how your grandson and this boy get to sit this fight out while the rest of us deal with the monsters they've unleashed?"

"Or about how the odds are being stacked against them?" she snaps. "How they'll still be expected to destroy enough varmints to make the cut, but they're being sent somewhere entirely different?"

Alister looks comically affronted. "I have no idea what you mean. Why, I've even volunteered my daughter for the task as well." He beckons to her, and Laurel moves forward.

"As have I," Pallavit says, stepping up with Jaleesa and giving her a proud smile. "This is about saving human- and magickind, and I know Jaleesa is up for the task."

Ori grabs fistfuls of his hair, tugging hard in frustration. "Could somebody please tell us what's going on? What is it with magicians needing to hear themselves talk without actually saying anything?"

"I second that," I say. He catches my eye, and I swear his mouth quirks up just a little. Finally.

"I'll leave you to it," Alister says. "Apprentices with me." He locks eyes with Laurel. "Don't mess this up."

Laurel winces like he's hit her. But with a vine over the balcony, Alister swings away without a second look. Every last member of the Guild, every single apprentice, follows him down to the portal on the first floor. Now it's just me, Ori, Jaleesa, Laurel, Meema, and Jameson. I'm so used to the Guild being full of noise and movement and magic. It feels eerily empty.

With a chill, I imagine what will happen if the Horde does free the Knife. Years from now, will the Guild stand empty just like this? Left to rot, with no magicians to tend to it? Will all of us be dead?

"Come on," Meema says, pulling me from my toadstool. "It's time to show you your birthright." She marches through the grass, heading to the balcony. "To the Hall of Destiny."

Ori laughs, loud and real, and for the first time I wonder if maybe things will go back to normal someday. If we fix this. "Hall of Destiny?" His words are jumbled thanks to his cackling. "Magicians are so predictable."

Ori catches me staring and his eyes dart away. He blinks up floor after floor, following Meema and me as we gallop on her bull to the topmost level. The twenty-fifth. The luckiest number in all of magic. I've never needed more luck in my life.

The twenty-fifth floor is unlike any of the others. Every time we crested the balcony to another level, there was always some new surprise—some spell enlarging the space, some jaw-dropping magical feature. But here, there's just pedestals, arranged in a circle around the circumference of the tower. Simple marble ones, twenty-five in all, with little etchings on their front. Envelopes lie on roughly the first third of them, gold with the deep blue emblem of the Guild.

"Each of these envelopes contains the history of a mega monster we've encountered since the founding of the Guild," Meema explains. "Most of them Depraved beasts, built from war, cruelty, hatred, and bigotry. But we're concerned with one in particular." Meema walks over to the first pedestal on our right. A gold engraving of a claw adorns it. It looks entirely unremarkable, a sort of misshapen crescent moon. My grandma, however, looks at it like it holds the secrets to the universe.

She swallows, her hands poised over the envelop atop the pedestal, her red nails catching the light. She flips a finger under the seal and turns to me. "Are you ready?"

Honestly, I don't feel any sort of reverence in this moment. I mean, how can I? We're hovering over glorified stationery. "Uh, yeah."

Meema scowls but flips the envelope open. The others crowd around to see what's written inside.

Nothing.

"I hate to state the obvious," Ori says. "But it's blank."

"Is it written in invisible ink or something?" I ask.

Jaleesa clears her throat. "I can probably sing it out. A revealing spell to show us what it's about."

Laurel rolls her eyes. "You're all such imbeciles. This is clearly—Ah!"

The entire rooms goes black. I can't see a single thing in front of, behind, or next to me, though I can feel people there, Ori especially.

"It's ironic how, in the absence of everything, nothingness is palpable," Jameson observes.

Suddenly, gold light erupts, and I snap my eyes closed at the intensity of it. When I'm finally able to blink them open, the Guild is gone entirely.

"Whooeee," I breathe.

We're in the middle of the greenest forest I've ever seen. The sky above is a cloudy gray, but the grass, the trees, every leaf is so green it's like we're in a filter.

"Where are the birds?" Laurel asks.

Her power over the elements must make her even more tuned in to nature than the rest of us. She's right, though. I can hear wind blowing, leaves rustling, a creek gurgling somewhere nearby. But no birds.

Then—

WHAM!

A mottled-green foot the size of a town house slams into the ground, sending ripples through the solid dirt and rock. Trees are crushed beneath the foot, revealing cracked and bloody toenails the size of a Fiat. All of us flinch, shielding our faces as tree trunks go flying, and we brace for impact at the ripples in the ground. But it's like we're not here at all. The ripples pass harmlessly under our feet. Shards of trees fly straight through us without leaving a mark. We're here, but we're not.

"The Knife," Meema says, craning her neck back to follow the massive leg up, up, up. Its body is so gigantic that its head is lost to the clouds. All I can see are skyscraper-high legs with thick, gnarly leg hairs the size of logs, leading to a torso with a belly so big this thing could swallow a town whole and still have room for seconds. Its neck bulges with veins so thick an entire Olympic swim team could butterfly stroke through them, easy as pie.

"One of the largest Depraved ever to be created," Jameson explains like he's reading from a textbook, bored, disinterested. "So monstrous thanks to the catastrophic levels of hate at the time, and to the stolen elven crown upon its head, linked to the creature's life force and fed by hearts. The giant is commonly referred to as the Knife, for its weapon of choice. Watch."

The Knife takes another thundering step, leaving a wide open path through the forest in its wake. The giant is bearing down on an old-time settlement: small, rectangular wood and brick buildings lining dirt roads that swarm with people. Some run to their little ramshackle houses and lock themselves in. Others flee to the woods behind their town. Most grab muskets and run to meet the Knife head on. It's brave, but compared to the monster, the people look like ants. Like nothing they can do will have any effect whatsoever.

My theory is proven as, with one swift kick, the Knife's leg topples half the town. Soldiers soar and fire pits scatter, setting the remaining buildings ablaze. The soldiers left standing swarm, firing their guns. Some hit their mark, but the giant acts like it can't feel the bullets as anything more than tiny gnat bites.

Finally, we see the Knife's face, which Ori sums up perfectly: "Rough."

The Knife's eyes glow so brightly in that rotten hue that it lights up the clouds. On top of its massive head sits a crown made of bone, a bloodred ruby in its center. A demonic smile cracks the Knife's lips so deeply you could fall into the fissures. It uses one baseball diamond-size hand to sweep across the gathered army, picking up dozens of screaming soldiers in the process. With its other hand, the monster pulls a knife from the sheath around its waist and, in one quick movement, slashes it across the line of soldiers, silencing their screams in an instant. Then, one by one, savoring each morsel, the Knife uses his thumb to pop the hearts out of the soldiers and gulp them down. It's surprising that something so big wants a snack that's so small. But with each heart, the Knife seems stronger, meaner, more bent on destruction, and the ruby at the center of its crown oozes dark red blood. As if every heart eaten makes it beat, makes it live. The giant throws the heartless human husks over its shoulder, ready for more.

"By this point, America's gruesome beginnings had already fueled so much destruction. Of its Native people by colonizers, of enslaved people by colonizers, of colonizers by Depraved, of Ancestrals by Depraved as well," Jameson says, listing off deaths with no emotion. "All that hate created the biggest Depraved ever seen in this country. The Knife held such terrifying power that it garnered favor among more common Depraved, who formed the original Horde. In the specific moment in time you see here, the Horde had already been destroyed by the Guild, buried away in our halls of marble. The Knife, however, lived on. The Guild was able to reconvene quickly, gathering what was left of their numbers to distract the Knife. Biding time."

Magicians of all abilities run out of the trees. Goblins shapeshift into dragons to dive-bomb the Knife from the air. Elves and fae cast spells that burn, pierce, or slow the giant. Nymphs make weeds burrow into the ground so deeply that sinkholes erupt, tripping the monster. Sprites even blink into the Knife's sheath in massive numbers and, daringly, blink back with its knife in hand.

"Even without its namesake weapon, the Knife fought on," Meema says. We watch as magician after magician falls, until only a few remain. "And then, finally, Barrett created the claw."

A frail old man with a wispy white beard growing past his knees wobbles out of the woods.

"Hey, Gramps," I say.

As if he can hear me, Great-Grandpa Barrett tilts his head in my direction. He takes a deep breath, magic gathering in his fingers as he runs them over his throat. His mouth gapes wide as he roars, fueled by his power. It's deep and thunderous and tree-shaking, echoing long after he stops. Then, the ground rumbles, branches snap, trees topple, and a herd of bears appears before him. At least fifty. Proving he lives up to his last name.

The largest of the bears, three times the size of any of the rest, steps forward. Grandpa walks to meet it, small as a doll next to the massive brown creature. It leans down, bending its neck so its furry forehead is just an inch away from my grandfather's. Gramps taps his against the bear's, and on contact, gold shoots from his heart directly into the bear's. His form crumples, unmoving.

"Grandpa!" I rush forward, but Meema grabs me by the shirt.

"It was his sacrifice, darlin'. He knew the mission of the Guild was greater than his human life. But he lived on as the bear, their hearts entwined through his spell. He gave up his life to take another's."

Rippling with gold magic, the bear takes off. He's faster than a lightning bolt. One second, he's at the edge of the woods, the next, he's bounding up the Knife's legs, swimming through its leg hair, clawing up its loin cloth, galloping over the Knife's back, crawling through its flaky scalp, until the bear stands atop the massive crown of bone. He raises a mighty paw, claws shining brighter than the sun, and with one swing, swipes his claws against the stone in the center of the Knife's crown. The jewel cracks, and the Knife instantly changes. It clutches its own heart, falling backward, creating a huge crater in the forest below. The bear carrying the spirit of my great-grandpa collapses, too, and is carried off by Guild members. One last magician lingers, picking up a bright gold bar that lays discarded on the ground. It's one of Grandpa's claws, still shining with magic. The magician joins the others, and using their powers, they transport the Knife's limp body across miles and miles of country, until they lock the giant away, deep inside the volcano that is Mount Rainier.

"The heartstone in the Knife's crown—the talisman that harnessed all the power of the souls it devoured—was cracked, but not destroyed," Meema says. "The injury was enough to subdue the giant, allowing us to imprison it. Guild members have renewed the spells keeping it caged every year. Over the years we've tried to completely destroy the heartstone, to separate the Knife from the source of its power, but it always rematerializes on the monster's head. The best we can do is keep the Knife in its enchanted sleep and safeguard the claw in case we need to knock the monster out again." Meema puffs her chest with pride as she turns to me and continues. "It's all thanks to the spell from your great-grandfather's sacrifice. A spell that lives on within that claw. Something so small, yet so powerful. And because it was made from the soul of a Barrett, only a Barrett can unlock its powers, as you've known all your life. But, to prevent any of our family from using the claw against the rest of the Guild, the organization hid it away and created a spell to find it that requires the willing participation of five magicians, one Barrett and four other Guild members, each from a different family."

Meema waves her hand and the scene disappears. We're back on the twenty-fifth floor, staring at the envelope-laden pedestal before us.

"That's where y'all come in. It's up to you to find the claw, using that location spell. We have four volunteers here." Meema looks at Jameson, Jaleesa, Laurel, and Ori in turn, then finally stares at me with her steely determination. "And a Barrett, giving us a star-sacred five. Find the claw and bring it to me. It will be our safeguard in case we cannot stop the Horde before they free the Knife." Her lingering stare says, *Don't fuck this up*.

I wish Bex were here. I wish Frosty were here. Anybody who could bolster me. Anyone but two apprentices who hate me, one senior magician who I can't get a read on at all, and a sprite who's magically connected to me but won't even look my way.

"Last thing," Meema says. "The spell to find the claw? It uses our blood. Barrett blood." She scans everyone else's face now. "In order for the whereabouts of the claw to be revealed, y'all have to drink it."

"What?" This could present a problem. Any time I see even one red drop, I get light-headed. If the whole group needs to *drink* my blood, I'm definitely going to pass out. And then who will get the claw?

Jaleesa gags. "God, pass. Nobody said anything about having to go all vampire on his ass."

Laurel looks equally disgusted. "And I thought this day couldn't get any worse."

Ori is straight-faced when he says, "Fine." A quick image of him with his mouth wrapped around my neck flashes through my mind, and I admit I'm not entirely against it.

Jameson simply nods.

"H-how am I supposed to retrieve my blood, exactly?" *Keep it together, Nigel!*

Meema gets straight to the point. "You have to be pricked by the Knife's namesake. It was spelled and transformed after we took it. No longer an instrument of the monster's destruction, but one to aid in destroying *it*, should the beast ever rise again."

So it'll be one big magical kumbaya over a feast of my blood. Fun.

"And where is the knife now?" I ask. "The weapon knife, not the giant."

Meema smiles. "That's the best part." She flips open the envelope again, and an image etches itself on the parchment within. It's a massive castle. Then, on either side, huge rectangular buildings, with window after window, a lot like a hotel. And in front of the castle, a gigantic, campy sign, lit up with one word: EXCALIBUR.

"You're kidding me. The Excalibur Hotel and Casino in Vegas?"

"Humans will go out of their way to believe magic's not real," Meema explains, "so it's sometimes best to hide things right under their oblivious noses. We've turned the Knife's weapon into a sword, hidden in the props department at the Excalibur. It even gets used for their knight tournament from time to time. It's harmless, unless it's wielded against magical foes or to draw Barrett blood."

Draw Barrett blood. I do not like the sound of that.

"You put one of the items needed to stop the worst monster the world has ever known in a Vegas show?" Ori asks. "Just want to make sure I'm hearing this correctly."

Meema glares. "You got it, sweetheart."

"Cool," Ori says in a tone that makes it clear it's anything but. "If I get in this group, I'm proposing a few procedural overhauls."

"Get the sword. Find the claw. Meet us back at the Horde when it's retrieved. Do me proud."

The *or else* is heavily implied. No pressure, right?

Without looking back, Meema conjures her bull and leaps over the balcony.

Jaleesa stomps forward, I guess electing herself leader. Her throat glows purple as she sings.

"The stage is set.
Enemies to gore.
Take us down
to the very first floor."

Her purple light covers her and Laurel before the two of them float into the air and gently descend to the entry hall. Ori and I are left standing there, with Jameson hovering a couple yards away. This is not a good sign of magical cooperation to come.

I glance at Ori. "We're screwed, aren't we?"

At first I think he's going to smirk, but the quirk of his mouth turns to a grimace.

"Seems likely."

At least we're on the same page about something.

Without a word, Jameson's hands glow gold and he snaps his fingers to make the three of us float. As we drift down to the platform, thoughts race through my mind. Maybe we'll find the claw but not stop enough of the Horde, and we'll fail the Culling. Maybe we'll find the claw and I'll get skewered by the razor sharp bones of a Horde soldier. Maybe we *won't* find the claw and the Knife will be freed and eat out all our hearts. I want just one last second to remember a time when I was confident I'd become a Guild member, that I'd make the world a better place instead of bringing so much chaos into it. I need to remember the hope I felt after succeeding in the first challenge. Because maybe, just maybe, I'll succeed here, too. And all I dreamed about for the first eighteen years of my life will actually become reality.

But that hope doesn't come. The halls are so silent that it's deafening. Everyone is far off, fixing my mess. I need to get out of this suffocating silence and do my part.

When we land, Jameson summons the portal, the rhyme he sings to trigger the fae magic quiet, ethereal, unsettling. A shimmering purple haze appears in front of us, highlighting the uncertain faces of a ragtag group of five magicians. As the descendant of Barrett, the guy who created the claw that'll get us out of this disaster, I feel some sense of responsibility to wrangle the group. To rally us to success.

I gather magic in my fingers, step in front of the portal, and say the only thing that comes to mind.

"Viva Las Vegas."

CHAPTER TWENTY-TWO

THE SUDDEN CHANGE IN SOUND AND SCENERY IS MORE JARRING THAN the fae magic that pulls us through the portal. One second we're in the eerie, empty Guild hall, and the next we're in the middle of a crowded street. Around us, tourists laugh, yell, cheer drunkenly though it's the middle of the afternoon; cars cruise past on the Strip, lights of every color flash, almost like magic, advertising the latest shows and All You Can Eat buffets. The brightest light of all comes from the glaring Excalibur sign, with its advertisement for the Tournament of Kings directly underneath. The crowds are so thick and swarming that nobody notices when we suddenly appear. Humans can't see the magic portal, but still. We're five bodies appearing out of nowhere.

"I'm not entirely sure anyone here would even notice if the Knife got free," I say. "They don't see magic happening right in front of their faces."

"I think they'd notice a monster popping their heart out and eating it," Ori says flatly. "Just a guess."

"And I, for one, don't want to be one of his snacks," Jaleesa says. She looks to Laurel like she's waiting for her to suggest what we should do next. But all Laurel does is give her a tight-lipped smile, her eyes darting away. She's doesn't seem nearly as sure of herself as she did that first day of the Culling. Maybe her dad is getting to her in the same way that Meema's pressure is getting to me.

Laurel notices me staring and sneers. "Can I help you?"

There's the Laurel I remember.

With a heavy sigh, Jaleesa marches down the street, heading toward a long walkway, the entrance marked by an open portcullis that welcomes visitors to the hotel castle and casino.

After a brief and uncharacteristic hesitation, Laurel follows, dashing to catch up to her girlfriend. Jameson strolls behind without a word to us. Ori and I move to follow the group, but we're blocked by an enormous bachelorette party. At least fifteen women and a handful of gays block the rest of our magician party from view. They're hooting and hollering and cackling as they down pink drinks in glasses shaped like swords, their tiaras and sashes catching the lights.

"Excuse us," I say, attempting to position my shoulder so that I can scoot by. But the nearest woman moves at exactly the same time, and my hand slips through her bride-to-be sash. I try to pull back, but my thumb catches on the fabric and tugs the bride toward me.

"Watch it!" she screams, her sword drink falling out of her hand and splashing to the sidewalk. The rest of her party snaps to attention and surrounds us.

"What do you think you're doing?"

"Get your hands off her, creep!"

"She's already spoken for, and her husband is going to kick your ass!"

Then there's a hand around my wrist, long, pale fingers gently extricating me from the sash. Warmth cascades through my body.

"Whoa, buddy," Ori says. "You all right there?" He turns to the fuming bachelorette's backup and gives them a full-on, every-tooth-showing smile. "Please excuse my friend here. I think he might have had too much to drink." It's such a shift from his broody vampire vibe that it does not look natural *at all.* But it's also kind of adorable. And the bachelorette, the ladies, that handful of gays all buy it.

I buy it, too. My mouth falls open and I get all googly-eyed, staring at Ori like a complete buffoon. It definitely supports his claim, but it's not an act. His touch makes me light-headed in the best way.

The group laughs, and the bride says, "Haven't we all!"

The bachelorette party cracks up and continues down the street while Ori leads me away, through the Excalibur portcullis. I don't say a word as we make our way inside the casino, too afraid that if I draw attention to myself, Ori will realize he's still got his hand in mine. This feels so right, just like it did before the second Culling challenge. Before everything fell apart.

A gambler screaming her head off snaps me back to reality. She's won the jackpot. Chimes ring and bells clang as coins shower into a metal basin and she scoops them up with glee. Everywhere I look, gamblers are hoping for the same outcome, pulling levers on thousands of slot machines.

My pounding heart joins all the noise. There are people *everywhere*, and none of them look like the folks I'm supposed to be teaming up with to find the claw. We're only ten minutes into this mission, and I've already lost three-fifths of my party.

Somehow, this one seemingly small thing makes it all too much. My breathing comes fast and hard, my palms start to sweat, and I burst into tears. I rack my brain for any spell that could stop them or make me toughen up, but I can't think of a single one.

I'm standing in the middle of the casino floor, in a packed Vegas hotel, bawling my eyes out.

"Nigel?" Ori's voice is curt as he tugs me to the side, out of the main walkway. Dozens of tourists look at me like I've lost my mind.

"I can't do this," I finally say through the lump in my throat. "I'm not meant to be a magician."

I look into his eyes, hoping to see pity, or comfort, or understanding. Any of it. But instead, his eyes reflect back what everyone else has shown me since I started the Culling.

"Do you know how selfish you're being right now? Standing here crying when *we* are the ones who ruined everything? There's literally a town that's being ransacked by dead Depraved warriors, and if those skeletons *leave* it, they're going to unleash a monster to *eat all of humanity*. And you think *you* have the biggest problem right now?"

Wow, way to pour salt in the wound.

"You don't think I know all this already?" I snap. "I know how epically I screwed up, I know how horribly things will turn out if we don't get this nightmare under control. But do you have any idea what it's like to feel so alone? To feel that, no matter what you do, you're not enough? To want nothing more than to form a connection with *anyone* to escape the torment in your own home? To live with the constant pressure to uphold some stupid family name, and to have no idea what it's like to be friends with someone who knows exactly who and what you are and actually still likes you?"

Ori steps back, the foot between us feeling more like the Grand Canyon. "You can't be serious. You're honestly asking me if I know what it's like to be *alone*?"

It's like that moment we touched when we fought, when I was

inside Ori's memories. I can see his sister again. I can feel his sadness, I can feel his shame that he wasn't able to save her, the pain that he could only watch helplessly while the Depraved killed her.

"Ori, I'm—"

But he barrels on, his voice quieter now but still seething. I have to lean in to hear him over the sounds of tourists screaming and coins clattering.

"The past four years of my life I've been nothing *but* alone," he says, "and I'm trying to do everything I can to make up for my inability to act that day. And now, in just the first week I've stepped foot in the Guild, my power is somehow even stronger than it was to begin with, but it has horrible consequences. My own *mother* voted against me being able to keep it. How alone do you think that makes me feel? No matter how many times I've told her my magic is what makes me *me*, she doesn't care. So, yes, Nigel, I know *exactly* what it's like to be on my own, to have my power not be what I expected. I'm doing so much more harm than good, all because I let myself get distracted by *you*. I allow myself to get close to someone for the first time after my sister died, after already knowing firsthand that connection leads to pain, and guess what? I was right! I'm losing focus, I'm losing sight of the whole purpose of this organization, all because of some stupid *tingles* when I'm around you. Because I believed for a second that this love thing could be real, when I don't even know you! It's ridiculous. Cassie deserves so much better than this."

His voice breaks, and he takes a deep, quavering breath. "You wanted somebody to finally know you for the real you? Well, now the entire Guild does. They know what we can do, and they know only a Barrett can fix it. So pull yourself together and get to it. Stop being selfish."

Ori turns on his heel and stomps off in the direction of the Tournament of Kings show, not looking back to see if I follow.

With every step he takes, the guilt in my gut settles deeper. Ori's right; I'm not here to feel sorry for myself. And breaking down in the middle of a casino is just more proof of how self-indulgent I am. All those books and TV shows where they show teens as the one person who can save the world? They don't make any sense. It's a lot of pressure to have your first moments of adulthood be focused on literally saving an entire planet. I'm just some lucky product of the genetic lottery, a great-grandson of one of the strongest magicians ever known, a kid who's more skilled at riding a horse or dodging angry roosters than taking up the mantle of Depraved giant slayer.

I slowly make my way behind Ori until a voice reaches me through open theater doors leading to the Tournament of Kings. "Are you the one, my boy? The strongest warrior, worthy of wielding your sword in battle?"

"Probably not." The roaring cheer of a crowd sweeps away my answer. I'm standing at the top of a massive arena, row upon row of seats filled with people eating Cornish game hen and potatoes and rolls, all with their hands, chugging down mugs of ale. Grease and butter drip down their eager faces as they yell at actors on horseback dressed as knights, who charge each other in a dirt-covered ring.

Slam!

Lances smash against shields, shattering to pieces, and the crowd goes wild. A green-clad knight falls off his horse. Half the audience is pissed—Team Green, I guess. The other half cheer on the yellow-wearing knight like their happiness hinges on this Vegas tourist trap.

A tomato smacks my cheek, and my yelp of surprise is lost to the roars of the spectators. I whip around to see Laurel looking as annoyed as ever, a tomato plant growing at her feet, providing her with the perfect produce projectiles. It's wild that we're just behind thousands of humans, but the veil on magic makes it so not a one sees it.

"Took you long enough. We've got to get this show on the road. Or did you forget you're the sole reason the world's about to end?"

No, Laurel. I definitely did not.

Laurel leads the way down a side hallway to a door that reads KNIGHTS ONLY, where the rest of our group waits. An electronic key pad sits to the left, and when I tug the doorknob, it doesn't budge.

"You honestly think we didn't check?" Jaleesa snaps.

"I'm surprised you didn't already barge through," I say.

Jaleesa rolls her eyes. "We were waiting for the great and powerful Barrett to show up, but you were acting like a scared little pup." She pitches her voice to sound like a little kid. And honestly, that's exactly how I feel right now.

With a deep breath and magic in my fingers, I craft a tiny keycard, like one you'd use to get into a hotel room, and imbue my magic with the intention of opening the door. Just one swipe and the door beeps, so Laurel is able to open it.

We step through into another hallway lined with doors. Each has ornate cursive labels painted on it. ELECTRICITY CLOSET. GREEN ROOM. SECURITY. We make our way down the hall, until Ori points at the last door on the right. PROPS CLOSET. "Here goes nothing."

He swings the door open. We collectively hold our breath, anticipating security, an attack, anything other than . . .

Nothing. At least in terms of anything trying to stop us.

"The most important weapon known to magickind, and it doesn't even have a lock on the door?" Ori asks, finding Jameson. "What is with magicians?"

We step inside to find shields in color-spectrum order lining the right wall; row upon row of flamboyant flags and tunics with different coats of arms sit opposite. Dozens of empty sets of knight armor stand at attention throughout the room, and on the back wall, placed safely on racks, are as many lances and swords. Meema said the Knife's namesake was turned into a sword, but not a one of these stands out as a legendary, Depraved-slaying weapon.

"All right, great and powerful Barrett," Laurel says. "Where is it?"

I look to Jameson for help. "Any ideas?"

"I'd venture you should start there." He gestures to the wall of swords.

They're stacked five deep, in three columns of six rows. Ninety blades to choose from. This is it. This is where I find the tool that gets us to the claw. And if I mess this up, we're royally screwed. My back itches as the group's eyes linger on me, waiting for me to act.

Waiting. Waiting. Waiting.

I could do a summoning spell, but I don't know which of the swords to summon. Maybe if I touch each weapon something in the one we need will react, but that could take a while.

"Okay, fine!" Ori says as if I asked him to do anything in the first place. He steps up beside me, but a thorn-heavy rose bush blossoms at our feet, pushing us apart.

"Not so fast, boys," Laurel says, her voice thick with contempt.

"Chill, Poison Ivy," Ori says. "I'm not going to touch him."

She eyes us up and down, until finally Jameson says, "Let them try."

I step next to Ori again, not touching him, but close enough that I can feel his warmth. Close enough that I can feel his breath against my cheek as he whispers, "You can do this."

My whole body lights up with his closeness, especially after how standoffish he's been since the aftermath of the second challenge. My magic responds in the most literal way possible. My fingers blare with gold, a lighthouse's worth of illumination.

"Turn that down, would you?" Jaleesa snaps, covering her eyes, but the light only grows brighter when, above our heads, another golden glow matches my own. In the middle column, fourth row up, three swords deep, one of the dozens of weapons shines back at us. I didn't even have to do a spell. Just the presence of my magic is enough to make it light up.

The Knife's knife. A piece of magical history, hanging in a prop closet.

"That's the one," I say, and let my magic pool into my middle finger and thumb. I bring them to my lips and blow, letting loose a piercing whistle. Effortlessly, the blade rises from its resting place, then floats down into my waiting hand. Its weight feels right, familiar somehow, even though I've never held a weapon like this in my life. With its hilt against my skin, I swear the thing vibrates a bit, and a dull glow lights its blade even though there's no more magic waiting in my fingers. With this sword, I feel unstoppable.

I turn to the group, the sword raised over my head.

"At least you didn't mess *that* up," Laurel says, dampening the mood so thoroughly I'd swear she was a water nymph.

Jaleesa gags. "I guess we better get on with the whole"—gag, heave—"swallowing your blood. What do you do, just slice yourself with the sword?"

Now I'm the one gagging at the thought of seeing my own blood. Which creates an opening for a grating, rattling voice to clamor from within a suit of arms.

"I think we can help with the slicing."

As one, five of the suits of armor step forward. In a flash of sickening green light, their metal plates burst outward, revealing five decaying Depraved, twisted grins gleaming, ready to kill.

CHAPTER TWENTY-THREE

The Depraved spring into action. A streak of green lightning blasts directly toward Laurel, who summons a mini-pine tree from the ground as a shield. Or at least, attempts to. The Depraved's magic slams into the newly formed pine and it bursts into splinters. The power pierces through and collides with Laurel. She falls to the ground along with a shower of wood, unmoving.

"Laurel!" Jaleesa cries, her voice cracking. But she's too busy dodging her own Depraved enemy to help; the monster's keeping her moving, preventing her from singing a spell.

I only have half a second to worry about them before the Depraved closest to me charges. Its clawlike fingers are outstretched, ready to inflict who knows what curse. My body reacts instinctively and I swing my sword.

Fwing!

The blade sings as it arcs down, then

Thwack! Thunk!

It slices through the Depraved's arm. The monster lets loose a blood-curdling shriek. Thick sludge oozes out of the wound at its elbow. It pours slowly, like molasses, and smells like a bank of porta-potties at a rodeo.

While my eyes are trained on my newly discovered amputation skills, another Depraved strikes my blade with its magic. The weapon flies across the room and slams against the wall of swords at exactly the same time that Jameson—with conjured golden ram horns—tosses a fourth Depraved head over heels into the same wall. Swords fall to the ground but bounce harmlessly off the monster. These are all props. The Knife's sword is the only one that can do damage.

Jameson takes advantage of the chaos and curses the fallen Depraved. He's over the monster in a heartbeat, dotting the air with his fingers, leaving tiny golden drops of rain that fall onto his attacker. Each time they land, the drops sizzle and hiss, acid rains that turns the Depraved to sludgy pulp.

Like a deranged spider, another Depraved scales the empty sword wall all the way to the ceiling, its fingers and toes finding purchase so it can hang upside down by one hand and use the other to blast us with its evil lightning.

Ori's found a toy knight and covered it in his pink power, turning it into an effigy of the Depraved that attacked Laurel. Ori uses the knight's fake sword to poke it over and over, and the Depraved jerks and twists, shrieking with each stab of the sword. But even as it becomes a living pin cushion, it still gets closer.

I let my power pool in my hands and conjure my lasso, forced to mimic the Depraved's jerky steps while I dodge its buddy's attempts to kill me from the ceiling. I'm jumping and dashing, hoping to find anything I can hide behind, but the shields in this room are all just cheap plastic. Then Jameson spells the ceiling so it turns to putty, causing the Depraved to fall with a thud.

My lasso is finally complete and I let the rope fly. It tangles in the stilted steps of the Depraved coming for Ori, sending the monster tumbling to the ground just as a blast of power leaves its fingertips. It zaps the knight figurine out of Ori's hands, leaving him defenseless.

I yank my rope taut, cinching it around the Depraved's ankle and pulling it toward me. My rope's tight enough that it also trips the other two, who were cornering Jaleesa.

"Now, boys, while the monsters are down." Jameson's chest heaves as he catches his breath. "It's time to test your focus. Use your magics together and stop this."

Jaleesa gasps. "Did I hear that right? They could make even more monsters for us to fight!"

Ori and I catch eyes and he gives one small shake of his head. I can't say I disagree.

"We can't," I say. "Too many innocent people could get hurt." I mean, there are thousands literally one room over, sitting ducks.

"You said yourself that your magics started this and might be needed to end it. All it will take is *focus.*" Jameson says it like it's the easiest thing in the world, like we weren't just put on trial by the other senior magicians for using our powers together. Like he can read my thoughts, Jameson adds, "Progress is never made by staying frozen in the past. You *can* do this. The innocent people outside of this room are precisely why you must act now. They're defenseless targets."

As if on cue, the Depraved nearest the door runs into the hallway with a cackle.

Jameson has one last blunt observation. "Your hesitation could cost lives!" He waves a glowing hand over his feet, then directs his glare at Ori. "You of all people know how much pain death at the hands of the Depraved can cause." Ori's mouth drops open while Jameson bolts after the runaway monster, his shoes spelled to run supernaturally fast.

Talk about dropping a bomb. But there's no time to deal with its aftermath. While we were distracted, the Depraved that I tripped have snapped to their feet and joined the third, all of them pulling in a breath in sync. They look exactly like I do when I'm summoning power.

"Ori, move!" He leaps to the side just as the three remaining Depraved vomit, sludge bursting from their lips like water from a fire hose. It coats the ground in front of them, sizzling. The tide of vomit pushes Ori, Jaleesa, and me toward the back wall, next to a crumpled Laurel. The room is covered in their bile, only the thin strip of floor where we're standing unaffected. Two of the three Depraved leave for the hallway as human screams float through the still-open door. The remaining one inhales, and a tendril of hungry drool drips from its mouth.

"You're gaining a reputation, Barrett," it says in its hoarse, cracked voice, licking its lips as more screams echo from the arena. "Chaos and fear follow you everywhere. So much to feed on. We thought the Guild was good for feasts before, but it has nothing on you!" With a hideous cry, the Depraved joins its friends down the hall.

As if I didn't feel bad enough already, the Depraved has found a way to make it worse. And we're trapped by the rotten vomit lapping at our feet.

"It really *is* you," Jaleesa says, wincing as the screams get louder from the arena. "Feeding the Depraved. If we didn't need you to get to the claw, I'd find a way to stop you myself." She inches along the back wall, directly in front of me, so I'm forced to press myself against it as she kneels next to Laurel.

"Get up and go.

No naps to take.

Heal. Rise.

Open. Wake."

Laurel's eyes snap open, and she shakily gets to her feet.

"What happened?" she asks, taking a step forward. Her foot slips through the pool of Depraved vomit and disappears into the floor, as though into quicksand. Jaleesa reaches out just in time and snatches Laurel back by the bicep. Her foot comes out of the sludge with a *pop*, her shoe pulled off and sinking into the floor.

"I thought I lost you," Jaleesa says quietly.

Laurel's eyes shine. "I'm here," she whispers.

Neither of them moves, Jaleesa's hand resting on Laurel's arm, saying so much without saying anything at all. My heart squeezes, wishing Ori would look at me like that again. We're supposed to be the ones with some sort of love connection. Not that you'd know it by the destruction we've caused, by how far apart we keep from each other, even when we're forced into close proximity like this.

"I hate to interrupt this moment, but we've got to move." Ori motions to the Depraved magic lapping dangerously close to his sneakers.

Jaleesa moves quickly, lacing her fingers through Laurel's. It makes my skin itch to remember how nice that felt when Ori did the same to me.

"The battle's not done.

No time to gloat.

Rise. Fly.

Move. Float."

They fly into the air with a purple glow and, pointing her fist forward like some cheesy superhero, Jaleesa leads them out of the props closet. Ori and I lean against the wall, the sludge threatening to swallow us if we don't get moving.

"Do you think it's possible?" Ori asks. "To do what Jameson said?"

"Focus our power?"

Ori nods.

"What if we can't?" I ask. "What if it's worse?"

"It's just . . . Jameson was right. I *do* know how terrible it is to lose someone to the Depraved. More people could be in that arena, dying at the hands of those monsters right now, and once again I won't have done anything to stop it."

"Ori, I—"

"Don't. Don't you think I know what he was doing? Jameson was trying to manipulate me to act using the memory of the person I love most. But it doesn't make what he said any less true." He winces as a fresh wave of screams barrels through the open door. "The way I see it, we have two options. One, we stay here and people die. Two, we work together, at least try to focus our magics, and maybe save someone."

"Or maybe kill them," I say flatly. Meema's scowling face gallops through my brain, warning me against teaming up with Ori again. Telling me to stay focused or destroy our family reputation. "Or unleash who knows what on all of Vegas. That Depraved said our magic can feed them. We can't risk making this mess *bigger*, Ori."

"It's not like I want that either." Ori stares me straight in the eye. "But we can't hide from this. Magic takes time to learn. There's this memory I have; I know you saw it. That time I spelled my sister and she hit her head on the ceiling?"

My mouth twitches into a small smile.

"You know the one," Ori says. "But even though she got hurt, she still wanted me to learn how to control my magic. The stakes might be higher now, but the lesson remains the same. We just have to harness whatever is going on between us."

He's got a point. I didn't know how to use my magic when it first manifested. I turned our chickens into pudding cups, I blew out the windows in our living room. But I learned. I got better.

A warmth builds near my shoulder. Ori's holding his arm out, leaving an open space against his side for me to lean into. The last thing I ever thought broody, grumpy Ori would do.

"Hey." He motions with his head toward his shoulder. This time, I don't hesitate. I lean into him, and Ori folds his arm around me. It's clumsy and awkward since I'm so much taller than him, but I don't care. My body buzzes, alight with his touch, and I know Ori feels it, too. He catches my eye and smirks.

We're going to do this.

My mouth breaks into a huge grin. Way to keep your cool, Nigel.

"Are you just going to grin like an idiot all day, or what?" Ori says, somehow still all sarcasm but now warm and accepting.

"Let's go kick some bad-guy ass," I respond, and Ori rolls his eyes before blinking us away.

We land with a gale force gust of air at the top of the Tournament of Kings arena. The wind pops a few of the buttons open on my flannel, and Ori's hair billows in the breeze of our jump.

"Shit," he breathes. "I just meant to go the hallway. I've never blinked that far with another person before."

"You all right?" I ask.

He nods, his eyes wandering down to my exposed stomach. His Adam's apple bobs as he swallows.

My cheeks blaze as I watch his throat. "I guess our connec—"

I'm nearly trampled by a stampede of people trying to escape the arena. Ori grabs my wrist and blinks us to the top of one of the nearby tables, from which we have a clear view of what's got everyone so terrified.

Jameson stands in the center of the ring over one of the Depraved, a lance now glowing with his power pierced through the monster's middle. He jerks the weapon out of its body and throws it at the other three Depraved. It must be spelled to hone in on the monsters because the lance zips and swerves through the air, trying to skewer our attackers. But the Depraved move fast, and they've changed now. All of them have shifted, grown taller, their limbs and bodies thicker than before, their sickly green eyes shining bright. Crimson scratches against Jameson's brown skin prove that they're even more dangerous in these new bodies.

"What the hell happened to them?" I ask. "I've never seen Depraved like that before."

"There's so much panic," Ori says. "It's a Depraved buffet."

While humans might not be able to see magic, they can see monsters in the flesh, and it's no wonder that these rotting assholes have freaked them out.

Jaleesa and Laurel fly above the action, Laurel blooming tangles of weeds and thistle to trip up the Depraved so Jameson can kill them. But the Depraved are so thick now that the weeds snap apart as their feet careen through them.

It's such a medieval-looking scene I'm surprised the showgoers didn't think it was part of the Excalibur act. But the very real fire spreading across the stands, burning tablecloths and Cornish hens and melting beer steins, must have snapped them to their senses.

Jameson's voice magically bellows through the arena as his magic lance returns to his outstretched hand. "Boys! End this!"

The Depraved turn in unison, squinting at Ori and me on our tabletop in the stands. They don't brace themselves for our attack.

None of them so much as takes a step in our direction. They just shrug and get back to battling Jameson.

"They don't think we'll do it," Ori says.

"Or they don't think we can control ourselves. They *want* us to combine our magic. They want it to get out of hand."

Wham!

"AAAAAARGH!"

I spin to see Jameson punched by a massive Depraved fist, smashing hard against the arena wall and sliding down it, unconscious. Instead of screeching with victory, the Depraved stand over him and throw up.

Ori gags. "They really need to get their stomach problems looked at."

It's the same sickening vomit from the props closet, covering Jameson. The sludge bubbles and pops as it pools beneath him, turning the floor into that quicksand. If we don't act fast, he'll sink through and drown.

From up above, Laurel shouts, "Just do something already!"

The growl in her voice reminds me of Dad's. The clear *annoyance*. Laurel thinks I'm pathetic, and even though it's for a different reason than Dad thinks, I can't help but feel small and pitiful at the blatant disdain.

I'm sick of it. There's a fire in my belly that is ready to prove them wrong. All of them. Dad. Laurel. Meema and the senior magicians who think my magic needs to be contained. These disgusting Depraved assholes who think I'm some tool they can use to wreak havoc.

Screw every last one of them.

I wind my fingers through Ori's. "Let's do this."

He looks at our hands, his thumb—whether absentmindedly or not—making gentle circles against my skin. "We're sure, right?"

"Never been more sure in my life."

"All right." Ori turns his glare on the Depraved. "This one's for Cassie."

We blink and my boots hit the dirt, where I'm instantly in my element. Earth, rocks, hay. These are the things I love to feel beneath my feet, the terrain where I know how to move.

"We need to curse them," I say. "Something that can do damage, and quick, to all three."

"I made just two effigies in that medical bay and it awakened the entire Horde," Ori says. "I think one will do here." He scoops up a pile of dirt and molds it into a ball, then jabs two fingers into the top and swipes one horizontally through the bottom half, a makeshift effigy head now in his hands. He soaks it with power. "Now's your turn, cowboy. What's the curse?"

As my mind whirs with ideas, I watch Depraved vomit pour down Jameson's body, tendrils of bile oozing like twisted snakes.

"Snakes!" I cry, just as Jaleesa dives from above, pulling Jameson out of the sludge. She carries him thirty feet up to join Laurel, still floating thanks to her girlfriend's magic. That leaves us totally exposed, three sets of evil eyes zeroing in on us.

But I'm ready.

Ori grips my shoulder, his fingers filling me up with his unstoppable warmth. My hands blaze gold with power, and in one swift movement I mold it into a yard-long tube. I channel my anger at these Depraved to give it some bite, pulling two fangs out of one end. The snake springs to life, hissing and slithering in my hands.

This is it. This is the moment when I need to focus. The moment when I unleash my power on Ori's effigy and our combined magics could stop the Depraved—or spiral out of control. *Poison the Depraved. Stop the Depraved.* Only *the Depraved.*

"Now!" Ori yells, and my magic snake strikes. It sinks its fangs into the muddy effigy in Ori's hands, just a second before the Depraved unleash their power on us.

But that second is all we needed.

On contact, Ori's effigy, my snake, and all the Depraved glow that brilliant abalone of our combined powers. It drowns out the rotten green of the monsters, so bright I have to shield my eyes. I feel elated; I feel powerful; I feel unstoppable.

Then come the screams, piercing and high. The light of our magic dims enough for us to see the Depraveds' mouths twisted in pain. Each has two gory wounds on their cheek, in the exact spot my snake clamped down on Ori's effigy. Our abalone magic gushes down their bodies from the holes, their decayed skin burning from their skeletons.

The first two collapse into a pile of bones. The third hangs on, its face warped with agony. But with one last fiery-eyed look, it points a cracked and bloody nail at me and says, "You will always feed the rest of us! While the Guild stands, we thrive!"

Guilt bubbles in my gut, draining my confidence. Yet another Depraved saying the work I do gives them strength. As my conviction dies, our abalone magic recedes from the last Depraved, whose pained shrieks turn to laughter.

"Don't listen to it." Ori laces his fingers through mine, and my whole body lights up like a carnival ride. "We can end this."

I feel his confidence through our touch, his need to stop the Depraved once and for all. His surety boosts me and our power grows stronger, fighting back until the monster joins its partners as bones. Ori's effigy crumbles back into dirt, and my snake curls in on itself before disappearing in a burst of gold.

I glance up at Jameson, Laurel, and Jaleesa, all floating down to the arena, completely untouched by our power. As their feet hit the ground, the warmth of a spell perfectly performed fills me.

Every Depraved in the arena, stopped. No other victims harmed. Our power did exactly what we wanted.

We *can* be a force for good. All it takes is focus.

Only, why can't I stop thinking about that Depraved's final words?

While the Guild stands, we thrive.

They don't seem to bother Ori. His face splits into the biggest grin, making my heart stop. "We kicked their asses!"

"About time," Laurel says as she wafts some magicked plant over Jameson's nose that brings him back to consciousness. "Can we finally stop messing around and get to the claw?"

"But what about—" I sweep my arms from the arena littered with the aftermath of our battle to the doorway from which all those tourists fled.

Jameson waves a golden hand over himself to clear the remaining Depraved barf. "There's an entire floor of the Guild dedicated to wiping memories of monsters from human minds. This will not be difficult for them to deal with. If the humans try to talk about it, they'll find they have no memory of the event. If they took any footage, it'll transform into an ever-distracting cat meme."

"I'm getting bored." Jaleesa snaps her fingers to grab my attention. "You got the sword?"

My fingers suddenly itch with their emptiness. Why is it that even when I do something right, I've also gotta make some birdbrained mistake? "I, uh, left it back in the props closet. I'll just—"

I use the charge from Ori's touch to let magic pool in my fingers, then place them in my mouth and blow. I laugh nervously while we wait for the sword, which finally bursts into the room, glowing gold, and lands in my hand. Everyone stares, expecting something to happen, but as seconds drag on, Laurel finally says, "Are you going to use that thing, or . . ."

My stomach twists into knots and my vision gets fuzzy at what I know we've got to do. But the rodeo must go on, so I squeeze tighter on Ori's hand to keep my head clear. "W-we need my blood." I look at Jameson, whose stare is unreadable. "Do I just . . ." I mock stabbing myself with the sword.

Jameson shakes his head. "Just a shallow cut to the palm would suffice."

He stares at me expectantly. Laurel and Jaleesa look at me hungrily. The only person who seems disturbed at all by this is Ori, his forehead scrunched with worry.

"Okay, then." I let out a shaky breath. "Here goes nothing."

I let go of Ori's hand, and the sudden coldness sends sickly goose bumps up my arm. With my left palm out, I squeeze the sword in my right. My hand is slick with sweat, and the hilt slips as I try to get a good grip. With my luck, this thing will slide out of my hand at just the right moment and I'll impale myself. I'll bleed out and be gone from the Guild and this earth. All because I'm an anxious, blood-phobic moron.

I will my shaky hands to steady, bringing the tip of the sword a centimeter over my palm. All it will take is one little cut, like slicing open a tomato—gentle so as not to squish it, but firm enough so the cut is clean.

I can do this.

My heart races.

I can do this.

I try to bring the sword to my skin.

"I can't do this." The words are out of my mouth before I realize I've made a decision.

Laurel throws her hands up, while Jaleesa says, "Not trying to be rude, but we are totally screwed."

"We are *not* screwed, you washed up Dr. Seuss." Ori wraps his hand around my own, steadying my sweaty palm on the hilt of the sword. "We can do this."

I catch his eyes, and I'm back in his mind. He knows what it's like to freeze. We're both envisioning that lakeshore, watching as the Depraved killed his sister, desperate to do something, anything, but unable to move a muscle.

"We can do this."

I don't know if he says it out loud again, if his words just echo in my mind, or if our connection is strong enough now that we can speak through our thoughts. But either way, I know without a shadow of a doubt that together, we can make this cut.

As one, we gently lower the blade and draw a thin line down the center of my palm. Red blossoms up, barely as wide as a needle, the cut so clean that I hardly feel it. I expect nausea to rise at any second, but it never comes. Maybe it's because my skin is so focused on Ori's contact, on how long and gentle his fingers are, on how he knows just the right amount of pressure to apply to the blade so as not to go deep while still piercing the skin. He's confident, assured, smooth, soft.

"Are you okay?" Ori asks.

"Mm-hmm."

"It didn't hurt, did it?"

I shake my head.

"I told you we could do it."

It takes everything in me not to lean forward and kiss his quirked lips.

"The spell will only work if we each consume a drop of Barrett's blood," Jameson says, and even still, I can't look away from Ori's mouth. Can't stop thinking about the fact that Ori's lips will be in contact with my skin in just a few seconds.

Ori takes his steadying hand off mine, leaving me to hold the sword by myself. I get a chill without his touch, but it only lasts a second. Just as gently as before, Ori uses both hands to take my cut one, holding it like it's the most delicate thing in the world, like one wrong move could break me.

I have the urge to snap my hand away out of fear that his touch might heal me and we'll have to do it all over again. But the healing doesn't come. It's not needed. Not wanted. Not our intent.

Ori brings my hand to his lips, then stops for the briefest second. I swear it takes everything in me not to groan. My entire being needs to know what it's like to feel his lips against my body, even if it is just my hand.

And then, finally, he moves that last inch. His soft, pillowy lips seal over the edge of my palm, his upper lip just far enough inside that it touches the edge of the cut. There's the briefest flare of heat, and I don't know if it's because the wound is agitated or because I can just barely feel the tip of his tongue caress my skin. And then it's over.

Ori pulls back, the smirk gone, something deeper written on his face. Some acknowledgment that that's the most physical contact we've ever had, and there's no forgetting that. There's no going back. No way we'd ever not wonder what it would be like to go further than a gentle kiss to my hand.

What else could we kiss?

My stomach does loops at the thought, a wild mustang running free.

And then, my hand is yanked away from his, and I'm disoriented by the sudden pull out of his spell.

"Okay, what part did you lick?" Laurel asks. "I am not trying to swap spit with all of you. Why was your great-grandpa such a perv, Barrett?"

She presses a tip of her finger to the opposite side of the cut, and it stings like hell as she swipes a smear of blood. With her eyes screwed shut tight, she presses it to her tongue and jerks my hand in Jaleesa's direction.

"Seriously, this is *not* hygienic," the fae says, pressing her thumb into the center of my cut, then sucking on it like a little kid.

"Using blood as a spell activator is one of the most sure security methods," Jameson explains, taking my hand with a surprising amount of care. "It must be warm, given voluntarily, and from a beating heart, ensuring no one will kill you or your offspring. Maybe Barrett was worried someone was after him and his family."

Jameson pads a bead of blood onto his finger, then licks it away with a flick of his tongue.

A flare of purple light pulls me out of my thoughts as a portal opens in the stands. It's opaque, offering no glimpse of what's on the other side, but something in my bones tells me we'll be okay. The sword glows gold in my hand, my body relaxing into the familiar comfort of elf power. But more than that, it feels like a part of me. A part of my blood. Like it's a wink from Great-Gpa Barrett, reassuring me from beyond the grave. Then, in a flash, the sword disappears, its mission accomplished.

"All that's needed now is a song to activate the portal," Jameson says.

Everyone turns to me, even though I'm not the fae of the group.

"Um . . ." Of course, I'm drawing a blank. I look at Ori. "Swiftie, got any ideas?"

His eyes flick to Laurel and Jaleesa. "Not here."

"Come on! I need some help."

Ori sighs. "Fine." He clears his throat. "Here goes nothing." He takes a deep breath and sings,

"The Horde ain't gonna stay, stay, stay, stay, stay.
Gotta stop the Depraved, 'praved, 'praved, 'praved, 'praved.
We'll shake 'em off.
To the claw!"

Triggered by Ori's remix, the portal glows brighter. Laurel and Jaleesa look at him, open-mouthed, while Jameson's blank-faced, but I'm smiling so big my face hurts. "That was perfect!"

"Yeah, let's never speak of this moment again." Ori covers his face with one hand and grabs mine with the other. There's a tickle in my palm and I watch my cut seal. Ori's thumb caresses my wrist, soft and gentle, almost as if he's wiping the pain away.

With each swipe, I feel my confidence boost. Ori and I *can* control our magic. We can get the claw, we can stop the Horde, we can defeat the Knife if it comes to that.

We'll do it together.

I look at Ori, look at those lips that, when all this is over, I'll do anything to feel on my skin again.

Then I turn to the group. "Y'all coming, or what?"

Pulling Ori behind me, I step into the light.

CHAPTER TWENTY-FOUR

Even when my boots hit the ground, it takes me a while to realize I've made it through the portal. There's just so much light, at first I think I'm still inside the swirling mass of magic. My eyes take a second to adjust, watering as they get used to the brightness.

When everything finally comes into focus, it takes my breath away.

"Whooee."

"Jesus," Ori breathes beside me. Laurel and Jaleesa actually seem impressed with something for once, too. Jameson, as always, is unreadable.

We're in a football field–size cavern full of gold, glittering from the floor, the ceiling, the walls. It's like the elf wing back at the Guild but on steroids. And the more I look, the more I realize this isn't just a random assortment of sparkling rocks; they're perfectly placed to form patterns, one specific shape repeating over and over.

A bear.

"Gramps." I can feel him permeating this room, somehow. Maybe it's some ancient spell I know nothing about. Or maybe it's just the pull of family, tugging at my heart from centuries past. I step forward and rest my hand on a bear glittering in gold. Steely determination settles in my gut.

Pulling back, I take in the hundreds of other bears glowing from the walls. Each looks in the same direction, toward the back of the cavern. I follow their path to the end of the room, and stop just feet away from a pedestal where the real-life claw lays on a gold surface.

It's . . . unremarkable, a chipped and scratched, grayish-black curve of keratin. The only hints at its power are the images on the back wall. They show Grandpa sacrificing his human form to become a bear, cracking the heartstone in the Knife's crown with one swoop of his paw. His claw—the same claw before us—glows brightest on the mural.

"That's it?" Laurel's skepticism echoes through the hall, mirroring my own uncertainty. "It was, like, glowing in the vision back in the Guild tower. You're telling me that little nub is supposed to stop the deadliest monster magickind has ever seen?"

Jameson nods. "It already has, and it will again." He turns to me, solemn. "If a descendant of Barrett wields it once more."

I stand there, unmoving. I'm not ready yet. Surrounded by these images of my great-grandpa, I'm not sure I can live up to his reputation. I'm not sure I can save the world.

"Come *on*." Jaleesa reaches for the claw. "Let's grab this thing and get gone."

"STOP!" Jameson's shout makes Jaleesa freeze, almost as if *he's* the fae. "Only a Barrett may remove it from the pedestal. If anyone else tries, it will kill them on the spot."

Jaleesa swallows. "I was just, um, stretching." She looks to Laurel for support, and the nymph nods her head once but steps back.

"Riiiiight," Ori says, but his face transforms from skepticism to encouragement when he looks at me. "Go on, Nigel. Grab it."

Looking into Ori's eyes, I take a deep breath and extend my hand. This is it. The moment I'll wield the greatest weapon the Guild has ever used. The moment that will connect me to my long-dead great-grandpa, whose legendary shadow I might finally be able to step out of.

My fingers wrap around the rough keratin, and I pull the claw from the pedestal. I expect something to happen, for the claw to light up like the Knife's transformed sword or, I don't know, harps to play, or Grandpa Barrett's voice to echo in my head. Anything at all. But the claw just sits heavy in my hands.

"I, uh . . . I guess we can go now."

Ori looks at me expectantly and Jameson has a soft smile on his lips, but Laurel and Jaleesa are turned away, whispering to each other. Laurel nudges Jaleesa, her hand tentative on Jaleesa's shoulder, and Jaleesa keeps shaking her head.

"Hey, look," I say. "I know as well as anyone that when you're *into* somebody, it's easy to get distracted. But this was my big moment, and I'd appreciate a little attention."

Laurel and Jaleesa turn, but they don't at all seem like lovestruck girlfriends. Laurel has a look of grim determination on her face while Jaleesa's eyes water.

"Another lover's quarrel?" I guess.

"Something like that," Laurel says. She turns to her girlfriend. "You ready?"

Jaleesa takes a deep, shaking breath, then nods. In a flash, her neck glows purple. She sings lyrics so fast the words practically meld together.

"Nowhere to go.

You're all out of luck.

Can't take a step.

You're simply stuck."

My feet fuse to the golden ground. Jameson's and Ori's, too.

"Oh hell no." Ori moves for his backpack, but Jaleesa's magical distraction is working. While we're focused on our feet, Laurel snaps her fingers, making three bursts of leaves wrap around our necks. It catches me so off guard that I drop the claw. The vines are spotted with purple flowers and berries so dark purple they're almost black, but they're free of thorns and loose enough that I can breathe.

Honestly, they don't seem that dangerous. "Uh, thanks for the snack?"

"It's nightshade, you idiot." Laurel sneers, tossing her auburn braids over her shoulder. "One of the most poisonous plants on the planet. A little will make you pass out, but if any of you so much as moves a muscle, or I see one sparkle of magic, I'll shove so much down your throats that you'll die."

"Laurel!" Jaleesa sounds genuinely surprised. "Nobody said anything about killing."

Laurel's sneer melts into a sympathetic frown. "You don't have to, babe. I promise. Just grab the nub and we'll get out of here."

Jaleesa dashes over to the claw.

"Jaleesa, I'd advise against it," Jameson says in his even tone. "Remember the curse."

Laurel grins wickedly, and I swear her canines have gotten longer. "Oh, we remember it perfectly. But we don't have to touch it, do we, babe?" She walks over to her girlfriend and grabs her hand. "I know this is a lot, but it'll be better for us this way. We can be together."

Jaleesa softens at that, but still she doesn't seem confident. Her eyes dart between Jameson and Laurel.

"Don't do this, Jaleesa," I say. "Whatever *this* is. Some play to get us out of the Culling? Don't take away our chance to join the Guild because of stupid pettiness. Think of your mom. Think of how much she loves magic. You'd willingly work to take someone's away, instead of proving you belong in the Guild with your own talent?"

Jaleesa tightens her grip on Laurel's hand, and a flare of magic passes between their palms. A flare of purple and green, twining together. For a second I think I see the colors of their magic start to blend into a new shade, and it reminds me an awful lot of the magic between Ori and me.

But Jaleesa's too frustrated to notice the power forming between them. Her face twists as she screams, "SHUT UP!"

My lips seal shut. Ori's and Jameson's, too. She looks at us, surprised, like even she didn't expect to spell us. It's clear that this was a sudden boost in her power, all while her fingers are wrapped up in her girlfriend's.

This is so familiar.

What if this magic of love is passing between Laurel and Jaleesa, too? But with my lips sealed, there's no way to tell them.

Laurel fills our silence with her harsh and bitter laughter. "You think *you* belong in the Guild?" With a snap of her fingers, tendrils of ivy curl around the claw and lift it from the ground. "You? *You* unleashed the Horde. Next comes the Knife. It would be best for all of us if you two disappeared, so you can't cause this kind of chaos again." Her nightshade pushes up against my lips. I'm actually grateful for Jaleesa's spell keeping them sealed shut.

"Laurel. Stop!" Purple magic slaps Laurel's nightshade away. But Laurel doesn't look angry or betrayed. She just looks sad.

"Hey." Laurel pulls Jaleesa in for a hug, and the fae's tears finally spill over. "It's going to be okay. This is going to be what it takes for Dad to finally let us be together. He won't worry about who I love if we can show that we're strong, that we have the Guild's best interests at heart. We'll prove we're so powerful together that he won't be able to deny us anymore. I know it."

Jaleesa runs a hand under her nose, sniffling. "How can you be sure? How can I know you won't just push me away again the second he hurts you?"

"All he cares about is power," Laurel says. "He was livid when I didn't get to the Guild first in the initial challenge. I only pushed you away because he made me. He said—" Laurel's voice catches, but with a defiant shake of her head, she clears her throat and continues. "He said our relationship wasn't natural, and the only proof he needed was that I wasn't performing up to his expectations. But if we can do this, *together*, I know we can show him that we're stronger as a couple than we are apart. This is what it will take to have my magic, my family, *and* you."

Jaleesa's quiet, contemplating, and we're just left to stand there while they decide our fate. I try to make eye contact with Ori, but he's staring straight ahead. Jameson, too, taking in our captors like he's watching somebody discuss the weather.

"Okay," Jaleesa whispers. She takes a breath and sings.

"Mouths unstuck.
Open wide.
Nightshade ready,
To turn the tide."

The spell sealing our lips vanishes, and the nightshade moves in. I slam my lips closed, but the berries smush against them, juice leaking from their skin.

"Come on," Laurel coos mockingly. "Just a little sip. Just enough to knock you out, so the Guild can come in when all this is over and take your magic."

Jameson blows out and a burst of golden air incinerates the nightshade in front of his face. In two quick huffs, he aims bursts of his breath at the berries taunting Ori and me too.

"Girls, honestly, do you think you could defeat a senior magician that easily?" Jameson says it almost playfully, lightly teasing. "You're good kids. I've known you your entire lives, and I'd hoped you'd come around on your own. You've always wanted what's best for the greater good, but in this case you're wrong. Your decisions will actively hinder the Guild's plans. The claw can only be used to defeat the Knife by a Barrett. You may be able to transport it, but you can't tap into its true power."

Ouch. Is that the only reason Jameson is upset that I'm being attacked? Because I'm needed to wield the claw? Why not because, you know, it's bad to go after your fellow apprentices?

Only, that's never been the Guild's stance, has it? Just like Bex said, this place was never about forging bonds.

"That's what Adela's for," Laurel says. "We don't need these morons. They'll only make things worse." Her fingers flare green, and the ground rumbles. Thorny tendrils burst from the stone, just like when we met during that first trial. I know if I don't do something, she'll be sure they kill me this time.

"Wait! You have our power, too," I blurt. "The same one that Ori and I have."

Jameson's head whips in my direction, while Ori says, "Say what now?"

Meanwhile, Jaleesa's mouth has fallen open and Laurel's vines recede. "We do?" they ask together.

"I saw it when you touched. The way your magics started joining, becoming one. It's what made you seal our mouths shut without meaning to, Jaleesa. I'm sure of it. I've done so many things I never saw coming since meeting Ori. When we touch."

"The Depraved have a magic fueled by hate." Ori's jumped in, and my heart pounds with conviction. It's up to us to convince them before they walk away with the claw—and our last chance at fixing this mess. "Is it so much of a stretch to believe there could also be a magic fueled by love? In magicians, it only makes our powers stronger."

Ori and I share a look. I wish Bex were here right now to see how she's been right all along. It's not just some theory; it's the truth, and we've got a second couple here to prove it.

Jaleesa looks hopeful, her lips parting to speak, but Laurel beats her to it. "That's a nice story, but we're not idiots. If this *love magic* was a thing, why wouldn't other people in the Guild have it?"

Ori laughs. "Come on, you know as well as anybody that the Guild isn't exactly the best training ground for leaning into your feelings. We're trained to distrust our fellow magicians from the start. Your own dad wants to pull you away from your girlfriend. How are feelings supposed to develop in an environment like that?"

"But despite having been taught to go for your competitors' throats, you two have found a way into each other's hearts." I cringe at how sappy I sound. I can't overdo it. "You've just got to lean into that."

Jaleesa sighs. "The more I've tried to lean in, the more she pushes me away."

Laurel, for the first time, looks genuinely hurt. "That's not fair. Once I prove to Dad that we're the best of our class, he'll get off our case. He won't be able to deny that we're better together."

"That's my whole point," I say. "You're better together. Just like Ori and me. *All* of us will be better magicians if we can just go back to the Guild with what we've learned. Show them how connection, not competition, makes magic stronger."

Jaleesa gives a hopeful glance to her girlfriend, while Laurel fiddles with a tendril of star jasmine she's grown at her feet, deep in thought. The longer she pauses, the more her plants wither and recede.

"What do you think?" she asks Jameson. "Do you buy any of this? Has the Guild heard of this kind of power before?"

Jameson eyes me solemnly, quietly, as though weighing what I had to say. I realize too late that we've bared our souls in front of a guy I've never been able to get a read on. Bex warned us not to say anything, and now we've let Jameson in on one more reason to wipe us out—and maybe Jaleesa and Laurel, too—to put a stop to our unusual power.

"I can't say that I have," Jameson says. "But that doesn't mean it's not possible." He glances my way, a slight smile playing at his lips. "And maybe now is the time to lead with love."

Laurel looks back and forth between us, her face furrowed, until . . .

"Never." She curls her fingers, making vines lash around my arms and legs, Ori's too. They squeeze harder and harder, cutting off circulation as they climb to our necks. "It's nice to have dreams about what the Guild can be. But you said it yourself, Nigel: What the Guild is *now* is an organization all about competition. With you two in the way, Jaleesa and I can never stand out."

Jaleesa clears her throat, readying her purple magic. I brace myself for her to sing some back up spell, giving Laurel the opportunity to finally end us. But then . . .

"Heart's changed.

Move about.

Ground soft.

Get out."

The gold caking our feet melts and we're able to crawl out of

Laurel's vines. Tingles shoot up my legs as blood rushes back into them. Ori's already on the move, shrugging out of his plant prison.

"Jaleesa!" Laurel's just as shocked as I am, but she doesn't move from her attack stance. Instead, she latches on to her girlfriend, a flare of their own connected magics supercharging her spell as she makes a massive cactus burst from the floor, spines big enough to impale.

Ori grabs my arm and blinks us out of the way just in time, while Jameson lets gold magic gather in his hands. He holds them out in front of him, ready to strike.

"Don't make me do this," he says. "I'm not in the business of harming apprentices."

Jaleesa shifts nervously. "Laurel."

But Laurel waves her hands so that three bonsai trees sprout in front of them, their trunks twisting together to form a shield. "This is for us, babe. For our future."

To Jameson, Laurel shrugs. "I'd like to see you try."

"So be it."

Jameson blasts power at Laurel's trees, breaking them apart in no time. Laurel goes on the run, growing ivy from the ceiling that snatches the girls from the ground. My first reaction is to laugh. How on earth does Laurel think she can beat a magician who's got thirty years of battle experience on her, especially with Jaleesa clearly not on her side? And how does she think she'll explain away attacking a senior member when she gets out of this?

Jameson moves fast. So fast that Ori and I don't even have to use a whisper of magic. He's one of those magicians who's so strong all he really has to do is flick an arm here, a wrist there to get what he wants to happen. Like now, as he holds one hand directed at each girl, and they stop in their ascent. They just hang there, suspended in midair like puppets hanging from plant strings.

"Enough." He doesn't even yell it. He just says it simply, no room for discussion.

Laurel roars with frustration. "God dammit!" She lowers her hands, sagging in her vines. "I just . . . I just wanted to win for once."

It's the most defeated I've ever heard her sound. Tears actually start to fall as Jameson lowers them to the ground with the wave of one glowing hand, snapping away Laurel's vines with the other.

"There's got to be a better way," Jaleesa says.

When Laurel's feet hit the ground, the tears stop instantly, replaced by a devilish grin, rivaling any I've seen on the Depraved. "There is."

Thunk

Jameson collapses to the ground, the claw clattering beside him.

He doesn't move, his eyes don't open.

"What just happened?" I look at Ori and he's wide-eyed with surprise, too.

Laurel cackles. "I had the claw hidden in my ivy, waiting just over Jameson's body! It's coated in nightshade juice." She points at Jameson, where a scratch mars his waves, blood trickling down his forehead. The claw next to him is glistening wet. "Enough to kill him. Never underestimate a nymph."

"Shit," Ori says as he blinks to his bag of tricks on the other side of the cavern. He's going to create an effigy. It's going to be okay.

I hope.

Meanwhile Laurel sends a new strand of ivy to twist and turn around the claw, creating a makeshift basket that she hoists over her shoulder. "Now that that's dealt with, I think it's time we got out of here, don't you, Jaleesa?"

Jaleesa's face is blank, sweat beading on her forehead as she looks at Jameson. "Y-you killed him."

Laurel pulls Jaleesa to her. "He'll be fine. These boys just have to act fast."

Ori blinks back then and grabs a Miles Morales doll from his bag. My whole body floods with relief when he coats it in his pink power. We can save him.

"They'll have ways of getting the truth out of you, Laurel," I say. "One spell and the entire Guild will know that you attacked a senior magician, that you trapped us here to prevent us from succeeding in the Culling. They'll take your magic for this."

Laurel stalks forward until she's inches from my face. "You don't seriously think we didn't plan for that, do you? There are enchantments to prevent truth spells from working. Magical ways to fortify your mind against intrusion. They've already been cast."

"Nymphs don't have that kind of magic," I say. "You're bluffing."

Laurel shrugs. "Believe what you want. But I think that's enough chit-chat for one day. I need to save my voice for when we tell everyone *exactly* what happened here. You two decided you weren't going to bring the claw back." Laurel's voice bubbles with twisted glee. "You wanted the Knife to succeed. That's what I heard them say, didn't you, Jaleesa?"

Jaleesa doesn't say a thing. It seems she can't even bring herself to look at Laurel, but the nymph is on a roll now. "We had to defend ourselves," Laurel continues. "*We* had to do what was best for the Guild." She walks toward me, slowly, ominously, each step making me wince. "I don't care if what you say is true. If you're stronger than us, Dad will never let us be together. What good is any sort of love magic if I can't be with my girlfriend? Getting rid of you gives me the leverage I need to get exactly what I want." She grabs Jaleesa's hand. "*Who* I want."

I hear Jameson take a shuddering breath. He's alive. But my

relief is short-lived when he coughs and blood spatters his shirt. My head swims, but Ori's voice keeps me steady.

"I can't get the nightshade out," he says, looking up from his effigy to meet my eyes. "Not alone."

With a last look at Laurel, I bend down to his side, placing a hand on his shoulder. Instantly, his effigy glows brighter and Jameson's coughs subside. His eyes remain closed, but his breathing seems easier.

Ori's mouth quirks into that cocky smirk. "It wo—"

In a flash, Laurel's ivy jabs forward, and the claw stabs straight into Ori's chest.

"Ori!" My vision goes red, a flare of heat blooming in the exact spot Ori's been stabbed.

Ori doesn't yell. He doesn't move, just bares his teeth in that smug smile, his grin covered in blood. "You'll regret that, you—"

Laurel's ivy pushes the claw deeper. Ori gurgles, his words cut off by blood. "Not so strong now, are you?"

"Laurel!" Jaleesa shouts. "What have you done?"

My entire body is on fire, our connection somehow sharing Ori's pain with me, along with a deep certainty that Ori is going to die. A knowledge that the claw is millimeters away from piercing his heart. The thought that this weapon—this claw that was supposed to get me out of this mess—is being used to kill the only person I've ever felt connected to sends a whole new emotion through my body.

Anger.

Red-hot rage that sweeps away the pain. I won't let her do this. I can't. Laurel can't take Ori away from me. Can't take that perfect smile, that snarky voice, those gentle fingers that can craft an effigy in a heartbeat, that can wipe away my injuries with a simple touch. Now it's my turn to wipe away his.

My anger runs so deep that my magic responds. This time it doesn't just rush to my fingertips, but makes my whole body glow gold with power. Laurel's confidence wavers. Her smile falls, and she edges closer to Jaleesa.

"You think you can stop us that easily," I say. "We unleashed the Horde, and you think *you* can get in our way?"

There's a flash of light from Laurel's hands. I act without thinking. A sharp golden spur appears in my grasp, and as Laurel sends thorn spears hurtling toward me, I slice each away.

Fwip! Fwip! Fwip! Fwip!

Laurel's hands fall limply to her sides, her chest heaving, drained of power. "Nice try," I say. "You wanted to make sure *we* were stuck here? I'll show you stuck."

All that time poring over elven texts is finally going to pay off. Sure, I thought it would be against the Depraved, but as Meema always says, *Desperate times call for desperate measures, darlin'*.

"I'll show you just how bad a curse can be."

Laurel whips her hand to the side, wrapping her fingers around Jaleesa's wrist. Her magic flares once more, and with a snap of her fingers, her ivy snags the claw from Ori's chest and raises it high.

"Not if I get you first," she growls.

Another snap and her ivy races forward, claw poised to strike. I ready my spur to slice, but I didn't need to bother. Jaleesa sings loud and clear.

"Impossible to use.
Strapped together with bands.
You can't feel your fingers.
You can't use your hands."

Laurel's arms snap to her side, her fingers fusing together. The claw clatters to the floor as her ivy falls.

"I'm so sorry." Jaleesa's eyes shine with tears. "This isn't you, Laurel. Not at all. You have to stop. Before you do something you'll regret for the rest of your life." She turns to me, motioning to Ori, who has blood dribbling from his mouth now. It pools on the gold floor. "Go to him." Then she sings open a portal and pulls Laurel through behind her.

In an instant, they're gone, leaving Ori and me alone, Jameson still unconscious. But I feel so much gratitude for Jaleesa. Whatever else she did, she gave me this opportunity, and I'm not going to waste it.

I fall to my knees at Ori's side, pulling his head onto my shoulder. I can still feel his heartbeat, a phantom pulse matching my own, but it's getting weaker. Ori's blood spurts with each breath, soaking his white shirt, and my head fogs with so much red. But I have to fight it. I squeeze my eyes shut and stroke Ori's back. Our touch has cured each other before. It has to work now, too.

With each stroke, Ori's breathing becomes less ragged. I hear him take a deep breath, as deep as he can manage, and there's no gurgle. He takes another, deeper this time, and I feel that phantom pulse between us beat stronger.

It's working.

But not nearly fast enough for my liking. With just my hands on his back, maybe there's not enough contact for the healing to work quickly. I scoop him up in my arms, our magic connection or maybe my conviction giving me the strength to carry his limp weight.

"Oh, so we're jumping to the wedding carry, huh?" Ori's voice is weak, but I can make out every sarcastic word. It makes me laugh out loud—it's so Ori, and for a second, I thought I might never hear that voice again.

Ori looks me in the eye and adds, "Don't worry. I kind of like it."

My heart races at full gallop.

"Can I try something?" I ask.

Ori nods, then coughs, a speckle of blood landing on his lip. I sway staring at it, but every time my vision starts to get hazy, the magic of our connection wipes it away. A push and pull keeping me from fainting, keeping Ori alive.

I gently lay him on the ground, on his side, then lie behind him. I put my arm around his shoulder, my heart pounding against his back as I pull him into me. Warmth flows between us.

"Is this okay?" I whisper.

Ori sighs, tension easing from his body. I feel him loosen up, feel that pulse beat harder, and I know with certainty it's not just because he's healing. It's because I make him nervous, too. The best kind of butterflies-in-your-gut nervous. He scoots back against me.

Neither of us speaks for a while, until Ori finally says, "I never pictured myself as the little spoon."

"Ha!" My laugh echoes across the hall. "And?"

Ori turns over so we're face-to-face. I glance down, and the hole in his chest where the claw once was is finally gone. I can see his smooth, blood-free pec through the open tear in his shirt.

I look up and find myself lost in the brown, amber, gold swirls of Ori's irises. His perfect lips get so close to mine you could barely fit a piece of paper between us.

"I'm into it," he whispers.

I swallow. Ori stares at my mouth.

Then, with that smirk, Ori leans forward and presses his lips to mine.

I thought I knew what magic felt like before.

Warm, tingly, *right.*

But it has nothing on this.

CHAPTER TWENTY-FIVE

I don't know how long we lie there, kissing, the sparks between us confirming that this magical connection Bex says we have must be real. It's so wild that I can feel so strongly for someone after knowing them for only a few days, but everything about this is just right.

My feet lie past Ori's, and I softly tip them up so the tops of my boots hit the bottom of his sneakers.

Tap, tap, tap, tap.

Matching the rhythm of our hearts against each other's chests.

Buh-bum.

Buh-bum.

Buh-bum.

Buh-bum.

In sync.

Even our magics have harmonized, our palms glowing with power as I lace my fingers through his. Pink and gold swirling together, creating that prismatic abalone light. The color of us.

"We can't stay here forever," Ori says. "We have a mess to clean."

I groan. "A lifetime of mucking stalls and I'm still not ready for this crap." I try to will myself to get up, but worry keeps bubbling in my gut. Something feels off. I know we need to fix what we started, and I'm dead set on ending the Knife if it comes to that, ready to fight to protect humanity. But Laurel's rant runs through my head. The way she acknowledged that maybe what we were saying is true, that we *could* harness love for good, and yet she still didn't want to. She had to be the *best*, just so she could fit in at the Guild.

"What is it?" Ori asks, pulling me close.

"It's just, everything that Laurel said. About still wanting to take us down because of our power, even if she could be that powerful, too. Because that's what it takes to succeed in the Guild. Maybe . . ." I can't believe what I'm about to say. It's the complete opposite of everything I've believed for the past eighteen years of my life. "Maybe the Guild isn't all it's cracked up to be."

I glance down at Ori, expecting him to look at me like I've lost my mind, like I've betrayed magickind. But instead his eyebrows are quirked, giving me the *Well, duh!* expression that looks so natural on his face.

"About fucking time!" he says. "I've been waiting for you to catch up. I've felt that way ever since Cassie. What kind of organization that considers itself good causes such heartache? Rips so many families apart? I've been so angry since Cassie died, knowing that to keep my power—the last thing that connects me to her—I have no choice but to join the organization that sent her to slaughter. But that connection is everything to me." Ori looks down at his feet, and his normally confident gaze swims with tears. "I'm convinced that just after she died, she *gave* her power to me. Or maybe, added to my power since she couldn't make effigies out of anything like I can. But I think she's given me some sort of boost. I swear I hear her voice in my head, guiding my power when I'm fighting. It's like she's looking out for me, wherever she is. The Guild is willing to rip that away if I don't meet their standards, even though they didn't give it to me to begin with. I hate them. And I hate that they've put us in this situation."

He looks away like maybe *I'll* think he's gone too far. But I gently press my hand to his cheek and guide his face toward mine. "You have every right to."

That Depraved's words come back to me then. *When the Guild stands, we thrive.* Dad's bitter, angry rants. His magic ripped away from him because he couldn't earn the Guild's approval. The monsters his hatred has created on the ranch. Ori, right in front of me, telling me how much the Guild's system of fighting to our deaths has affected him.

"What if this is what they meant?" I ask. Ori scowls with confusion. "The Depraved. 'When the Guild stands, we thrive.' The distrust of our fellow Cullingmates, the way we discard those who don't make it, the way we move on and forget the ones who've died for the group." My stomach swirls with guilt at how little thought I've given my grandpa, Dad's dad, since he died on a mission. "Could *we* be creating monsters?"

"We *are* the monsters."

This. *This* is what's been nagging at me ever since we woke the Horde. This fear that something within me made me dangerous, made me bad, when all my life all I ever wanted was to be a force for good.

But it's not my power that makes me bad. Not when it feels so right, especially now, with my body and my magic tangled with Ori's.

Maybe what made me bad was not seeing what needed to be changed all along.

The Guild.

I twine our fingers together, the color of our magic shining bright. "But when we have this," I say, holding up our hands, "maybe we can change that."

Ori leans in and kisses me, our light glowing brighter behind my closed eyes.

All feels right again, until a hacking cough snaps us back to reality. Jameson, coming to. I don't know how much he's heard, if anything. But if he wants to stop us now, he's going to have a rough go of it with how weak he looks. He's clammy with a sheen of sweat glistening from his forehead—but at least he's alive.

"Jameson!" Ori gets to his feet, my chest immediately feeling cold in his absence. But he reaches for me with his pink-glowing fingers, and when his hand closes around mine, my body settles. I'll have to get used to the temperature changes, to only really feeling right when we're together. With Ori beside me, I'm so sure of myself that my fingers work on their own as we get to Jameson's side. In seconds I've molded my power into a pillow that I fit under his head and fill with the intent of peace. Jameson winces with the movement, but lets out a sigh when his head hits the pillow.

"What else do you need?" I ask.

Jameson waves me off. "I'll be fine with a few more hours rest." His eyelids flutter, like he could pass out again at any moment. But he wills them open and looks between us, dead serious. "Thanks to your connection. It's about time you used it to stop the Horde. I know it will work."

There's something in the way he says it that hints at more. "*How* do you know?"

Despite his nearly fatal wound, Jameson's eyes sparkle. "There's more at play here than even you know, boys. More magic out there that the Guild knows nothing about."

I can hear Bex again, saying she was ready to start the Resistance. I don't think it was a joke.

"You know about Bex's dads," Ori says. It's not a question. Jameson nods.

"Yamato and Kenneth have shared theories about their connection with me, yes." A rough cough interrupts Jameson, but with Ori's hand over my own, I imbue my magic pillow with more calm, more peace, willing his body to relax and heal.

"It truly is a magical development," he says, no hint of irony at his choice of words. "Bex's fathers have kept me abreast of what they've learned over the years. For some, like the girls, their power grows as their love builds over time. Apparently, anyone can harness it as long as their heart is open to making that bond. Or it can happen between magical family members and friends, when deep love is felt in times of crisis."

I remember Cassie telling Ori she loved him just before she died. "That must be what happened with your sister," I say. "Cassie was thinking of you before . . ." I pause. I don't mean to suggest that Cassie's death was a good thing.

"Before she died," Ori finishes.

Jameson gives him a sad smile. "From what I've heard, it's very probable her last thoughts of love did give you powers unlike any sprites before you. A familial connection like that is often unseen in the Guild, where interactions are so focused on competition and success. Then there's another type of love—what I believe we're seeing in you two. A bond that's instantaneous, built on unexplained yet undeniable attraction. The same bond that formed between Yamato and Kenneth. It can be summed up simply: You're soulmates."

It feels like the air is sucked out of the room. Ori grimaces, but when I make eye contact, he shifts to an apologetic smile. It's silent in the cavern until he whispers in a soft voice, "But I don't love you."

I'd be lying if I said it didn't feel like my heart was just impaled by the claw.

"Ouch" is all I can muster. My mind jumps back to that moment in Torchy's, getting dumped out of the blue, surrounded by tacos and queso. Sure, the scenery's different, but I don't want what's going on between me and Ori to end before it even starts.

"Hey, cowboy, don't get like that. Hear me out." He tilts my chin so I'm forced to look at him. "Do I feel something when I'm around you? Yeah. Can I open up to you more easily than anyone else? Absolutely." He takes my hands and laces our fingers together. "But to say I'm in love with you after knowing you for only a few days would be ridiculous, right? You can't honestly say you already love *me*, can you?"

My chest loosens just a bit, the sad grip around my heart letting up. He's right. I feel all kinds of connected to him; I want to be around him at all times. But to say I'm *in love* already seems naive and outrageously clingy. Outside of the Culling, I barely know him.

"Please don't take that to mean I don't want to see what this is about," Ori says. "Or to use our connection. It's just, I don't want to call this something it's not . . . not before I'm ready, anyway. So if the moment comes that we can honestly say that, it'll mean so much more."

"I *did* get dumped less than a week ago," I say. "I'd hate for you to be the rebound." Still, I already know for a fact, even if this isn't love yet, I have more feelings for Ori than I ever did for Jeremy. "Let's give this thing the time it needs."

Jameson nods. "That's the spirit. Soulmates are about so much more than fairy-tale notions. The bond ties two magicians together in ways most will never experience. But that connection is built on openness with each other, on laying your hearts on the line for one another."

Ori crosses his arms firmly over his chest. "This information would have been *very* helpful a few days ago," he says. "Might have saved us a lot of trouble."

"It's knowledge we have to keep close to our chests," Jameson says simply, unbothered by Ori's snark. "There are those who would destroy anyone whose power can't be easily understood or categorized. Use these details and your power to the best of your abilities, to stop the Horde, and to stop the Knife if it comes to that. Then find the others who know of your magic. Who want to help."

I instantly think of Bex. Those who want to help sound an awful lot like the Resistance. I hope she's found them, if they exist. Or maybe she was able to get to her dads and they've helped hide her from the Guild. Maybe her dads are in hiding now, too. Wherever Bex and her family are, they're the first folks I'll want to talk to when all this is over.

If we make it out alive, that is.

Jameson starts coughing again, but he forces out two words. "F-f-f-find them." He gets lost to another fit of hacking, and faints.

"Seriously?" Ori shouts, shaking Jameson's shoulders. "*Now's* the moment you decided to pass out? Talk about a movie cliché." He stands abruptly, reaching to pull me up. "I guess it's time we get this show on the road."

I look around the hall, hoping to see a door. The portal that brought us here has faded; Jaleesa's, too. And without fae magic, we can't open a new one. "Uh . . . how do we get out of here? And how are we going to get Jameson out? I know he said he'll be fine after some rest, but what do we do when he's healed?"

Ori doesn't say anything. He just keeps staring at our hands, where our magics are working on their own now, pouring out of our fingers to make that abalone light. It really is beautiful.

I squeeze his hand. "You in there?"

"Oh, you think I'm getting all googly-eyed over you because you're my soulmate, huh?"

My cheeks blaze. "I just thought—"

"Get over here." Ori tugs me forward, a smile on his lips as he presses them against my own. More magic, a blaze of light from our hands, so bright I can see it behind my closed eyes. Ori pulls back just a bit and says, "Thanks for the recharge. It'll help me get us out. And when all this is over, we'll find a way to use that Barrett blood to get Jameson. Ready to blink?"

"Wait, where to?"

"To the battle, obviously. To the Horde."

I gawk at him. He said himself that blinking from the Excalibur props closet to the arena was the farthest he'd ever jumped with someone. We don't know how far we are from the Horde, or if they've left Hood River. What if this goes wrong? Maybe we'll get stuck in some in-between place. Maybe our bones will crush like that Depraved's in our second task. Maybe we'll—

"Stop," Ori says. "Don't think about all those things. It's not going to go wrong. Not when we work together."

"Right." I try to sound more confident than I feel. "You've got this. I mean, this is what sprites do. Blink."

Ori clicks his tongue approvingly. "Got that right, cowboy."

Cowboy. I love the way he says it. How he likes the me that wrangles cattle and rides horses. "I'm spitballing here," I say, "but maybe I could channel the energy of horses. Great-Grandpa Barrett transformed into a bear, and Meema always summons her bull. What if I call on the energy of my own favorite animal and, I don't know, hope it gives your blinking a boost? Literal horsepower."

"That's thinking on your feet." Ori taps my shoe with his. "Or, your boots."

I laugh, which helps dissipate my nerves. It makes the magic gathering in my hands glow bright as stars as I close my eyes, put my pointer finger and thumb in my mouth, and blow.

'Yup! I envision a herd of wild horses, manes whipping in the breeze, galloping with nothing holding them back. *Run like the wind.* I chant it over and over in my mind as magic fills me with hope. A pressure builds in my chest as I picture the horses, feel their freedom in my bones, and watch another horse join my imagined herd.

Frosty.

Neighing, tossing their mane, the glistening blue of their icy hide casting brilliant light on the browns, beiges, tans, whites, and blacks of the rest. And, typical Frosty, they make sure they're at the front. When they take their place leading the others, I feel that pressure in my chest build until I can't contain it.

My eyes snap open to see a herd of golden horses burst from my torso, casting prisms of light everywhere I look. The horses circle the cavern before charging us head-on. The herd splits in two, galloping for Ori and me until they enter both of us, Frosty leading the way into Ori's soul, charging him with their speed. My chest swells with gratitude that Frosty found a way to help us. I guess even death can't keep Frosty from doing exactly what they feel like doing. Ori grins as the magic hits him, each horse sending a ripple of gold over his skin.

It's the most beautiful thing I've ever seen.

Finally, when the whole herd has vanished, Ori rubs a hand over his heart. "Thanks, buddy."

I know he's talking to Frosty, wherever they are now.

I've never wanted Ori more.

"Ready?" he asks.

I grab the claw from the floor and shove it in my back pocket. "Ready."

"Focus on the Guild. Think about meeting up with them, no matter where they are, so we can fix this once and for all."

I try to center my thoughts, but as I look into Ori's eyes, I don't know how to focus on anything but him. How safe I feel with him. How much I trust him. How I know we could go to the ends of the earth together, fighting off every last Depraved until the world is safe. How when the Horde is defeated, we'll change the Guild for the better.

With those feelings washing over me, I wrap Ori in my arms, and we're whisked away in a swirl of abalone light. It's not like a portal. Here, in this in-between space filled with the color of us, Ori pressed tight to my chest—it's so much better.

Our feet hit solid ground, and we stand steady, not even swaying. Chest to chest, Ori's head resting gently on my shoulder, his wild hair tickling the side of my neck, my body feels more sure than it ever has, even on horseback. And that's saying something.

My heart jumps. "We did it!" That's twice now we've done exactly what we wanted: destroying those Vegas Depraved, and now blinking together, to wherever we are.

Which is . . . the center of pure chaos, apparently.

"GET DOWN!" Ori pulls me with him just in time so that a jet of twisted green magic zaps over our heads. But the bolt of power is just one of *thousands* bursting and flashing around us.

We're on the edge of a volcano, surrounded by craggy gray

rocks, snow melted here and there by the onslaught of magic. There are Depraved everywhere, battling hand to hand with Guild members. Magicians mingle with the Horde, and skeletons strike whoever they can with their razor sharp bones. Fae sing to slow the Depraved, nymphs blast apart the Horde, elves use their golden power to trap or disintegrate or liquefy their foes. Goblins flash silver and transform into all manner of beasts, from unicorns piercing Depraved through to gorillas grabbing the Horde and literally pulling their skulls from their bodies. There's blood and shattered bone everywhere, but that's not the worst part.

The worst part is the mottled-green arm, the size of a cruise ship, that rises over the rim of the volcano.

The Knife.

Horde soldiers surround the monster's arm, dancing in triumph, their bones clacking sickeningly. The Depraved let loose their high-pitched shrieks.

Another massive arm joins the first, crashing down over the edge of the volcano with a ground-shaking thud. And in one massive heave, the Knife pulls its torso out of the volcano's mouth. Its gaping, rotted-tooth maw lets loose a bellow that stops everyone in their tracks. Magicians, Depraved, Horde, demons lured by the chaos.

For the longest split second of my life, no one moves. The only sound that cuts through the silence is that of the helicopters swarming the Knife's head. News choppers. Six of them, circling Mount Rainier as they video the battle.

I know the Guild has ways of wiping memories, but this? All of humanity is going to know about the existence of monsters and magic.

The Knife tenses muscles so large that I can hear them move, the rocks groaning beneath its weight. Then, in a single movement, way too fluid for a creature of its size, the Knife launches its body into the air. Its bloated torso and skyscraper legs burst from the mountain, sending boulders flying. As it soars higher and higher, the Knife swipes every last helicopter out of the sky. They fall in chaotic rotations, half a dozen explosions burning the mountain as each of them crash.

The first deaths at the newly wakened Knife's hands seem to jog the magicians back into action, while the Horde and the Depraved let loose more warped cries. The Depraved nearest the explosions take deep breaths, feeding on the fear felt by the pilots and reporters just before they died. In green bursts of light, the Depraved grow, their muscles expanding, their eyes getting brighter, as they become the decaying, bulging monsters we saw in Vegas.

It feels like the entire world shakes as the Knife lands on the volcano's side, knocking magicians off their feet. Magic of every color blasts from all directions. But a vibrant streak of gold stands out the most, bursting through the chaos to stop at our side.

Meema pants atop her golden bull. "Nigel! Did you get it?"

I hoist the claw into the air.

A flicker of a smile perks her red lips, but she won't meet my eyes. "Good work, darlin'. Now give it here."

She puts her hand out, but the way she's avoiding my gaze makes me pause, the claw still in my grasp. "What's wrong?"

"Damn it, Nigel, do as you're told. Nothing's wrong, I just can't trust you to get this right. Look what you've done already!" She motions to the pandemonium around us, and I feel like she's slapped me in the face. I guess when they say the truth hurts, they're not kidding.

"You're too young to handle this. Now"—she beckons with her fingers—"give it here."

I slowly lift my hand, holding the claw out to her, so focused on the weapon that it takes a second to notice the avalanche building behind my grandma.

"Meema! Watch out!"

A wave of snow crashes down the mountain, sweeping up Depraved, Horde soldiers, and magicians alike in its roiling mass. We have about two seconds to move or be moved.

"Nigel!" Ori's hand is outstretched, ready to blink us away. But I can't leave Meema to be swept up in all that snow and ice.

"Nigel, grab my h—" But the words are knocked from Ori's lips by a taloned foot that snatches him into the air, grabbing me a second later, the claw still clutched in my hand. The snow sweeps over Meema below us, drowning her in a wall of white as she's hurled down the mountain.

"No!" I pound on the scaley toes holding me tight. "Take me back! Take me back!"

"She'll be okay."

My body is a swirl of emotion: Deep worry for Meema pierces my stomach, but my heart leaps into my throat when I recognize the voice.

"Bex!"

She's in phoenix form, staring at me with one golden eye, her pupil widening as she takes me in. "Never thought you'd see me again, did you?"

"So you escaped the Guild's clutches only to fly right back into their grasp?" Ori asks, incredulous.

"I'll be fine," she says. "I've got folks on my side. There's a lot the Guild hasn't told you. Like how they aren't the only ones with magic, for starters."

Jameson basically said the same thing, but a new realization makes my heart stop. "How? If there were too many non-Guild magicians, we'd all be dead from the power overload."

Bex's body vibrates with an angry shriek. "It's all a lie, Nigel. The Culling isn't needed. It's—"

Whack!

One of the Knife's flailing fists knocks Bex out of the sky. We slip from her claws, free-falling. Ori flies too far away for me to reach him.

My thoughts race as fast as our fall toward the hard rocks of Mount Rainier below. I've been lied to, since birth. Meema. Dad. Everyone. If magicians *can* exist in larger numbers, what purpose does the Guild serve? Why hold the Culling? Why *not* boost our numbers to match the growing threat of demons and the Depraved?

"Nigel!" Ori's panicked voice is almost carried away on the wind. "Cowboy up!"

It's such a ridiculous thing for him to say. I've heard it in so many country songs, read it in stupid memes, but never when about to be flattened like a flapjack, like he wants me to throw on my boots so we can honky-tonk in the air. But Ori points toward Bex, and I catch on in an instant. Bex has righted herself, this time out of reach of the Knife's fists, her bright red body straight as an arrow as she dives. But there's no way she'll make it to us in time.

Unless I do something to close the distance.

I gather magic in my windmilling hands, then force my arms to move against the whooshing air to coil a lasso around my elbow. I give it some slack, knot it, then twirl it around my head. Only seconds to go. I've got to make this count. It's going to be the farthest throw I've had to make in my life. But fortunately, I know a guy who can give me a little boost.

I stick my glowing middle finger and thumb into my mouth and blow: a summoning spell. Ori zooms within reach just as I thrust my foot out. "Grab on!" The second his hand makes contact, magic surges through me, and I let my rope fly.

Bex sees it and moves so fast air whistles around her body. The rope continues to soar upward, defying gravity with my supercharged magic.

The rope climbs and climbs while Bex shoots forward like a bullet, but finally gravity takes its hold and the rope starts to dip. Bex isn't going to make it, and the ground is just feet away. This is it. We're going to—

"Oof!" The rope pulls taut as Bex's talons close around it, the air yanked out of me at the sudden change in direction. We swing upward, Ori clinging to my ankle for dear life as Bex dips toward the ground, placing us on our feet, her fiery warm body melting a circle of snow as she lands. She shifts back to her human self in a silver flash, and I throw my arms around her.

"Bex!" I cry. "We would've been dead without you."

The words nearly stop my heart cold, because there *is* one person who could be dead right now, lost to a tidal wave of snow.

Bex reads my mind. "I'm sorry I couldn't get her, too."

I swallow, unable to speak, while Ori puts a hand on my shoulder. His touch does nothing to remove my dread.

We're standing apart from the battle, bursts of colorful magic lighting up the sky. Goblins shifted to dragons, griffins, and gargoyles dodge the Knife's fists. But the Depraved giant isn't discouraged by their ability to escape his grasp. Instead, it swings one massive hand and scoops up a group of magicians climbing the mountain on foot. In one fluid movement, it snaps them in half. It doesn't matter that it no longer has its namesake weapon. The Knife is out for blood.

Bile burns my throat as the Knife brings the halved magicians to its mouth, sucking at the torsos to get their hearts. For the first time, the magicians below show fear. Some retreat farther down the mountain, the Depraved near them growing with the feast of terror. The more of us it kills, the stronger the Knife will become, and the Depraved with it, feeding off our fear for our lives.

"Oh my god," I breathe. "We did this. We brought this upon the Guild."

Ori swallows, while Bex shakes her head. "You can't blame yourself. It was a total accident. And the fact that you and Ori, two barely adult magicians, were able to awaken the Horde just doesn't feel possible. Even for soulmates."

Ori thrusts his arm out, pointing at the Knife. "Then what do you call that? That seems possible to me, Bex."

"You shouldn't be *that* powerful. More powerful than most, thanks to your connection? Sure. But no offense, my dads are way more experienced, yet their powers have never been strong enough to awaken a Horde, even when their experiments did go haywire."

I want to say her words are a relief, but without another explanation, I can't shrug off the blame. I watch as the Knife swipes up whoever it can get its massive hands on. I can't tell who's fallen victim to it already, who's still fighting and with what magic. I just know that, with each swing of its fist, the Knife is dwindling the numbers of the only people who can fight back.

I've got to get over there and stop this, before it gets worse. But I can't. I'm panicking, my breath coming in short, sharp bursts that stab my lungs.

"How do we stop it? If all those magicians can't keep it caged, what could we possibly do? I graduated high school three weeks ago, I'm not some chosen-one warrior!"

"We can't just sit here," Ori says. "You'll regret it more than anything else in the world."

I know he's thinking of Cassie. For a moment I wish that I could take that pain, craft a golden hankie, and wipe it away. But I can't erase his memories. They make Ori who he is, that snarky, protective guy who my body and my magic can't seem to get enough of. They shaped his path to this moment. They shaped his path to *me*. And I'd never wipe that away.

Would I change the past if I could? Absolutely. But change his memories? No.

I know that he believes everything he's saying with his whole heart. If I turn my back on this responsibility now, he'd still try to stop the Knife. Alone, it'd probably kill him. And I can't be the cause of his death. Or that of one more person.

"We've got to get close enough to his crown to smash the heartstone at its center," I say. "But with those flailing fists, there's no way we'll get up there."

"You're gonna lasso that thing right off his head, and I'm going to turn his crown into an effigy." Ori says it like it's *simple*. "We're not just going to put the Knife back to sleep and bury it again. We're going to kill it, once and for all."

"Do you really think we can do that?"

Ori nods once. "I don't see why not. Even if it's impossible for our magic to be this strong, somehow we woke up the Horde. We're soulmates, right? Why wouldn't we be able to kill this guy?"

"It just sounds too easy." I look to Bex, but she seems as lost as I feel.

"I don't know how it's working, but Ori's right. Your connection is there and for some reason it's stronger than anything I've ever heard of. But this has been my mission all along, right? To show the power of love. What better time to start than now?"

I look at Ori, his perfect eyebrows set in grim determination. He laces his fingers through mine, my body buzzing with our bond, with his confidence and courage.

We got this.

"Well, then." Ori said I should lasso the crown, so lasso it I will. With a burst of magic, a golden rope appears around my elbow. "Let's get this show on the road."

CHAPTER TWENTY-SIX

The more I repeat the plan, the more absurd it seems.

"So we'll just blink up there, snag the crown, blink back, and destroy it with the claw?" I ask for the third time, checking to make sure the weapon is tucked safely in my pocket.

"Yes," Ori says. He glances up at the Knife, who's currently swatting a pack of goblins-turned-dragons trying to burn out its eyes. "We can't stall anymore." He takes my right hand and I grab Bex's with my left. "Ready?"

Bex's stare is steely and determined. "Ready."

I can only nod.

"All right then." Ori lets out a breath. "Imagine being on top of that monster's head. Got it? On three. One, two, three."

Blink

We're in that shiny abalone space for a split second. One brief moment of peace before we're dropped on top of the Knife's decaying scalp. It smells like hot garbage up here, the spikes of the Knife's bone crown blocking out the orange light of the late evening sun. Even still, I can make out a sharp point of the headpiece, the perfect spot to snag my lasso before we blink back to get rid of the Knife once and for all.

I grab my lasso, stepping out to steady myself as the Knife jostles this way and that, swinging at the magicians attacking it. I twirl my rope over my head and say, "Here goes no—"

WHAM!

The Knife slams its hand onto its scalp, missing me by inches. Its sequoia-size fingers scratch incessantly, forcing me to run to avoid being crushed. Sheets of flaky, rotten skin come up with each scratch, making it harder and harder for me to keep my footing.

I slip just as a massive finger hovers overhead, ready to flatten me. A second before I'm halved by the Knife's cracked and bloody nail, Ori blinks to me, grabs my hand, and blinks us both to the side of the crown, pressed flat against it.

"I'll distract it!" Bex cries, shifting to a phoenix again and taking off in a burst of angry flame. In a heartbeat, she's up and over the crown. There's no time to wonder what she's up to as the Knife keeps digging around its head. Ori blinks us away every few seconds.

"I need a—"

Blink

"—second to—"

Blink

"—throw my rope!"

Ori opens his mouth to reply, but he's interrupted by the worst sound I've ever heard.

"YIIEEEEEEEEEEE!"

The Knife's cry is a million times worse than the Horde's portal-opening shriek. But luckily, the monster's hand yanks back, letting us catch our breath.

"Here's your shot," Ori says.

The sharp point of the crown looms above us, ready to be cinched.

I can do this.

I grab the lasso.

It'll just take one throw.

I twirl it over my head.

All I've got to do is let it fly.

So I do. The loop goes soaring, soaring, soaring.

The golden light of my rope reflects off slick bone as the lasso snags the crown.

"That's it, cowboy!" Ori screams, his elation lighting up my insides. "Go, go, go!"

I quickly tie the loose end of my rope into another knot, throwing it over my head and tugging it tight around my waist. I figured if it's attached to me when we blink away, the crown will have to come with us, right?

Ori tugs me close, his hand fitting around my waist, his fingertips grazing my stomach.

"Ready?"

I nod, too caught up in the butterflies at his touch to be able to speak.

"Here we go."

And we blink.

It's our gold and pink twisting together again, creating the color of us. Until, somehow in this space that's just meant for Ori and me, a shadow hovers overhead. The crown. The Knife's headpiece, the source of its twisted life force, fueled by death, overpowering our light.

My stomach twists.

Something's wrong.

I think it just before we materialize. Too soon.

We reappear in a crash, the crown sliding against the stone and snow. Ori and I are pulled along behind it, still holding on to each other, our touch healing every gash and bone break as we tumble down the mountain. It's a whirlwind of pain and warmth and adrenaline until we finally screech to a stop.

I'm on my back staring at what would be the sky, if it wasn't for the angry, monstrous glare bearing down on me from the clouds. We've landed at the Knife's feet. Much too close. It could reach down and scoop the crown back onto its head at any second. The Knife roars as its bends to do just that.

"Cloudy with a chance of hell spawn," Ori shouts, jumping to his feet. "We have to go! Leave the crown."

He reaches for the rope around my waist, but just before his fingers can close around it, we're swarmed by blasts of magic. Like fireworks all around us. Not magic directed at us—magic to protect us.

The Guild has our backs. Senior magicians send bursts of magic flurrying around the Knife's arms as they get closer to the crown, spells and vines and flames and ice forcing the giant to turn its focus to them. Curses, fae and elven, push back the Depraved as they try to back up their master.

And then, brightest of all, a beacon of gold rampaging through the battle. Meema on her bull.

"She's alive!" Even from here I can see the bruises covering her body, see how her denim blouse is untucked, how she looks more disheveled than she's ever allowed herself to look in her life—but she's freaking *alive*.

Surviving an avalanche hasn't set her back at all; she charges the Knife on her bull and rams the giant's hideous toes with her sidekick's long horns. That pride I've felt my whole life at her bravery swells in my chest. But it's quickly met by a rush of shame. I screwed up so badly to begin with that she and the rest of the Guild are having to fix my mess. And when all this is over, how do I even go about acting like everything is normal between us? If what Bex said is true and the Culling has never been necessary, if the Guild has been feeding the Depraved . . . what part did Meema play in it?

But these questions will have to wait. Depraved swarm the crown, demons right behind, Horde skeletons clacking after them. Unmoving bones and magically decimated Depraved remains litter the ground at their feet. The Guild has put up a good fight, but it's not over yet.

Meema, Alister, Pallavit, and dozens more Guild magicians give it their all. Each of them here to defend magic and humanity. To show the humans who are no doubt watching this on the news—a new pack of helicopters has come to stupidly fill the places of those lost before them—that there is a group of people equipped to battle threats they've only known in their nightmares.

"Time to get to work!" Ori slips the lasso off my waist and blinks us to the crown's side, right in front of the cracked heartstone. All the heads of the nearby monsters swivel in our direction, ready to kill before we can destroy their master.

Ori immediately drops to his knees and builds miniature snowmen, his hands blinking fast. I'd laugh if I didn't have to dodge a group of Horde soldiers who leap at me. I pool magic in my fingers and blow, a summoning whistle that makes a shining gold horse materialize, just like Meema does with her bull. I swing onto the horse's back and direct it to buck and kick, toppling skeletons and shattering their skulls with its hooves. Those that get too close, I slash at with the claw, pulling it from my pocket and swinging like a scythe. It slices through their skulls like butter.

Magicians blast their power in every direction, keeping the Knife busy so it can't reach for the crown. Alister trips as many Depraved as he can with vines, or sends bamboo shoots bursting from the ground to pierce demons' bellies. Ori has his little snowmen lined up in a row, and when he has a dozen glowing sprite pink, he swipes them all through the middle. Twelve Depraved double over, writhing on the ground and clutching their stomachs.

Then there's Meema, her hair slicked back with snow, her shirt tucked in again. She almost seems to be having *fun* with it all. She soaks her favorite lipstick tube in gold magic, then applies it expertly to her lips, not a stray mark outside her lipliner despite the bumpy ride on her bull. Instead of her favorite shade of red, the makeup now glows gold, and with it coating her lips, she blows kisses. Comic kiss marks float through the sky, landing on Depraved, demons, and Horde soldiers, each time smacking right onto their cheeks. When the magic kisses land on their face, her victims disintegrate. A kiss of death.

But every time one of us stops an enemy, there's another to take its place. Another skeleton jerkily swiping with its deadly elbow blades, another Depraved sending jagged lightning streaks at our faces, another demon—possessed cougars and wolves and porcupines—using their hate-enhanced bodies to create more destruction.

"We need a distraction," I yell to anyone who can hear. "Or we'll never be able to use the claw!"

Ori drops a rock on a snow effigy and the Depraved looming over him splats as if flattened by a boulder. Five more Depraved stalk up the mountain toward him. "I'm a little busy."

In all the chaos, a woman steps out of the crowd of magicians, and Ori and I spot her at the same time.

"Mom!" Ori shouts.

Lyra Olson holds a pink-coated sprite wood figure in her hands, and in one clean move she snaps it in two; the nearest Horde soldier's head pops right off its body. With her bare hands, she grabs the skull and smashes it against a boulder with a guttural scream.

Lyra blinks to her son and wraps him in her arms. "Go! You have to get out of here!"

"We can stop this," Ori says. "Nigel and me."

"No!" Lyra's eyes go wide as a Horde skeleton sprints toward them. She blinks herself and Ori ten feet away, leaving the skeleton to stab at empty air. "You're not ready."

"I'm more than ready." Ori scoops a discarded bone from the ground, bathes it in pink, and snaps another would-be-attacker in two, then stomps on its skull. "You know I can do things other sprites can't do. Things even *you* can't do." He blinks again, back to my side, and grabs my hand so our power blazes.

"And it's more than that. I'm not alone." His eyes never leave his mom's as he says, "Even before this connection with Nigel. Cassie's with me, Mom. She's always been with me. *She's* why I can do what I do. No matter how many times you try to change that, I won't let you take her away from me."

Lyra is a blur of motion as a trio of Horde skeletons surrounds her: all pink magic and wooden effigies and curses liquefying enemies. She's a practiced magician, moving through her attacks so seamlessly it's hard to imagine there was ever a time when a Depraved could sneak up on her and take her daughter. But through all the commotion, through the limbs both human and bone, Lyra's eyes never leave her son's. Realization dawns on her face, and whatever conclusion she's come to makes her grimace.

Her enemies downed, Lyra blinks to her son's side. "Ori. Baby.

I'm sorry. I never wanted to take her from you; I just couldn't have *you* taken from *me.*"

"Nothing ever could. Even if I die, Cassie's shown me that we're always together. Always."

"I love you."

Lyra pulls her son close just as a streak of jagged green light blasts in their direction, but Lyra's faster. She holds up her glowing sprite wood and intercepts the spell. The Depraved who cast it explodes, destroyed by its own magic.

She is *good.*

"Ori, go to Nigel!" she says, jerking her head in my direction. "Adela and I've got your distraction covered!"

"You bet your bottom dollar!" Meema yells, then conjures a shining gold jockey's whip and bounces it from flank to flank on her bull. With each smack her bull glows brighter.

"Get to the crown!" Lyra yells, and as we run she flings even more effigies, the enemies in our path flying out of our way. It'd almost look like a synchronized dance routine if not for the mangled and broken limbs after each leap, followed by the Depraveds' tortured shrieks.

In no time, the magic that's been gathering in Meema's bull finally lets loose. It charges forward, a gallop that boosts to light speed in seconds, Meema and her magic companion becoming a golden blur with a streak of red at the top. I smile. Meema's perfectly dyed hair always makes its mark.

They run in a circle, the blur solidifying into a gold wall that only my grandma and her sidekick can traverse. Demons swipe at it, but their claws are vaporized on contact. Depraved try to push through, but they snap back as if burned.

We have a force field. The golden walls grow and bend, meeting above our heads to form a translucent dome. Nothing coming in from the sides or above.

I'm amazed at Meema's power, at Lyra's—at the skill of *all* the senior magicians. Their ability to maintain this much strength in battle—and without a recharging soulmate by their sides—is wildly impressive. But still, they won't be able to last forever.

"I don't know how long that will hold," I say. "We've got to move!"

Ori's hands are already glowing pink and pressed against the old bone crown, the heartstone looming overhead. "You honestly think you need to tell me that, cowboy?" He shoots me that smirk that makes me want to kiss him, long and deep, charging our powers in a way nothing else can. "Just because you're my soulmate doesn't mean you get to call all the shots. Get over here and supercharge my power, lover boy—or am I going to have to do this on my own?"

My body buzzes, and as I reach forward to put my hand on his shoulder, I feel an emotion that I haven't felt for days.

Hope.

Hope that we can get through this. Hope that we'll have a future. Hope that I'll get to hear Ori's playful jabs again and again, all while we use our magic for good. With or without the Guild.

That hope filling my heart, I hug him from behind, nuzzle his neck, kiss the soft skin there.

Ori's magic bursts outward with so much force that we're pushed back. His hand is no longer touching the twisted bone of the crown, but it doesn't matter. Ori's magic has soaked every last inch of the headpiece, infusing it with a pink glow.

"If that's not the gayest crown I've ever seen . . ." Ori says. "But more importantly, it's an effigy." He looks to the sky, where shape-shifted goblins have the Knife distracted. They fly into its eyes, zoom up and out of its nostrils. I hope one of those magicians flitting back and forth is Bex in phoenix form. Down on the ground, Meema's bull field still stands. Everything's lined up for this to work.

"Batter up," Ori says, stepping aside to give me a path to the heartstone. "Get to clawing."

I hold the claw in my palm, which is surprisingly not sweaty. This is it. The moment I live up to my great-grandpa's power. The moment I prove that I can clean up one of the biggest magical messes ever created by me and my . . . soulmate. The moment we start to pick up the pieces, get the chance to learn what the Guild is really about, set our paths back on track. Get out of Dad's depressing shadow. Start moving past the regret Ori feels over his sister. Start forging a path *together*.

I hoist the claw over my head, ready to slice down. The little nub of keratin glows bright gold while the heartstone stares at me like so many of Dad's glares, daring me to do anything. Doubting I have the courage or the strength to do what needs to be done.

With one swing, I'll show them that I'm Nigel Barrett, and I'm one of the greatest magicians the world has ever known.

I tense my muscles.

And swing.

The claw arcs through the air, soaring straight for the center of the heartstone.

It's feet, inches, centimeters away from contact.

But at the last moment, just before we can end this once and for all, a golden lasso loops over my great-grandfather's weapon and yanks it from my grasp.

Mission failed.

I look over my shoulder, gathering magic in my palm to fight whoever is trying to keep this battle going. Whoever's using my magic of choice to thwart me and keep the Knife alive.

There, holding the claw in her hands, is the last person I ever thought I'd see.

"Meema?"

CHAPTER TWENTY-SEVEN

My heart feels like it's left my body completely, like the Knife has sucked it out.

"How *could* you?" The question is barely more than a whisper, but I know she hears it.

"Don't worry, darlin'," she says with a soft smile. "It's not what you think."

Her boots crunch on the rocky ground as she saunters forward. My senses hone in on this tiny bubble inside Meema's bull ring, intended to protect us. Or is it intended to keep everyone else out so she can personally stop me from my mission?

She pulls me in for a one-armed hug, keeping the claw out of my reach. The familiar smells of hay and Chanel No. 5 flood my nose, a combination that's always comforted me, but now turns my stomach.

"I know you're going to be mad. This is goodbye."

Is this what Meema tried to tell me would happen? Her warnings that I'm earning enemies, that I'm befriending the wrong people, her coldness even after she stood up for me in the tribunal. Maybe all along she only needed me to retrieve the claw, and now that I've done that, she's going to make sure I can't cause any more messes. That I can't degrade the Barrett name any further.

Ori's hands glow. "Hurt one hair on him and you're dead."

"That's where you've got it all wrong, kiddo. I'm the one who's dying."

My heart stops. Even now, even as she holds the claw out of reach, preventing me from ending this. Maybe she's on the wrong side, maybe she's helped the Guild do more harm than good. But I don't want her to die.

"Look at me, Nigel." She tilts my head down so I can see her eyes swimming with tears. "You listen and you listen good, you hear? I'm so sorry I ever made you feel like you weren't a worthy Barrett. You're the best of us, darlin', and always have been."

I want to say I keep it together at that, but finally hearing the words I've been so desperate for makes my eyes burn with tears. "Meema, I'm the one who's sorry. This wouldn't have happened if I—"

"None of that now, sweetheart," she coos. "There's no time. We've got to end this." She bites her lip, a completely uncharacteristic show of nerves. "But there is something I didn't tell you. This claw?" She looks at it like it's a long-lost member of the family. "You know it's the greatest weapon against the Depraved. Hell, you sure cleaned up some of those varmints with it on your own. But for a monster as huge as the Knife? It will only stop them if the user sacrifices themself. An act of love for the greater good that is so strong it can defeat the ugly negativity that created the Knife in the first place. It's what your Great-Grandpa Barrett did all those years ago." She pulls me in again, this time with both hands, the hard side of the claw pressing against my back as she holds me. "It's what I'm going to do now."

"Meema, you can't. There's got to be another way." My heart beats at a full gallop. I pull away, hoping if she looks her only grandson in the eye, it'll convince her.

She steps back. One step, two, three. Creating distance between us. We both know that even if I tried a spell, it'd do nothing to stop her.

"There isn't, sweetheart. I love you."

She hoists the claw over her head, and a million thoughts race through mine. *I* might not be strong enough to stop her, but what about me and Ori together?

I snap my hand back and grab onto Ori's. But suddenly a newcomer joins us in the circle, just as Meema brings the claw down in an arc.

Alister. Burrowing up from underground, his magicked Venus flytrap bursting through the rock and snow and belching him out in one fluid movement. A flash of green magic flies from his hands before he even gets to his feet.

A huge thorn shoots from the rock to stab Meema right through the gut. Her blood splatters my face. The thorn stabs over and over, too fast for me to react.

"NO!" I fall to my knees, willing my magic to heal Meema as it does Ori. I grab her arm, her leg, I hold her to my chest and feel her blood soak my clothes. My heartache is so strong I don't even feel any nausea at the sight of it.

It's not working. I let magic pool in my hands, gather it like gauze and press it against the wound, hoping to stem the flow of blood. But as I shift Meema to get a better hold, her head falls limply to the side. When I see the gray in her roots, where her magic always kept it dyed, I know she's gone.

Meema's dead.

Murdered.

By Alister.

"I'm going to kill you!" Golden magic swells in my hands, so hot and angry that, for the first time in my life, it burns.

"Not so fast," Alister says lazily. He snaps his fingers, and thorns burst from the ground again to imprison me and push me away from Meema.

It's so ridiculous I laugh. "Are you kidding me? I'll burn these to ash."

"Is that so?"

"Nigel," Ori says, tight-lipped, jaw-clenched. From the corner of my eye I can see he's surrounded in his own plant prison, crouched like he was about to build a snow effigy, a thorn pressed ever so slightly against the skin under his chin. If he opens his mouth too wide, it'll pierce his jaw—and I just *know* that if Alister sees any sign of me using magic against him, he'll send that thorn shooting straight through Ori's skull. And if Ori blinks, it's me who'll meet that same fate.

"Now that I have your attention," Alister says, a cool smile spreading across his face, "you're going to do exactly as I say. I'm going to release you, Nigel, and you're going to take that claw from your grandmother's corpse and destroy the crown. If you make a single wrong move, if I see any hint that you're going to act against me, I will kill your boyfriend."

He moves the thorn so it just barely pierces Ori, and I feel the pinch in my own skin. The thought of Ori dying makes my stomach turn. If I have to watch him die, just like I watched Meema . . . I won't make it. I'll die of heartache right then and there.

"Don't do it, Nigel." I can feel the tightness of Ori's jaw as he struggles to speak. "Don't be stupid. You'll die."

Alister lets out a deep chuckle, one I'm sure he's used to patronize his political opponents. It disarms me, makes me feel small. "That is precisely the point. Nigel will kill the Knife, die along with it, and leave you here alone, Ori. Grief stricken and easy to pick off. Another victim of our battle against the Depraved."

Meema's hand falls limply, and her favorite tube of lipstick tumbles to the ground. The memory of her blowing deadly kisses, confident and ready to fight for what's right, comes back to me in a rush. I feel her energy, her passion, her will to survive burn inside me. "I'll never do what you want."

Alister's face falls into a look of mock surprise. "Not as altruistic as we first believed, are you, Nigel?" He sounds genuinely amused. "No, you're just like every other magician. In it for *you*."

"What the hell are you talking about?" Ori asks. "Typical magician, saying things nobody understands just to hear yourself speak."

Alister raises an eyebrow. "Oh, you didn't know? The Guild may have been created to stop the Depraved all those years ago, but it's grown to be so much more than that. The few humans who were granted the Ancestrals' gifts knew what a wellspring of power they had access to. Many were poor farmers, tradesmen, hunters, all trying to make something of themselves. They realized if they hoarded their new skills, they could do just that. Which is exactly what they did, by creating the Culling."

Alister steps forward, his wicked grin getting wider the closer he steps, relishing this moment. "Magic doesn't saturate the air, Nigel. Magic doesn't *destroy*. The Culling was never about *balance*. It was created to ensure that only those who are worthy of the riches that come from our magic are allowed to keep it. And you two . . . *soulmates* . . . are anything but worthy."

So Bex was right. The Culling was never necessary. I immediately think of Dad. Forced to live without magic, for no reason. The cruelty of having his gifts ripped away repeating over and over as the bitterness it caused created demons and Depraved that Meema has to fight.

Had.

"You're a fucking monster," Ori says. "Without the Culling, think of how strong we could be against the Depraved. They're on the rise, they're killing humans. They're killing other magicians!" He's yelling now, trying to push forward, but the movement just drives thorns deeper into his skin. "Cassie could have lived! So many more people could have lived!"

His sadness and rage burn in my veins. Without the Culling, who knows how many more magicians might have fought beside Cassie, killing that Depraved before it killed her. Instead, the Guild has just created more monsters, the hate left in failed Cullingmates' hearts festering, the cruelty of taking magic for no reason birthing more and more Depraved.

This. This is exactly what that Depraved meant. The Guild has been feeding them all along, thanks to their greed. They just stand by while people die at the hands of monsters, when they literally have the power to stop it. What could be crueler than that?

Alister waves his hand dismissively. "The Depraved may be on the rise, but we're still standing. We can *handle* it. But only if we elevate the strongest among us, which your sister clearly wasn't. We can't let just *anyone* have magic. If it's a gift for all, it's a gift for none. But those of us who remain—we're unstoppable. Just think of our members. With the strength of Pallavit's voice, she is one of the leading opera singers in the world and can cast spells with simply a note. We have goblins able to shift away imperfections to become world-famous celebrities while mauling Depraved with one transformation. I've used my way with earth to become a political powerhouse in a state that booms with agriculture. We all have money and influence beyond your wildest dreams."

"That's what all this is about?" I spit. "Money?"

Alister rolls his eyes. "Don't be so high and mighty. Magic may bring a lot of good, boy, but money is what makes this world go 'round. Do you really think you could live the life you lead if it wasn't for magic keeping the livestock on your grandmother's ranch strong? We *all* use our gifts to our advantage." He stands tall, lifting his chin with haughty arrogance. "It's our right. The Guild started with nothing. Poor beggars, all of us. And it's not like we don't generously offer our skills to help. We *do* hunt the Depraved. We kill those we can. After all, we need a world to be powerful in.

"But *you*—you threaten all of that." His thorns close in tighter until I can't move an inch. "You came along and freed the Horde. All with your *love*." I flinch. How could a magician so cold and heartless know about the power of love? "Yes, Nigel, I know of your connection, but very few do. And I aim to keep it that way. To stop the two of you, so you can't grow even stronger. Stronger than all of us. Strong enough to dictate what we do in the Guild.

"I tried to stop you before this. Compassionately, at first, simply taking your magic away instead of your life. Pairing you together in the second task, hoping you'd lose control. Baiting that demon and Depraved to cut into your time for the challenge while you retrieved cursed victims. Working behind the scenes to show senior members what a threat you are to their children, to their Guild legacies. Hoping you'd feel so alone that you'd lose your heart to compete. But still, you were strong enough to make it to this point. *Too* strong. I have no choice but to eliminate you both. And you taking out the Knife in the process will just be icing on the cake."

He says it like the decision's already made. But without my cooperation, his whole plan falls apart. "What if I refuse?"

Alister motions to the battle raging outside the golden dome. The circle of protection still stands, even after Meema's passing, empowered by the force of her conviction, her *love*. But nothing can outlast death for long, and her spell is fading. Above us, the Knife is winning against the onslaught in the sky, grabbing dragons from midair, ripping off their heads and sucking out their enormous hearts.

"Are you honestly going to let this monster live?" Alister asks. "You'll stand by and watch as it destroys all of the Guild, then turns its eyes to humanity? Just to—what? Prove a point? When *you* were the one who unleashed it in the first place? You'd be willing to allow *what you did* to destroy every last human, when you and you alone have the ability to stop it? When you could do what even your great-grandfather Barrett couldn't, and actually *kill* the beast? If you thought Depraved attacks were getting worse before, imagine the destruction they'll cause if the Knife continues its rampage. Could you live with yourself while thousands die? Hundreds of thousands? Millions?" He stalks forward until he's a finger's length away from my cage of thorns. He bends down, his murky green eyes staring deep into mine. "What is the number, Nigel?"

"N-number?"

"How many people have to be destroyed before you're happy? You've already forced every Guild member to battle for you here today, and the body count continues to rise. Why, even your grandmother would still be alive if it weren't for you. And where is my daughter? Where is Pallavit's? Have they become more of your victims? When will it be enough for you?" He's whispering now—not grandstanding, not performing for an audience as he's done so many times. He knows the only person he needs to convince is me. And with every word, he looks more and more like Dad, more and more like the person who told me all my life that I'd screw up. That I'd never be able to rise to the challenge.

The least I can do is make this better.

Alister's right. The golden barrier separating us from the

Depraved is nearly gone now. I have a clear opening to destroy the crown, still glowing pink with Ori's power, but in moments, I'll lose it.

"I'll do it," I say.

Alister grins, triumphant.

"Nigel, it'll kill you." I feel Ori's sadness hit me like a bucket of water. "I need you. *We* need to see how our connection plays out. We need to change things."

I know he means we need to change the Guild. But what good will it do to change the organization if there's no world left for it to be in? No humans for our magic to protect?

Alister snaps his fingers, and my thorny prison is gone in a green flash. The path toward the crown is clear.

"Quickly," Alister says. "Before it's too—"

Alister's body stiffens and he falls to the ground, a faint pink glow coating his body. He's paralyzed, but I can see his pupils constrict with anger. I look to Ori, at his perfect smirk even though that huge thorn is pressed against his chin.

"I may not be a good artist, but—" Ori motions to a glowing pink stick figure he's scratched into one of the thorns of his cage.

I blow a magic bubble through my thumb and forefinger, and when it pops against Ori's prison, a portion of the vines and thorns turn to bubbles themselves. Ori's scratched effigy remains, keeping Alister still.

Ori stretches his jaw, massaging his chin, but his look of victory falls the second he meets my eyes. "There has to be another way," he says. "Don't do it, cowboy."

I take in the Knife battling the Guild, the Depraved and Horde fighting senior magicians as well, and beyond them all, the Seattle skyline. What if we're beaten? How long before the Knife decimates this city? Who knows how many people the giant Depraved will eat, how many it will stomp to death on its route.

"You always said if we did nothing, we couldn't live with the regret. Do you honestly think we could live with ourselves after this, knowing we had a chance to end it now?"

"The Guild stopped the Knife before," Ori insists.

I heft the claw. "Using this." Tears slide down my cheeks as I look to Meema's unmoving form. "I'm the only one who can use it now."

"But I don't want you to die," Ori whispers.

I lace my fingers through his, and the feeling that spreads inside me is so much more than warmth. It's caring and hope and the promise of the future. It's not wanting whatever strange, mysterious journey we've unwittingly started to end. But it's also the certainty that we must make this sacrifice, because it's what's right. Ori knows as well as I do that this is what has to be done.

I pull him along until we're right in front of the heartstone. The Depraved shriek behind us, beginning to push through the remnants of Meema's barrier. We have to hurry.

"Switch hands with me, would you?" I say, shifting the claw to my right so Ori can hold my left. "I may be magic, but I'm not ambidextrous."

Ori's lips don't perk up at my sorry attempt at a joke. He just looks into my eyes, and I feel his fear, his guilt that he's not doing enough to save me. I know, for him, this is Cassie all over again.

"Don't do that," I say. "You have to know that Cassie's death wasn't your fault. You were just a kid. Even if you could've used what little power you had, it wouldn't have been enough. Cassie knew that. Your mom knows that."

Ori's silent for a long time, biting his lip, soft pink pillowing out. I'm going to miss how perfect he is.

"I think about that moment every day," he says. "I wish I could go back and change it."

"I know. And if there was some way we could, I'd go to the ends of the earth to help you. I'm so sorry there's no spell for that, no magic we can unlock to go back." I think of Meema. If we had that magic, I'd use it on her the second after we revived Cassie. "We can't change the past, but we can change the future. Will you do that? With me?"

Finally, Ori nods.

"Good," I continue. "And just so you know, *you* make me better. I wouldn't be able to do this if it wasn't for you. You give me the strength. With just a touch. With just a—"

Ori brings his hands to my face and pulls me in for a kiss. It's hard and soft, tender and intense, loving and needy and everything I've ever wanted to feel. In this moment, I feel loved.

Electricity travels down my spine, saturating my bones, lighting me up with power. The claw lights up in my fingers, too, that perfect abalone shade of our magics combined.

The color of us.

Ori's fingers slip back into mine, and even though it's freezing on Mount Rainier, a fire burns in my belly. The fire of knowing what we're doing is right. No matter the sacrifice.

I heft the claw above my head.

"'Yup!" I yell, and let my arm fly.

The Knife roars, Depraved scream, and demons shriek, all of us watching this little nub of keratin travel toward the heartstone that's coated in Ori's magic. As the claw gets closer to the crown turned effigy my heart sings.

This is it.

My hand shakes so hard when the claw meets the jewel that I fear I might drop it. But with an abalone flash down my arm, my grip becomes firm. As firm on the claw as it is on Ori's fingers. In this last moment, I feel our victory over the Knife as strongly as that perfect connection, that certainty that I'm next to someone who was meant to be in my life.

I look back into Ori's brown eyes—filled with sadness and pride and loss and triumph—for one last second. Then, I get a glimpse of the crack deepening down the heartstone's center, see it start to shatter, take in how the blood red of the jewel dulls to earthy brown.

It worked. The ground shakes as the Knife goes down, goblins in many forms directing its body away from us. Hundreds of trees snap and break as the giant falls.

My entire body glows from within, brighter than any magic I've seen before.

And then . . .

Everything stops.

CHAPTER TWENTY-EIGHT

ORI'S HEART STOPS WHEN NIGEL'S DOES. ONLY, FOR ORI, IT'S A SPLIT second that feels like a lifetime. For Nigel, it's permanent.

As soon as Ori's heart beats again—and again, and again—while that phantom pulse he could always feel from Nigel is silent, he knows the plan worked. He sees the Knife fall, truly dead this time—the spells they cast did that. Its massive corpse slides down Mount Rainier, taking the forest with it. He sees the Horde minions crumble, too, lifeless bones littering the side of the volcano. Demons flee as the remainder of the Guild celebrates the victory, the positive emotion from the magicians driving away the monsters' cruelty. The Depraved are close behind, knowing they don't stand a chance against the magicians now.

But for Ori, there's no victory.

Only emptiness.

He doesn't feel a thing.

He shuts himself off again, just like he did after his sister, needing to run from the weight of his sadness or else drown in it. He *can't* drown in it. Because the one person whose touch could heal him is going cold in his arms. And no matter how tightly he squeezes, no matter which limp limb he presses against, desperate to trigger the healing magic they once shared, nothing will bring back Nigel's warmth.

"You're so stupid, Nigel," he sobs. "So, so stupid."

He doesn't really mean it. Not in the slightest. But he knows now he never should have let someone in again. It always leads to heartache.

If only his effigies could wake the dead.

"Wake the dead!" Ori screams it, the sudden realization such a rush that the words burst from his throat.

He's woken the dead before. The Horde. All it took was creating an effigy and attaching a magical heart, like the ones Nigel made in their second Culling task. And laying at his feet are dozens of pieces of a stone fueled by hearts, plus a centuries-old weapon with power that's tied to Nigel's blood, to Barrett *life*. He could use it as an effigy. That's his thing, isn't it? Making effigies out of the unexpected. All thanks to Cassie. Thanks to her love.

Ori's lips quirk up, a movement entirely outside of his control, the smirk that always comes when he knows he's on the right path. It sparks a realization that he might be able to *do something* this time. He didn't have this power when Cassie died. There was nothing he could have done. He knows that now. But today, he just might change the outcome.

He has to.

His hands are hurried, hovering over the claw and glowing pink, sending his power down the length of the weapon—careful not to touch it—nothing but Nigel filling his mind. Nigel's quiet, observant personality. Nigel's desire for belonging, for family. Nigel's open heart, his willingness to let Ori become a part of that family, even if Ori *had* decided to close himself off. Nigel didn't want Ori to have to protect himself alone. Nigel would protect him, too. Nigel was *meant* to.

They're soulmates.

And with that knowledge filling his heart, Ori grabs one of the broken pieces of the heartstone. At first, it's just a cold lump. But one second in Ori's hand, with his mind and heart racing with memories of all the good in Nigel, with the certainty that they are meant to be, that their lives and powers are linked, the broken piece begins to glow. It no longer looks like a shattered remnant of some evil weapon. Now, it's its own jewel, a solitary beating heart belonging to one person and one person only.

Nigel.

Ori slams the heartstone into the claw with a force even he didn't know he was capable of. With a glow of red and pink and gold that swirls into their beautiful abalone light, the jewel fuses to the claw, to that piece of keratin that belongs to Nigel and his blood. Ori braces himself for the curse of the claw to kick in, for it to send him reeling, refusing the touch of someone who's not a Barrett. But rather than push him back, it pulls him in, like it's gripping *his* hand. And from that position, Ori can just feel the quiet, soft *buh-bum* as the jewel beats once.

Ori reaches out and grabs Nigel; his skin is still cold. "Come on, Nigel. Come on."

Buh-bum.

A vibration runs through Nigel's hand.

Buh-bum.

A finger twitches.

Buh-bum.

A heaving, coughing breath.

Buh-bum.

"Ori."

CHAPTER TWENTY-NINE

He's the first thing I think of the second everything comes back.

Ori.

And somehow I know he was the only thing I thought of wherever I went when I died.

"Nigel!" He screams my name and scoops me into his arms. The second he presses his lips against mine, my heart beats so strongly it hurts. Maybe the pain's a side effect of beating so hard after not beating at all, but whatever the case, it's worth it.

We kiss and kiss and kiss, Ori's perfect lips pressing harder, deeper, after each breath. His tongue gently touches mine, creating sparks throughout my body.

Finally, Ori says into my mouth, "Took you long enough."

I pull back so I can look in his eyes, see the happiness there, the relief. "Just trying to make a grand entrance."

Ori laughs, that playfully judgy eyebrow quirking up. "Oh, so you're some rodeo clown looking to put on a show now, huh?"

"Unfortunately, I only know one trick." I pull him in so we can kiss again.

When we've finally had enough—for now—Ori says, "That's a good trick."

I prop myself on my elbows and survey the scene. No enemies, anywhere. Guild magicians already swarm the massive swath of forest cleared from Mount Rainier, working to get rid of the Knife's hulking, rotten corpse.

I glance up to the sky and see the helicopters are long gone. "Word's going to get out about this."

A gentle, melodic laugh comes from behind us. Pallavit. Scratched and bruised, her lips bloody, her chest heaving with exhaustion. But still, she's laughing.

"Your insistence on underestimating magic is pretty impressive," she says. "Even after you've seen all that you two can do." She gives me that appraising smile, the same one she shared the night we fought our first Depraved. Maybe now that we've killed the Knife, we're back in her good graces.

"The Guild is working as we speak on wiping this incident from human memory," Pallavit continues. "You can't honestly believe the Knife is the only monster of its size we've had to deal with. Not with how terrible humans are. Think of how many wars there have been in just the short life of this country. But through it all, magicians are here to clean up the mess."

She's right. In a way. The Guild *does* defeat monsters, the ones humans unknowingly create. There is a good side to the group.

But they also *create* monsters. The Culling needs to stop. The Guild needs to change if we're to ever truly say we make the world a better place.

Maybe Pallavit can help with that. Maybe change starts now.

"Where's Jaleesa?" she asks.

Or not. Pallavit's throat glows purple with power, a mother protecting her only child. She'll kill the magicians she thinks harmed her. A dozen other Guild members materialize behind her, Alister among them—freed from his magical paralysis—their hands or necks all glowing with magic. Ready to fight. To kill us. Ori and I may have saved the day, but we're still a threat to their power.

Pallavit strikes first.

"*You cannot m-moo-mooov-moooooooo.*"

But I'm faster, Ori's grip fueling my power, my renewed heart ready to fight for what I know is right. With my free hand I've molded a cowbell, ringing it over and over, my magic cursing Pallavit's voice so she can't sing her spells. She can only moo.

Ori laughs, loud and clear, in spite of the other magicians baring down on us. "Leave it to a cowboy," he says.

More senior magicians stalk toward us, hands outstretched with power, ready to strike.

WHOOOOOOOSH!

A searing hot flame pushes the Guild members back as a massive black dragon flies by. Just as its tail whips past my head, a frog hops off, changing into my best friend in midair.

"Bex!" I cry.

"Now *that's* a grand entrance," Ori says as the senior magicians contend with the literal fires that separate them from us.

Bex beams. "Dragons love living inside a good ol' volcano. I had to scare the poor guy to get over here quick. After dive-bombing the Knife's nostrils for twenty minutes, my magic's running low."

"You did what?" Ori asks, disgusted.

"How else was I supposed to distract the Knife? Just popped up there and blasted its brain with fire from the inside."

"I'm so glad you did," I say. "Or we never would have been able to get the crown. We couldn't have done it without you."

"And don't you forget it." Bex's smirk totally puts Ori's to shame.

"Guys." Ori motions to the senior magicians, the dragon flame keeping them at bay nearly gone. "We've got to go."

"Where to?" I ask.

Bex turns to Ori. "Can you blink us to the Great Smoky Mountains?"

I've heard of them before, thanks to Meema's taste in music. Music we'll never get to listen to together again. "You a Dolly Parton fan or something?" I ask.

"Just do it! It's where somebody important is. Somebody who can explain everything."

"Who?" Ori asks.

A blast of golden light erupts just inches away from Bex's face. We've got to hurry.

"I can't tell you!" Bex says, grabbing Ori's hand. "I've been spelled."

"Classic magician," Ori says. "Always saving the most important info for some big reveal." He rolls his eyes. "But don't worry. I can blink us." He reaches into his pocket, pulling out the claw. "Take this. We can't lose it in the jump."

"H-how? How can you hold that?"

Ori smirks. "I guess being your soulmate has some perks."

I want to lean in and kiss his perfectly quirked lips, but when the claw strikes my hand, a sharp jab stabs my heart. I clutch my chest in pain, but the feeling is gone as quick as it started. What's left behind is a low-burning coal of anger, of vengeance. A malice, building in my soul, that wants to be let out.

Magic pools in my hands, and I turn toward the magicians readying powers of their own. I could stop them right here. End them once and for all, so they'll never come after us again, so they'll regret the day they ever—

"Nigel!" Ori squeezes my fingers, and the warmth that follows washes away my thoughts.

I look down at the claw and see that it's changed. A dark red light glows at its center, a familiar jewel pulsing there.

"Ori?" I ask, a sense of doom creeping into my gut. "How did you bring me back?"

He looks at me, and I can tell he feels my worry. He feels my certainty that he's fused me with the Knife, with the most powerful evil force this country has ever seen, by merging my great-grandfather's weapon with a piece of the Knife's heartstone. He feels that scratch of hatred against my heart, that desire to do damage to the people who have damaged me.

Ori swallows, dread seeping through his bones.

It's the last thing I feel before we blink out of existence.

And jump into the unknown.

ACKNOWLEDGMENTS

It really felt like some kind of feat of magic to get this book from idea to finished novel. A heaping farm-full of thanks to:

Rachel Stark! Thank you for all the talks, lassoing me away from the edge of some huge plot holes, and painstakingly going through this magic system to make sure it tracks. You are a true magician!

Melissa de la Cruz! For seeing something in my writing and giving me the best boosts with your comments. Your notes made me feel like a real writer, and I can't thank you enough for that. Torchy's trashy tacos on me the next time you're in Austin!

Brent Taylor! You have a magic all your own that makes authors' dreams come true! I am so, so, so honored to get to work with you and am continually in awe at all the career milestones that have been manifested because of your powers.

The MDLC Studio team! From marketing to copy editing to cover design. I am so grateful to all of you for taking such great care of Nigel and Ori and making their love one for the elven texts . . .

I mean history books. I'm so excited to get to work on more books with you!

Thea Harvey and Marci Senders! Thea, this cover is everything I could ever want it to be and more! Marci, the design is simply magical!

Erin Watley, Sahrish, and Stefanie! Thank you for your heartfelt notes on how to make this magical world still feel inclusive and real.

The librarians and teachers and booksellers across the country who constantly work to get queer books into the hands of queer readers! I know it's not easy, and I know you regularly have to deal with the soulless Depraved who want to strip the world of compassion and love. You are all heroes!

Readers! From your notes and DMs, to your book talks with friends, to your shout-outs on social media, there's this special spark of connection we have through a shared love of words and stories. I'm so honored that you choose to spend time with mine. I can't thank you enough.

Jerry! There's no doubt in my mind that our love makes real magic.